DEAD MAN TALKING

*Recent Titles from Richard Woodman from
Severn House Large Print*

The Privateersman
The East Indiaman

DEAD MAN TALKING

Richard Woodman

Severn House Large Print
London & New York

This first large print edition published in Great Britain 2004 by
SEVERN HOUSE LARGE PRINT BOOKS LTD of
9-15 High Street, Sutton, Surrey, SM1 1DF.
First world regular print edition published 2002 by
Severn House Publishers, London and New York.
This first large print edition published in the USA 2004 by
SEVERN HOUSE PUBLISHERS INC., of
595 Madison Avenue, New York, NY 10022.

Copyright © 2002 by Richard Woodman

British Library Cataloguing in Publication Data

Woodman, Richard, 1944-
    Dead man talking. - Large print ed.
    1.   World War, 1939-1945 - Naval operations, British - Fiction
    2.   War stories
    3.   Large type books
    I.   Title
    823.9'14 [F]

    ISBN 0-7278-7341-5

Except where actual historical events and characters are being described
for the storyline of this novel, all situations in this publication are
fictitious and any resemblance to living persons is purely coincidental.

Printed and bound in Great Britain by
MPG Books Ltd, Bodmin, Cornwall.

For Captain Lennart Granqvist
to whom I am indebted for my own
Arctic adventure

PROLOGUE

Throughout the drive into Suffolk and right up until the old man started talking, I recall a sense of deep irritation. A strong sense of guilt was to overwhelm me on the homeward journey, but I cannot forget the intensity of my annoyance at being summoned to meet yet another veteran of the Second World War. A few years earlier I would have happily undertaken the task which I had now been inveigled into. I had then been writing what I had presumed to call the definitive history of a naval campaign waged fifty years previously and I had been eager to glean anything germane to my research. A few years earlier I had been keen as mustard, but now I was exhausted with the effort of the task I had accomplished and, having survived the assaults of critical review relatively unbruised, wanted only to lay the job aside. Now to be told that there was something my researches had failed to unearth, something of such critical importance to the historical record that my book would have to be rewritten, simply infuriated me.

But I could not refuse to go out of sheer petulance and, in the end, what I learned on that golden autumn afternoon was something quite extraordinary, in the fullest sense of that oddly abused word.

My churlish irritation arose from the simple fact that I had received a telephone call from a woman who said that my book was inaccurate. Moreover, it was suggested that this inaccuracy was profoundly serious and it touched upon one of the most notorious disasters of the war at sea: the destruction of convoy PQ17.

This news was a mighty blow to my self-esteem, for veterans who had served in the Barents Sea had flatteringly described my book as comprehensive and accurate. It was my tyro work as a naval historian and I was heady with my own success, so to receive a message suggesting that it was very far from what I had believed it to be kept me from proper sleep in the four days between the telephone call and my appointment at the end of the drive up into a remote corner of Suffolk.

To write what was described as 'a magnificent book' and have it 'thoroughly recommended' seemed like fair comment after the labour of research and reconstruction. I felt that in interviewing and corresponding with some remarkable old men, in poring over charts, analysing weather conditions, dragging official reports from the dusty archives, reading unofficial documents and personal letters and staring at literally hundreds of old photographs, I understood *something* of those dreadful wartime voyages through the extremes of the Arctic Ocean. I thoroughly immersed myself in my subject so that, with the conceit of the artistic creator, my version had surpassed Voltaire's definition of history: it was more than a fable upon which we, my sources human and documentary, agreed upon. It had become the absolute truth. Now I was the victim of my own hubris, hoist by mine own petard!

And this disagreeable news concerned an event, still controversial, upon which I had laboured in order to establish what I considered to be the fairest account yet written. Now a woman's voice had told me that my account was inaccurate, and that inaccuracy was relevant to convoy PQ17.

Perhaps I had better explain. Convoy PQ17 had been a major operation, one of many convoys designed to force the material of war through to Soviet Russia which had been treacherously invaded by Nazi Germany in July 1941. Up until Adolf Hitler unleashed his forces upon the Russians, the two totalitarian states of Nazi Germany and Soviet Russia, although occupying the theoretically opposite ends of the political spectrum, had been allies. In 1939 they had carved up Poland between them, a circumstance that caused hostilities between Germany and Great Britain and France, though it was only the German action which attracted the declaration of war from London. Hitler, however, had imperial designs upon the grain-producing regions of the Ukraine as living space for the Master Race, hence the unprovoked attack on his quondam ally in June 1941. In London the hard-pressed British government, standing alone against Germany after the Nazi occupation of much of France, had begun to send arms to Soviet Russia in an attempt to reconcile the hard-line Communist state to an alliance with the hitherto hated capitalist monarchy on the Atlantic coast of Europe.

By the summer of 1942 the Japanese had bombed Pearl Harbor and the United States of America was in the war alongside Great Britain. American armaments were also being sent to the Soviet Union in American ships and, for the first time with convoy PQ17, the heavy escort of the British Royal Navy was reinforced with American warships, operating under British command. The convoy formed up at a rendezvous off Iceland and sailed north-east in a great arc round the North Cape of Norway, whose coast was a base for aircraft, submarines and, significantly as it turned out, some heavy units of the German fleet, most

10

notably the battleship *Tirpitz*. The convoy route was not only round this flank of the extended German Reich, it was hemmed in to the north by the ice fields of the Arctic Ocean.

Nevertheless, it was well provided for with an experienced close escort under Commander 'Jackie' Broome in the destroyer *Keppel*, and an attending 'covering force', a squadron of British and American cruisers under Rear Admiral Hamilton in HMS *London*, which would accompany the convoy for part of the way. Distant heavy cover was provided by the British Home Fleet, which, with some American men-of-war, including the battleship *Washington*, provided a powerful disincentive to any meditated interference from the heavy units of the Kriegsmarine. Lying in the remote fjords of north Norway were, besides the *Tirpitz*, the heavy cruiser *Hipper* and the two pocket battleships *Lützow* and *Admiral Scheer*.

To watch for any sortie by these menacing warships, patrol lines of British, Free French and Russian submarines guarded the Norwegian coast, Norwegian spies were observing the movements of the German ships and the Royal Air Force were overflying their anchorages. Moreover, a dummy convoy sailed shortly before PQ17 to act as a decoy, and a westbound convoy of empty merchantmen was making its way home from

11

the previous outward convoy. This was routed closer to the Norwegian coast as an easier and possibly more tempting target, so that in theory the thirty-five laden freighters and tankers of PQ17 were ring-fenced by steel, sinew and all the cunning possible.

The Germans knew all about convoy PQ17 and planned to strike it in an operation denominated *Rosselspring*, or Knight's Move. Ten U-boats were mustered to attack it, with air support by Luftwaffe aircraft from Bardo and Bardufoss aerodromes. Meanwhile *Tirpitz* and *Hipper* had left Trondheim, a movement reported by air reconnaissance, and while this failed over Narvik, *Scheer* and *Lützow* were also moving northwards towards Altenfjord where the mighty *Tirpitz* lay.

By the fourth of July convoy PQ17 was well on its way towards Russia. It had beaten off several attacks by U-boats over the preceding three days, along with air assaults by Heinkel torpedo bombers, but that morning the American Liberty ship *Christopher Newport* had been hit by an aerial torpedo and had to be sunk after her crew had been taken off. That afternoon Admiral Hamilton and his cruisers were ordered by the British Admiralty in London to continue to support the convoy further east than initially planned. Hamilton responded with a signal stating that he intended to withdraw that night, but the Admiralty countered this by telling him to hang on. Among the officers responsible for the safe arrival of the convoy an atmosphere of impending and escalating threat began to be generated. In London the first whiff of confusion was forming.

Air reconnaissance over north Norway was unproductive and the precise whereabouts of *Tirpitz* was beginning to cause concern to the intelligence analysts on the staff of the First Sea Lord. Meanwhile, in the light evening of the Arctic midsummer, PQ17 had sustained a combined bombing and torpedo attack by the Luftwaffe. Two merchantmen were lost, but the damaged Russian tanker *Azerbaidjan* pressed gallantly eastwards, a manifestation of the spirit uniting the crews of the Allied merchant ships. Despite the enemy successes, the attacks had been beaten off with some heartening losses of enemy aircraft and the mood among Broome's men was elated.

At the Admiralty, Sir Dudley Pound, the First Sea Lord and operational chief of the Royal Navy, called a staff meeting. The staff appreciation of an assault by the combined enemy forces thought to be in the vicinity of the North Cape concluded that both Hamilton's cruisers and the convoy would be annihilated. This was an odd assumption, given the forces originally deployed to protect the convoy, but it was weighted by the assumption that the *Tirpitz*'s intervention would be decisive, for by this time the British Home Fleet had turned back for its base in the Orkney Islands. At the time, Pound and his advisers, uncertain as to the position of the German heavy warships and somewhat confused by imperfect intelligence assessments and the failure of vital aerial reconnaissance, thought it best if the convoy was broken up. Broome was therefore ordered to disperse the convoy; a little later he was told that the merchant ships should scatter. At the Admiralty the dispersal order was felt not to have instructed the merchant ships to diverge widely enough in their respective courses to avoid too many of them being sighted by German aircraft or U-boats. Pound afterwards admitted that he had meant to say 'scatter', rather than 'disperse' in the first place. He was tired and unwell and the error in terminology was nothing more than that.

Thus it was that the merchantmen of PQ17 were ordered to scatter *after* they had been told to disperse. This modified instruction was precise in its interpretation as regards the divergence of courses and was designed to spread the ships as quickly as possible. In fact it was designed to counter the mutuality of convoy integrity and reduced each merchantman to an individual unit. To the officers in those distant ships this change of orders was not seen as a mere amendment. To them it appeared to be an obvious escalation of the order and indicated a rapidly deteriorating situation. Both Broome and Hamilton considered attack by *Tirpitz* and her sisters to be imminent and, in accordance with their own orders from the Admiralty, withdrew their warships in the direction they expected the overwhelming German attack to come from. To steer towards the sound of the guns was in the best traditions of the Royal Navy and, while as yet there was no gunfire, it was anticipated at any moment. It was only later they realised they had been fooled. In a dawning of the enormity of the error they had unwittingly committed was brewed a terrible sense of desertion and dereliction of duty. The tradition of the Royal Navy as the protector of trade had been destroyed at a stroke.

In the succeeding days the almost helpless merchant ships were picked off in a turkey shoot, twenty-three being lost to the shadowing U-boats, who had watched with glee as Hamilton and Broome ran past them to the westwards. As for the remaining merchantmen, and the handful of lesser warships of the close escort whose task ended with the scattering of the convoy, they and their crews endured ordeals of almost epic proportions. The perception of the British

Royal Navy by the United States Navy was dreadfully compromised by the Admiralty's decision, but more serious was the damage to the relationship between the Royal Navy and the officers and men of Allied merchant ships. *They* thought, and went on thinking long after the event, that the Royal Navy had run away. Years after the war a celebrated libel trial in London argued over the matter and one of the challenges of my own book had been to try and get to the bottom of this matter. I thought I had done it. It had been due to a bungled order, a product of fell circumstances and the problem of the British Admiralty overriding the men on the spot as it exercised its prerogative as the remote command centre for naval operations.

It seemed that all the tragic consequences flowed from the simple fact that Pound was deprived of the accurate information he required and made a misjudgement. It was a decision confused by the fog of war but one that could, just, be argued on the face of the available evidence to be justified. Of course, realising his error, the First Sea Lord should have turned the escort and cruiser squadron round and sent Broome and Hamilton back to try and mitigate things. Hamilton could have defied the Admiralty and ordered the same thing. On the bridge of one British destroyer, as they heard the plaintive transmissions of merchant ship after merchant ship reporting an attack, they thought of pretending they had had an engine failure, dropping astern and then turning round and racing back to the scene, but the matter had passed beyond redemption. In the event, it was not that twenty-three merchant ships were lost, but that not one warship was lost in their defence.

It was a sad story, but I felt that in my book I had dealt with it as compassionately and fairly as was possible, given what fifty-odd years later we knew of 'the facts'. As I have said, Pound was a sick man. His change of the order from dispersal to scattering was eloquent of a person distracted by pain. It was no excuse, of course, but it had been an explanation. He made a gross misjudgement, the consequences of which were fatal for a lot of people. His subordinates on the spot were chained by discipline and the notion that, as the operational director, Pound at the Admiralty knew a great deal more than they did. My version was what I thought in my presumption to be the historic truth.

And then a few days ago I had had the telephone call that suggested there was more to the matter. It seemed incredible, but it had me driving into a lonely corner of Suffolk, annoyed, irritated and, God help me, angry that some old fool had challenged

17

the fable that had been agreed upon!

It was a state of mind that worsened as I was shown into the room where I was to meet my informant. What, I asked myself, could this emaciated old fellow tell me that was new?

I was about to taste humble pie.

I had driven east out of Woodbridge, along narrow straight roads that cut through forest, behind which one caught occasional glimpses of steel fences and the remnants of the American occupation of air-force bases, abandoned since the fall of communism. Breaking out of the pines and the low scrub I drove through farmland rolling down to the North Sea, which gleamed intermittently on the horizon. I came upon the house suddenly. It stood alone, behind a high brick wall and a series of laurel bushes, a red-brick, four-square, two-storeyed building. I gingerly edged the car on to the entrance to the gravelled drive. Beyond the gate an elderly, mud-spattered Rover was parked. I shut the gate and approached the house across a shorn patch of lawn. The rest of the garden seemed out of control, and although a handsome *Magnolia grandiflora* rose against the red-brick wall, the paint on the window frames was beginning to flake. A little apprehensively I knocked on the dark-blue door. Though this too could have done with a coat of paint, the brass, dolphin-shaped doorknocker gleamed in the brilliant sunshine of late morning.

I was met by his daughter. She was a little older than myself, sixty-one or -two, I guessed. A tall, handsome woman with short grey hair and an air of quiet competence. She invited me in and we shook hands in the hall.

'I'm Charlotte ... His daughter.' She did not add what I learned later, that she was a widow.

The house smelt of long occupation and a tall clock ticked sonorously beside me as I noticed a handsome seascape in the rather gloomy light.

'It's good of you to come all this way,' she said, half smiling. 'I hope you did not mind my phoning, but my father particularly wished to see you and it *is* important, *very* important I believe.'

'It's a pleasure,' I lied.

She caught my gaze and held it, briefing me before we met the old man. 'You see, he greatly admired your book but ... Well I'll let him tell you himself, but he gets very tired and may drift off. Please make allowances...'

'Of course,' I responded politely.

'You'll see there's nothing wrong with his mind, nothing at all, that's what is so remarkable; he's as sharp as a tack, though rather deaf.' I smiled and nodded, not

19

certain what was expected of me. 'And you may stay the night if you think it is necessary. You must allow him to tell you everything.'

The air thickened with mystery. 'About PQ17, you mean?'

'Yes.' She nodded and then turned on her heel. 'If you'd like to follow me...'

She led me through into a room flooded with sunshine. I was aware of a fireplace, above which hung another marine painting, a brigantine working her way through Arctic ice among fantastically shaped icebergs. The flanking alcoves contained filled bookshelves, and on an end wall hung two portraits, an eighteenth-century naval officer and, presumably, his wife. The furniture was heavy and in the window, looking out over the rear garden – a sweep of mown lawn ending in bushes, trees and a tangle of undergrowth – sat the old man himself.

She accelerated her pace, crossed the room and bent over him. 'Father, your visitor is here to see you.' She enunciated the words clearly, raising her voice as she did so.

As the old man turned and I saw his face, I wondered what the hell I was doing there. The prospect of staying the night was not attractive and I wished simply to hear what criticism he was going to level at my book and get away as fast as possible to assess what damage his 'revelation' might do to its accuracy and to my credibility.

He began to stand up, waving aside his daughter's outstretched hand. I sensed a fierce pride in front of a complete stranger. He faced me, his thin figure silhouetted against the sunshine so that I could not at first make out his features. I stepped forward and took the claw he held out in welcome.

'Very pleased you have come,' he said, his voice a little wheezy. 'Very pleased. You've been to sea yourself, haven't you?'

'I have, yes, sir.'

'Don't call me "sir", there's no need; besides, you're a captain yourself, aren't you?'

'I've been a shipmaster, yes, but not a naval officer, and I've found some naval officers object to the use of the title, so since leaving the sea I only use it rarely.'

'Huh. There are some damned fools in the navy. If you've been in command you've borne the burden. I'm a master mariner myself,' he said as, now leaning upon Charlotte's arm, he tottered round the arm of a large settee and fell back into it. 'Do sit down,' he offered, waving me to an adjacent chair. 'You'd better call me John,' he added.

'I'm Richard,' I replied awkwardly.

'I know, it's on your book.' He held out a hand and looked up at the hovering Charlotte. 'Pass it over, would you, m'dear? It's on the bookshelf there.'

I watched him take the familiar red-and-silver book, a paperback edition by John

Murray, the red for blood and slaughter, the silver for the ice and cold of the Arctic. Carefully his ancient fingers turned the pages.

With the light on the side of his face I could see him properly now. The skin was stretched tightly over the skull and the grey eyes were rheumy behind magnifying lenses. But he wore a shirt and I recognised the neat club tie under his dark-green cardigan. His pair of fawn trousers were immaculate and his tanned shoes bright with polish. He was clean-shaven and clearly he or Charlotte had taken some pains over his appearance.

'Tea or coffee?' she asked.

'Er, coffee please,' I replied, distracted from my scrutiny of her father.

'Yes,' he said slowly as he continued to search through the pages, 'I was a master mariner before I joined the Royal Navy, but I only made commander,' he looked up and gave me a disarmingly charming and rueful grin. 'I didn't get up to very much after PQ17.'

'Then you were involved with PQ17?' I said, though what I wanted to say was 'I've never seen your name or any reference to you in any document or account that I have read about that disastrous event,' but I held my tongue.

There was a silence and then he found what he was looking for in the book and gave me his full attention.

Nodding, he said, 'Yes, I was. I was at the heart of it...'

'At the Admiralty?' I asked. I had interviewed people who had been at the Admiralty that fateful day and had no knowledge of this old boy's presence.

He shook his head. 'No, I was in the Arctic...' he paused and I waited for more. Then he said, tapping the book, 'this is a very fair account but you have to conclude that Sir Dudley Pound acted very foolishly, however you try and mitigate things.' I nodded. 'All that stuff about his arthritic hip and his lack of sleep, the stories Alanbrooke told of him being like a dead parrot and falling asleep at the Chiefs of Staff meetings and then the diagnosis of the brain tumour and his death on Trafalgar Day a year later...'

I held my tongue and waited as he drew breath before resuming.

'You know he went into Churchill's bedroom when they were both in Washington and told the Prime Minister he couldn't go on?' I muttered that I had heard the story. 'And you know Churchill said in his *History of the Second World War* that he knew nothing of the background to Pound's decision to scatter the convoy?' Again I muttered that I was familiar with the passage in *The Hinge of Fate*, the fourth volume of Churchill's monumental history. 'Winston was lying, of course, he knew *all* about it.'

'I did know that,' I interrupted, still irked by my summons and wondering where all this was getting us, 'and I said so in my book...'

'Oh yes, you said Churchill dissembled, but you did not say why, because you did not know why.'

'And you do?' Aware that my tone had been challenging and rude, I added quickly, 'I mean, you know *why* Pound ordered the convoy scattered? That there was a reason, a real, justifiable reason?' I must have sounded quite incredulous at this point, and I think it was at this instant that I forsook my peevishness and felt the first tug of enthusiasm, because the old fellow leaned forward and fixed me with those grey eyes in the same way his daughter had in the hall outside a few minutes earlier. This was the cusp of our encounter.

After it everything changed.

'Oh yes,' he said. 'Why d'you think I've asked you to come and see me?'

At this point Charlotte arrived with the coffee and there were a few moments as we sorted out cups, saucers, sugar bowls, teaspoons and the milk jug. When we were settled she announced she would leave us alone and would be in the garden if we wanted anything. She announced that she would bring some sandwiches in an hour, if that would be all right. I thanked her and turned again to her father. I remember at this point all my feelings of irritation had certainly vanished. I was not in doubt that what the old man had to tell me was important, nor did I care that it nullified two chapters of my book. I was only conscious, with a thrill, that I was glad I had come and that I was in a unique position to hear an historical and official secret. I was quite un-prepared for the fantastical story I was about to hear.

'Like the boys and girls at Bletchley Park,' he said, 'I was afterwards told to keep my trap shut, firmly and for ever, but the secret about Ultra is well known now and I am very close to my end. Perhaps I should not have decided to break my imposed silence now had I not received a copy of your book for my birthday, but I don't think any of the secrecy matters any more and it is a pity that the truth should be lost.' I remained utterly silent as he sucked coffee and then, with a trembling rattle, put the cup carefully back on the saucer on the little table Charlotte had set before him. Then he looked directly at me and I caught something of the man he had once been, and of the injustice I had done him as he said, 'You say in your book that the tragedy of PQ17 was that not one man-of-war was lost in the defence of the merchant ships. That's not true. My ship was lost and I was the sole survivor.'

'What ship was that then?' I asked, and I remember that my mouth was dry.

He seemed to gather himself for a great effort, moving his shoulders and drawing himself up a little in his chair. I watched him swallow, his Adam's apple bobbing under the thin skin of his neck. 'I had better start at the beginning.'

I did stay the night and most of the next day. A week after I had left, while I was already busy reworking my narrative from the notes I had made, I received a second telephone call from Charlotte.

'I thought you should know,' she said, and I think I already knew what she was going to tell me, 'my father died peacefully in his sleep last night.'

'I'm so sorry,' I said, genuinely moved.

'He forbade me from placing any notice in the papers,' she went on, and then added after a brief pause, 'You *are* going to tell his story, aren't you?'

'Yes,' I replied.

HAMBURG

August 1939

Had he known it at the time, John Clark's war started a few days earlier than history's convention records. He was not alone, for the world had been sliding towards a second cataclysm since the vindictive terms of the armistice ending the First World War extracted punitive terms from the German nation. The Chinese had been fighting the Japanese for several years and the first Nazi pogroms against the German Jews had already split many families, sending hundreds into exile. But for people like John Clark, who was better known to his contemporaries as Jack, the busy occupations of daily life excluded any real appreciation of the palpable movements of history, still less of the ineluctable quality of their consequences.

On that fine late summer morning the sun rose over the great maritime city of Hamburg in a blazing orb, burning off a slight mist that lay over the turbid waters of the River Elbe. It caught the greened copper spire of St Michael's great church and, just as its first tentative light had released the song of birds a few hours earlier, now it initiated the excruciating din of the hammers of a hundred riveters as they commenced another day's work in the city's busy shipyards. To the uninitiated, few places on earth can convey such an impression of hellish disorganisation as a shipyard in full production. The cacophony of the riveters is but a part of the dislocating horror of such places. That which Clark entered that morning was no exception. Beyond the offices from which the construction of a dozen vessels was being simultaneously planned and overseen, lay the huge 'shops' and rolling mills which processed the steel plates and joists brought from the stockyards. With a skill equal to true artistry these inanimate grey rectangles assumed graceful curves which were then despatched towards the building ways that sloped down to the great river. Here they were united to a thousand similarly treated plates and grew into the elegant lines of unlaunched hulls which towered above the concrete slips, each one surrounded by scaffolding and staging. The scene teemed with the movements of hundreds of men; overhead the cranes and gantries moved newly formed plates into position; here and there the blue flame of oxyacetylene cutting torches blazed, elsewhere the small portable furnaces of the riveters and their mates glowed redly. Drills screeched as they bored through adjacent plates and then incandescent rivets were thrown with apparent disregard, caught by the expert wielders of tongs and inserted into the holes, to be hammered by pneumatic power until they drew steel so tight that even the pressure of the ocean four fathoms below the surface could not intrude.

Beyond the building ways those hulls nearing completion rode high in the water at the fitting-out berths. Here a more complex process was in train, for they were receiving the final fittings, from accommodation blocks to the light fittings in individual compartments, from masts and derricks, to bureaux for the cabins of their officers. In such an environment, as he walked to a smartly painted hull riding high in the water alongside number one fitting-out berth, Clark's thoughts were very far from considerations of international tension, let alone war, for his mood in standing-by a brand new cargo liner was far from gloomy. On the contrary he was optimistic, for the splendid new ship was unequivocal evidence of global reinvestment and marked an easing of the economic depression that had held the world in thrall since the Wall Street crash ten years earlier. Clark's entire life for the past four months had been devoted entirely to the completion of the new ship, one of a class of powerful twin-screw, eighteen-knot vessels intended for the Far Eastern Service of the Eastern Steam Navigation Company of Liverpool. The ESNC was more familiarly known as 'Dent's' or 'Dentco', after the family who had founded the shipping house in Liverpool 120 years earlier. They had then owned sailing vessels, largely employed in the India and China trades which had been opened up when the old East India Company lost its monopoly, but when Dent's moved into steam, the new name was coined to reflect this shift of technological gear. Clark's new ship, in common with her seven sisters – four of which were being built in British yards, with one just launched in Rotterdam and another almost completed in Copenhagen – was a motor vessel, not a steamship. However, it was not anticipated that the board of the Eastern Steam Navigation Company would change the company's name again. Perhaps a more relevant tradition, instituted in 1870 when Dent's had ordered the first of their line of famous steamers, was that of the new ship's name. The introduction of steam had brought a predictability about schedules unknown to the world of sail, which, allied with the telegraph, transformed the operation of merchant ships into a thoroughly modern business. This shift in culture had resulted in what a later age would call 'branding' and manifested itself in a company house style designed to impress potential shippers both in Europe and in the Far East. Thus, along with distinctive funnel designs and hull colours, Dent's fast cargo ships all bore the names of explorers.

As had been his custom for many weeks, Clark walked up the gangway of the *Ernest Shackleton* that bright morning with a list of queries to review before his morning meeting with the builder's representatives over coffee at ten o'clock. Each daily conference threw up queries and differences as the *Ernest Shackleton* neared completion and the ceremony of handing the ship over to her new owners approached. Clark was the ship's designated chief officer and with the second engineer formed Dent's representatives presiding over the final phase of the building. Whatever deficiencies the new ship revealed in service would not be attributed to her German builders, but to Clark and his colleague, Gerry Hunter, an outspoken Ulsterman. This point was emphasised by Dent's harassed marine superintendent when he paid his fortnightly visits to inspect progress.

'I have eight ships to supervise,' he would

complain, 'and it doesn't help to have three of them building on the ruddy Continent. I might as well be at sea again for all the time I get at home!'

Clark and Hunter tactfully and dutifully commiserated with their superior and, after he had left for Copenhagen, or Rotterdam and the ferry at the Hook of Holland, got on with their own task. This was demanding enough, and ranged from the relatively trivial to the complex and apparently more important. Thus, in addition to such matters as ensuring that the correct fittings were put in the wardrobes of the dozen passengers the *Ernest Shackleton* would soon carry, it was equally vital that the pipework and pumping arrangements of her ballast, oil, water and deep cargo tanks all functioned correctly. The arguments over the specification and the realities of construction were usually reconcilable and amicably settled. They rarely provoked anything more than merely technical disputes with the staff of the German yard, who were, it seemed, eager to get the job finished. If, in this busy time, Clark or Hunter were unaware of greater events impinging upon their lives, it was simply that the shipyard, in common with others in Hamburg, had very full order books. They could not blame the German officials for wanting the British order completed and the *Ernest Shackleton* on her way to the Oderhafen to start loading her first cargo for the Far East. They were eager to be finished themselves, though they wanted the ship in serviceable order, for Dent's were exacting masters.

Both men observed that the radical National Socialist government of Adolf Hitler had galvanised German shipbuilding. That much was clear to the two busy officers as they did their morning rounds of the ship, ticking off items in their notebooks or making additional comments, taking measurements or discussing details with the foremen and chargehands each assigned specific work aboard. But, at a more personal level, the lack of rancour aroused in the daily meetings was also due to the popularity of Hunter and Clark. The former because he was a man of outrageous opinion whose extreme Northern Irish accent made his English incomprehensible to German ship managers eager to practise their linguistic skills, but who made them laugh; and the latter because he could not only understand and interpret Hunter, but spoke German fluently. It was this ability which had recommended Dent's board to order Clark to stand-by the new tonnage being built in Hamburg.

Dent's were well aware of this talent, for Clark's father was a director of the company. Clark senior had married a beautiful German girl named Lisa Petersen, whom he had met in Hamburg when he had been second officer of the company's steamer *Henry Hudson*. In 1901 this ship had conveyed members of the board of the Eastern Steam Navigation Company to Hamburg, where she was scheduled to dry-dock and where her passenger accommodation was used as a boardroom for negotiations with a rival German shipping company. On the evening of their arrival Dent's held a reception which the ship's officers were obliged to attend. Lisa Petersen accompanied her widowed father, the chairman of F.G. Petersen Reederei, and in his distraction as he met Sir George Dent lay his daughter's fate: she and the *Henry Hudson*'s second officer fell head over heels in love.

Predictably Herr Petersen heartily disapproved of the marriage, but for two years the young lovers were intransigent. In the end Lisa's angry but indulgent father capitulated, extracting only a promise that the offspring of the young couple would be taught German and would visit Hamburg as often as possible. The match did the young Christopher Clark little harm, for the board of Dent's had come to an arrangement with their German competitors and were by then running a joint service to Chinese ports. Certain difficulties arising over the operation of ships in Chinese waters persuaded the joint boards to consider a common representative in the Treaty Port of Chinkiang. Christopher Clark soon found himself promoted to master and, after one voyage in command and with the title of 'Captain', the young couple were sent out to Chinkiang, where Captain Clark acted as marine superintendent, presiding over the interests of both companies until the arrangement foundered in the First World War. Life in the International Concessions of the remoter Treaty Ports took on a slightly surreal air, with the small isolated British and German communities abandoning their personal friendships and pretending neither group existed. Christopher and Lisa were almost totally ostracised, their prestige and, to the local population, the important fact of their 'face', diminishing with the severing of the joint service provided by Petersen's and Dent's. This strained life ended when Clark was posted to Hong Kong, where few knew of Lisa's nationality and where the couple continued to live, as far as was possible, a life of social inconspicuousness until the war ended. By this time they had two children, Carl and little John, who was eight years old and destined, in due course, to follow Carl aboard the static British public-school-cum-training-ship *Conway* as a cadet. Carl, passing out of *Conway* in 1915, joined Dent's and while still only an apprentice was torpedoed twice by U-boats of the Imperial

German Navy. He did not survive the second attack.

After the war Captain Clark returned to sea and made several voyages before being invited to join the board of the Eastern Steam Navigation Company. By then the brief post-war boom had turned sour. The depression in shipping was followed by a greater universal economic disaster. British shipowners felt beleaguered; mergers and takeovers occurred; the board of Eastern Steam were steered through these difficulties in part by the skill of Captain Clark, whose partnership with the new chairman, Sir Desmond Cranbrooke, was crucial to the company's survival. Curiously, both of these men were destined to play small, circumstantial, but significant parts in the fate of convoy PQ17.

During his stay standing-by the *Ernest Shackleton* in Hamburg, Clark had ensconced himself in a small hotel not far from the shipyard. It was a neat, family-run establishment which enjoyed the patronage of ships' officers like Clark, understanding their needs and providing them with modest facilities for them to undertake the considerable amount of paperwork which they brought home from the shipyard. Although the builders provided Clark and Hunter with a tiny office, neither man much enjoyed working there after hours and it served as little more than a place in which to change in and out of their boiler suits. Both preferred to relax in their hotel and sort out and co-ordinate the problems of the day over a stein of beer and a cigarette.

Ironically, as Hunter's engine room came nearer his expectations, his work eased, whereas Clark, as chief mate and therefore executive officer of the ship, had increasingly to consider the domestic arrangements necessary to have the ship stored, manned and in commission ready to enter service on the due date. Fortunately the hotel provided him with a telephone and he was able to contact Eastern Steam's Liverpool head-quarters with reasonable ease. The previous evening he had put in his requests for key personnel to join the following week and reminded the chief store clerk of outstanding indents. He knew the clerk, a Mr Wilson, quite well. Wilson was a quiet, efficient man with a sickly wife and a son with a club foot; Clark always thought Wilson possessed the intelligence and drive to have done better in life, but the clerk bore his twin burdens uncomplainingly. Nevertheless Clark often spent a few moments chatting to Wilson, partly out of a feeling of pity for the man, partly because he knew Wilson to be dis-creet. Thus the previous evening he had asked Wilson if he could find out who the company were intending to send over as the *Ernest Shackleton*'s bosun. Clark was anxious to get hold of a man named Dixon, but feared that an older petty officer would be given the new ship as a mark of confidence, though everyone knew a new ship was a work-out and the old boy, Perry by name, would be better left aboard the *James Clark Ross* where he had been vegetating happily for years.

'They haven't decided yet, Mr Clark...'

'That means it's Perry,' Clark had said, disappointed.

'Er, I don't think so, sir...'

'Well, if it isn't Perry and it isn't Dixon, who are they thinking of, Wilson?'

'You haven't seen any English papers, Mr Clark?'

'Fat chance,' responded Clark, considering his own fraught existence and at first missing Wilson's point.

'The news isn't too good, I'm afraid, sir.'

There was something about Wilson's tone which was both ominous and somehow intimate, as though the man wanted to bridge the distance between them, and Clark was quite unaware that this was because he himself was situated in Germany.

Instead Clark assumed the bad news was of a domestic nature, something to do with the ship or the company.

'What's up, Dent's share prices diving

again?' he asked with an air of flippancy that increased Wilson's apprehension.

'No, no, nothing like that, it's a consequence of the troubles in Danzig...' And that was as far as Wilson got, for the next moment the line went dead and Clark became aware that he had been chatting for longer than he ought to have done. Moreover, neither Danzig nor its troubles meant much to Clark and he so far forgot about the matter that he failed to mention it to Gerry Hunter over dinner that night, preferring to grumble about the indecisiveness of the company in the matter of choosing a bosun.

That Clark, a German speaker, was unaware of the manoeuvrings of the Nazi government from any local newspaper, or the conversations of those about him in the shipyard, needs some explanation, but it is easily given. By nature seafarers are not usually politically inquisitive; politics are the province of those who dwell on land and, if he read newspaper headlines, Clark read the Nazi version of events with a naïve and uncritical eye. Moreover, Jack Clark was a man whose interests were entirely absorbed by the sea and, in his youthful conceit, he had conceived a vague contempt for the machinations of faction and party. He would by nature have rather read a book than a newspaper and an early adventure had diverted his attention away from the cut and thrust of commercial acumen that had decided his father's career. Whilst still at school aboard the *Conway*, Clark and another senior cadet had been selected to accompany what turned out to be the last British Arctic expedition under sail. Led by Commander Frank Worsley, whose name had been made by his part in Sir Ernest Shackleton's ill-starred *Endurance* expedition, Clark's experiences as an ordinary seaman aboard the small brigantine *Island* in which Worsley visited Spitsbergen and Franz Joseph Land had entranced him. By way of a diversion from the drudgery of life in the shipyard, what leisure hours he possessed were spent reading books on exploration, which he collected. Currently, and for the third time, he was reading Cook's journals. It was for Clark not only fitting that the shipping company to which he was apprenticed on his return from the Arctic named its vessels after explorers; indeed, it was a private delight that his present appointment was to a ship named after Worsley's heroic 'Boss', Shackleton himself. Had he known how these almost infantile connections were to intertwine in his life, he might not have viewed them with such enthusiasm.

Thereafter, sufficiently cushioned by circumstance and influence against the worst deprivations of the depression, Clark had, unlike many seafarers, escaped the despair of protracted unemployment himself. His career as a junior officer as he rose in rank with the acquisition of his certificates of competency had not been greatly interfered with by the decline in world trade. Moreover, Dent's, with their fast liner services, had secured two government contracts and thereby saved most of their ships from enforced idleness.

Clark might still have gleaned all was not well in the world during that fateful summer had a number of other circumstances not hidden the facts from him. Had Hunter been the remotest bit interested in current affairs, *he* might have drawn his colleague's attention to the impending crisis between Germany and the Anglo-French. Hunter, however, was no more interested in politics outside Ulster than in flying to the moon. But Hunter's parochialism was of little account when set against the smokescreen of family, for Clark's German relations had played host to him on several occasions since his arrival in Hamburg. To be fair to Clark, he had declined their invitation to him to stay with them in their large house in Altona, a pleasant residential suburb of greater Hamburg that lay some miles below the city centre on the north bank of the Elbe. During the early weeks of his sojourn at the shipyard, Clark had regularly spent his weekends in the company of his mother's older brother, Uncle Reinhard, and his family. Reinhard Petersen had two sons: Johannes, at thirty, was a year older than Jack, while cousin Kurt was thirty-three. Kurt was an officer in the Kriegsmarine, so only Johannes lived at home with his parents and strutted about in what Jack thought was a rather ridiculous brown uniform bearing the red, white and black armband of the Nazi swastika. Clark found Johannes' constant eulogiums upon the virtues of Adolf Hitler and of the progressive nature of the National Socialist movement tedious but, because he quite liked Uncle Reinhard and Aunt Eva was a kindly soul, he took little notice of them. Clark had been accustomed to Johannes' bombast since childhood. The political discussion that did take place in the Petersens' household was not unnaturally weighted in favour of the national government's policies and their successful regeneration of the German economy, particularly insofar as it affected Hamburg. Although F.G. Petersen's had long since passed into liquidation, Uncle Reinhard was eager to re-establish the former Anglo-German links and would have liked to have resurrected his family's fortunes in shipping. What was never mentioned was the intimidation of minorities, though occasional veiled allusions to 'riff-raff' were made by Uncle Reinhard, and Johannes referred darkly to the 'scum' which were being removed from their parasitical positions in German business.

Unable to judge the extent or nature of outrages being perpetrated by Nazi Party members, blinded by the familial ties of blood, and working daily with Germans whom he had come to respect as they all went about their business of building the *Ernest Shackleton*, Clark was almost hermetically sealed from any objective appreciation of the deteriorating European situation. Nor had he taken much notice of another circumstance which had occurred about a month earlier, before the progress of the ship's building became increasingly absorbing and his duties less easy to lay aside in favour of visits to Altona.

He had arrived at the Petersens' house one Friday evening at the end of July to be greeted by Johannes with the news that he had better get a good night's sleep because Kurt had arrived from Berlin and the three of them were all going out wildfowling on the following morning.

'Where is Kurt?' Clark asked.

Johannes pulled a face. 'Oh, he has gone to see some piece of tail he likes. She is a silly cow but then Kurt is a sailor like you and,' Johannes lowered his voice so that his mother could not hear, 'he likes to fuck anything.'

'I see,' Clark responded with a chuckle, hoping to embarrass his cousin. 'I thought it was you Nazis who liked to fuck anything, you said you had fucked Austria...'

'Ah, Jack, you think you are a clever bastard.' Johannes grinned back, then added in a lower tone, 'This girl is no good for Kurt and I think he has some stupid idea he is going to marry her. I am very worried about him. He cannot marry her.'

'Why? What's the matter with her?'

'Oh, she is not right for Kurt. He is stationed in Berlin and I keep asking him to bring back one of those smart Berliners with an educated arse for his little brother, even if he doesn't want one for himself. He says they are not worth the trouble, which is a clear indication that he has got it bad for Magda...'

'Magda?' Clark frowned. 'Magda ... er, was it Liepmann?'

'Yes ... You see, now you know, you don't approve...'

'I haven't seen Madga since we were kids,' Clark said, remembering a skinny dark girl with unsightly pigtails and huge eyes who had once played with them during some family gathering. 'But isn't she some relation?'

'Yes, that's what makes it worse, she's a second cousin besides being a Jew.'

'Does that make any difference?'

'What? Being a Jew?'

'No, being a second cousin?'

'Not as much as being a Jew does, for God's sake!'

'Well, if Kurt doesn't care, why should you worry?'

'You don't understand, do you, Jack?'

'Apparently not.'

But they got no further, for at this point Uncle Reinhard came into the room and Kurt's marriage plans were hurriedly dropped.

'Time for a little schnapps, I think,' Uncle Reinhard proposed, rubbing his hands, 'and you can tell me how your ship is coming along, Jack.'

Clark did not see the elder of his two cousins until the following morning, and even when Kurt appeared in the first light of dawn, he seemed disinclined to talk. Clark attributed no significance to this. Neither the hour nor the purpose of their excursion was conducive to idle chatter. He declined a gun and offered to row the skiff which the family kept in a boathouse on the Elbe. Pulling across to the river's southern bank where an area of marsh lay, bordering the river with the shallows beloved by duck, Jack pottered happily while his cousins blazed away for two hours, their English spaniels throwing mud and water over their masters as they brought back the booty. Jack lay on his oars between the two marksmen as they stalked through the shallows in their waders, collecting the haul until Kurt and Johannes had had enough and announced a strong desire for breakfast.

On the walk back to the house carrying their bag and with the spaniels romping about them, it was Johannes who extolled the virtues of the vigour induced by their early-morning pursuit so that Jack gathered such manly activities formed some part of the Nazi creed. For the first time a sense of unease crept into Jack's mind. He possessed an innate suspicion of linking the personal with so obviously a national movement as the Nazi ethos. Something of his scepticism must have shown on his face, for Kurt caught his eye and Jack sensed he too felt something of his own awkwardness. But he dismissed the notion as silly; how could he possibly know what Kurt was thinking? Kurt was a serious, reserved man and was probably simply embarrassed by his younger brother's rather preposterous enthusiasm. Indeed, this seemed confirmed when Kurt snapped, 'Please shut up, Hannes. Adolf Hitler is not God!'

Johannes shut up as Kurt had commanded, but the mood of the morning had been shattered. The younger brother's face bore a stony, resentful expression with which his English cousin was unfamiliar and they trudged the rest of the way in silence. Even now Jack Clark attributed Johannes' mood to mere sibling interaction: it was only much later that he realised it was evidence of the ideological chasm that was opening up between the two brothers.

But there was one moment that weekend that left Jack truly perplexed and it occurred just as he was leaving to return to his hotel late on the Sunday afternoon. In his honour, Aunt Eva had served tea in the English mode, and both Uncle Reinhard and his two sons were in decorous and rather awkward attendance.

'I shall carry your bag down to the tram-stop,' Kurt announced as Jack laid his cup and saucer down and turned to take leave of Johannes.

'He is going to his Jewish tart,' Johannes said in a disagreeable stage whisper which, Jack thought, both Kurt and his father could hear.

'Well don't be long, my dear,' Aunt Eva said, looking at her elder son.

Kurt spread his hands and shrugged. 'You would not think a Korvettenkapitän in the Kriegsmarine would need so much mothering, would you Jack, eh?'

Jack, not knowing quite what to say with Johannes' remark still in his ears, smiled wanly.

'Come,' said Kurt, 'let me have your bag.'

'There's no need...'

'I insist.'

They had left the house and garden behind them before Kurt spoke. 'I heard what Hannes said to you and it is true, I *am* intending to see my Jewish tart.' Kurt said. 'Do you remember Magda Liepmann, Jack? She played with us once or twice when you came to stay as a little boy.'

'I recall a dark girl with long plaits.'

Kurt chuckled. 'Oh, you should see her long plaits now...'

'I should like to meet her again,' Jack said conversationally.

'Perhaps you will,' Kurt said, before going on, a note of urgency in his tone. 'But there is something I wanted to speak to you about; something between ourselves. I know you are fond of Hannes, Jack, but be careful what you say to him; he is a Nazi and not to be trusted.'

'I must say I don't particularly warm to his zeal,' Jack responded. 'He's rather too dogmatic for my taste.'

'You don't understand,' Kurt interrupted, 'and I have no time to explain, but it is best that you are circumspect in your dealings with him, as with all Nazis. He is typical, a convinced Nazi, and now father has joined the Party.' Kurt paused a moment and set Clark's bag down to change hands.

'Here, let me.' They shared the weight

48

between them, then went on.

'Anyway,' resumed Kurt, 'it is not circumstantial that I am in Hamburg. I have a job to do and you may see me in the shipyard in the next few weeks...'

'That would be pleasant...'

'No, it would not, Jack.' Kurt's tone was unhappily vehement. 'I only wish it were so. I tried to get another assignment, but I could not pull enough strings. Of course, I knew you were standing-by the *Ernest Shackleton*, but I did not wish to meet you, not on board, at least.'

'Why not?' Jack looked sharply at his cousin.

Kurt remained silent for a moment as they walked in step, each holding a handle of Jack's bag. 'Because, like sleeping with a Jewish girl, having an English cousin is beginning to look dangerous in this country.'

Jack digested this news. 'And that is why your mother told you not to be out long?'

'You begin to understand, Jack,' Kurt said. 'Look, there is the tram stop, so I must tell you quickly that it is better that if we meet in the shipyard, you *must* pretend not to recognise me. And, forgive me Jack, but don't come to the house too often any more. I shan't be staying there, I've naval accommodation in the city, but it is best for all of us that no direct connections are made by other people.'

'But Hannes...'

'Hannes will keep his mouth shut about you, if he knows what is good for him, unlike that Austrian dogshit he thinks is Jesus Christ. Besides, he has applied to join the Kriegsmarine like his big brother...'

'You don't approve?'

They were approaching the tram stop and a small queue waited for transport into Hamburg. Kurt stopped, jerking the bag swinging between them and compelling Jack to face him. Jack took both handles and held out his hand to Kurt.

'What do you think the opinion of a non-Party Korvetten kapitän counts for in these matters?' he asked ironically. 'No, I shall recommend him. I may need the protection of a Nazi brother, God help me. Goodbye, Jack. I hope we meet again.'

'I was hoping to meet Magda,' Jack said, trying to introduce a flippant tone to counter the depressing gloom that seemed now to have enveloped Kurt ever since they had set out on the duck shoot.

'I think you will,' said Kurt.

'We could have dinner together.'

'Yes, we could,' Kurt said doubtfully. 'Perhaps we will. Here comes your tram. Goodbye.'

And then he turned and was gone into the summer night, striding away towards his dark lover with the transformed pigtails.

So absorbing had the work of completing the *Ernest Shackleton* become that Jack, to his retrospective shame, almost forgot about this odd encounter. Kurt's sombre character lent an air of personal dramatisation to the affair and this had tended to demonise his younger brother. Johannes was not such a bad fellow and probably nursed no more than the prejudices of many young German men. In this reflection Jack Clark forgot the perceptive notice he had taken of his aunt's concern, taking refuge, as many do, in hoping things were not as bad as they sometimes appeared. Long afterwards Clark could see with fateful hindsight how these circumstances had bound him and his life inextricably with events to come.

It was this personal entrapment that had enabled him to remain silent for so long after the climacteric to which these minor events were but the opening gambits. Perhaps too, his later secrecy was an expiation for his failure to perceive the seeds of tragedy, a tragedy which was as much personally as historically disastrous. But such consequences and reactions that bright morning as he went aboard the *Ernest Shackleton* lay far in the future.

In the weeks since his encounter with Kurt he had not seen his cousins at all. Clark had not returned to Altona to visit Johannes or his parents and, although he had observed a group of uniformed naval officers once or twice in the shipyard, he had not recognised Kurt among them.

But that morning he and Gerry Hunter walked into their meeting with the shipyard managers and found Kurt sitting at the table. There was a palpable air of awkwardness among the men, with whom they had discussed matters for months and whose moods and methods they had grown familiar with. The ship manager, Herr Eberbach, explained the presence of Korvettenkapitän Petersen as an observer and the discussion commenced. As they concluded and gathered up their papers, Kurt spoke for the first time. 'You speak excellent German, Herr Clark.'

'Thank you,' responded Clark, meeting his cousin's gaze and sensing the charade was for the benefit of Kurt's fellow countrymen, if not a test of himself. 'As I have told my friends here,' he said, gesturing at the shipyard personnel, 'I have German blood and it was a second language at home...'

He did not think he had ever said more than that to any of the casual acquaintances he had worked with in Hamburg, but he was not 100 per cent certain. No one seemed particularly interested, however, and if he had ever mentioned his relatives' name to Gerry Hunter, the engineer did not appear to have made a connection with the dark-uniformed German naval officer just then rising from behind the table. Of course, he could not be sure, and the presence of the Korvettenkapitän seemed to inconvenience the men of the shipyard, so that Clark felt a lingering unease that he had let Kurt down.

'I shall be interested in observing your inclining experiment,' Kurt said conversationally, looking down at a paper before him. 'And I see that is scheduled for next week. You will be ready for it I hope, Herr Eberbach?'

'Certainly, Kapitän.'

'And you are already bringing members of your crew over from England, Mr Clark?'

Clark met Kurt's gaze and nodded. 'I have requested them, yes, but I am waiting for confirmation from my owners.'

'But you both hope to have the ship in commission by October?' Kurt's gesture took in both Clark and Eberbach.

'By the end of the first week,' Eberbach said emphatically.

'Provided everything is in order and as promised,' Clark added with a smile.

As the conference dispersed, Clark avoided Kurt's eyes as he left the room with Hunter.

'Something funny about that meeting,' said Hunter the moment they were outside, so that Clark's heart missed a beat and he felt the breath tight in his throat.

'Yes,' he managed, 'the presence of that German naval officer...'

'Oh no, it wasn't that,' Hunter broke in. 'He wants the fitting-out berth, I heard. They're now in a hurry, falling over themselves to oblige the navy. They've a hull in Bremen they want to tow round here to complete, so there's no mystery in that. Old Korvetten-what's-his-name just wanted to make sure that if the yard completed we'd have the ship away without a delay. No, it wasn't that...'

It was odd how Hunter, with no knowledge of German, could find out so much more about what was going on in the yard than Clark himself, but he had little time for this reflection with the engineer in full flood.

'I was just taken by the way Eberbach went all sheepish when I said that they were leaving the fitting of the poop accommodation and the completion of the centre-castle contactor houses a bit late. They've been dragging their heels on those areas for a fortnight now...'

'They said there was a delay in the supply of switchgear and the accommodation won't take long to finish off.'

'Oh come on now, Jackie, don't you go swallowing all that crap. Did you not see how that little bastard Kessler was grinning?'

'The electrical foreman?'

'That's the one, the little weasel. And have

you seen the badge he wears in his lapel? He's a fucking Nazi right enough...'

'Well, so what?'

'Have you not yet rumbled the fact that the Nazis are a bunch of shits...?'

Clark laughed. This was Ulster prejudice taken too far! 'So they're like the Fenians, are they, Gerry?'

'You can laugh, Jackie, but you mark my words! You get on to Liverpool and let's get a crew and fuck off out of this place. I've had Hamburg up to my eyeballs. I don't care if the Chink firemen down aft sit and shit in buckets and I'll build a contactor house myself wi' a bit of help, but let's get this ship to sea.'

They separated, Hunter to go and harass Kessler, and Clark to telephone Liverpool. In the little office he picked up the phone and got through to the shipyard's switchboard. For twenty minutes he waited impatiently while the operator tried to contact Liverpool but in the end the poor girl admitted defeat.

'Never mind,' he said, 'I'll try again in an hour or two.'

He went back on board the ship and, for half an hour, immersed himself in checking through the specification. He was expecting a stores delivery that day and, to his delight, several large packages had been carried aboard and left in the near-completed wheelhouse. He knew what they were instantly, the folios of British Admiralty charts without which no Eastern Steam Navigation Company ship ventured far. They covered the entire world and came with sailing directions, the *International Code of Signals* manual, the company's volume of *Standing Orders* and several other books and documents. A few minutes later one of the shipyards' storemen, recognisable in the brown cotton overall coat worn by such functionaries, came into the chartroom, where Clark was putting the books in the neat shelves shiny with new varnish. The man carried a neat brown-paper-wrapped package in each hand.

'Ah, the chronometers,' Clark said with relish.

'Good German chronometers, Herr Clark,' the man said with a grin. 'To go with your good German ship.'

Clark cut the sisal string round each, peeled back the paper and looked at the first of the clockfaces staring up at him from its double ring of brass gimballing. The name of the maker was set over the word: London.

'These are...' he began with mild astonishment, looking up, but the storeman pre-empted him and closed the chartroom door.

'Yes, they're British and,' the man interrupted, speaking perfect English, 'it pains me to have to tell you to leave them behind, but I take you for Mr John Clark.'

Clark frowned. 'Yes, and who are you and,' he added looking down at the chronometer face again, 'what d'you mean by...?'

'My name is Sanders and I'm from the British consulate. Be a good fellow and get your men together. I want you out of this country by tomorrow morning. You won't get through to Dentco, the authorities here will prevent it. I don't think they are interested in interning you or your colleague, but they want your ship and I'm afraid it looks as though they are going to get her by default. You must get yourself to the Hook of Holland and on a ferry to Harwich by tomorrow night.'

'Why should the German authorities want this ship? I don't understand ... and if they do, I can't just walk off...'

'That's exactly what I want you to do and what we have persuaded Dentco is the only solution to the problem. We had hoped to get her away before the situation became volatile, but Berlin and Moscow signed a non-aggression pact five days ago and we've just formalised our arrangements with Poland into a full alliance.'

'Poland? What the hell has Poland...?'

'There's going to be a war, Mr Clark,' Sanders said with a faint air of exasperation. 'Or at least I think it most likely. I have been living with the possibility for weeks now

57

while you, it seems,' he added with a mild sarcasm of penetrating accuracy, 'have been too involved with your ship to notice.'

'A *war*?'

For a moment an incredulous Clark stood stock still and Sanders was intelligent enough to let the full import of his grave news sink in. Clark rallied his scepticism once more.

'How do I know you are who you say you are? I mean, if the Germans want the ship, you could be...'

'Yes, yes, I understand your misgivings, Mr Clark, but here...' Sanders held out his diplomatic pass. 'You'll have to trust me, old man. I know you have German relatives...'

Clark's response was sharp, prompted by an old family fear and compounded by his distaste for Johannes' National Socialist dogma. 'I hope that you don't consider me a sympathiser with the German government,' he snapped.

'Get yourself and your men to the Hook, then. I'll not be far behind you.'

'You've known about this for some time,' Clark said, pushing the chronometer, which, he found, he had been clutching to himself.

Sanders nodded. 'As I have said, we hoped to get the ship completed before things got to this pass, but it's too late for worrying about that now. Be on your way home and prove your patriotism. Dentco will approve,

I assure you.'

Clark emerged from his shock under a flood of comprehension. 'They *do* want the bloody ship, by God! That's what Kur ... Korvettenkapitän Petersen's doing here! And that's why they're delaying work on the poop. There'll be a gun there and others forward on the contactor houses! They're going to make a commerce raider, or a Q-ship out of her!'

Sanders nodded again. 'Bravo, Mr Clark.' He sighed. 'Now look, we've left all this a bit late, I'm afraid, so we're going to provide you with transport. There will be a Volkswagen parked outside your hotel this evening. Get yourself to the Dutch border as quickly as you can and don't hang about when you have crossed it. Get a train from Groningen to the Hook. I want you back home telling Dentco I've done my bit.'

'Why don't we sabotage the ship and prevent...'

'Look, Clark, neither you nor I are Bulldog Drummond. Let's just go home like good boys and then, if you feel so inclined, you can embark on any number of escapades.'

Clark felt suddenly foolish and nodded sheepishly, looking down at the exposed chronometer. 'It seems a pity to leave this behind,' he said.

'Take it with you then if it bothers you,' said Sanders curtly, 'I've got other things to worry about.'

'A Volkswagen, you say...?'

'All ready to go. Full of fuel. You can drive, can't you?'

'Er, yes.'

'And you have some money? A ship's imprest, or something?'

'Oh yes.'

'Then take the lot and consider yourself lucky we're helping you to the extent we are. We don't normally do so much for Distressed British Seamen.'

'Is that what I am now? Most kind. I'd better go and find Hunter, the Second Engineer.'

'Good idea, and by the way, I wouldn't mention this to anyone apart from your colleague. Don't say anything to the yard people. Just bugger off quietly at the end of the afternoon.'

'There're going to notice we're not here tomorrow morning.'

'Well,' Sanders shrugged, 'so be it.' He held out his hand. 'Goodbye and good luck. I think we're going to need quite a lot of it.'

Clark could not find Hunter immediately. A workman in the engine room told him that he had heard the Irishman talking to one of the chargehands and they had gone aft to take a look at the steering gear. When Clark reached the steering flat it proved empty, though its steel door was tied back and it smelt of wet paint. He stared briefly at the gleaming quadrant which seemed ready for instant use. As he hung a moment in the doorway, Clark felt a creeping anger that it would be a Nazi voice that would order its first operational movement. Ironically, his 'God damn!' of fury was enunciated in his perfect German.

As he went ashore it occurred to him that he ought to try and get through to Liverpool again. If he understood the spirit of Sanders' instructions, he should behave normally. Once again, he could not get through. It was clear now that he was not meant to, and he recalled being cut off when he had last spoken to Wilson.

'Well, I'm damned,' he muttered in English.

It was when he left the shore office and began to hurry back to the ship that he bumped into Kessler.

'Herr Clark, you are in a hurry...'

'There is a great deal to be done, Herr Kessler, as you know. Have you seen Mr Hunter?'

'I have just come from speaking with him. He is in the conference room, talking with Korvettenkapitän Petersen. Korvetten-kapitän Petersen is most interested in the engines, you know, and the maximum speed of your ship. I have told him that she is designed for eighteen knots. That is correct, is it not? But I expect that she can make twenty!'

'Excuse me, Herr Kessler...'

'Of course, Herr Clark. I had forgotten you were in a hurry.'

Clark found Hunter in the meeting room alone with Kurt. He stared from one to the other, not sure what to make of this odd mismatch under the circumstances.

'Ah, Jack, there you are,' Hunter said, turning to face his shipmate. 'The captain here has been telling why he is interested in the ship's movements. It's just like I guessed, the German Navy is fitting out some naval auxiliaries in this yard and they want our berth...'

'I see.' Clark's heart was hammering in his chest. 'Well Gerry, we have some problems arising on board...'

'Nothing serious, I hope, Herr Clark,' Kurt broke in, catching Clark's eye.

'Er, that depends upon whose point of view you are taking,' Clark responded, holding his cousin's gaze and feeling a tightening of the muscles in his gut. 'It's pretty bad for us ... on the ship...'

'What the fuck's up?' Hunter asked, standing up in a posture of alarm.

Clark turned to Hunter. 'Bit of a problem on board, Gerry. Not something we can talk about in front of strangers.' He threw Kurt a final glance with the last word and saw a slight frown cross his cousin's face. 'I'll see you in the chartroom in half an hour. In the meantime, I want a word with the Captain here, and I think you should take look at the steering gear.'

He watched with relief as Hunter reacted. 'What the fuck have the bastards done? It was all right an hour ago.'

'Go and have a look,' Clark said coldly, adding, 'and I'll see you in the chartroom in half an hour.'

'I'll be there, don't you worry!' Fuelled with uncertainty and concern Hunter hurried from the room.

Shutting the door behind him, Clark rounded on his cousin. 'You might have told me you were intending to take over *my* ship!'

'I'm sorry, but how do you know?'

'I've just been ordered to head for the Hook of Holland!'

'Who by?' Kurt frowned.

'The British consulate.'

'God damn!'

'I understand that war is imminent.' The impact of these words clearly surprised Kurt.

'No! Not between England and Germany! If we requisition a ship being built in Germany we would pay compensation.'

'You are beginning to sound like a Nazi. Who are you going to go to war with? I know it isn't the Communists, you've just signed a

63

pact with Moscow...'

Kurt's mouth dropped open in unfeigned astonishment. 'How do you know *that*?'

'How do *you*?' Clark responded.

'I don't.' Kurt looked genuinely astonished. 'I have no knowledge of any pact with the Soviet Union.'

'Well, I have to be gone, cousin, and we look like becoming enemies.'

'No, this is not possible,' Kurt said, clearly distressed, his voice edged with despair and desperation. 'Not even Adolf Hitler would want to go to war with Great Britain, while it is impossible he has allied himself with the Communists!'

Clark's news had quite clearly discomposed his cousin, who ran his hand through his hair in a frantic motion.

'I hope you are right, Kurt, but I am not keen to hang about on your evaluation of the situation. There is clearly a requirement in the minds of your masters for my ship...'

'Yes, but that is part of a long-term plan ... My God, what am I saying?' Kurt paused and stared at Clark. The admission was quickly followed by the true state of Kurt's thoughts. 'When are you going?' he asked, swiftly adding, 'You must take Magda with you.'

'*What*?'

'Get her out of Germany for me! Please, I beg you!'

'For God's sake, Kurt...'

'I'll get you a car...'

'I've got one.'

'Good! Tell me where to be with her. What time are you going? Come, quickly, I don't want to be found talking to you like this!' Sweat stood out like glass beads on Kurt's forehead and he moved like a chained dog.

'I can't just take Magda...'

'Why? I know hundreds of Jews have gone to England since the Night of Broken Glass. Even you have heard of that, for God's sake!'

'Yes, of course, but what's the panic? A few businesses smashed up...'

'Good God, it was more than that! Why do you think so many Jewish families abandoned their livelihoods here? They are being treated like shit, Jack, you really have no idea!' Kurt paused as Clark wrestled with his conscience. He and Hunter had a car. It should not be too difficult, simply driving across the border into the Netherlands. What had he got to fear? They could pretend Magda was his girlfriend ... Yes, that was it.

'All right, I'll do it.'

'Thank God.' Relief was plain on Kurt's face. 'Tell me where you will pick her up.'

'At the tram stop.'

'You'll come out to Altona?' Kurt's delight was manifest. 'You are a true friend, Jack. God bless you!' Kurt paused a moment, tears filled his eyes and then, clapping Clark on the shoulders, he said, 'I must go.'

A moment later Clark was walking back to the ship. The sun rode high in the blue sky but the glory had gone out of the day. It was then that he realised that to drive out to Altona took him in the wrong direction, away from the Elbe tunnel and the Reichsbahn to Bremen and the Dutch border beyond.

'Bollocks!' he swore in English.

MAGDA

August–September 1939

If Clark anticipated any difficulties with Gerry Hunter, he was surprised by the ease with which the second engineer accepted the course events had taken. It was clear, when he reached the steering flat, that he had been sent on a fool's errand, but he was intelligent enough to realise at the same moment that Clark had had his motive. Having heard what Sanders had told Clark, the Irishman sat in silence for a moment or two staring at his colleague, then he shook his head.

'Bugger me,' he swore quietly, 'we've done all this work for nothing, Jack; all this

66

coming and going and now we've got to go home and leave the ship.' Incredibly, Hunter's eyes were bright with tears. Then he banged his fist down so heavily on the chart table that he made the half-unwrapped chronometer jump so that Clark, distracted for a moment, feared for the safety of its delicate mechanism. 'Fuck it, Jack, I need a drink. Then I'll pack and I'll be ready for you. You say we've got a car?'

Clark hesitated a moment. 'Yes. And we have to pretend that nothing is wrong until we leave the yard this evening.'

'That's going to be fucking difficult.'

'And there's something else.'

'It never rains but it pours. What?'

'We're taking someone else with us.'

'Who?'

'A Jewish girl.'

'A Yid? Oh, God Almighty, Jack, what are you, some kind of fucking hero? Have you been dolling a Yid while I thought you were off taking tea with your Auntie?'

'She's a distant relative, Gerry, and we're going to get her out of Germany.'

'So that's where you went,' Hunter said, relieving Clark of explaining the awkward gap of half an hour, 'to telephone.'

'Yes,' Clark lied.

'Well that's settled then. And how do you propose I spend the next few hours play-acting?'

'As best you can. Go and give that bastard Kessler a difficult afternoon. Be ready to go at ten o'clock tonight.'

'*Ten*? Why are we waiting that long?'

'Because it won't be safe to move the girl before then.'

'This is crazy, Jack.'

'We're going home on leave. God knows we've earned it.'

'Who goes home on leave at eleven o'clock at night?'

'A couple of British sailors after a last spree in St Pauli. Now let's get back to normal. Oh, and by the way Gerry – and you must forgive me for saying so – but I'd rather you had a decent meal before you go, rather than a lot to drink. You can act the drunk.'

'Don't worry, Jack. I'll just have a stein. I'm in no mood for the German stuff now, anyway.'

The Volkswagen was not there when the two men sat down to dinner in the hotel; but it was when they looked afterwards. Regarding the beetle-shaped vehicle they exchanged glances and Hunter said in a low voice, 'There's fuck all room in that thing.'

'Just an overnight bag, then, Gerry.'

'Let's hope the woman coming along understands the concept of travelling light,' Hunter murmured disagreeably. With a wan smile Clark recalled Gerry was married.

They both retired to their rooms to complete their packing and put their feet up. They had left their working clothes in the little office, where, in one final act, Clark had again attempted to get through to Liverpool. Once again the girl on the switchboard had been apologetic. Clark had affected disappointment and announced he would postpone the call until the following day. Now packing, Clark stared at the chronometer which he had brought back to the hotel with him, ostensibly to start on a radio time signal from Berlin. Taking it home was a foolish thing to do, he thought now, and he considered leaving it behind in the hotel room, along with the full sea kit both he and Hunter had arrived in Hamburg with.

At ten o'clock they quietly left the hotel and got into the Volkswagen.

'It never occurred to me to ask if you can drive,' Hunter said as he waited for Clark to start the ugly little car.

'Oh yes, I think I can manage this,' Clark said as the air-cooled engine fired and he switched the lights on.

'I can too, if and when you want a relief,' Hunter offered. 'And I've got three small bottles of beer so that we can appear drunk at the border.'

'Thoughtful of you,' said Clark grimly as he let in the clutch and they began to move over the cobbles. 'I was only intending to convey the impression of mild merriment, not get us arrested for inebriation.'

'Tell me Jack, I've wanted to ask you for a long time, but why, with a father on the board, did you have to go to sea?'

'Because my father wasn't always on the board and he thinks a man should have a trade.'

'Well, I hope you haven't lost it,' Hunter said, adding a mild blasphemy as Clark coped uncertainly with a corner and recalled which side of the road to drive on. He then fell silent as they headed west, catching intermittent glimpses of the river shining darkly on their left. The traffic was light, though they regularly passed trams, reminding them of their rendezvous.

They reached the tram stop nearest to Altona. There was no sign of a soul and Hunter swore. Clark felt a coldness about his heart and considered for a moment driving directly to the Petersen house, but reflected that Kurt was unlikely to have taken Magda there prior to spiriting her out of Germany. Nor did he have the slightest idea where Magda lived. For ten long minutes they sat in the car consumed by anxiety. Clark had switched the engine off and was telling himself that they were doing nothing in any way illegal, indeed he was about to comment on the fact to Hunter when the Irishman, staring over his shoulder, suddenly nudged him.

'Is this them?'

Clark craned round in his seat and instantly recognised Kurt bareheaded in the fitful street lighting, his blond hair slicked down upon his head. The woman's face was invisible, cast down under a broad-brimmed hat, but it was clear her advance was reluctant and Kurt was hastening her along.

Hunter had noticed the same thing. 'Methinks the lady doth protest,' he quipped.

'Sit still,' said Clark, realising that Hunter might recognise Kurt as his interlocutor of the morning. He felt suddenly protective of his cousin. He got out of the car and walked towards the approaching couple.

'Good evening Fräulein Liepmann. Perhaps you remember me,' he said in a low voice, raising his trilby hat and breaking into the hissed remonstration between the two lovers.

'Please, please, please just go and trust me,' he heard Kurt saying, bending over the girl as he came up to Clark.

'Jack,' he said, looking up. 'Thank God.' Then he slipped into English, explaining in a low voice that Magda had opposed his idea of her escaping to England alone. 'She wanted you to take her whole family, but I said that that was impossible. Only her mother and her father's pleas persuaded her to come, but she is not at all happy.'

'I understand,' Clark said. Then reverting

71

to German he said kindly, 'Magda, we must go. I am sorry, but we have many kilometres to drive tonight.' He held out his hand to Kurt for her bags. 'Don't come any closer, Kurt, I don't want you recognised by my colleague.'

'No, of course not. Thanks.'

Clark turned to the sobbing woman. 'Say goodbye to Kurt, Magda.' He turned and, opening the bonnet, squashed one of the bags in beside his own and Hunter's, then placed the other on the back seat of the car, standing aside for her to get in behind the driver's seat.

'I'll get in the back,' volunteered Hunter.

'Stay where you are for a bit, Gerry.' Clark bent down to prevent Hunter getting out of the car. 'We can change later. Let's be on our way.'

'Come, Magda,' Clark pressed.

The two lovers were clasped in each other's arms and the lights of a passing car caught them for a moment as it drove by. Further down the road a tram rumbled towards them. Suddenly Magda broke away and came towards Clark as he stood beside the car. Kurt watched her go, a forlorn creature, wracked by his own misery – an image that long remained in Clark's memory.

Madga pushed past him and climbed into the car. Clark raised his hand to Kurt, let down the driver's seat and got in beside

Hunter. A moment later they were heading east for the Elbe tunnel.

They drove in silence until, beyond the tunnel, they turned west along the Reichsbahn to Bremen. In due course they were in open country, where the moonlight bathed the landscape in a pallid, almost surreal light. Occasionally a sob came from the back seat, but soon that was replaced by quiet until Magda coughed. Whether or not she had been asleep, neither man could tell, but Hunter broke the silence, turning in his seat and holding out his hand in an oddly distorted but formal gesture.

'I'm Gerald Hunter, Fräulein,' he introduced himself. 'I don't know if you speak English, miss, but may I say I'm glad of your company, though sorry you've had to leave home like this.'

'Thank you,' she said in English. 'That is kind of you. I am sorry for not being, er...' she faltered and spoke a word in German.

'Grateful,' Clark translated.

'I remember you,' she said in German. 'You are John and were once a thin little boy. I remember looking for you when we played hide-and-seek in Kurt's house, but that was a long time ago.'

It occurred to Clark that this benighted creature had had even less time to prepare for her unexpected departure than he and

Hunter. Moreover, while he and the Irish-man were going home, Magda had not the faintest notion of where she was going, nor with whom she would spend her future. He thought of his own family home on the Wirral peninsula. It was not huge, but a spacious family house which no longer contained a family. His father had lived there alone except for the married couple who provided him with a gardener-cum-driver and a housekeeper, his only companions since the death of Jack's mother in 1933. Would he be glad of company? Clark could not tell, but he knew his father would not turn the destitute Magda away.

'My mother died six years ago, but my father will make you welcome, Magda,' he said over his shoulder.

'Kurt said you were kind...'

'Don't be silly, you are part of our family.'

'Kurt says he thinks there is going to be a war.'

'Yes. So do we. That is why we are going home.'

'That is dreadful.'

'Yes.'

Silence fell upon them again. It was past one when they drove into Bremen and picked up the signs for Delmenhorst and Oldenburg. A little light late-night traffic masked them as they continued west. Clark's heart slowed as they pulled out of the second great German port, and he began to feel tired. He began to yawn compulsively and then he dozed off momentarily. The sensation of reawakening shook him. For a while he drove on but at half-past two, with Hunter snoring in the seat next to him and with no response at his enquiry after Magda's wellbeing, Clark eased the little car off the main road and pulled into the side under some trees. Neither of his passengers protested or stirred as he switched off the engine. After he had relieved himself he tried to ease himself more comfortably into his seat. It was a warm night and he was sticky with perspiration, but he soon fell into a fitful and uneasy doze.

Hunter woke him. It was already light, though his watch showed it was still very early.

'Here, I'll drive.'

'No. It's better if I do, as I speak German.'

'Suit yourself.'

'Where ... Oh, God...!' Magda stirred in the back and both men turned round. The sight of her hit the jaded Clark like a blow, and even Hunter murmured in appreciation. She had removed her hat and even in the dishevelment of the moment she was strikingly beautiful. Her fine-drawn features were sculpted in the morning light, her dark eyes seemed to the overwrought Clark to be limitless in their depth, while her hair tumbled enchantingly down over one eye and fell about the shoulders of her navy blue jacket.

'I am not surprised Kurt wants you taken care of,' Clark said awkwardly as he recovered himself. 'You have changed, Magda!'

Observing his surprise, she could not resist a smile. Strong white teeth showed between the parting of her wide lips.

'God, she's a dazzler to be sure,' Hunter said in a low voice. Then he added, 'Aren't we supposed to be over the border by dawn?'

'Yes,' Clark responded, turning his back on Magda and starting the engine.

They passed through Oldenburg observed by a milkman and three labourers, heading for Leer – touching the outskirts of Emden at Hesel, where the road looped northwards. They were all feeling hungry and stiff but agreed not to stop and eat until they had crossed the border. By the time they had left Weener they had agreed that they should tell nothing but the truth, that Hunter and Clark were British merchant-marine officers going home for a spot of leave and that Magda was a distant cousin of Clark, who had met up with them in Hamburg and was going for a short holiday in England.

They crossed the border at Nieuwe-Schans. The German guards stopped them and they all got out, producing their passports.

'How did you get this car?' Clark was asked in halting English. 'Oh, I speak German, Corporal. As for the car, I was lent it by a friend at the Howaldswerke shipyard. We, Mr Hunter and I, are standing-by a ship being built there and we are going home for some leave. Miss Liepmann is a distant relative of mine, my mother was German, you see...' he smiled as he saw the border guard's attention transfer to Magda as her passport was being examined by his junior colleague. 'She is coming to England for a holiday.'

The corporal nodded in Magda's direction and then stared at Clark. 'If she's as Jewish as I think she is,' he said, 'you had better get her out of the Reich as soon as possible, Herr Clark. She is breaking the law without her armband.'

He called across to his younger colleague. 'Let them through, Helmut.'

'I think this one's a Yid.'

'What? With legs and tits like that?' the corporal called. 'No, she's pure, a relative of this nice Englishman here, who has a German mother.'

The corporal followed them back to the car and bent down to peer in past Clark. 'Take a long holiday, Fräulein, as long as you can bear.'

As the barrier lifted Clark let the clutch in with a nervous jerk. The Volkswagen lurched and the border guards laughed. A moment later they were in the Netherlands and heading for Groningen.

'Well, that went all right,' said Hunter, while in the back Magda sobbed with humiliation.

They reached the Hook of Holland in time to board the night ferry to Harwich. Despite dozing on the train, they were exhausted after their disturbed night. Clark secured first-class cabins after seeing the purser and, having wished Hunter a good night outside his cabin door, he carried Magda's bags along the alleyway to her accommodation.

'Come in,' she said with a sudden intensity as he made to withdraw. 'Wait.'

In the tiny single-berth cabin the proximity of the beautiful young woman had an unbalancing effect upon Clark. He had not slept with a woman for a long time and this sudden propinquity filled him with an overwhelming concupiscence. Magda was bent over her bag, in which she was rummaging for something, and Clark was on the point of touching her when she straightened up and swung round to face him. She was holding up a brown-paper envelope.

'Kurt made me promise not to give you this before we were safely in England, but I cannot think of a better time than now.'

'What is it?'

'Something he said was of great importance to our families. I think he meant something else, but I don't care much. D'you have a cigarette? Or a drink? I need a drink.'

Clark produced a cigarette, recalling the three bottles of beer Hunter had put in the car. They had forgotten all about pretending to be drunken seamen, and the three bottles were either in Hunter's possession or still in the car parked near Groningen station, many miles away.

'I don't have a drink,' he said, lighting the cigarette for her, 'though we could get one from the ship's bar.'

She shook her head. 'No, I don't want to be sociable.'

'No, I can understand that.'

'No you can't John. You're a decent man, but you can't understand what I feel at all; no Englishman could, and don't be silly and say you're half-German. That's going to cause you enough trouble without claiming it to get on the right side of me.' She must have seen the impact her words had upon him, because she leaned forward and kissed him on the cheek.

'What the hell are you and Kurt going to do?' he asked, with a reciprocally brutal frankness.

She shrugged and blew smoke at the

yellowing paint of the deckhead. 'I rather think it depends upon Herr Hitler, M' sieur Daladier and Mister Chamberlain. We are just pawns.' She gestured at the brown envelope. 'Put that away for now and keep it safe. It is very important, I think, and I am certain Kurt has risked a great deal to make sure you have it.' She paused and then said, 'John, I do not think I shall ever see Kurt again...'

'Why ever not? Even if there is a war...'

'Kurt will not survive contact with those bastard Nazis. His brother or his father will betray him, or he will give himself away.'

'He is an officer in the Kriegsmarine. If he does his duty, which may include killing me just as my brother was killed in the last war...'

'I'd forgotten that you had a brother,' she said, then shook her head, adding, 'What Kurt has given you is enough to have him shot, war or not. He has worked on Grand Admiral Räder's staff, that much I do know. Just make sure it falls into the right hands.'

'I'll do my best,' Clark said doubtfully. He had never heard of Grand Admiral Räder.

'Your father has influence,' Magda insisted.

'Yes, but he is in commercial shipping and has no access to government or the Admiralty.'

'Surely someone on his board will know

someone who knows someone. Isn't that how you English arrange things?' She changed from German to English and added, 'The old boys' networking, yes?'

Despite himself Clark smiled ruefully at her distortion. 'Yes,' he replied. 'Now, I had better wish you goodnight.'

'Yes,' she responded, still in English: 'Goodnight.'

Then, leaning forward, he kissed her on the cheek. He felt dizzy and lightheaded as he stepped out into the alleyway and walked to his own cabin. The ship was under way and, peering through the small porthole, he watched the lights of the berth and the railway station alongside fall away.

Clark contemplated the package Magda had given him. Its plain surface was un-addressed. He considered leaving it sealed until he was safe ashore in England, but then curiosity got the better of him and, after a momentary hesitation, he opened it and drew out a thick wad of tightly folded fool-scap sheets. They were stapled together and handwritten in German. Clipped to the first was a smaller sheet of paper; one glance told Clark that it was a personal note to him. It read simply:

My Dear Cousin,
You must see the importance of the attached, both to Germany and to Great

Britain. Please ensure that it is shown to a senior officer in your Admiralty. You will understand the danger I am in by this confidence.

K.

'Oh, my God,' Clark breathed, his heart pounding in his chest. He laid the letter aside and turned to the foolscap sheets. He read halfway down the first, then rose and locked the cabin door. As he turned, the ferry cleared the breakwaters and met the first swells of the North Sea. He had lost his sea legs and staggered a little, catching sight of his face in the mirror over the small sink the Great Eastern Railway Company had thoughtfully provided for him. He recalled Sanders's remark about neither of them being Bulldog Drummond, an allusion to a popular, fictional British Secret Service agent. Suddenly he gave an involuntary shiver, then he sat on the edge of the bunk and began to read again from the beginning.

When he had finished he stared at the bulkhead for a long time before he folded the papers, put them back into the envelope and secreted it in his bag. Then he stripped to his underwear and turned in.

But for a long time he lay staring up at the deckhead in the darkness.

ENGLAND

September–October 1939

'How did you get this, Mr Clark?' The naval captain looked across the desk over Kurt's papers, which trembled slightly in the ageing officer's hands. He was in his fifties, with thin grey hair plastered back over his head and a gaunt face which bore a stonily sceptical expression. Clark felt his mouth go dry. He was beginning to realise that his action in producing Kurt's document laid a burden of suspicion upon himself. He was also beginning to feel angry, suspecting the source of that suspicion. He looked at the other officer sitting alongside the naval captain's desk, to whom he had already spent the previous hour explaining himself. Having pronounced himself satisfied, Commander Gifford had asked him to wait and then, a few moments later, ushered him into the office of Captain Inglis, his superior. Gifford, whose manner had been perfectly amicable up to that moment, now avoided Clark's eyes.

'Captain Inglis, I have just explained all this to your colleague, Commander Gifford.' Clark's tone was exasperated, but Inglis was unmoved.

'Then you may repeat it.'

Clark shifted uneasily in his seat. 'Look, gentlemen, I am acting in good faith over this after having discussed the matter with Vice-Admiral Bulteel who initiated this appointment...'

Inglis slowly laid the sheets of paper down on the desk in front of him. 'Under the Emergency Powers Act, Mr Clark, I can have you locked up if you do not cooperate and answer me as I wish.'

Clark gave up on Gifford, who was studying his nails, and met the captain's eyes; anger removed the threat inherent in Inglis's intimidation. 'Very well,' he began. 'As you seem to be aware, my late mother was German and I have German relatives. I have been standing-by a ship being built in Hamburg for the Eastern Steam Navigation Company of Liverpool. My family has long-standing connections with this shipping house and my father is a member of its board. Up until the last war Eastern Steam and a Hamburg shipping company ran a joint service to China. My familiarity with the German language made me an obvious choice as the chief officer of the new vessel. From time to time, whilst in Hamburg, I was in contact with my aunt and uncle in Altona, just outside...'

'I know where Altona is,' Inglis interrupted. 'Pray go on.'

Clark paused after the interruption. 'My cousin Kurt, a Korvettenkapitän in the Kriegsmarine, came home from Berlin, where, I gather, he has been serving on the staff of an Admiral Räder. Kurt is not a Party member and I contrived to bring his Jewish fiancée out of Germany when I returned home. It was she to whom my cousin had given the document you now have in your possession.'

'Very well...'

'There is a little more in which I think you might be interested.'

'Oh?'

'When I was told to leave – by a man named Sanders who claimed to come from the British consulate in Hamburg and, incidentally, appeared perfectly genuine, with diplomatic papers to prove it – it occurred to me that events might be linked with a circumstance that had recently arisen in the shipyard.'

'And what was that, pray?' Inglis asked archly.

'I had become aware that the presence of my cousin, along with a small party of German naval officers active in the shipyard, might bode ill for my ship. To be strictly accurate, the notion had been put in my head by my colleague, the second engineer who was also standing-by the vessel.

'Accordingly, just before I left, I confronted my cousin with my sense of outrage and – somewhat unfairly I suppose – invoked the family connection. For his part, he admitted to there being a plan to commandeer the ship. I got the impression that the admission was an indiscretion, an unguarded remark that he regretted, but it may be that it precipitated the confidences in the papers you have before you. I formed the opinion on this slender evidence that a plan for German naval reinforcement was in train whereby ships such as the *Ernest Shackleton* could be acquired as naval auxiliaries or commerce raiders. The odd thing...'

'Yes, yes, Mr Clark, this speculation is all very interesting, but I hardly think you as a merchant officer are able to analyse...'

'Damn it, sir,' Clark snapped as Gifford looked at him sharply, 'Admiral Bulteel thought my modest speculation of sufficient interest to extract an undertaking that I laid it before someone in the Admiralty capable of having the courtesy to listen...'

'Admiral Bulteel is a retired officer and you had better mind your tongue, young man!'

Gifford coughed, then brushed some imaginary dust from the knee of his immaculate uniform. Clark ignored him. He was thoroughly irritated by Inglis's tone. For a moment he and Inglis glared at each other in silence, then Clark said, 'I think you had better arrest me, Captain Inglis, and let me explain this to an officer from military intelligence.'

The effrontery of the remark took Inglis by surprise, and even Gifford momentarily ceased preening himself. 'I am in *naval* intelligence, Mr Clark,' Inglis said savagely, 'and if you were a naval officer, I should...'

'But I am *not* a naval officer, Captain Inglis, and I suggest you either hear me out, or do as I suggest and place me under arrest. The war is only five days old and it strikes me we should be fighting the enemy that carried out the air raid of yesterday, rather than each other.'

Gifford coughed again and leaned forward to murmur something in Inglis's ear. There was another silence as Inglis weighed Clark up. 'Go on,' he said at last.

Clark paused to compose himself and then resumed his story. 'The odd thing that struck me at the time was that although it was clear the German naval authorities had some sort of contingency plan to requisition or seize the *Ernest Shackleton*...'

'That being the name of the ship you were standing-by?'

'Quite so,' confirmed Clark, slightly surprised at the captain's question. 'Nevertheless,' he went on, 'my cousin seemed genuinely surprised that I had been recalled home...'

'You *told* him you had been recalled?' Inglis asked sharply.

'Yes. Perhaps it was a slip on my part, but please don't forget that until a few days ago we were not at war with the Germans and Kurt was a relative with whom I was friendly. Besides, I think it did little harm and, quite fortuitously, it revealed what I think may be an important point.'

'And that is?'

'Well, for all the high-handedness of the plan to take over the *Ernest Shackleton*, Kurt seemed very genuinely surprised that total rupture with Great Britain was a possibility.'

'That is tautological.'

Clark frowned. 'I'm sorry, I don't understand. What is tautological?'

' "Very genuine surprise", Mr Clark.' Inglis seemed oddly pleased with his little victory.

'Tautological or not, sir, Kurt seemed discomfited by the intelligence. If he was a staff officer...'

'Yes, yes. You mean Berlin might have been surprised at our reaction, proceeding to an outright declaration of war.'

'Well, the German Admiralty at least.'

'Does that really square with an alleged *plan* to seize a foreign ship building legitimately in a German shipyard?' Inglis asked, laying a sarcastic emphasis upon the noun 'plan'.

'Well, I'm not certain myself, but in discussing this point it was Admiral Bulteel who pointed out that I should mention it to you, because, as he said, it has been Hitler's policy to advance by stealth, taking a little and then, when he gets away with it, taking a little more.'

Gifford grunted and Clark saw him nod to Inglis. 'That is a point, sir.'

'Possibly,' Inglis admitted. He fell silent and regarded the sheets of foolscap in front of him again.

'It is, of course, the other intelligence that I think my cousin most wished you to see. You will appreciate the considerable risk he has exposed himself to by passing on the information in this document.'

'What do you think *his* motives are?' Gifford asked, speaking directly to Clark for the first time since he had ushered him into Inglis's office.

'Well, he is clearly opposed to the Nazis and I think that whatever else one can say about him, he is a man of honour. I formed the opinion that he did not think Hitler's government was in the best, long-term interests of Germany. The spectre of a second war with this country clearly rattled him. His family fortune was ruined by the last war...'

'Yet he is an officer in the German navy.'

'That does not make him dishonourable,' Clark argued with unconscious irony.

Gifford suppressed a smile. 'Perhaps not, but it would suggest an act of treachery.'

'Or of conscience,' Clark said. 'And one must recall that he is engaged to a Jewish woman.'

'Is that so very significant?' Inglis asked, looking up.

'It would seem so, Captain Inglis. Moreover, he is also aware that I lost a brother sunk in the last war by a German U-boat.'

'You have a somewhat confusing family history, Mr Clark,' Gifford said, not unkindly.

But Clark was unmollified by Gifford's late intervention. 'I should have thought the fact that my family's confusion has laid those documents before you, gentlemen, was a matter for some expression of gratitude.'

Gifford looked pained and Inglis stared at him again. 'You are an impertinent young man, Clark,' he said.

'It seems necessary, sir,' Clark said standing up, 'in order to do what I conceive to be my duty. Now, perhaps you will be kind enough to let me know whether I am to be arrested, or allowed to go home.'

'Gifford, get Clark out of the building.'

In the corridor outside, Clark felt his elbow taken by Gifford. At first he thought Gifford's precipitate action sinister, but at the end of the corridor Gifford apologised.

'I'm very sorry about all that, Clark. You have to understand Captain Inglis is anxious, very anxious, about the activities of German intelligence.'

'You mean I am under suspicion of being a spy?' Clark asked incredulously.

'Well, not exactly a spy, but this information – or perhaps I should call it *disinformation* – could have been planted on you.'

'Damn it, Commander, the circumstances under which I was given it don't in the least suggest such a thing.'

'Come, come, Clark, consider: you are asked to help evacuate a young Jewish woman by a relative of whom you are fond. You are a kind man and are sympathetic, but the fact of the matter is that your cousin is an officer in the Kriegsmarine who was on *duty* in your shipyard.'

'But Commander, you cannot seriously think that the facts contained in that document can be false information, surely? I mean, it simply does not make sense. It is clearly a hurriedly produced memorandum outlining the enormity of the threat to our commerce, a threat similar to that which nearly brought this country to its knees in 1917. Kurt clearly states the general plan of the German navy is to...'

'I understand your anxiety, Mr Clark,' Gifford broke in, 'but this is neither the time nor the place. You must leave the matter with us. You are staying with Admiral Bulteel, I gather.'

'Yes, he has a flat in St John's Wood, but I was only availing myself of the Admiral's offer of hospitality until after this interview. I shall be returning to Liverpool tomorrow.'

'Very well. You will be serving with the Eastern Steam Navigation Company, I imagine?'

'Yes. I can hardly see you offering me a commission in the Reserve after this afternoon.'

The two men smiled. 'Not if the war's over by Christmas, but who knows?' Gifford said with a rueful smile, 'Unfortunately they have a habit of lasting rather longer. Thank you anyway for coming to see us. Now follow me and I shall find someone to escort you to the street.'

And there, Clark thought, the matter would end.

'Over by Christmas? What a bloody preposterous thing to say!' Vice-Admiral Bulteel spluttered over his cheese and biscuits, refilling his port glass. 'You seem to have had your nose bloodied, my boy.'

'Well, I suppose that when a merchant jack walks in off the street with a document purporting to reveal German naval plans...'

'Damn it, Jack, you're hardly an ordinary

merchant jack!' Bulteel crunched the Bath Oliver into a powder, some of which he discharged across the table as an expression of his outrage. 'Inglis, Inglis?' Bulteel drummed his fingers on the table as though the gesture would tease the recollection out of his ageing brain. 'Ah yes, I recall the fellow now. Not particularly gifted, though a reasonable staff man if left to himself. Not quick on the uptake, though. How on earth do such johnnies get into intelligence?'

'I don't know, sir, but that sounds like the fellow. His deputy, Gifford, seemed like a brighter spark.'

'Hmmm,' Bulteel grunted. 'Don't know him. After my time, I suppose,' he added with a sigh.

'Never mind. The matter's been dealt with and we can do no more.'

'You'll be off tomorrow then?'

'Yes, I had better see how my father is coping with Magda Liepmann.'

'What is the poor girl going to do?'

'I really have no idea, sir, but I daresay she will find some war work in due course.'

Their conversation was interrupted by the sinister whine of the air-raid warning. The Admiral sighed and laid down his knife, then he picked it up again and cut the apple he had just selected from the bowl in front of him. 'I'm damned if the Hun is going to interrupt *my* dinner. Pass the port before you run off.'

'I'm in no hurry, sir,' Clark said.

'Good man. I suppose you'll be appointed to another ship?'

'I imagine we'll all be needed.'

'You will if it's anything like the last flap. Ever thought of joining the Reserve?'

Clark laughed. 'I think I've blighted my chances of that, sir. As I mentioned to Gifford, my little contretemps with Inglis should have put paid to any such idea.'

'Oh, Inglis isn't the Royal Navy. You'd be wasted at sea in a merchantman, Jack. What with your fluency in German.'

'I think to commend me to their Lordships I have to have that ability without the inconvenience of a Hun mother, Admiral,' he countered with a note of irony.

Bulteel looked at him. 'Damn it, I meant no offence!'

Clark met the old man's eyes. 'There's none taken.' Clark smiled at him. 'None at all. Anyway, I'm not at all sure that I want a shore posting. I'm a seaman...'

'Oh well, if that's your objection there'll be plenty of opportunities on a seagoing flag officer's staff where navigation and a knowledge of the German tongue would be useful.'

'Perhaps...'

'You're not persuaded?'

'It's all so uncertain, sir. I'm thankful I'm

not married.'

'Wife and children hostages to fortune, eh?'

'Yes.'

'Never got round to it myself. Been a bachelor too long to consider anything else now. Not that any filly would consider an old warhorse like me nowadays,' he chuckled. 'Got a girl in tow?'

'No. I came close to an engagement last year, but she declared her preference for a teacher at a prep school in Lancaster. She's married now.'

'Serves her right. Come–' the admiral rose – 'let's go and have a brandy next door.' In the admiral's book-lined study he poured a cognac and handed it to Clark. Both men sank into the clubbily comfortable armchairs while, with a quiet clatter, Bulteel's man-servant cleared the table in the dining room.

'I daresay they'll find something for me to do, even if it's only as a convoy commodore. A lot of my contemporaries have taken the job on. Perhaps we'll meet at sea and you'll be in a ship under my command!'

The prospect seemed to brighten the old boy, and Clark, who had not thought of a future beyond the obligation to discharge the duty that Kurt had laid upon him almost a week ago, wondered where the war would lead him. Then he dismissed the thought with the lack of concern the young have for the future. If there was a future it was muddied by images of Magda. The consideration turned his thoughts backwards. What a week it had been, Clark reflected as the two men sat in companionable silence and sipped their brandies.

From Harwich he and Magda had gone straight to Liverpool, where, crossing to Birkenhead and the rolling countryside of the Wirral beyond, he had installed her as a guest in the family home. There they had dined with Clark's father, who had insisted that Clark came into Liverpool the following day and made a verbal report to the board, outlining the fate of the *Ernest Shackleton*. Amid the board's anxieties over war insurance, government compensation agreements and the immediate requisition of several of their first-class cargo liners, the account of the loss of their newest ship had visibly struck the silent directors. When Clark had finished, the chairman had formally thanked him. Turning to his fellow directors, Sir Desmond Cranbrooke had added, 'So, gentlemen, Dent's have suffered their first war casualty. At least there was no loss of life.'

That night Magda and Clark had dined with Cranbrooke, his charming wife Diana, and Captain Clark at the Cranbrookes' beautiful house about two miles distant from Clark's home. Lady Cranbrooke had promised to take Magda under her wing, and

Clark had felt his anxiety over Kurt's fiancée lessen. During their journey to Liverpool he had been much taken with Magda and had had to tell himself she was officially engaged to his cousin in order to suppress his own inclinations. Whatever the true state of Magda's mind, she seemed vulnerable under an artificial carapace of toughness. As he had watched the two women leave the gentlemen to their port and cigars, he had resolved not to enmesh himself with a woman while this war was on. Instead he had leaned forward and, having taken the two older men into his confidence and explained the importance of Kurt's document, had solicited their advice as to how best to contact someone with influence at the Admiralty.

'I shan't ask to read it, Jack,' Clark's father had said, 'but give us the gist of it.'

Clark had outlined the contents and Cranbrooke had spoken for them all when he observed, 'That is pretty significant for merchant shipping and we ought not to sit upon it a moment longer than necessary.'

'No doubt of that,' Clark Senior had concurred.

'I think an approach to John Bulteel would be the best thing to do to cut corners. I dare say both you and I will soon have more up-to-date contacts in the Admiralty in a month or so,' Sir Desmond had said, speaking directly to Clark's father, 'but this sort of thing can't wait.' He had turned to explain himself to Clark.

'All merchant shipping is coming under the control of the Ministry of War Transport, and your father and I have both been assigned roles for the duration. As for Bulteel, I've known him for some time. He's related to my wife and he used to occupy a staff post in the Admiralty as a senior captain. Despite his age, he keeps his finger on the pulse and is very friendly with the First Sea Lord. I'll give him a phone call and furnish you with a letter of introduction.'

'That should be fine, Sir Desmond.'

'I certainly hope so. We cannot afford to squander a godsend like you have brought us.'

'I wonder what will happen to Kurt?' Captain Clark mused.

'I don't know, Father,' Clark said, 'but his allegiance to Adolf Hitler is decidedly suspect.'

'It sounds non-existent,' said Cranbrooke.

'I wonder how many more there are like him?' Captain Clark asked.

'I wish I could say a lot of them,' remarked Cranbrooke, 'but you've seen those films of the Nuremberg rallies, and the Sudeten Germans and the Austrians didn't seem too disappointed to see Herr Hitler's legions strutting into their towns and cities.'

'We shouldn't have trodden on them so

hard in 1919,' Clark Senior said.

'No, you're right, Christopher,' replied Cranbrooke, 'it's certainly brought a deal of woes upon us in shipping.' He turned to the younger Clark with a smile. 'Well Jack, what are we going to do with you? You've lost us one ship, d'you think we can trust you with another?'

'That's a bit hard, Sir Desmond...'

'I'm joking, my boy, though I admit to the poor taste. Besides, *I'd* give away someone else's ship if I swapped her for a young beauty like Magda Liepmann.'

'She's my cousin's fiancée, Sir Desmond.'

'Good heavens, Christopher,' Cranbrooke had laughed, waving his cigar at Clark's father, 'you have failed utterly to breed a son ruthless enough to make a businessman! I think he will have to stay at sea.' Then he had sighed and his voice had grown serious again. He had addressed Jack. 'You will find that tough enough, I think.'

Clark was torn from this recollection when Bulteel, whom he had thought was dozing off, suddenly spoke. 'You know,' the old admiral said vehemently, 'if we give the Huns long enough to bring the plans your cousin outlines to fruition, they will strangle us, just as they nearly did twenty-two years ago.'

'I pointed that out to Captain Inglis.'

'Well *he* should know that in 1917 Their

Lordships went to the government and told the Prime Minister that they had lost the war at sea! Can you imagine such a thing? It took David Lloyd George himself to overrule them and to order them to organise merchant shipping into convoy to stem a defeat. And it wasn't just Their Lordships who took their medicine with a grumble; a lot of shipowners made immense sums of money from the compensation they were paid for their losses.'

'Yes, I know. The Chancellor of the Exchequer made his infamous speech boasting about his personal gains from shares in shipping the same week my brother was killed. My mother was never the same afterwards. I think father had done well out of the war and she felt she had paid too high a price. She couldn't believe a British politician could be so callous, unfeeling and insensitive.'

'Ah well, women have a different view of these things.'

They fell silent again and then Bulteel set down his glass and tugged out his watch as through the night the all-clear sounded. 'Time for bed, my boy.'

They rose and, as they moved towards their respective bedrooms, Bulteel fired his parting shot: 'You should think about joining the navy.'

★ ★ ★

Clark returned to Liverpool. The war was only a week old and a mood of unreality seemed to prevail throughout the country. British troops of the Expeditionary Force were moving towards the Channel ports to embark in the vessels that would carry them across the sea to France; air-raid sirens and occasional tentative bombing raids interrupted daily life, but it was only at sea, where the first British merchant ships were succumbing to the torpedoes of German U-boats, that the war was showing the first signs of the horrors to come. Unlike in the First World War the Admiralty had been swift to herd commercial shipping into convoys, but the country's vast merchant fleet was too widely dispersed about its normal business to avoid many dreadful encounters. The sinking of the passenger liner *Athenia* within hours of the outbreak of hostilities had sent a shiver of apprehension down the spines of shipowners and seafarers alike.

Since there was no immediate vacancy for Clark, he availed himself of a few days' leave. Back home he invited Magda out to dinner and they crossed the Mersey to enjoy an evening in the Adelphi hotel.

'Try not to speak German,' he warned as they went up the wide steps from Lime Street.

'Of course not,' she laughed. 'Anyway, I must learn to speak English like a native, at

101

least until this is all over.'

The menu was, as yet, unaffected by the strictures of war. They dined well and then joined the couples circling the dance floor. Warmed by the wine and the proximity of the beautiful young woman whose lissom body he held as they danced, Clark ventured upon an indiscretion.

'Do you love Kurt?' he asked with a gauche abruptness that surprised them both. For a second he felt Magda stiffen at the impropriety of his question and then, in an almost fluid sensation that raised his heartbeat, he felt her relax.

'Not as much as he loves me,' she answered enigmatically, but her true response was physical and, though they exchanged no other word on the dance floor, they ceased to move formally but clung together as intimates.

That night they kissed goodnight with a mutual passion. Magda prevented him from entering her bedroom and Clark lay awake for a long time, his heart thundering, debating whether to force the issue. He half hoped, half expected her to open his door and come to him, but the house lay still in the darkness and, in due course, sleep overcame him.

He woke happy, the first time his spirits had felt light for a long time, and he realised how burdensome had been his sojourn in

Hamburg. There might be a war on, he thought with an almost merry disregard for coming danger, but he had some leave and a burgeoning romance with a stunningly beautiful young woman whose rival was not only overseas, but separated by the mighty distance of war. He was glad he had not succumbed to the crude urges of last night; he wanted to enjoy the sights and sensations of wooing Magda. Today, tonight, tomorrow would be different!

He had almost finished his breakfast when Magda appeared. Clark and his father lowered their newspapers and half rose in their seats. After her formal good morning, she avoided Clark's eyes as she refused the housekeeper's offer of eggs and helped herself to toast.

'Have a good evening with my ne'er-do-well son, Magda?' Captain Clark asked with his brusque kindness.

'It was very pleasant, thank you.' She shot Clark a glance. Was there a twinkle of complicity in it, or was there a hint of conscientious remorse?

But Clark's romantic speculations were dashed by his father's next remark. Laying his paper aside, the older man said, 'I was talking about you to Lady Cranbrooke, Magda. This is not a very happy environment for you under the circumstances. Jack here will be off to sea soon and I'm not good company myself. Besides, when the current reorganisation is completed I shall have even less time at home than I have now, and that is precious little. Diana Cranbrooke's going to be in a similar position when Desmond takes up his new post in London with the Ministry of War Transport, so she has offered to do more than merely provide you with some war work, she suggests you join her as a companion. There will be plenty to do in the coming months and she feels that you will be happier and more comfortable living with her. There's an element of self-interest in her suggestion, of course, but I think it a kind offer and one that will be of benefit to you. If you rattle around this place you'll become bored and introspective, worrying about your parents and so forth. With Diana, you can get on with helping us bring this fellow Hitler and his gangsters to book...'

'She doesn't have to go to the Cranbrookes' to do that,' Clark put in indignantly.

'No, but I'd like to go,' Magda said, looking at Captain Clark and ignoring his son's intervention. Clark, hardly believing his ears, felt a keen sense of disappointment. 'It is kind of Lady Cranbrooke,' Madga was saying, 'and it will be for the best. Will you tell her so, or should I write to her?'

'Give her a ring on the telephone. She'll be delighted to hear from you.'

Clark could hardly hide his distress and caught Madga later that morning.

'Magda, please...' he began, but she cut him short.

'No Jack, it is all too quick ... too sudden ... Yes, you are a nice man and I like you, but I cannot turn my back on Kurt so quickly.' She shrugged and cast about her. 'All this is so strange ... How can I explain?'

'You don't have to *explain*, Magda,' he said desperately. 'I want to see you.'

'I am not going to be far away, Jack, my dear...' She had lapsed into German and he did the same.

'Good God, Magda, I am falling in love with you, can't you see that?'

'Yes, and it frightens me. I thought I was in love with Kurt, and I have lost him. Now you are saying ... Jack, please understand...'

'But what about last night, for God's sake?'

'Last night was wonderful, Jack, but it is best that we do not see each other for a few days. Please try and understand I want a little time to myself.' She broke away and ran up the stairs to her room. He heard the door of her bedroom slam shut and cursed.

'Bugger!'

By that evening Magda had been whisked away in the Cranbrookes' Daimler and Clark dined alone with his father.

'Pity she's gone,' remarked Captain Clark. 'She certainly brightened this place up.'

'Yes, she did that,' Clark mumbled.

'How long did Harry Linton give you leave for?' Clark Senior asked, referring to Dent's personnel manager.

Clark sighed and, shoving all thoughts of Magda aside, gave his attention to his profession. 'Well, I was appointed to the *Shackleton* and now with her gone there isn't an immediate vacancy. I suppose I'll relieve someone in a day or two. The *John Chancellor*'s due to arrive in a couple of days, I hear.'

'Yes, and the *Francis Drake* isn't far behind her, but both are going into Cammel Laird's to have guns fitted.'

'Well I really don't want to sit in another shipyard. I had enough of that in Hamburg.'

'Don't be too eager to get back to sea, Jack. It's a dangerous place at the best of times; in a war it will be awful.'

They both sat a moment and thought of Carl, then Clark said, 'I know Dad, but I can't dodge things for ever...'

The older man sniffed. 'No, I knew you'd think like that, but I could pull some strings...'

'No, I really don't want you to do that.'

'Well at least you can enjoy your leave and I'll be glad of your company. It gets bloody lonely here.'

Clark sighed again. 'Yes, it does.' Then an idea struck him. 'Look, can't I come and do something in the office? It would be an opportunity to get acquainted with what's going on.'

And so Clark, a victim of unrequited love, commuted daily with his father across the River Mersey to the headquarters of the Eastern Steam Navigation Company, which occupied two floors of a large office building in Water Street. Here he was soon immersed in the extraordinary reorganisation that rapidly transformed every shipping company in the land, irrespective of whether they owned passenger vessels, cargo liners, oil tankers, tramp ships or coasters. Although each of these owners remained responsible for the manning and management of their own property, their vessels were rapidly requisitioned by the state. As each came in from its voyage and discharged its last peace-time cargo, all operational control passed from its beneficial owners to the growing Ministry of War Transport whose offices and officers, though directed from London, sprang up in the great ports of England, Scotland, Wales and Northern Ireland.

Clark spent ten hectic days in this fluid atmosphere. Beneath a superficial chaos which brought howls of frustration from many of the ship's masters, officers, engineers and ratings, there emerged an underlying order which slowly but surely integrated with the nascent convoy system.

Its weakest link was the docks and the uncertain, traditionally capricious mood of the dock workers. Too long neglected, these men now sensed a power passing inexorably into their hands.

In those ten days Clark was literally run off his feet. He sped between meetings in Water Street and visits to incoming ships, not all of them owned by Dent's; he helped foreign masters of ships for whom Dent's were Liverpool agents, whose fates were uncertain or who wished for nothing to do with Great Britain's war with Germany; he liaised with the naval authorities and the shipyards of the Mersey, Tyne and Clyde, making arrangements for months ahead when all the company's ships would receive a modicum of defensive armament. On two occasions, on account of his ability to speak German, he was sent to explain what was going to happen to German crews whose vessels, caught in British ports by the outbreak of war, had been impounded. He wrote reports, made written suggestions and helped streamline procedures as only a practical seaman can when confronted with a frustratingly obdurate administration. And then, on the tenth day, two things happened. The first was a simple, internal matter. He arrived at the desk that had been made available for him to find a note that Harry Linton wished to see him.

'I think this'll be my marching orders, Jenny,' he said to the plump and comely typist who had become his temporary secretary.

'I do hope not, Mr Clark,' she said, watching him with a tear in her eye as he went off in search of Linton. The previous ten days had been among the happiest, most breathless and most extraordinary in her life. Mr Clark was thought to be one of the company's most handsome officers and many of the younger girls in the typing pool had outspokenly envied her. Nine years Clark's senior, Jenny O'Neil had long ago abandoned any hope of marrying. She had a widowed mother to look after and only her small salary to live on. The temporary appointment as assistant to Mr Clark had passed like a whirlwind.

'We want you to go up to Glasgow, Jack,' Linton said to Clark as he entered the personnel manager's office, 'to stand by the *Matthew Flinders*. She's going into dock there...'

'Oh, for God's sake, Harry! Not another bloody shipyard...'

'It's a board decision, Jack, so there's no point in trying to persuade me otherwise.'

'The old man is trying to keep me from going back to sea, on account of having lost one son in the last war.' Clark expressed his exasperation.

'That's not how I see it, Jack. The *Matthew Flinders* has been requisitioned by the navy. She's to be altered and refitted as a fast fleet-support transport. Your old man wants to discuss it with you later. We're retaining officers on board familiar with the machinery and they want one company officer with cargo-handling expertise. God knows what they've got in mind for the ship, but in a war you can never tell. Anyway, you've been selected. I think they'll want you to double up as the navigating officer.'

Linton paused a moment to study a letter he had on his desk. Clark digested the news; several questions arose in his mind and he was about to voice them when Linton, having reprimed himself, went on.

'Now, it seems that the company officers retained on these ships – the *James Cook* is to be another, incidentally ... Anyway, as I say, all the company's officers retained on board are to be given temporary commissions in the Royal Naval Reserve, so in addition to standing-by the ship you'll go through some training programmes. I see you've done the Merchant Navy defensive gunnery course...'

'That hardly qualifies me for much,' Clark protested.

'Well, never mind, the navy will take you up and teach you how not to eat peas off a knife and how to march...'

'*What?*'

'Look, don't start cutting up awkward, Jack. There's a war on. Anyway, I told them you were a chief officer in our service and they said you'd probably jump being a sub-lieutenant...'

'That's bloody generous of them. Christ, Harry, I'm twenty-nine and a master mariner! Sub-lieutenants are commissioned midshipmen.'

Linton ignored the protest. 'And you'll probably get accelerated promotion to lieutenant commander...'

'Oh, how bloody jolly,' Clark snapped sarcastically.

He made his way slowly back to his desk and told Miss O' Neil the news. 'It's worse than I thought. They've got me in the navy, Jenny.'

'You'll look lovely in the uniform, Mr Clark,' she said dreamily, smiling up at him bravely.

She wasn't bad looking, he thought, as an image of Magda swam into his mind's eye. With a sigh he submitted to his fate. 'I thought I looked *lovely* in Eastern Steam's uniform,' he said with his disarmingly engaging grin.

'Oh, you do, but it's not the same as the *real* navy.'

He stared at her for a moment, affronted by her remark, but not wishing to hurt her by showing it. *Real* navy? Carl had been wearing the Eastern Steam's uniform when he had been killed in action. 'Real navy, be damned,' he thought to himself.

But to Miss O' Neil he said, 'You'd better let me take you to lunch, Jenny. I may not get another chance.'

They returned from their meal a little tipsy, for Clark had splashed out on a bottle of wine and Jenny O'Neil had taken full advantage of her host's generosity. Besides, it was not every day the son of a director several years your junior took you out to dine! She had taken Jack Clark's arm rather familiarly on the way back to the office and had been rewarded by the dark, envious glances of a number of her fellow typists. A few minutes later she announced there was a call for him. To Clark's astonishment it was Commander Gifford, calling from the Admiralty in London.

'I hear you're joining the navy, Mr Clark. My congratulations. Now look, can you be in London by this time tomorrow?'

'Er, yes, I suppose so. But I'm not in the navy yet, you know. I've my hands full here at the moment.'

'You'll have to oblige me,' Gifford said abruptly. 'Now listen, report to the main gate in Whitehall and ask for me by name. Bring some sort of identification like you did the last time, your British seaman's card'll do. I'll see you tomorrow afternoon.'

He put the phone down and an expectant Jenny caught his eye. 'That was the real navy,' he said absently. 'It seems I'm off faster than I thought.'

'Oh, dear,' she said, putting a hand up to her mouth.

Gifford asked him to sit down. There was a palpable buzz about the place, Clark thought, and Gifford almost immediately explained why.

'There's been a bit of a shake-up since you were last here, Clark. Captain Inglis has been, er, transferred. He'd been over-working, you know.' The expression in Gifford's eyes invited Clark to appreciate the euphemism. 'Now, we've a first-class director and I've got some new instructions, which is where you come in. We need your help.' Gifford paused and offered Clark a cigarette.

'I'm totally confused,' Clark said as Gifford, having lit Clark's cigarette, lit his own. 'Yesterday I was told that I was to be temporarily commissioned into the RNR and sent to Glasgow to stand-by one of our ships requisitioned for conversion. Now I find you asking for my help.'

'Ah,' said Gifford, blowing a plume of smoke at the ceiling. 'The two things are not irreconcilable. I'll come straight to the point. Inglis gave you a difficult time but in doing so he did me a favour. He made me aware that you were an astute chap. Not only had you done the right thing with that document, but you fought your corner hard under what, to many fellows, would have been very intimidating circumstances.'

Clark shrugged. It hardly seemed the order of courage to win a war, he thought.

Gifford paused and then confided, 'He was a difficult man. Anyway, since that little encounter, I've done a bit of digging about you. Partly, I admit, we wanted to check out the possible risks implied by your German parentage. Don't be angry, it's a necessary formality. I've consulted several people including Sir Desmond Cranbrooke, and I've learnt of your connections with the Eastern Steam Navigation Company. Rather than a potential spy,' Gifford said wryly, 'you would seem to be a chap with a fair insight into merchant shipping and the likely impact of the contents of your cousin's paper. Now, what I want you to do is to write an appreciation of what *you*, you personally with your experience and understanding of things, make of the intelligence revealed by the document.'

'Well, I doubt that I'll tell you anything you can't work out for yourself, Commander.'

'Let me be the judge of that and don't be diffident. Now look, I've booked you a room in the Regent Palace Hotel. Have another

114

read through the paper now, then leave it with me. Come back in the morning after you've had a think about it and I'll make the document and a desk available to you. You can be back in Liverpool tomorrow night.'

Twenty-four hours later he sat in the same chair and smoked another of Gifford's cigarettes while the commander sat and read his 'appreciation'. When he had finished, Gifford laid down the paper with a nod. 'That's very good, Clark. Thank you.'

'But hardly revolutionary.'

'No, but another man's perspective is often useful.'

'You seem, if I may say so, a little dis-appointed.'

Gifford shook his head and looked directly at Clark. 'No, not at all. I'll admit to being rather frightened though.' He paused and referred to Clark's notes. 'I'm interested in the list you call "priorities of inherent danger". That's a nice touch worthy of a naval staff officer,' he added, looking up at Clark again.

'Thanks. I take it that's a compliment?'

'Very much so. But to the point: you seem less concerned about the commerce raiders than I would have supposed a master mari-ner to be.'

'Well, I understand they'll have a certain success, but I hope the resources of the

Royal Navy can soon eliminate them.'

'It might be more difficult than you think.'

'Yes, I admit they can hide in remote locations and use the opportunity to disguise their appearance, but I'd have thought their potence lower than the U-boat threat, and in particular, the threat of large, submarine cruisers.'

'Yes, that is a new departure. There has been absolutely no indication of such large submarines being built by the Germans. We have known for some time that they have two aircraft carriers under construction, and their completion will have a profound effect on things in due course. We know too that they will put a lot of effort into building conventional submarines in considerable numbers, but this is the first intimation we have had of long-endurance, super submarine cruisers of the sort of size and submerged speed your cousin indicates.'

'Well, perhaps they are still on the drawing board,' Clark offered.

'Yes, possibly,' Gifford ruminated. Then he sighed and added, 'What a pity your cousin could not tell us a little more.'

Clark nodded. 'Yes. Perhaps he didn't know; perhaps ... Well, I know he wrote the paper in a hell of a hurry, between the time I told him I'd been ordered home and meeting me with his fiancée. If you deduct the time it must have taken him to detach himself from the shipyard, get to Altona and prepare Magda, he would have been in a tearing rush.'

'I see.' Gifford looked at Clark. 'There is just one other consideration, Clark. One that I think you may have overlooked.

'Oh? What is that?'

'It is just possible that, if your cousin is no Nazi-lover, and if he thinks this war may go badly for Germany, the submission of this document may act as, well, shall we call it an insurance policy?'

Clark frowned. 'No, I hadn't thought of that.' He paused, then said, 'But then, does that actually matter?'

'It would if this was a tissue of lies.'

'Well, we know it's not; you yourself said we know about the aircraft carriers and I've as good as clear evidence of a commerce-raiding programme with the seizure of the *Ernest Shackleton*.'

'Yes, but all those facts are known to us. Only the super submarines remain enigmatical. He may have made them up so that, if he is caught by his own side, he can claim he was spreading *dis*information to confuse us and, perhaps, to make us waste resources.'

Clark shook his head. 'This gets more and more bizarre. It didn't strike me that the concept of super submarines was not at least feasible.'

Gifford pulled a face. 'Perhaps. The French

have built one, the *Surcouf*, and I can tell you that we've toyed with the notion again since we built the M-class with their twelve-inch gun in 1918. All the same, I'd like confirmation. It's a pity we can't get in touch with your cousin.'

'I really can't help you there, Commander.'

Gifford paused. 'No, of course not, it is unfair to suggest that you should.'

There was a brief pause and then Clark said, 'Irrespective of whether or not these super submarines are a figment of the imagination, on the drawing board or being built yet, if this war goes on for long, the probability is that they will be.'

'Yes,' Gifford agreed, 'like the aircraft carriers *Graf Zeppelin* and *Peter Strasser*, they could alter the whole balance of sea power in the North Atlantic. It is something we must bear in mind.'

'Surely time will tell, one way or the other?'

'Of course. Well, thank you.' Gifford stood and held out his hand. 'Good luck.'

They stood and shook hands. Gifford rang for someone to escort Clark out of the building and, while they waited, Gifford said conversationally, 'Whilst I was ferreting among the skeletons in your personal cupboard I discovered you had been with Worsley in the Arctic.'

'Yes,' responded Clark, his eyes widening with enthusiasm. 'Commander Worsley was

118

a fine man.'

'You obviously enjoyed the experience.'

'Oh, very much; very much indeed. It's an extraordinary, beautiful place.'

'I don't suppose His Majesty's Transport *Matthew Flinders* will be going anywhere near the Arctic,' Gifford said with a laugh.

'I'll take that as a hint not to pawn my tropical kit,' Clark quipped back.

'Probably very wise,' Gifford said.

A few moments later Clark hailed a taxi and instructed the driver to head for Euston station. As the vehicle swung round Trafalgar Square, Clark looked up at the statue of Nelson and wondered what assistance he had personally rendered the war effort by the fruits of his odd duty that day.

'Not joined up yet then, mate?' called the taxi driver over his shoulder.

'Yes I have,' Clark said wearily.

'I went all through the last lot. Royal Navy. Finished in the old *Lion*. Battlecruiser. Marvellous ship. Scrapped the fucker though. Stupid bastards.'

HMS *Daisy*

There was one further intervention fate made in order to propel Clark into his unusually personal war. Curiously enough it at first seemed to set him upon a course which, for most of his fellows in the Royal Naval Reserve, would have proved conventional. History has given the Battle of the Atlantic a glamour, largely from its attenuated nature, as an epic struggle that lasted from the very first to the very last day of the European war; but for those who endured it and survived, it consisted largely of unremitting discomfort interspersed with intermittent desperate and nerve-wracking action.

The fatal intervention in Clark's life was entirely circumstantial. A smart young reserve officer whose name is irrelevant, but who occupied the post of first lieutenant of a relatively new corvette, HMS *Daisy*, fell down an icy bridge ladder one morning in the spring of 1940. His corvette was not at sea, but about to leave the James Watt dock in Greenock, and his trip to the bridge had been for nothing more exciting than to check the vessel's gyrocompass repeater, but the ice of a raw Scottish morning caused him to slip, and in falling he struck his head. Concussed and with a suspected fracture of the skull, he was sent to hospital in Glasgow.

Under orders to join her escort group, which was assigned to a convoy already forming up off the Tail of the Bank, the corvette's commanding officer cast about for a replacement. He was not in good odour with the escort group's senior officer and the loss of his young first lieutenant was a severe blow. The little ship's previous trip had been her first in attendance upon a convoy and she had not performed well; the only officer the corvette's captain had found totally reliable was his young first lieutenant, a former second mate from the Blue Funnel Line who, like himself, wore the interwoven braid of the Royal Naval Reserve.

The escort group's senior officer, Commander Brenton-Woodruffe, was a short-fused regular naval commander whose despair at the inept state of his group, and HMS *Daisy* in particular, was not improved by his own temper. In sending Brenton-Woodruffe a signal explaining his plight, the corvette's captain, Lieutenant Commander Hewett, considered the only way of mollifying so ferocious a man was to offer a solution along with the problem.

By the grace of Almighty God, or so he consequently believed, Lieutenant Commander Augustus Hewett had been on a solitary drinking spree at Gourock two nights earlier. He had forgotten the name of the hotel in the bar of which he had run into an old friend, but he instantly recognised a former shipmate. Hewett and Lieutenant Jack Clark had been apprentices together, and shared the half-deck of the Eastern Steam's oldest ship at the time, the SS *George Bass*. Later Hewett had been second mate of another of the company's elderly steamers, the *Robert Fitzroy*, in which Clark had served as third. His delight was therefore genuine.

'Jack? Good God, it *is* you! What in hell's name are you doing in the uniform of the Reserve? I took you for a blue-eyed boy, Jack, what with Daddy being on the board,' he guyed, with a familiarity that was only partly due to the drink.

'Good God, Gus Hewett!' Jack had exclaimed with equal pleasure. 'Whatever are *you* doing here?'

'Oh, I've been in this silly suit for ages, Jack, and tonight I'm drowning my sorrows,' Hewett had said.

'Well I knew you were in the RNR. What are you? Not in command?'

Hewett nodded. 'Yup, 'fraid so. Their Lordships have been pleased to place a brand new corvette in my charge.'

'Heavens! They obviously have no idea what you did in Surabaya when the old *Robert Fitzroy* hit the...'

'Sod off! That wasn't my fault, Jack, and you know it. I was only second mate and...'

'You managed to get a mooring wire round the screw...' Clark laughed. 'Poor old Huggy Mandeville shoved me out of the way when the ship wouldn't answer his orders! He nearly dismembered the engine-room telegraph before he grasped that you had a wire fouled round the prop!'

'Well you could hardly describe it as a collision. We sort of drifted into that Dutch ship.'

Hewett gave a rueful grin and finished his gin. Clark, who recalled his old shipmate as somewhat prone to misadventures, had no idea that Hewett had not lost his habit of ineptitude and had recently repeated his sin. At least Brenton-Woodruffe held him personally responsible, though Hewett blamed one of his two sub-lieutenants, just as he had once blamed the Chinese bosun's mate of the *Robert Fitzroy*.

'The mate let the anchors go far too late,' Hewett went on in further self-exculpation, referring to the ancient incident.

'Oh well, at least you only make that sort of

mistake once,' Clark laughed consolingly. Hewett knew better and remained glumly silent. Then, over a few more drinks, he poured out his heart. He had been called up before the war and had been appointed as first lieutenant to a new corvette directly, before she had been completed. His pre-war experience and training with the Reserve had made him an obvious choice for command, at least on paper, and after a few months he moved on. His commanding officer had been glad to see the back of him. Gus Hewett was charming, an asset at a wardroom party and could be guaranteed to round up some female company in the most unlikely circumstances, but he was not a particularly good first lieutenant. His commander recommended appointment to a bigger ship, where he could do less damage, though he failed to explain his suggestion on paper. Contrary to this intention, Their Lordships, mindful of Hewett's rank and the need for corvette officers, had appointed him to HMS *Daisy*.

Lieutenant Commander Hewett hated the name of the ship, hated his senior officer and had found himself at odds with two of his own officers. With the exception of his first lieutenant, they were men of the Volunteer Reserve, the RNVR, men who at best were yachtsmen and at worst had what he called 'an enthusiasm for the sea engendered by some fucking uncle giving them the *Wonder Book of Ships and the Sea* for their tenth birthday!' adding, as he slipped from the general to the personal, 'One fraternises with the hands, of whom he is fundamentally frightened, thinking he can ingratiate himself by criticising me, while the other is a supercilious little turd who spoke of his privileged ownership of a ten-ton cutter with the gravity of a master mariner describing his last ship.'

Clark pulled a face. 'Ah, the *last* ship, eh. Always the best one was on, and certainly always better than the present one.'

'Exactly! Little cunt.' Hewett spoke with vehemence.

By the time the war was six months old, Hewett had escorted several convoys and they had lost a few ships. Then had come his promotion into *Daisy*. The corvette was the least popular ship in the escort group, largely on account of the misjudgements of her commander and her consequent failure to be in the right place at the right time. As other commanders developed instincts for anti-submarine warfare, Hewett remained intellectually obdurate. His ship became known as 'Drooping *Daisy*'; ashore his men were in regular fights with their colleagues in the other ships in the group.

Clark was to learn all this later. That evening, acting as Hewett's confessor, he learned

125

that there were insufficient escorts in the North Atlantic and what there were, were poorly manned by inexperienced ship's companies. It was a disaster, Hewett explained, and it was getting worse as the Germans got into their stride. During the previous convoy, his first in command of *Daisy*, they had had a real mauling. Hewett had been blamed for the loss of two merchantmen and his senior officer had said as much, castigating Hewett in a blistering interview in his cabin. It was only with difficulty that Hewett's failure had not been exposed in Brenton-Woodruffe's *Report of Proceedings*.

'I tell you, Jack, it isn't the bloody Jerries who fuck you, it's your own side. My bloody boss, Commander Guy Brenton-Woodruffe, is a scalp hunter and is out to get me shifted, so, here I am, enjoying a quiet one or two beers before I shove off in a day or two to do another stint out there.'

'If you're not happy, why don't you let him transfer you...?'

'No! It's a matter of pride, Jack,' Hewett bristled. 'Anyway you know I'm no coward.'

'Of course.' Clark remembered that Hewett had rescued two Chinese firemen from a nasty engine-room fire aboard the *Robert Fitzroy* some months after he himself had left the ship. Hewett had received a Lloyd's medal and the decoration of the Royal

Humane Society for the act, though Clark noticed neither ribbon adorned his naval reefer as it had done his Eastern Steam Navigation Company uniform. He imagined Hewett had turned aside the wrath of Commander Brenton-What's-his-Name by pleading his previous gallantry. No, Gus Hewett was not a bad chap to have alongside in a tight corner when an animal reaction of raw courage was required, but he was no man for quick, cool decisions in a crisis, and his charm masked a congenital laziness.

'But Gus, this war isn't going to be over in a few months,' Clark reasoned.

'You're telling me!'

'Well then, submit to a transfer and time will give you another opportunity.'

Hewett waved Clark's commiserating advice aside. 'Oh, never mind, Jack, never mind. I got Brenton-Woodruffe to see that it wasn't all my fault, that we had developed gremlins in our festering Asdic set at two critical moments, but you do, you *really do*, begin to wonder which bloody side the gods are on. Fortunately, the Asdic specialist who came aboard when we got in here threw half the bloody thing over the side and wrote a report which exonerated me but, you know how it is, give a dog a bad name ... Anyway, enough about me. What about you, you old sod?' he asked, ordering two more gins.

'Well, I'm a sort of chameleon at the

moment. I'm standing by the *Matthew Flinders* as the resident derrick expert...'

'Ah! I knew you were on your Daddy's yacht,' Hewett interrupted gleefully, glad of the change of subject.

'Well, she's not quite Daddy's yacht these days.'

'Well, she's one of Dent's new eighteen-knotters, isn't she? Pretty much the same thing.'

'Yes, she's a cracking ship, but she's undergoing conversion into a fast transport, so she's anything but yacht-like. I'm still half wearing my Dent's cap, but then, as you see, I'm actually wearing the King's uniform.'

'She's a white ensign ship then?' Hewett enquired.

'Oh yes. And I'm undergoing some crazy conversion myself, metamorphosing into a King's officer, with square bashing and sword drill.'

'Just like the *Conway*, eh?'

'Well similar, I suppose. I don't recall us waving swords. Anyway, I think I graduate, or pass out in a week or two. I certainly hope so, I seem to have been buggering about like this for months. They send me back here to Glasgow periodically to run over the *Flinders*, then they take no notice of what I say while I'm learning the difference between the bands on an armour-piercing shell and the rings round a commodore's arse, or something like that.'

'You are clearly not the stuff of which the real navy is made, Jack...'

'Please don't you witter on about the *real* bloody navy. There seems to be precious little difference between us at sea, though ashore the merchant jacks are treated like shite. Mercifully, most of them are used to it. Anyway, all I want to do is get to sea and do some proper work. I've never felt so bloody well wasted. The work on the *Flinders* has been stop-start, stop-start for months now.'

And in that vein they consoled each other until the barman asked them to leave.

It was therefore of Jack Clark that Hewett thought when faced with the necessity of replacing his first lieutenant. Dictating his signal to his leading telegraphist he concluded with a flourish of his cigarette, 'Request immediately available services of Lieutenant J.P.J. Clark, currently standing-by HMT *Matthew Flinders*, Govan.'

Brenton-Woodruffe forwarded the request to the flag officer commanding the Clyde. The admiral's staff, aware that a delay to the convoy was unacceptable and grateful that an officer was readily to hand, drafted Clark accordingly. They made no further enquiries before issuing the order for Clark to shift his traps instanter. Thus Clark, without ever completing his basic induction into the

RNR, found himself aboard HMS *Daisy* in March 1940.

Clark was to spend nineteen months in *Daisy* and thereby become a veteran of the great battle in its early stages. An administrative flunkey, discovering the irregularity of his appointment, remonstrated briefly, but the exigencies of war soon confirmed the circumstantial wisdom of his post. Commander Brenton-Woodruffe was soon aware that the new first lieutenant of *Daisy* had transformed the ship and, as the Royal Navy gradually built up the resources with which it was to fight the threat to the survival of Great Britain, anxieties about *Daisy* subsided. It was no reflection on the abilities of the concussed young lieutenant, whose concussion kept him in hospital long enough to ensure that Clark remained in Hewett's corvette; upon recovery, he was sent to a newly commissioned ship. The fact was that the old association between Hewett and Clark simply continued. Hewett's charm and personal courage were impressive; he was also exceedingly tough, in the physical sense. He could stand on the bridge for hours, apparently impervious to fatigue, but he was slow to react, inclined to be indecisive at a critical moment and often failed, through lack of intuition, to understand what Brenton-Woodruffe required of him. Such deficiencies were not uncommon in those first months of anti-submarine warfare, but most escort commanders, honed in the early, inadequately prepared days of total war at sea, rapidly acquired the necessary skills. Later, with the establishment of training facilities at Tobermory, where every commissioning escort was sent for the most rigorous exercises before being despatched on active service, most of this undesirable in-theatre learning was eliminated. Later still, the combat skills of senior officers were developed and honed at the Anti-Submarine Warfare School in Liverpool. But all this lay in the future.

What Clark brought to HM Corvette *Daisy* was an understanding, adaptable cushion between Hewett and his inexperienced crew. Only a little younger than Hewett, and yet carrying the weight of his pre-war experience in the merchant service as a credential necessary to awe the hard-bitten regular petty officers appointed to every corvette in order to help transform the majority of 'Hostilities Only' sailors into proper seamen, Clark filled the bill to perfection. He immediately hit it off with the *Daisy*'s coxswain, who had served on the China station and with whom he shared common experiences of the Far East. Dentco's ships were as familiar to a regular RN seaman as were those of the P & O, Blue

Funnel, Glen and Ben Lines.

But it was in his relationship with Hewett that Clark crucially affected the reputation of *Daisy*, and it was soon apparent to her consorts that something had happened aboard the corvette. Initially, of course, her late joining of the escort was considered highly typical. Scoffing was common on all the bridges as *Daisy* approached, but especially on that of Brenton-Woodruffe's destroyer, HMS *Vortex*, as he assigned her to her usual rear station. Clark, ignorant of these undercurrents in the group, had nevertheless swiftly realised the poor state of the ship's company's morale. A few probing questions had the coxswain spill enough of the beans to reveal the source of the trouble: Lieutenant Commander Hewett was a very nice gentleman, but his idleness prevented him from taking much trouble over details. Sadly, the otherwise exemplary former Blue Funnel officer had not been able to have much effect. As for the two sub-lieutenants, Clark discovered the supercilious yachtsman was only eager to demonstrate his knowledge of seamanship, while his tedious references to his experiences aboard his yacht were essentially only expressions of surprise that the principles of basic seamanship were common to most craft. It was a congruous fact that Their Lordships had acknowledged in their admission of such young men to the brotherhood of naval officers. The other sub was a rather colourless character who, while he lacked a degree of confidence when confronted with the rougher elements of the crew – the like of which Clark judged he had never encountered in his life before – nevertheless possessed an obvious gift for mathematics and trigonometry. Under some wise nudging from Clark, he was soon demonstrating the potential to become an able navigator. Long ago Clark had learned to harness the skills a man possessed, in order to get the best out of him and, within a week of joining, he had succeeded in turning over much of the duties of navigator to the young man. In company with a convoy these were not arduous, but they allowed Clark to concentrate on his own greatest deficiency, a deficiency that exercised the unknown Admiralty clerk who noticed it in Clark's service record: his lack of any experience of anti-submarine warfare. He had mentioned this to Hewett as soon as he had reported aboard, but Hewett had pooh-poohed his misgivings.

'Oh, don't worry about that, Number One. We've especially trained ratings for all that sort of thing.'

Then, as they bounced round the Mull of Kintyre and the two of them were on the bridge, Hewett asked publicly as Clark peered into the Asdic compartment tucked away under the forward part of the compass platform, 'D'you think you'll get the hang of it, Number One?'

The laxity of Hewett's approach to his dilemma in losing his experienced first lieutenant, and his present apparent lack of concern, appalled Clark and caused him to undergo a momentary, stomach-churning anxiety. Clearly he himself was supposed to be an expert. Looking at the slightly incredulous faces of the bridge messenger and the lookouts in this very inept and public exposure, he suspected he was supposed to be *the* expert. He presumed that Commander Brenton-Woodruffe, somewhere beyond the steady lines of grey merchantmen deployed ahead of *Daisy*, expected him to be one. Doubtless the admiral confirming his appointment to *Daisy* thought he was. The realisation hit Clark like a blow. It was clear that Hewett's breezy revelation, unconsciously delivered to further batter the morale of the Drooping Daisies in the mess decks when the word got below that the new Jimmy had no idea what an Asdic set was, had to be turned round.

'Of course I don't know anything about it at all, sir,' he jested. 'I'm a merchant-navy man in disguise.'

The joke was feeble in the extreme but, linked with the buzz that the new Jimmy and the Old Man had sailed together before, it was taken to be evidence of an irreverent, chi-ike-ing relationship. Mercifully, any lingering notion that the new first lieutenant was as big a prat as the captain was swiftly dispelled in the days to come.

But that evening Clark had quietly and tactfully confronted Hewett in his cabin. 'You know, what you have done is bloody silly, Gus...'

'I didn't know you hadn't done the Asdic course,' Hewett expostulated.

'Oh, I've done the basics...'

'Listen, chum, that's all there is, for Chrissakes. I told you the bloody box of tricks is unreliable. We've had a lot of problems with it. Now I'll trouble you to remember, for the purposes of good order and discipline, you don't come bursting in here covered in indignation, and remember that I'm the commander.'

Clark regarded Hewett. 'Fuck you, lieutenant commander, sir.'

'That's more like it. Now have a drink.'

'No, not at sea.'

'Then fuck *you*, Number One.'

In the few hours left to Clark before they reached the open Atlantic, Clark sat alongside the duty Asdic operator, a rating named Carter. As though idly flicking through the operator's handbook, he surreptitiously observed the man's technique as Carter swept the surrounding sea with the questing

135

sound beam. The 'noise' of the churning screws of the convoy ahead rendered a wide arc obscured, but away out on either beam, the attenuated sound seemed to dissipate into the ocean with an almost mystical beauty.

It was an odd notion, Clark admitted to himself, but he was addicted to such strange things. They were part of what made the sea life so enduringly seductive to him. Just as watching the sweep of a fulmar petrel quarter their wake with motionless wings moved him to wonderment and pleasure, or as the sunlight upon Arctic ice had once struck him with an infinite beauty, or as the aurora had touched him, so that strange, scientific sound of the Asdic impulse, similarly fascinated him.

It was this novel fascination and a natural talent, inherent in most sea officers, for spatial conceptualisation, that caused him to transform *Daisy*'s reputation on the third day of the westbound convoy. At about ten in the morning Brenton-Woodruffe's destroyer signalled she had a contact with a submarine, then another of the escorts ahead confirmed she, too, had echo-located a U-boat. The Drooping Daisies closed up to action stations and Clark ducked into the Asdic compartment, where, in a sweat of apprehension, he tried to understand what was going on.

For two hours in the distance the low grey shapes of the two escorts rushed about, busy with their counter-attack as the convoy, stoically maintaining its methodical zig-zag, moved steadily westwards. Although Clark could not see the tall columns of water that the attacking escorts threw up from their detonating depth charges, he was aware of the crumps of the explosions and swiftly formed, in his mind's eye, a mental picture of the tactical plot. Deprived of sight, he, like Carter, relied upon the underwater sound transmissions, not of *Daisy*'s transmitted echo-location, but of the incoming noises and the rapid shift in their modulation and azimuth. While Carter unknowingly pulled faces as the noises came in to them through their headsets, Clark had no difficulty sensing what was happening. Afterwards Carter told his messmates the new Jimmy was 'all right', that he had 'the gift', but for the moment the sounds of combat drifted astern.

As *Daisy* shifted her station in conformity with the orders that provided for the detachment of escorts attacking contacts, Hewett called him on to the open bridge and pointed out what was happening.

'They won't find anything,' he said. 'Jerry, if he was there and it wasn't a bloody whale, will have done a bunk by now.'

Clark picked up a pair of Barr and Stroud

binoculars and peered astern. He could see a flurry of wakes criss-crossing, and white columns where *Vortex* and *Nemesia* tossed their depth charges. The explosions thundered through the water while the shapes of the attackers faded into the grey murk. The convoy ploughed on and Hewett began a desultory conversation. And then Clark heard it: the echoing ping of a contact nearby.

Long before the fact had registered with his captain, Clark was beside Carter.

'Green one-one-zero,' Carter said sharply, indicating the initial bearing of the contact, 'moving right.'

'Yes,' Clark responded excitedly, his heart racing. He repeated the information to Hewett.

'Very well, er, hoist the attack pendant, Yeoman, and make to *Vortex*: In contact.'

'Come to port sir!' Clark exclaimed. He was closely watching the mean of the arc of bearing in which the echo responded with its greatest magnitude shift as Carter manipulated the questing beam. 'Hard over! Steer one fifty and reduce speed!'

He said it without thinking, the logic of it simple to him, and Hewett repeated the order as if his own. After a second, as *Daisy* heeled to the turn, Hewett queried, 'Reduce speed, Number One? Are you sure?'

'Yes!' Clark snapped, almost resentful at

the interruption as he continued following Carter's manipulation of the controls and visualised the track the U-boat was following. It was clear to him that, having successfully evaded the noisy demonstrations of *Vortex* and *Nemesia*, she had slipped in immediately astern of the convoy.

'Depth charges!' Hewett sang out.

'Shallow setting!' shouted Clark. 'No, mixed pattern,' he yelled. 'Can you do that?' he asked Carter as the operator wound his controlling wheel. The man nodded, unwilling to break his own concentration with speech.

The U-boat commander had no advantage in speed below the surface, he would have to take a peep through his periscope if he intended to attack. Unless he sought the shelter of the convoy's collective underwater noise, the fact that he had turned inwards towards it argued he might be intending to attack before he lost the chance. He was clearly a bold man and Clark did not think *Daisy*'s Asdic had deterred him amid the noise of the convoy's screws and the bangs of the depth charges exploding astern. It was a gamble but, even if he had gone deep, another depth charge going off over his head would not hurt.

Clark heard the response of the coxswain on the wheel below inform Hewett they were steadied on the new course. Sweat was pouring off Carter's forehead as he kept the Asdic beam on the target. 'He'll be hearing us now sir. He's bound to dive.'

Concentrating, Clark detected the imbalance of arc as Carter adjusted the machine. 'He's moving left ... And diving!'

'Yeah!' Carter agreed.

'Port twenty, sir, and increase speed!' Clark yelled.

'Port twenty and nine-oh revs!' Hewett sang out obediently.

For a few long seconds they waited as the ping interval shortened. Then Carter called out: 'Instantaneous echo!'

Clark never heard the order to fire, nor the clang of the gongs that sent the depth charges out from the mortars on each quarter and over the stern from the after racks. He was staring into Carter's eyes as the rating ripped the headset off with an intensity that, in any other circumstances, would have been indecent.

The explosions rocked *Daisy* as she made off from her handiwork. Without prompting, Hewett turned her round to retrace her steps as Carter and Clark bent again to their task. Carter caught an echo, then it was gone.

'The wake's fucking it up, sir,' he explained.

'Yes, I see that.' They waited. 'There it is again...'

'No, I've lost it...'

The faint noise of cheering came to them and then Hewett's bulk loomed in the doorway. 'We've got the bugger, Number One!' he said with a broad smile.

Clark and Carter looked at each other. 'I *can* smell diesel oil, sir,' Carter said.

Clark was unconvinced. 'We may have damaged a tank, or they may have released some...'

'There's oil on the water, Number One,' Hewett was calling. 'We *have* got the bugger, by God!'

Clark and Carter remained unconvinced. As the word spread like wildfire through the corvette, and the news was flashed to *Vortex*, rushing up in a smother of foam, the sense of exhilaration was almost tangible.

'I'm not convinced,' Clark muttered to Carter. 'Keep looking.' Carter bent to his controls again.

'We've got the bugger,' Hewett was repeating, 'we've got the bugger! We've got the bugger!'

'Christ, it sounds as though they're fucking dancing! He must think his DSC's in the bag,' Carter muttered as he sent the sound wave out all round them.

'Pay attention,' Clark reproved him gently.

But the echo resonated out into the vastness of the ocean unimpeded. 'Nothing, sir,' said Carter as the captain's bulk filled the doorway. Clark patted Carter on the shoulder.

'Well done, anyway. At least none of the convoy were lost.'

'Come up here you two and fill your lungs with that glorious stench,' Hewett commanded.

They lost three ships in the next few days, and the Admiralty would only credit them with a 'possible', but the Daisies drooped no more. *Vortex* and *Nemesia* had lost the contact and, as far as they were concerned, the *Daisy* had saved the day. Moreover, Lieutenant Commander Hewett was generous enough to attribute the success of the attack to his new second-in-command: Lieutenant Clark had established himself as a man with a potent skill.

It was the nearest *Daisy* came to glory. Later, in the summer of 1941, *Vortex* 'killed' a U-boat and *Daisy* was mentioned in complimentary terms in Brenton-Woodruffe's report, but for the most part victory went to the enemy and the *Vortex*'s escort group grew weary with their inability to prevent heavy losses in the slow convoys under their protection. But they made hundreds of attacks and, though most were unsuccessful and a few achieved the ambiguous status of 'possibles', Clark's expertise as a submarine hunter remained undiminished. In fact, though he was not to know it at the time, promotion was withheld from Clark because, as long as he was saddled with Hewett, Brenton-Woodruffe wanted Clark riding shotgun.

But Norway, Denmark and France had fallen under German occupation by the summer of 1940, the British Expeditionary Force, minus its equipment, had been evacuated from the beaches of Dunkirk, and Fascist Italy had joined the Germans. Britain, under threat of invasion until the Luftwaffe was defeated in its attempt to gain control of English airspace, stood alone.

Clark had been in London on leave when the blitz began. He had learned that Magda was in the capital with Diana Cranbrooke and the two women were attending meetings in connection with plans for dealing with the expected intensifying of air raids. To his relief, for he feared a rebuff, she had agreed to join him for dinner, after which they had gone dancing.

'It is so good to hold you again,' he had whispered as they moved among the other dancers.

He felt her press against him as she had once done at the Adelphi. 'I am glad too,' she whispered back. 'I was horrible to you before. I'm sorry.'

He drew back and looked at her. He had never seen so beautiful a creature. It was as though the misery to which she had consigned him vanished in an instant. 'Forget it,' he said. 'I am only glad that you remember me,' he said, thinking of the broken romances and shattered marriages among the *Daisy*'s complement, revealed by his censoring the men's private mail. 'This war has made people different.'

'I could not forget you, Jack. You were very kind to me.'

'And Kurt?' He asked.

She did not hesitate. 'As you say, people change in war. Kurt belongs to another time. Besides, we were never actually engaged. We had, I think you would call, an understanding. It is all in the past now.'

'Can we go somewhere?'

'I have a room to myself. Diana is close, but it is quite private.'

'And you will not shut the door in my face?'

She smiled, a beguiling curve of her wide and lovely mouth. 'I did not shut it in your face before.'

'Oh, I rather thought you did.'

'You should have discovered that I did not lock it.'

'You mean, had I come to you that night, you would not have turned me away?'

'Perhaps that night I would, but as you're asking me now, all this time later, I do not think I should have.'

For Clark, the brief interlude he enjoyed during *Daisy*'s boiler clean proved the happiest period of his life. As London submitted to German bombing he was caught up for a few days in the intensity of life lived under such extraordinary circumstances. They revelled in the wild, hedonistic, devil-may-care atmosphere. With the clubs, restaurants and pubs full of the remnant pride of expatriate Poles, Norwegians, Free French, Czechs and Belgians, he imbibed a slightly manic defiance that was in stark contrast with the dour aspect of the grey North Atlantic.

Magda and Diana Cranbrooke returned to the Wirral a day before the expiry of his short leave. He travelled back with them, his attachment to Magda clear to anyone who cared to notice.

But if his affair made him happy on land, it made him miserable at sea. He had experienced similar pangs before, but nothing so excoriating, so demoralising as this. He was wracked by the misery common to lovelorn sailors, intensified by the risks of war.

'Marry her,' advised Hewett, observing Clark's dejection on the eve of sailing when they were enjoying a glass of gin together. Hewett had himself long since tied the knot to a pleasant, dumpy young woman who had reminded Clark of a younger version of

Jenny O' Neil. It did not prevent him flirting extravagantly with other women, but, as far as Clark had observed, Mrs Hewett possessed the ability, even at long range, to keep her husband faithful. 'Otherwise she'll run off with someone else, mark my words,' Hewett concluded.

Clark grunted. He had proposed to Magda as he had lain beside her after their last night together. He could not believe his good fortune in making love to so sublime a creature, and had taken her acquiescence for reciprocated wonder. But his proposal had met with less eagerness and he had been disappointed, if not entirely surprised, by her response.

'Perhaps, darling,' she had said in her husky, post-coital voice, 'when this war is over and if we are both still alive.'

'We could be so happy...'

'We are happy now, aren't we?'

'Of course.'

'Then that is all that matters.'

And with that he had had to be content.

'Well, she won't agree until the war's over,' he said now to Hewett.

'Bloody shame,' said Hewett. 'If only because I don't think I can stand the sight of a lovesick first lieutenant mooning about my bridge. You're too old for such nonsense, Jack. Next time we get a break I'll get Dierdre to ask you both to stay and we'll see

146

what we can arrange.'

'You'll do no such bloody thing!' Clark protested.

'Don't forget who's in command here, Number One,' Hewett said with his engaging grin.

'How can I, sir?' Clark said with an expression of mock pain upon his face. 'Anyway, I'd better go and do my rounds,' he said, rising and picking up his cap.

'You ponder my advice, Jack,' Hewett said as Clark drew aside the door curtain. And when he had gone, Hewett murmured, 'or you'll be too bloody late, old chap.'

The war in the Atlantic dragged on. After the debacle of Norway and the occupation of France, from which U-boats now operated, merchant-ship losses mounted alarmingly. But so too did the loss of escorts. Brenton-Woodruffe's *Vortex* was torpedoed one night in May 1941 as she hunted a contact. As she steamed past a burning tanker, silhouetted against the blazing oil, she had formed an irresistible target to Kapitänleutnant Johannes Petersen, peering through the periscope, his white covered hat reversed. Round his neck he already wore the *Ritterkreuz*.

In the aftermath the corvette *Daisy* was assigned the task of searching for survivors. She picked up twenty men. Brenton-Woodruffe was not among them and Hewett was profoundly disappointed. He should have liked 'old Bee-Double-You' to have owed his life to him. But this indulgent dream was cut short by the cry of 'Torpedo!'

Hewett watched as the pale streak missed *Daisy*'s bow by a few feet.

'God damn the bastards!' Hewett raged as he watched the trail disappear into the darkness, compelled to hold his ship stopped while Clark and the seamen scrambled over the side and helped *Vortex*'s oil-soaked survivors inboard. It was not a battle that men of Hewett's courage could shine in; Hewett wanted the bruising contact of aggressive action. For Clark, superintending the wounded and saturated wretches, it had simply assumed the qualities of a bad dream. Their struggle had ceased to be a battle in the sense that they had imagined a battle to be; it was simply a matter of endurance, of warding off attack, of countering it when it came and of picking up the survivors when they failed, as they so often did. For Clark it seemed like some inglorious playground scrap against a monstrous bully from which one could only emerge beaten; except that the metaphor was too trivial.

They were all growing tired, increasingly aware of the looming possibility of defeat, their only respite the boiler cleans which kept the *Daisy* operational. A month later they were ordered to the Clyde for their next.

During that leave in June of 1941 Clark was with Magda when they heard the news that Hitler had turned on his ally and invaded the Soviet Union. Russia had reeled under the blow.

'Can Hitler be as stupid as Napoleon?' Magda asked as they listened to the BBC news. They had the family home to themselves, apart from Captain Clark's staff, for he himself had gone to Glasgow on company business.

'Can he win?' Clark countered. 'At least we are not in this alone any more,' he added, brightening, 'and hitting at the communists is going to make things awkward for their sympathisers here.'

Despite the fact that Russia shared in the dismemberment of Poland, the British Prime Minister, Winston Churchill, offered Stalin help, and in the succeeding months convoys began to sail north, into the Barents Sea, round the North Cape of Norway, taking war supplies to the Red Army and the Soviet air force by way of Archangel and Murmansk.

HMS *Daisy* took no part in this new theatre, though Clark entertained a vague hope that he might go north once more. He had long ago forgotten his interview with Inglis and Gifford. Those events of the first few days of the war seemed to belong to another age. But the tales that filtered back from the Barents Sea, of the convoys being hemmed in to the north by ice and attacked from the south by the Luftwaffe's aircraft from their bases in occupied Norway, began to persuade them that perhaps the North Atlantic was not such a bad place to be after all.

'We've only got submarines to worry about,' Hewett remarked as they steamed towards the convoy with its lines of merchant ships, each flying their column numbers in the bright colours of the International Code of Signals above their rusty grey hulls. 'The poor buggers in the Arctic have got the lot: U-boats, ice, the Luftwaffe *and* a frosty reception when they get to Uncle Joe's wonderful bloody Workers' Paradise.' Hewett lifted his binoculars and studied one of the merchantmen, a Ropner tramp. 'And, of course, there's all that midnight sun and midwinter gloom that you'd remember, Number One,' he added conversationally.

'Oh, I was only up in the Arctic during the summer,' Clark replied.

'Damn me, but isn't that a bloody periscope?' Hewett suddenly cried. 'Wheelhouse! Ring on the revs! Action stations! Hoist the attack pendant! Make to *Seymour...*'

* * *

150

And so it went on until, berthed in Londonderry in December, they heard two pieces of news. The Japanese had bombed Pearl Harbor and Clark was to leave the ship.

'I must say I find it difficult to be downhearted,' said Hewett, referring to the news of Pearl Harbor as he handed Clark the signal. 'This'll bring the Yanks into the war properly, by God!'

Clark read the signal, his heart beating. He hoped for promotion and a command. Or just a ship of his own; several corvettes were commanded by lieutenants. From down in the wardroom, where the wireless was on, came cheers as the import of the news sank in.

'The Admiralty?' Clark said, looking at Hewett. 'What in Hades can I do at the bloody Admiralty?'

'Have a gin, Number One. I'll be sorry to lose you.'

'Thanks,' Clark said, raising his glass to Hewett. 'It had to come, I suppose, but I rather expected a command, or a half stripe...'

'Or even both, you deserve 'em...'

'Good of you ... But the poxy Admiralty ... I just don't understand it.'

'Well, it only says "*Report* to the Admiralty". Doesn't mean they're going to give you a desk there.'

'Well, that's true,' replied Clark, somewhat

151

mollified.

'Anyway,' Hewett went on flippantly, 'what do you know about what goes on at the Admiralty?'

'Bugger all...'

'Oh my, Number One, *that* could qualify you for flag rank!' Hewett laughed and refilled his glass. 'By God, it's beginning to look really serious!' Hewett held out the bottle. 'Such rapid promotion calls for another gin.'

CHRISTMAS CHEER

December 1941

'Good to see you, Clark.' Gifford held out his hand.

'I see congratulations are in order, sir,' Clark said, referring to the augmentation of gold lace upon Gifford's sleeve.

'Oh, thanks. Actually we're going to do the same for you. Between ourselves, your half stripe is overdue and I'm rather to blame.'

'Oh?'

'Well, for reasons that will become clear later, I've been keeping an eye on you and I blocked your promotion earlier in the year.'

'I see.'

'No, you don't,' Gifford said with a boyish smile, 'but you will. Now, first things first, a cigarette and a cup of tea, I think.' With the tea and an ashtray between them, Gifford sat back and became more expansive. 'How would you like to go back to the Arctic?'

'Russian convoys?' Clark said, thinking of Hewett's strategic summary of the polar theatre.

'Yes and no. Well?'

'Well, er, I'm not sure whether I'd actually *like* it, sir, but I go where Their Lordships direct these days.'

'Huh! Don't we all!' Gifford smiled at him and added, 'It would have delighted Captain Inglis to hear you say that.'

'I'd forgotten him.'

'He's forgotten himself, these days. I'm afraid he's lost his marbles, poor fellow. He's in Netley Hospital and likely to stay there.'

'Oh, I'm sorry to hear that.'

'It's hard on his wife. She has two children...' Gifford ground out his cigarette and leaned back in his chair. Drawing a thin file towards him with an air of resolution he said, 'Now to the heart of the matter. I'm in a quandary: I want an officer for special service, and you are the obvious candidate because of your familiarity with the subject.'

Clark frowned for a moment, and then the

past caught him up. 'My cousin's document?'

'Exactly. My quandary is that there are aspects of this assignment that I would have to conceal from any other officer in the Service, *any* other officer, mark you...'

'My cousin again?'

'Yes. He is a very brave man. He runs incredible risks, but he has secured a post of great use to us.'

A torrent of thoughts rushed through Clark's brain. Kurt, Kurt rising like a spectre to haunt him, to come between him and Magda. Kurt wanting to survive for Magda Liepmann's sake! But then another thought, too terrifying to contemplate, except that he must consider it, if only to preserve his own chances with Magda!

'Look, Captain Gifford,' he said sharply, 'I am executing the duties of a naval officer in the North Atlantic, I hope to Their Lordships' satisfaction...'

'Of course, my dear fellow...'

'Well, you had better understand that I am not the stuff of which lonely heroes are made. Whatever virtues I may possess do not include being sent into Nazi Germany to make contact with my cousin. Call me a coward if you will, but the thought makes my blood run cold. I would simply funk it.'

Gifford's look of growing astonishment changed to a grin. 'My dear chap, relax. The

154

idea never crossed my mind. Your cousin is too precious an asset for us to go clumsily blundering about by trying to make contact with him. In any case, we don't have to. He's perfectly capable of making contact with us. Besides, the Director of Naval Intelligence is, believe it or not,' he said wryly, 'intelligent enough to passively allow your cousin to tell us what he wishes to, without us *asking* him things. We don't get much, but a diamond is not a very big object, you know.'

'I see.' Clark felt the prickle of the sweat of relief under his shirt. 'I thought my speaking German...'

'Oh, that may come in useful in due course, but no, not now. Actually, we're more impressed with your talent as an Asdic analyst. You impressed Brenton-Woodruffe and your present SO, Godfrey Talbot, thinks you're red-hot.'

'That's very flattering, sir, but I'm not aware I've killed any U-boats yet.'

'There's evidence that you've helped materially in several possibles. It isn't your fault if the attack fails at the point of delivery. It's the picking up and holding the spoor that's important.'

'I'm not certain where all this is going, sir.'

'No, of course,' Gifford smiled. 'I'm a bit off-track myself. You recall your cousin's paper and the super submarines?'

'Yes, of course.'

'Well, they've built three. We've managed to get the RAF to damage two, one in Hamburg and one at Kiel, but the third has been completed and is undergoing trials in the Baltic. Thanks to information received, we know enough about it to realise something of its potential. It's not all due to your cousin; since our last meeting we've learnt a lot from Dutch sources. As you may know, the terms of the Versailles Treaty prohibited Germany from building any submarines. So the design team from Krupp's Germania yard were sent off to the Netherlands, where they set up a company called, if I can pronounce it, *Ingenieurs Scheepsbouwkantoor*. Behind this front, the Germans built what amounted to prototype U-boats, but they were in fact for Finland, Spain and Turkey. They also secretly made parts for a building programme which, by the time you and I were cosily chatting about the potential dangers of the war at sea, quickly provided Grand Admiral Räder with a fleet of over sixty boats. Apart from various classes of attack types, Jerry was also designing larger hulls for use as underwater cargo carriers and supply tankers, as well as the big super U-cruiser that concerned us in September '39. We know that the U-tankers are about to be deployed now, along with the U-cruiser. Clearly the U-tankers are intended to refuel and resupply boats already at sea. We can therefore confidently predict that they'll operate in the Atlantic. The question is, while they might have used a wolf pack of this super-class in the Atlantic, what are they going to do with one by itself?'

'Well, she could operate as a wolf-pack leader, a flagship,' suggested Clark, 'as well as an oiler to her sidekicks.'

'She'd be wasted.' Gifford shook his head emphatically. 'No, we think – and we have some grounds for thinking it which you will have to take on trust–' Gifford said with a quiet emphasis – 'that she'll be deployed in the Arctic. You see, while the interdiction of the Atlantic route is directly important to us, keeping us in the war and so forth, interdiction of the northern convoy route to Russia is directly important to Germany. Every tank and aeroplane we send to Archangel or Murmansk is destined for the field to serve against the German Wehrmacht. Our appreciation is that it is actually more important to Berlin that the Russian convoys are stopped, and soon. Don't forget, with the United States in the war now and with Hitler and the Eyeties declaring common cause with Japan, Berlin's under increasing pressure. Besides,' Gifford said cheerfully, 'it is winter now and Jerry is probably having a grim time of it in Russia.'

'I see. What about the Russians?'

'They seem to be holding up very well.

157

Quite surprising really, but there we are. They're a pretty tough lot.'

'Yes. Perhaps that shouldn't surprise us.'

'Perhaps not,' Gifford nodded agreement. 'Now, if we are right about the theatre of operations for which this super U-boat is intended, we need to take measures to ensure she either does not get there or, if by some mischance she does, we destroy her in the Barents Sea. This in turn raises another problem. We need to protect our sources of information, in particular your cousin. We don't want to go crashing about in either the Baltic or the Barents Sea as though we expect the bloody thing to pop up there; we want a surgical operation undertaken by an officer who understands the absolute, repeat absolute, necessity for secrecy.'

'Haven't you already indicated to the Germans that you know about their big U-boats by bombing two of them?'

'We don't think so. They were both caught in general raids on U-boat construction yards. We think they will assume the fate of those two boats to be circumstantial.'

'I see.'

'Well, as to the secrecy element of what we are proposing, there are things we can do to help. We hope intelligence from the Norwegian resistance will help us destroy this thing before it gets up to the Barents Sea, but bombing her in the Norwegian Leads may not be easy. If I was Räder I'd send her north submerged, fill her up with fuel when she gets to Hammerfest, or Tromso or Altenfjord and then let her loose on our convoy route. Having the support of other U-boats and the Luftwaffe, she will have the impact of a cruiser, for she has heavy guns. That is what is concerning Their Lordships upstairs and they have warned the Joint Chiefs. Between ourselves, Admiral Pound has long worried about the presence of *Tirpitz* in Norwegian waters. She is free to attack a convoy at a time or place of her own choosing and other capital units of the Kriegsmarine are known to be in north Norway, or on their way up there, so, with the augmentation of their forces with this super-submarine, a major attack upon a Russian convoy is confidently apprehended.'

Gifford paused and, picking up a chart from a side table, opened it and, laying it over the papers on his desk, turned it so that Clark could see it. The long, eastwards curve of the Norwegian coast trended round past the North Cape until, beyond the indentations of Porshanger Fjord and Varanger Fjord, lay the Kola Inlet and the Gourlo, leading to the White Sea. Ice-free Murmansk lay at the head of the Kola Inlet; Archangel at the innermost part of the White Sea. To the east of the entrance of the Gourlo lay the barrier of Novaya Zemlya, two islands separated by a narrow strait. Far to the north of Norway's North Cape lay the South Cape of Spitsbergen, a polar irony, between which was the isolated hump of Bear Island. Gifford ran his right index finger along a dotted line that wandered from Novaya Zemlya westwards until it curved round and met the South Cape of Spitsbergen.

'If you wanted to conceal a ship you'd take her up here, inside the summer ice limit. She could sit up there dozing, out of the way of the prying eyes of the Norwegian resistance, the Royal Air Force, or the Russkies, until the moment came to strike at one of our convoys.'

'A big submarine could make the entire passage underwater,' Clark said. 'She could even get into a Norwegian fjord submerged if she had a small surface escort to lead her in, and would only have to surface to refuel.'

'I see you're warming to the subject.'

Clark looked up from the chart. 'Where exactly do I come in?'

'Well, Clark,' said Gifford, folding up the chart and putting it to one side. 'It's a simple enough matter on the face of it: we want you to go up there and sink the bloody thing.'

Clark raised his eyebrows and let out his breath. 'As you say, it's a simple enough matter. What do I get to do this with, sir? A corvette?'

Gifford shook his head. 'No, sorry, we've

160

got to consider the security aspects of the affair as paramount. The whole thing must be undertaken as a clandestine mission. We can't afford to send a corvette, partly because their movements may well be known to the enemy, and partly because the complement is too large. Someone's tongue will wag. No, we've found a vessel more suitable. A whaler...'

'A whaler...?'

'Not a naval pulling boat, but a whale catcher,' Gifford said with a smile. 'Good turn of speed, built to a high standard and specially fitted for the job. We have given her long-range fuel tanks and one or two other refinements. At the outbreak of war she was being built by Smith's Dock on Teesside for Norwegian owners. Moreover, she has a number of sister ships which have been requisitioned for service with the Kriegsmarine. It will not be immediately obvious to the curious who happen to see her that she is a British man-of-war.'

'I suppose that will help,' Clark said thoughtfully. 'What about armament, sir?'

'A four-inch gun, same mark as you had on *Daisy*, two depth-charge mortars, one on either quarter, plus a small rack aft. The most potent weapons we intend to fit you with are two torpedo tubes. At the present moment the vessel looks like a pretty standard auxiliary anti-submarine vessel. We've had a number of such hybrids in hand since the beginning of the war. The problem is that the fitting of torpedo tubes is most emphatically *not* standard, so we are going to do that secretly at Scapa Flow. In fact they are fabricating the units in Rosyth now; they'll be taken north to meet you.'

'It would seem, sir, that the matter of the commanding officer is all that is left to be considered.'

'Not quite, Clark. As I say, we've had you earmarked for a while, but yes, the crew is the last thing. We don't want a word of this breathed outside these walls. The crew is being put together piecemeal. A chap in the Second Sea Lord's department has been cherry-picking commended ratings and POs out of Home Fleet and Western Approaches ships for some time. Apart from officers, we've a list of about twice as many as we need so that we have a good chance of getting what we want, when we want 'em. No good wanting Able Seaman Jack Tar if he's sitting on a bar stool in Halifax, Nova Scotia, or sunbathing on a cruiser in the South Atlantic.'

'No, of course not.' Clark paused a moment. 'Do I have any choices, sir? I'm thinking in particular of a second-in-command, if you'll allow me that luxury, and an Asdic operator.'

'No, you don't,' said Gifford bluntly.

Clark pulled a face. 'That's a shame, because a good Asdic operator may prove important, especially in the ice. I'd need to be up north early enough to get some experience in the ice and I was hoping to have someone as good as my best man in *Daisy*.'

'Are you pleading with me?' Gifford said, his face serious.

'Yes,' answered Clark, meeting the commander's rather stony expression. 'I rather think I am.'

'Well, there's no chance of changing things now. You'll have to put up with what you get.'

'That's a pity.'

'Don't you want to know his name?'

Clark shrugged. 'Does it make any difference?'

'How does Carter sound to you?'

'*Daisy*'s Carter?'

'Don't look so bloody incredulous, Clark, it ruins your good looks! Of course it's *Daisy*'s Carter!'

'Well, that's wonderful,' Clark responded, beaming. Then he added, 'So you're already selecting people, from your shortlist.'

'Oh, yes. Time's pressing and the ball's already rolling.' Gifford went on crisply. 'As for your first lieutenant, we've got a chap whom I don't think you'll know, but I am pretty confident you will get along with. He's a regular and has already made a name for himself by some very distinguished service. You'll understand that I can't go into details, just as I can't tell him all that I've told you. The only facts germane to the matter presently in hand are that he is a very good navigator and is very cool under fire.'

Clark wondered what the man had done to get such an understated recommendation. 'Is he a destroyer man?' Clark hazarded, seeking a chink in Gifford's reticence.

'Yes. Shrewd of you.'

'Any other officers?'

'Yes, a Norwegian naval lieutenant and a sub from the RNVR. Both come recommended. We've got an engineer officer for you, another Norwegian chap, and he is quietly selecting his own black-gang. He has experience with Norwegian whalers in civvie life. As for the rest–' Gifford withdrew a brown envelope from his file – 'they're all good men, and we've given you just enough to maintain watches for a longish trip with the possibility of manning the gun and torpedo tubes in a surface action. The alternative scenario is an underwater attack, in which case you are equally well provided for. We've given the details a lot of thought.' Gifford handed the envelope over. 'There's the final list of your complement, the men we've selected from those available in the country at the moment...'

Clark took the envelope and opened it,

giving it a quick glance as Gifford went on. 'You should all arrive on Teesside on Friday evening. Naturally, you're the first to know, we thought you ought to have a couple of days to sort things out, get your half stripe put up, make your will if you haven't already done so, though I'm sure you have...'

'And the others?'

'We'll leave you to tell them. I want you to return here on Thursday and we'll have a number of pro formas for you to take with you. It'll make things easier. Now, there will be written instructions, of course, but you won't get them until just before sailing and you won't be able to open them until you are over the Arctic Circle, but you clearly cannot go to sea without a full and fundamental understanding of what this particular mission is all about, and what is expected of you. Oh, and I almost forgot, on Thursday the First Sea Lord wants to see you.'

'Admiral Pound?'

'Sir Dudley himself.' Gifford smiled. 'I don't suppose you'll have time to have your half stripe up by then, though...' Gifford looked at his watch. 'I don't know, you've probably got time to catch a taxi to Gieves and get a new uniform ordered. Anyway, I expect he'll forgive you for being improperly dressed in the circumstances, Lieutenant Commander.'

Gifford held out another envelope. 'That's

the only document you can take with you this afternoon.' Gifford leaned back in his chair and took out his cigarettes. 'Go on, read it now,' he said, waggling the unlit cigarette between his lips.

To the flick of Gifford's lighter, Clark opened the envelope and read of his promotion. Folding it he replaced it and tucked it in his breast pocket, taking the cigarette Gifford held out. 'It's been quite a day, sir.'

'I suppose it has. Congratulations, anyway.' Gifford smiled. 'I shall pay you a visit before you sail to keep you abreast of the latest intelligence information and hand you your written operational orders. On Thursday you'll get detailed orders to prepare your ship, but nothing more. The rest of it I leave up to you.'

There was a moment's silence as Clark digested this information and then he asked, 'By the way, sir, what's the whaler's name?'

'By heaven, haven't I told you that?'

'I don't recall it.'

'She goes by the name of His Majesty's Armed Whaler *Sheba*. Rather regal, I thought.'

'And my objective? Does she have a name, or just a number?'

Gifford ground his cigarette out and stood up, shaking his head. 'We don't know, but our informant calls her *Orca*, after the killer whale.'

166

'Seems appropriate,' Clark said, uncomfortably reminded of Kurt and reflecting briefly on the thin thread of kinship and circumstance that linked him with his distant cousin.

'I'll see you on Thursday,' said Gifford. 'Go home and enjoy forty-eight hours of fun. It may be a while before you get another opportunity.'

Fun, he thought, as he left the Admiralty and hailed a taxi in Whitehall. But then the image of Magda's white body swam into his mind and he felt the quickening prickle of lust.

'Savile Row,' he told the cabbie, climbing in.

' 'Ome fer Christmas, Guv?'

'Hope so,' said Clark. There was not a snowflake's hope in hell of such a thing, he ruminated, but a night with Magda seemed a wonderful substitute, and beyond that...? Well that was not to be thought of. Except that it was north into the pack ice and the white nights of the Arctic.

From Gieves's establishment in Savile Row, Clark took a second cab to Euston where he caught the last train to Liverpool. He submitted to a cold, stop-start journey during which he fitfully dozed and dreamed, curled in his heavy naval bridge coat and ignoring the other inhabitants of the carriage. In his waking moments he thought of his mission and it dawned on him that, in the torrent of Gifford's briefing, no mention had been made of how he was to locate this mysterious super U-boat. But then he consoled himself with the thought that this was not something they could consider in anything other than the light of the most recent intelligence; Gifford had said he would personally come up to Scapa Flow and pass that on to him in due course. In the meantime, Clark had a ship to commission.

As the train rumbled over the Manchester ship canal at Runcorn one of the compartment's other occupants – an army major – lifting the window blind, peered out into the darkness and swore.

'What's up, Freddie?' his companion, a half-colonel, asked, stirring grumpily from a doze and waking the others.

'Bloody air raid, that's what's up, sir!' the major explained, and they all peered in turn at the distant prospect, the searchlight beams probing the night sky, the dull and distant flashes of bomb bursts and the faint lines of tracer fire from the ack-ack batteries and the anti-aircraft guns fired from ships in the docks lining either side of the Mersey. They were rumbling over the great river itself now, their view blocked as the curve of the track led round towards the city. The blackout blind fell back into place and they

168

all resumed their seats, staring at each other.

'Poor old Liverpool getting another pasting,' the major remarked. 'Had several bad raids since last May.' He looked at Clark. 'If he can't get you chaps at sea, he'll get you when you and your convoy get into port, eh?'

'Yes.' Clark said, nodding.

'Don't know where it'll all end,' a dark-suited, elderly civilian offered.

'In victory, by God,' the major affirmed.

'God knows what time we'll arrive now,' the lieutenant colonel groaned, 'let alone what time we'll get to bed!'

'It's a real bugger,' agreed the major. 'You joining a ship?' he asked Clark.

Clark shook his head. 'No, going on leave.'

'Won't have much fun in that lot,' the major responded, nodding at the blanked-off window.

'No. What about you, sir?'

'Oh we're, er, well, you know...'

'Don't like to say too much about it,' the half-colonel put in, rolling his eyes towards the civilian.

Clark nodded. 'I've been in the North Atlantic,' he said, 'and I don't like to say too much about that either.'

'Bloody business, eh?' the major asked.

Clark nodded. 'Pretty awful, yes.'

'Need you chaps, though, keep the stuff coming through – and now we've got the Yanks in, things should start looking up.

Drink?' The major held out a hip flask towards him.

'Kind of you, sir, but no thanks.'

The major grunted and offered the flask to the colonel. 'No thanks, Freddie.'

The major hesitated a moment before offering the flask to the civilian. 'Not for me, but thanks all the same.'

'Oh, well,' said the major, holding it out towards Clark. 'Here's to the navy.' Clark smiled and nodded.

'Thanks,' he said as the major took a nip.

It was an hour later before the train finally drew into Lime Street station. The air raid was over, but the air was gritty and smelled of burning. Hefting his overnight bag, Clark headed to the street, debating his best course of action. He was extremely hungry and it was very late. His only chance was to see if he could get something to eat at the Adelphi, where, he decided, he had better take a room for the night. It was not what he had planned, but the delay to the train made getting across to the Wirral too difficult and he was too inured to the vicissitudes of war to concern himself; besides, he was bone-weary and longed for a bed that did not move up and down and from which no one would summon him at some ungodly hour.

Once through the blackout curtains shrouding the hotel from the street, the atmosphere of disregard for the effects of

German bombs was remarkable. The sound of the dance band carried up into the large foyer, through which a few couples moved, men in uniform and women in bright dresses, taking off or putting on their coats. Along with the music came the chink of glasses and the seemingly irrepressible noise of voices and laughter. Clark thought of Magda but, without her beside him, he was too weary for the most superficial distractions of this brittle gaiety, and he approached the reception desk. They would serve him with some food if he took a room, to which he happily agreed. He carried his own bag up to the third floor. Inside the room he threw his bridge coat on a chair and removed his shoes, wiggling his toes with a luxurious pleasure. Slipping off collar and tie, he found the 'Do not disturb' sign and went to the door. As Clark opened it he came face to face with a couple arm in arm, a couple clearly intent upon a night of passion together as the man fumbled in his jacket pocket for his room key, and the tall, dark young woman nuzzled up to him.

'Magda!'

They stood staring at each other for a second, the shock of recognition mutual. But an instant later it was swiftly followed by all that the encounter implied.

Clark fell asleep as dawn broke over the

great sea port. The agony of having discovered Magda's betrayal had bitten deeply, but at last fatigue had overwhelmed him. It was after noon when he finally awoke to the misery of realisation. The change in his life and hopes insinuated itself into his consciousness like a knife blade, almost imperceptibly at first, but then with a mounting crescendo of pain. He turned his face into the pillow and wept; a long and bitter release which drained from his soul not only his anger at Magda's infidelity, but, once tapped, all the horrors of war in the Atlantic. Magda was no longer the one bright expectation against which he could set the awfulness of convoy escort: the fear, the privation, the cold, the inequity of the struggle and the personal humiliations of helplessness as he, as *Daisy*'s first lieutenant, presided over the deaths of oil-sodden seamen pulled from the ocean's cold waters. Magda, herself a victim of the indifferent cruelty of war, had shone in his imagination with the promise of a perfection which he knew existed, for he had tasted it in the depths of her body.

But Magda's dark and passionate eyes had been upon another's face, her arm had been entwined with another man, her legs about to clasp the eager waist of another lover. Clark could reconcile an old affair with Kurt, could absorb Kurt's part in the small triangle of their own private and familial eternal quandary; but he could not hold with that triangle assuming the outline of a square; or worse, perhaps, of a polygon.

Yes, that was it! He knew with a sudden intuitive conviction that Magda had buried her German past, her memories of her abandoned parents and even of her relationship with Kurt in the ready appeal of hedonistic pleasure. What was the point of subjecting herself to the painful anxieties of falling in love with a seaman who might never come back? She had lost Kurt, she might lose Jack. Why worry about one man, when there were plenty of them eager to sleep with her? Why, she could lose the particular in the general! She could have her pick, play the field, enjoy herself to excess!

Christ! Clark thought as he recalled their most intimate moments. Had she been behaving like this all the time? And one thought swiftly bred another: what in God's name had she been up to with Diana Cranbrooke? Her ladyship was, he thought wildly, not beyond making a cuckold of Sir Desmond. The two of them would attract spectacular notice in London, if they chose to, while in Liverpool, with her husband in the capital, Diana Cranbrooke could have her pick of lovers. And Magda was a perfect decoy too. Good God, they might even act as a pair, together...

Clark lashed himself into a frenzy of furious jealousy. What had she said? War changed people? Was that a half-confession of her own deep metamorphosis? How the hell would he know anyhow? He had been blinded by his own devotion! She might have been as enthusiastic a whore in Hamburg!

He thrashed around the bed wallowing in his misery until, in due course, a chamber-maid knocked on his door. He had nowhere to go, now; the thought of calling upon his preoccupied father and dining in that echoing house appalled him. He wanted to hide in the grubby, knocking-shop anonymity of the Adelphi.

'I'll take the room for another night,' he told the woman. 'Now leave me alone and let me sleep.'

'It's two o'clock in the afternoon, sir,' she remonstrated with scouse truculence.

'I don't care what the bloody time is, just leave me alone.'

She must have had a colleague with her, as he heard her say grumpily, 'He thinks it's blooming Christmas already.'

Christmas! Christmas, with all its over-tones of family and gifts, seemed as remote as the dark side of the moon! He drifted in and out of rage and sleep, finally waking at six o'clock. He wanted a drink, wanted to get drunk and drown his unhappiness in the sailor's remedy, but the thought of his mission intruded. It was the only thing he had in life now; a hard, difficult thing, but a thing to be embraced like a piece of timber floating circumstantially alongside the floundering survivor. He must seize such an improvised lifesaver with the tenacity of desperation.

Clark was not a man to give up.

He drew a bath and put on a clean shirt and collar. He would go for a walk, a long walk, air raid or not. He would call in at a couple of pubs and allow himself a few drinks. Then, when it was late and he had tired himself out, he would come back and fall asleep again. Tomorrow he would go home and muster his sea kit, then travel up to London for his meeting with Gifford and Admiral Sir Dudley Pound. After that he would be on his way north to join his ship on Teesside.

The streets were dark and rain was falling, driven on a strong wind that caught him on corners and pressed against the heavy serge of his bridge coat. It would be a foul night in the Atlantic, he thought. It was funny how the notion brought him a grim comfort, as though the gale sought him out to remind him of his true habitat.

'But I wasn't cut out to be a monk,' he muttered to himself, articulating the great dilemma of the natural seaman: to fuck or float? And he took the seaman's traditional medicine, that quantity of alcohol rendered down into a reasonable 'few beers'. Not that he was drunk at ten o'clock when the air-raid sirens wailed and those in the street began to flow towards the shelters which had become familiar to them. Hunching his shoulders against the wind, he pressed on. Sod the bloody Jerries!

At the end of the street he was confronted by an air-raid warden. 'Not that way, sir,' the man said, holding up an arm and seeing Clark's naval cap. 'Shelter's down there. Follow those people, sir.'

Clark hesitated, the beer warming him to a contentious disobedience. 'I'm going for a walk,' he said. Overhead the rumble of bombers was met with the stabbing divergence of the searchlight beams, probing up through the falling rain.

'Don't make life difficult, sir. I've got a son in destroyers and I know you're having a rough time. Just bugger off after those people and sit quiet in the shelter.'

Clark gave in. The man had a kindly voice. The sideways reference of sympathy moved him and the beer added its sentimental influence. He felt a sudden and unmanly desire to cry, turning away to hide the brightness in his eyes which, even in the blackness, he thought the ARP warden could not fail to notice. He stumbled after the retreating forms hurrying towards the shelter.

Once inside he sought out a corner. Benches lined with huddling men and women, a few young people and a number of children, talking softly, as though unwilling to draw attention to themselves. An elderly man began to sing an Irish song in a fine baritone voice. A thin accompaniment joined him, growing in volume until almost everyone who knew the words of the old rebel song was singing. Those who were unfamiliar with the Fenian plaint knew the tune and hummed. The origins of the song did not matter; its historical inappropriateness at this intense moment of British patriotic anxiety was immaterial. Its power lay in its defiance.

Clark knew the words, and if he disapproved of their sentiment, he roared out the passion of their universality as it summoned up their conjoined courage. If a German bomb had destroyed them in that moment, they would have died victorious. As the song reached its end, he was quite unaware that tears were flowing down his cheeks. It was some moments after they had finished singing – so that they were once more awkward, individual and anxious selves, as the sudden silence gradually gave way to soft, half-embarrassed laughter and low conversation – that the first crumps of exploding bombs made the earth tremble and shook the dust from the ceiling overhead. At that moment he saw Jenny O' Neil watching him.

She had been watching him as he sang and, as recognition dawned on him, she came over and sat beside him.

'What a nice surprise, Mr Clark. I had no idea you were at home. Your father never said a word.'

'Jenny!' Clark said, genuinely brightening at the sight of her. She was smiling at him, her face, wrapped in a headscarf, looking older than it was. 'Well,' he said, 'my father has no idea I'm in Liverpool. Anyway, how are you?'

'I'm all right. I'm the captain's personal secretary now. Mary Logan has joined the Wrens; she's commissioned too. How about you?' She regarded him with an almost maternal concern.

'Oh, I'm fine,' he blustered. Then, as she continued to stare at him he asked: 'Why?' as though he wore some sign that he had been made a fool of by Magda.

'You looked sad while you were singing,' she said simply, not mentioning the tears.

'Sad? Good heavens no.' He attempted ironic laughter. 'It's good to be back in Liverpool and share the joys of war with you lot. Haven't had such a good sing-song for a long time!'

She was rummaging in her bag and produced a handkerchief. 'Here,' she said quietly, handing it to him. 'Blow your nose and wipe your eyes. You look terrible.'

He stared at her a moment in astonishment. Then he took the offered handkerchief and was about to blow his nose when he recovered himself.

'It's all right,' he said, handing it back, 'I've got one of my own.'

'Don't be silly. Use mine.'

He hesitated a moment, then did as he was bid. 'I'll, um, take it and wash it, and send it back to you.'

'There's no need,' she said, taking it from him. 'You've had a bad trip,' she said, lowering her eyes and facing straight ahead, the moment over. It was not a question, rather a commiserating statement, as though Jenny O'Neil wanted no explanation other than the one she herself offered.

'Pretty bad,' he said quietly, entering into the spirit of the wordplay, though unaware of her motive, seeking only to conceal his own.

'You poor dear,' she said, and without turning her head, she slipped her arm through his as she drew their bodies closer. He was touched by the kindness. Under the circumstances, there seemed nothing odd in this gentle gesture of solidarity as they sat and waited for the Luftwaffe to desist from bombing their city and the homes of their fellow citizens. Nor did it seem odd when the all-clear sounded and they emerged into

179

the windy street, Jenny's arm still tucked inside his, and she said, 'Would you walk me home, Jack? It's not far.'

'Yes, of course.' They pulled up their collars and leaned into the wind and rain. 'What were you doing out on your own?'

'Oh, once a week Maureen McCarthy – you know her, the head of the typing pool – well, we go to the cinema. We wanted to see *Gone with the Wind* again and it came back on at the Empire.'

'Did you enjoy it?'

'Oh yes, Vivien Leigh is so lovely...'

'And what about your mother?'

'Oh, she passed over last winter with the bronchitis. It was a relief really. I don't think she could have coped with all this. It's no time to be old...'

They walked on in silence, turning into a street of terraced houses, down which the wind thrust at them with its full force. Instinctively they drew closer together.

They passed the remains of two houses. The debris had been cleared up so that the heap of bricks, flapping wallpaper and jags of splintered timber joists, all visible in the gloom, only occupied the precise, bounded area of the property.

'We've had a few visits from our German cousins,' Jenny remarked matter-of-factly with an unconscious irony.

'Yes, so I see,' replied Clark, regarding the

English nicety of the clearing-up operation.

'So far, I've been lucky,' Jenny said, stopping at the door of her house, detaching herself from Clark and taking her keys from her bag.

'Come in for a cuppa,' she said over her shoulder as she turned the key in the lock.

'I ought not to.'

'Why?' she said, standing in the doorway, her bag tucked under one arm, her other hand extricating the key from the lock. Her face, constrained by the headscarf, was a pale oval. The threshold lay between them like the Rubicon.

Clark chuckled. 'On a night like this there's nothing I'd like more than a cuppa,' he said.

Inside, he stood in the utter darkness of the hall until the flare of a match lit the gas light in the room beyond and the incandescence spilled through from the kitchen.

'Come through,' she said. 'It's not much,' she added apologetically, taking off her coat and laying it on the single armchair beside the range. It bore obvious traces of having been her late mother's. 'What with father dying and mother being left to me to look after ... Well, you know how it is. I wanted to move out to the new housing estates at Aigburth, but mother wouldn't hear of it. Perhaps one day...' She sighed and, filling the kettle, she put it on the hob. 'You're used to better things,' she said, not looking at him

181

as she bent and stoked the fire.

'Not on a corvette, I'm not,' he said, regarding her rump in its cheap tweed skirt. What he could see of her legs in their thick brown stockings disappeared into short, ugly boots.

Straightening up she turned to face him, pulled off the scarf and shook her short brown hair. 'Do sit down.' She removed her coat from the armchair. 'It's too cold in the parlour.'

'After the bridge of a corvette,' he said with a trace of awkwardness as he sat down, 'this is absolute heaven, I assure you.'

She too sensed the awkwardness. The moment of impulsive invitation and acceptance had passed. They had seized the moment and were now not quite certain what to do with it. Jenny fetched the teapot, then reached up for the tea caddy on the mantelpiece over the range. He watched her uplifted arm and the soft curve of her breast beneath the dull woollen cardigan. He wondered about her life, wondered about the men in it.

'It'll be a moment, I'm afraid,' she said, pottering about folding a tea towel and picking up her coat from over the back of a plain upright chair that, with three others, ringed a small, square table. She had tossed it there when offering him the armchair and now she put it on a wooden hanger. 'If mother was still alive, I'd have left the kettle on the hob, but now I'm alone I don't like to go out and leave it. I'm sure it would be all right, it always used to be. It's just that if anything were to happen while I was out – you know, a bomb, or something – I'd ... Well, it worries me a bit.'

She closed the door to the hall and hung the coat and hanger on a hook on its back. The warmth of the stove filled the room. 'But if I go out,' she went on, 'I always keep the range in. It's horrible coming into a cold house.' Jenny's remarks, uttered nervously in the tension of their proximity, made Clark think of the privations of civil life: of rationing, of coal and coke in short supply and of the war of small, disrupting inconveniences being fought on the home front amid the greater terrors of the blitz. She gave a quick smile. 'As a treat, I have some home-made biscuits...' Again she reached up to the mantelpiece, again he regarded her body. 'Mrs Gilbert makes them, her husband works on the docks...' And Clark glimpsed the irregularities in the smooth running of civil society in wartime, of the pilfering and cheating that eased indigence, and of the tip of the greater evils of the black market. Jenny's remark hinted at the profiteering which would leave its exponents wealthy, whoever won the war, while less fortunate men died, their throats and stomachs seared by oil, or scalded by escaping superheated steam. Did war change people, or did it just reveal them in the dreadful truth of their inequities?

Jenny placed the tin barrel on the table and took off the lid. Then she fetched a plate and shook a few of Mrs Gilbert's home-made biscuits on to it from the tin. The irregular discs rattled out just as the kettle began to sing.

'Shall I warm the pot?' Clark asked, pulling himself up from his soporific lolling, embarrassed at her activity.

'No. I'll do it.' And then, as if realising her refusal had been unintentionally abrupt, as she picked up the oven glove and lifted the heavy kettle, she smiled at him. 'I like doing this for you.'

He looked at her. She avoided his eyes as she busied herself, the hot steam rising in the drab little room.

'There's not much else we can do for each other this Christmas...'

He was aware that her voice had changed. She was pushing at the threshold of propriety and he felt his heartbeat quicken. There could be little doubt of her desire; only of his.

'That's kind of you,' he said as she put the kettle back on the hob. As she turned back to the table, he caught her wrist. 'Jenny...'

That night, or on the one that followed, Clark's daughter was conceived.

THE FIRST SEA LORD

December 1941

Clark found Gifford less chatty when he returned to the Admiralty. Despite his new assumption of the two and a half bands of gold lace on his cuffs, changed into at Gieves' on his way, his reception was brief. Not uncordial, Gifford was clearly preoccupied with events of some moment elsewhere. He unbent to the extent of remarking as he indicated that Clark should take a seat, 'Some rather mixed news from the North Atlantic snookered by some not so good from the Med.'

It was a long time afterwards that Clark drew the conclusion that the 'rather mixed' news from the Atlantic concerned the destruction of several U-boats by an escort group under Commander 'Johnnie' Walker, helped by a support group centred on a small carrier and the loss of that carrier, HMS *Audacity*, which had been torpedoed and lost a few days later. The 'not so good' news from the Mediterranean was in fact disastrous, for Gifford's understated admission referred to the complete immobilisation of two battleships – which only failed to sink by sitting on the seabed in Alexandria harbour – and the loss of two cruisers, a destroyer, a corvette and serious damage to several other men-of-war. Although these events had been preoccupying the Admiralty for some days, Gifford's attention on Clark's previous visit had been entirely focused upon the matter he had in hand. Now Clark was left to kick his heels amid an impression of muted turmoil based solely upon the comings and goings of the denizens of the Admiralty. To the waiting Clark those in uniform seemed rarely of rank above his own, while the others were not only civilians, but females, naval wives recruited into the Admiralty's service when the RNVR officers originally deployed on clerical tasks were sent to sea in answer to the U-boat offensive in the Atlantic. These, Clark learned, were known as 'The Second Sea Lord's Ladies' and he was impressed by their bustling efficiency. All had husbands at sea and all knew the Royal Navy and its ways. In passing, one or two of them smiled at Clark, and a motherly forty-year-old brought him a cup of tea.

'There you are,' she had said. 'They're keeping you waiting an awfully long time,

Commander. I thought you might like a refresher.'

It was the first time anyone had given him the inflated courtesy title and it was, in fact, vastly more refreshing than the stewed tea.

He was left alone with the tea and the turmoil of his thoughts. He had buried the overwhelming betrayal of Magda in his brief affair with Jenny O'Neil. Both he and Jenny knew it to have been an encounter born out of circumstance and mutual expedience. But while Clark had come to Jenny's bed bruised by Magda, it was Jenny who was left the more so. Apart from the yet imperceptible effects of Clark's physical invasion, he had disturbed her with longings she knew to be impossible. An unworldly woman, life had offered her only one previous love, a man to whom she had become engaged at nineteen and to whom she had eventually lost her virginity. The engagement had dragged on, dogged by the complications of parental objection and unemployment, and ended abruptly when the young man vanished, to marry another within a month. The suspicion that she had long been deceived took root deep in Jenny's heart and flowered in due season whenever any prospect of a new romance appeared. That she had so precipitately surrendered to Clark had in part been due to the disruptions and strains of war, in part to their sudden, unplanned propinquity, but mostly to the fact that Jenny had become susceptible to her boss's handsome son.

Clark knew nothing of all this. She was a 'girl' from the typing pool, a woman who had raised herself from the grinding poverty of her class but whom a dependent mother had held in thrall to her locality. Such 'girls', it was assumed by many of the officers of the Eastern Steam Navigation Company, made jolly dancing and dinner partners; often they provided inter-voyage inamoratas, but rarely wives. Clark assumed she had sexual experience, certainly she knew how to enjoy herself and to pleasure him. But Jenny was not Magda; she did not possess the wanton abandon or the outrageously liberating impulsiveness of an equal. There was a submission about Jenny's lovemaking that, in his moment of emasculation, Clark needed as much as he needed her affectionate kindness. He too had been engaged and he too had lost his lover; he too had taken casual consolations, but, with a male incontinence, attached less importance to the coital act than the receptive Jenny.

'Write if you can,' she had pleaded as he left her. It had been her only articulation of her love and her hope that she would not be discarded. She knew that, even had they not been inhabiting a world made topsy-turvy by war, theirs would not be a romance that endured. Clark was no ordinary deck officer of Eastern Steam, he was the son of a director and would, one day, be on the company's board himself. No one doubted that in the Water Street offices. Jenny's consolation was that she had had her dream; her tragedy that it was over. Clark's consolation was the binding up of his wound, while his tragedy would be in the long aftertaste of guilt.

Not that he felt guilt that late December Thursday in the Admiralty, for he was full of nervous anticipation. Jenny's plump and eager body had interposed itself between him and the self-centred agony of Magda's infidelity, but its interposition was insufficient to obscure the purpose of his presence that afternoon in Their Lordships' waiting room. He wore a black reefer, bright with the gold of promotion, and was aware of its import. He was in attendance upon Their Lordships for a fell purpose: naked he could bring forth a life, uniformed he was empowered to destroy it. Such grim considerations steeled him as he sipped the bitter tea.

Three-quarters of an hour later the same motherly lady returned. 'My word,' she remarked, seeing him still patiently waiting his summons, 'one would think this war was all about waiting around and queuing.' She picked up Clark's emptied cup, adding, 'I'm sure they won't keep you much longer.'

'I rather hope not,' Clark responded,

thanking her for her thoughtfulness.

'There's rather a lot going on at the moment,' she said obliquely.

'So I gathered.'

He watched her go, a comely enough creature though running to fat. He wondered who her husband was and where he was. Their eyes met as she turned in closing the door and she smiled again. The touch of loneliness and anxiety in her glance lingered in Clark's mind as the closing door obscured her, and he was still staring at it when it was abruptly opened by Gifford's four-striped arm. Gifford remained outside and it was clear that he was opening the door for someone else. Standing up, Clark heard the heavy, uneven tread of a man limping with a stick, and a moment later Sir Dudley Pound confronted him.

Clark would never forget the preoccupation evident in the expression of the First Sea Lord. Much later he heard opinions damning the Royal Navy's operational chief, the kindest of which explained his failures, especially that relating to the destruction of Convoy PQ17, as attributable to his lack of sleep. This in turn was caused by the constant chronic pain of an arthritic hip. Others added the explanation that the brain tumour that was to kill Pound in October 1943 was already compromising his intellectual abilities, but for Clark none of those conclusions even obscured that first impression of a deep and abiding concern. Just as he had divined the loneliness of his genteel tea lady, Clark's perception – he was convinced to the day of his own death – was of Pound's utter devotion to his beloved Service.

Pound studied him for a moment, then his eyes relaxed, his brow smoothing, his narrow mouth smiling. 'Lieutenant Commander Clark?'

'Sir!'

'Do sit down.'

Clark resumed his seat and, as Pound eased himself stiffly into the upright chair opposite, Gifford closed the door.

'Captain Gifford has appraised you of this operation, I know. For no good reason, we are calling it Operation TREE-TOP and Captain Gifford will give you the latest operational intelligence available, along with your communication schedule, before you leave Scapa Flow, but I wished to meet you and to wish you luck. You will not need me to emphasise the importance of the absolute secrecy with which this mission must be concealed...' Pound paused.

Clark shook his head. 'No, sir.'

'Not a word of it should leak out and you must therefore keep as much as you can from your crew. When you brief them you are to tell them your mission is to gather meteorological information to facilitate our convoys through the Barents Sea and enable us to route them as far north as possible, close to the ice, but as far distant as possible from enemy aircraft operating out of Banak, near the North Cape. In addition you are to search for and destroy German weather ships on a similar errand to your own. If and when we transmit *Orca*'s nearest known location, it will be as though she too is a weather ship. There is one other fact that you should know about, capture of any German vessel is not a matter for broadcast. This is a standard precaution, allowing us the possibility of channelling disinformation to the enemy, and this is the reason you should give your ship's company if you are success-ful in achieving your objective. It lays an absolute compulsion to secrecy upon them, a breach of which will be regarded as trea-son.'

Pound paused again to let the medieval import of the word sink in. 'You under-stand?'

'Yes, I do, Sir Dudley.'

'Very well.' Pound turned to Gifford. 'Any-thing else, Captain Gifford?'

Gifford shook his head. 'I think not, sir.'

'The DNI doesn't want to see Clark?'

'He's left it to me, sir.'

Pound smiled at Gifford and stood up, turning towards Clark again. 'Well, Com-mander Clark, it only remains to me to

192

congratulate you upon your promotion and to wish you and your ship well.' He transferred his walking stick to his left hand and held out his right. 'God speed.'

Clark shook Pound's hand. 'Thank you, sir.'

A moment later Clark was on his own and Gifford's footsteps merged with the receding stump of the First Sea Lord's.

Clark hesitated a moment before putting on his greatcoat and picking up his hat, gloves and respirator box. He was about to leave the room when a breathless Gifford reappeared. He was holding a brown envelope with the familiar *OHMS* superscription.

'You made an excellent impression, Clark. Well done.' Gifford handed the envelope to Clark.

'Thank you, sir.'

'And I'm sorry we kept you so long. We've had a succession of flaps, I'm afraid.' Gifford looked at his watch. 'I've a car outside ready to take you to King's Cross. Where's your sea kit?'

'Already at King's Cross.'

'Good man.' Gifford indicated the envelope Clark was putting into the breast pocket of his reefer. 'Those are your operational orders. They tell you to proceed to Scapa by way of Rosyth and place yourself under Commander-in-Chief, Home Fleet. Report to Sir John Tovey in the formal manner. He knows enough about you to ensure you get your torpedo tubes fitted, but thereafter you're on your own. You're to keep those tubes under cover from the moment they come aboard and you're to let the C-in-C's staff know when you are satisfied with them. There will be one practice shoot from each but you will not be able to carry these out locally. You'll have to take it on trust that the installations will work, and there's no reason why they shouldn't. You'll load your torpedoes at Rosyth. Theoretically they're intended to re-arm Home Fleet destroyers and you'll discharge some to maintain the pretence.' Gifford paused a moment. 'I think that's all, for the time being. The moment the C-in-C lets us know you're operational, I'll be on my way up to see you. All right?'

'Yes, sir.'

'Good luck then.' They shook hands. 'Oh, and happy Christmas.'

The simplicity of the brief meeting concealed its momentous nature. In the months to follow Clark became aware of its primary importance amid the scandal and aftermath of the destruction of PQ17. But it was only many, many years later that he realised that he had been brought as near privy to Great Briatin's best-kept wartime secret as he could have been. For the most junior lieutenant commander on the Navy List to be informed that silence over the capture of German warships was to allow the Admiralty the possibility, in Sir Dudley's phrase, 'of channelling disinformation to the enemy' was as close as it was possible to get to telling him of the decoding of German signals sent by Enigma that was then being undertaken at Bletchley Park. He realised all those years later that he had not been ordered to attempt the recovery of an Enigma machine or any of the Kriegsmarine's codes because of the risks he might thereby incur. In principle his mission was simply the destruction of the German submarine cruiser the British knew as *Orca*; as usual, it was in the detail that the devil resided. So much for the reason which he should give his ship's company if he were to be successful in achieving his objective. The threat implicit in the treasonable nature of any revelation, unwitting or not, was a chilling finale to a briefing he had thought might be little more than a pep-talk.

As he shivered in his unheated railway carriage, Clark thought the cold the warning radiated far exceeded any he might encounter amid the ice floes of the Barents Sea. The professional cordiality of that trio of officers holding the quiet, low-key meeting in the informal environment of a waiting room, seemed horribly portentous. Between them had yawned the deep crevasse of naval rank and of naval obligation, a crevasse dark with the uncertainties and forebodings of war that might yawn yet wider with the passage of time and Clark's distance and isolation from the Admiralty. And yet Clark was not insensible to the honour done him, of the perception that there, in the Admiralty, the operational headquarters of the Royal Navy, he was part of an extraordinary brotherhood. Notwithstanding his status as an officer of the reserve, his mission had warranted the personal involvement of the First Sea Lord.

He wondered how long that sensation would last.

HMS *Sheba*

December 1941–February 1942

For no discernible reason, Clark's train was held up south of Doncaster for several hours. It had previously lingered outside Peterborough, from where distant flashes, the faint probing of searchlights and the occasional crumps of bursting bombs, indicated air raids somewhere far to the west of them. Despite this it was unclear why their train had sat stationary in the darkness of flat farmland, nor why it now waited in the middle of nowhere for some unseen intelligence to beckon it onwards. Uneasily, he tried to sleep, but he found it impossible in the cold and, as dawn broke, he watched his breath form into frost on the inside of the train window as he lifted the blackout. War was indeed all about waiting, a resented suspension of the personal life so that even the basic necessity of sleep was withheld.

He fell asleep for about half an hour, aroused when the train suddenly jerked into motion, as though jolted from illicit sleep itself. Clark swore with deep sincerity and rubbed his eyes. His mouth tasted foul, his eyes ground grittily in their sockets and, he cursed again, he had none of the consoling tasks he had come to rely upon to make this ghastly morning moment tolerable. When occupied on escorting convoys in the North Atlantic there had been a cup of kye to ease the misery, merchant ships to count up, signals from the escort leader to respond to, and sometimes a miserable schoolboy look-out to chastise for some real or imagined inattention. All he had that morning was the sticky chill of his cramped body, the rasp of the melton collar of his bridge coat on his stiff and sensitive neck, the disgusting taste of himself and the abrasive quality of his conjunctivae.

'Oh, fuck, fuck, fuck...' he growled, clasping himself for warmth and trying to rearrange his stiff legs and aching body into some more comfortable posture on the seat. But it was no good and, in the end, he gave up. He was saved by some selfless soul on Doncaster station who, even at that ungodly hour, had a trolley from which what passed for tea was available to the wretches travelling north that winter morning.

Clark descended to the platform, walking like a man whose joints had seized up.

'Not much of a Christmas, is it, sir?' a soldier remarked as he warmed his hands round the brown brew and sought some goodwill amongst his fellow travellers.

Clark shook his head, grasping his own mug and taking a sip. He did not feel like talking, but clearly the young soldier was of a different mind.

'Going home on leave, sir?'

Clark shook his head. Home? On leave? What the fuck for? He thought bitterly of Magda and how she would enjoy Christmas with the Cranbrookes and the irony of her Jewishness in such a social setting. It would, of course, glitter unrestricted by wartime austerity. The Cranbrookes' were wealthy, possessors of old, East India money, it was said; certainly Sir Desmond's family had been in shipping longer than the Holts and Bibbys, the Cunards and the Ellermans;

older, he used to claim, than the Brockle-banks of Whitehaven. Bugger Magda *and* the Cranbrookes!

'No,' he said to the soldier, 'no such luck. Off to join a ship.'

'Bad luck, sir.'

'Yes, it is, isn't it.' Clark roused himself. 'What about you?'

'Bit of leave. Newcastle, like. Not long but, well, nice just the same.'

'Very nice,' Clark said with little conviction.

'Should make it nicely,' the soldier said with a happy smile. 'Can't wait to see their faces when I walk in on them.'

It occurred to Clark that it was Christmas Eve. He made an effort and smiled at his young companion who seemed satisfied with such a plethora of English niceness.

'No, it will be quite a shock for them, I imagine.'

The soldier grinned and nodded. 'Aye, it will that.'

The piercing note of the guard's whistle made their ears ring, so that his subsequent order of 'All aboard!' was imperfectly heard. The two men tossed off their mugs, thanked the lady behind the tea trolley and turned to their respective compartment doors.

'Good luck, sir,' the soldier said.

'And you,' Clark responded, slightly ashamed that he had not been more cordial.

'God bless you and happy Christmas,' the woman said to their retreating backs.

In due course, and what to Clark seemed like half a lifetime later, they drew into Stockton-on-Tees. Clambering down and assembling his sea kit on the platform, he caught a porter's attention. As the train pulled out he saw the friendly grin of the watching soldier going on northwards to Newcastle. He nodded and smiled back.

'Middlesbrough train,' he told the porter.

Clark was very hungry when he finally arrived at Middlesbrough and the shipyard at South Bank. Making his way to the offices of the Smith's Dock Company he found he was not too late for lunch, and could get something to eat in the managers' canteen. It was therefore almost mid-afternoon before he found himself trekking across the disordered yard. Though humming with industry the place could not shake off its appearance of a wasteland. Steel is not a material sympathetic to man; it is cold to the touch and cruel in appearance, its virtue lying in its utility. It is devoid of charm, is worked by fire and, unlike a yard building in wood, it never forms a landscape to which the romantic eye is drawn.

The building slips and dry docks were all full. Two colliers lay in the latter, their decks more or less level with the ground, their rusty grey-black hulls being repaired. One had struck a mine and was lucky to have been saved, salvaged from a timely grounding in shallow water; the other had received damage from a near miss, her shell plating buckled and strained so that she leaked badly. On the building slips the hulls of two corvettes rose grey inside their greyer cocoons of scaffolding. Erected above ground level they seemed to Clark so much larger than they did at sea. Over, on and around, and moving back and forth between these ships, the men of the workforce spun a web of activity, their individual garb of old clothes combined with the ubiquitous flat cloth caps of the working man assuming a uniform grey under the grey sky which leached a cold and drizzling rain. In his present mood, Clark was easily persuaded that this too was grey, for it fell into a river grey with filth and sediment. Only the swirl of the tide as it tugged at a midstream trot of moorings told of its relationship with the raw, clean and biting tang of the Atlantic somewhere far beyond its outermost debouchement.

Between the mooring buoys two vessels were secured alongside one another. One was a battered and rusty anti-submarine trawler, beyond her, partially hidden, lay what Clark had been told was His Majesty's Armed Whaler *Sheba*. From the trawler a damp white ensign showed a flash of colour to break the melancholic monochrome of the afternoon.

But even as he watched, the keen note of the piped 'still' came to him and the flag descended. Amid all this greyness, in defiance of the meteorological conditions of the miserable day, the ceremony of sunset went on at its prescribed moment. Clark saw the movement of figures, the upsweep of arm in salute, and in that defiant little moment an unmanly lump formed in his throat and he found himself drawing himself up into a half-heartedly erect pose until the 'carry on' bade him relax.

'I say, are you *Sheba*?' The imperious enquiry broke into his moment of reflection. Sniffing, he turned. His interlocutor was a short, portly individual in rather grubby blue battledress. His epaulets proclaimed him an equal in rank to Clark, though the accumulated verdigris emphasised the fact that he was clearly Clark's senior by some time. 'I'm *Nottingham Forest* and if you're *Sheba* I must say it's about bloody time you turned up. They made me look after your ship as well as my own...' Having closed the distance between them by crossing several apparently discarded coils of rusty wire, some steel plates of ancient and uncertain origin and a small, almost neat pile of emptied paint kettles, 'Nottingham Forest' stopped, looked up at Clark and held out his hand. 'John

Forrest, late of the Clan Line and now, alas, commanding one of His Majesty's less grand men-of-war.' As they shook hands, Forrest went on, 'Yes, it's a damned bad joke, but I suppose it is evidence that the Admiralty has a sense of humour or, God forbid, they haven't noticed the irony...' Forrest paused, cocking his head to one side. 'Christ, you don't understand it either, do you?'

'You will have to forgive me being obtuse,' Clark apologised. 'I spent last night on a train and got no sleep. I take it your trawler is named after the football team and, by co-incidence, or perhaps design, you have been appointed to her...'

'That's about the size of it. My crew think it's sublimely bloody funny.'

Clark gave a tired grin. 'Well, I suppose that's understandable. I'm Jack Clark. Late of the *Daisy*...'

'Christ, that's worse than Nottingham Forest,' Forrest exclaimed with glee. 'Any-way,' he went on rapidly, 'I've got a long way to go, so enough of the courtesies. You can do me a favour. I think I'm right in claiming seniority – anyway, I'm past caring. I'm in for essential repairs and I want to get home and buss the wife for Christmas. You can look after both ships until the day after Boxing Day. I've a subby and the blue watch on board. You've had some hands arriving all afternoon, so I guess you'll manage.' Forrest peered at him. 'You look a bit P & O to me...'

'Eastern Steam,' Clark explained, somewhat overwhelmed by Forrest's robust decisiveness.

'Ah, Dentco, good outfit ... Anyway, on board you've also got some strange creature who might be a naval officer, though he might equally be a stick insect, I'm not sure. He seems to entertain a prejudice about uniform, or indeed pyjamas, for he doesn't appear to have removed the flannels and hacking jacket in which he arrived yesterday. Says his ship's not in commission so it doesn't matter...'

Clark frowned. His fatigue had produced a few grey spots which danced across Forrest's face like some sinisterly mobile acne. He had no idea to whom Forrest might be referring.

'Claims to be your first lieutenant,' Forrest hinted darkly. Seeing Clark shrug he went on, 'Well, old boy, you look as though you could do with a kip. Get yourself aboard and do me a favour by letting me leave with a clear conscience. Make yourself at home in my cabin. I've a new baby to see and I'd really like to get away.' Forrest hesitated a moment and then asked, 'Are you all right?'

'Perfectly.' Clark realised the import of Forrest's abrupt manner and smiled. 'Of course, and congratulations.'

'Poor little bugger's nearly three months old. Still, I could have been up the Hooghly or the Perishing Gulf on two-year articles, so perhaps this isn't so bad after all.' Forrest sank his head into his shoulders and stared about him with a pronounced grimace. The coarse serge of his battledress blouse sparkled with raindrops. 'Though it's bloody hard to see how,' he added. Forrest held out his hand again. 'Well, I'll be off then. Got my kit in the car...' he waved towards a row of wooden huts. An Austin saloon stood behind them.

'Hail and farewell,' Clark said, and watched the rotund little man as he scrambled over the wires, plates and paint kettles. A moment later the Austin moved off and Clark was left alone on the quayside. As if to emphasise his desolation, the yard's steam whistle hooted the end of the working day. Faint and irregular cheers came from workmen who had, Clark realised, been drifting away from the building slips and the colliers in dock for some time. The notion of 'knocking off' mildly offended him, quarrelling with his notions of wartime duty. At sea in convoy the only respite would be the change of watch, on man-of-war and merchantman alike. Then he realised it was Christmas Eve and supposed that even the work of building and repairing ships should stop for a few hours. Perhaps, on the other hand, he thought wearily, it was just a change of shift.

'You aren't wanting to go out to one of

those bloody ships, are you?' The voice was accusingly hostile. Clark looked round. A tall workman with a ruddy face confronted him. Clark realised the man had just ascended from a motor boat tied up at the foot of a flight of wooden steps set into the staithing.

'Er, yes, I was, actually.'

The man sighed. 'They're supposed to run their own boats after four o'clock...'

Clark looked at his watch. It was just past three forty. He stared up at the boatman. 'You want to knock off early...'

'It's Christmas Eve, mate,' the boatman said, 'and you heard the siren. I'm not knocking off early, there's a war on.'

'I hadn't noticed.'

The boatman ignored the sarcasm and eyed Clark's epaulets. 'You the commander of the whaler?' Clark nodded. 'I saw you talking to the skipper of the *Notts Forest* and guessed who you was.' He jerked his head. 'Come on, I'll take you out before I go. Call it a Christmas present. Goodwill to all men, and all that claptrap.'

The man threw the last words over his shoulder as he turned and stumped back down the steps. Clark picked up his holdall. He had left his heavy kit in the ship manager's office and would pick it up later. He stepped into the wooden workboat just as the boatman threw the engine into life. As they pulled away from the wooden staithing and swung into the ebb tide, Clark rummaged in his pocket. A few minutes later they passed under the bows of the two vessels and ran alongside the low grey sides of HMS *Sheba*. Two man-ropes and a short, wooden-runged rope ladder hung down the side. Clark passed the boatman half a crown. 'I'm obliged to you. Get something for your children,' he said.

'Oh, thanks skipper, thanks very much. Go on, up you go. I'll bend your bag on to t'man-rope.'

Clark watched as the motor boat headed for the shore, churning the grey River Tees into yeasty foam in the last of the daylight. He lifted his hand and the boatman responded, then Clark turned his attention to the ship. The narrow side deck was bounded by a deckhouse, above which rose the funnel. In the gloom forward he could see the edge of the foredeck and the forecastle bulkhead. Aft the plating curved round to the stern with its two depth-charge mortars on the port quarter. She did not seem much of a ship, he thought, nor was she very welcoming, despite the news that her crew had been arriving, for she was cold and had every appearance of being uninhabited. Although Clark had no very great expectations, this was a somewhat depressing anticlimax to his tedious journey, not helped by the onset of night, his exhaustion or his mood.

'Anyone aboard?' he shouted, but it evoked no response whatsoever. A brief walk round the unlit deck and a stumbling progress through the blackness of the accommodation confirmed his impression that the ship was deserted. It was only as he walked down the starboard side deck that he heard laughter. This came from the trawler *Nottingham Forest* moored alongside, separated from the *Sheba* only by the squashed volume of a dozen rattan fenders that creaked between the two hulls as they worked together in the tide. The trawler betrayed her occupied state by a fingernail of light escaping from a porthole over which the deadlight had not been properly secured. Clark's riddle was solved. Leaving his holdall on *Sheba*'s deck he scrambled over on to the *Nottingham Forest*. The trawler had steam up and was warm to the point of cosiness. It took him only a moment to discover that what passed on the extempore warship for a wardroom was empty. Another gale of laughter erupted and this was quickly traced to the mess deck.

Clark descended the steel ladder, aware that he was revealing himself from his shoes upwards, a gradual process which was at first unremarkable, but then resolved itself in kid gloves and brass buttons, reaching a climax with his epaulets, face and cap. The noise of mirth became subdued in proportion to the exposure of his figure. At the foot of the ladder Clark confronted them. Sitting on benches, lounging across the mess tables, a few leaning on radiators, were the men of *Nottingham Forest*'s duty watch, the blue watch Forrest had mentioned. They possessed an almost palpable immunity from any unpleasantness arising from Clark's intrusion. The handful of men assigned to *Sheba*, and who were playing hookey from their own vessel, kept still in the manner of small animals caught in the open by a possible predator. All, however, nursed bottles of beer. Only the *Nottingham Forest*'s sub-lieutenant, dressed like his absent commander in battledress, drew himself up, put down his beer bottle, donned his cap and saluted.

'Afternoon, sir,' he said, looking round at the assembly with a half-embarrassed, half-defensive expression.

Clark returned the salute and removed his own cap, a gesture designed to acknowledge his presence as an intrusion into their privacy. 'Good afternoon.' He stared about him. 'I'm Lieutenant Commander Clark of the *Sheba*. D'you have any of my men aboard?'

From beside the *Nottingham Forest*'s sub-lieutenant a man stirred. In reverse to Clark's own appearance on the scene, he now watched a straw-blond head rise, followed by houndstooth check over a yellow pullover. As the apparition elevated itself, the blond head had to curve over and tuck itself under the deckhead so that it was half-hidden behind the bulb-angled deckhead beam before this curious elongation ceased.

'Ah,' said Clark quickly, recognising the stick insect Forrest had alluded to, 'my first lieutenant...'

The blond head inclined itself graciously. 'Dirk Frobisher *á votre service*, Commander,' he enunciated facetiously in an accent that would cut glass and provoked a snigger from the young seamen assembled about him. Intuitively Clark knew it was Frobisher who had been amusing the ratings. 'We were just discussing the ship-keeping arrangements for Christmas, sir,' Frobisher explained, 'the air-raid precautions and the action stations necessary to make best use of the combined armament of the two vessels.'

Clark inclined his head, only half believing Frobisher's explanation. 'Very well. Perhaps, when you have completed your dispositions, you would come aboard.'

'If I might suggest, sir, we meet in the wardroom above? Charlie here,' Frobisher nodded at the sub-lieutenant beside him, 'won't mind.'

'Go ahead, sir,' volunteered Charlie.

'Very well.' Clark looked at his watch.

'I shan't be a moment, sir. Incidentally, we've decided to mess together over the next couple of days.'

'It wasn't that, Mr Frobisher. I'm more concerned with the time. I understand you are running a ship's boat from 1600.'

'Charlie's chaps are doing that, sir.'

'Well, I've my kit to get on board and time's getting on...'

'I'll send someone up to the yard for it.'

'Thank you. It's in the ship manager's office.' Clark turned and ascended the ladder. Below, the noise of laughter and conversation revived. Clark was too tired to care much about the improprieties in the conduct of Lieutenant Frobisher, but as he sank into a chair in the trawler's wardroom, he realised that much would depend upon the relationship he established with the man.

'Ah, there you are, sir,' Frobisher's cheerful greeting woke Clark from the depths of a profound sleep. He looked at his watch: he had been asleep for no more than ten minutes. 'Gin, sir?'

Clark shook his head. 'No thanks.' He was befuddled and caught at a disadvantage, cross with himself for dropping off to sleep.

'Mind if I do?'

Clark shook his head again. As if reading his commander's mind, Frobisher added, 'We've rather made ourselves at home here, sir. It seemed the sensible thing to do. I don't know what you've been told, but *Sheba* won't be ready for service for some time.'

'Oh? That's not what I understood.'

'I thought not. Well, there's trouble with one of the boilers. That's what the yard says, anyway, though they're very cagey about our Asdic set and I'm convinced there's a problem there.'

Clark nodded. 'Could be,' he said, affecting disinterest. He did not feel mentally capable of embracing his command wholeheartedly, let alone appearing eager. He simply wanted to sleep. It was quite dark outside. 'We can talk about this tomorrow,' he said. 'Do we have a steward aboard?'

'Yes we do, but it's bloody miserable aboard *Sheba*, sir. I'm sleeping aboard here. It's easier than getting ashore and looking for digs. Shall I get the bedding changed in L'tenant Commander Forrest's cabin?'

Clark was inclined to go aboard *Sheba* but he was desperate for a proper night's sleep and, recalling Forrest's kind offer, capitulated to Frobisher's suggestion. 'Very well.'

'We're still supposed to be sleeping ashore, sir. I thought you knew. Mind you, I only found out when I got here. It's all a bit odd, if not downright disorganised.'

'I, er, guess it's up to us to organise it then,' Clark said, yawning. 'Look, I'm all in, Number One. Pass word that I'm going to occupy Forrest's bunk and that I'd like a mug of kye when that's been done.' He hauled himself out of his chair and stretched. 'Under other circumstances I'd join you in that gin but, if

212

you'll excuse me, I just want to hit the hay.'

'Of course, sir. I'll go and rouse out the steward.' Frobisher dipped his head and made for the door.

'Oh, and Number One...'

'Sir?' Frobisher turned.

'Uniform tomorrow. In commission or not.'

Clark met Frobisher's bright blue eyes and saw the sparkle kindle in them. 'Aye, aye, sir. Battledress all right?'

Clark wrinkled his nose. He loathed the utility uniform. 'Only while we're in the shipyard's hands. Once we commission, proper reefers.'

'Have you been to the Arctic, sir?'

Clark smiled to himself. He knew what Frobisher was driving at, but he had gone just a smidgin too far. 'Oh, yes, Number One. And under sail, too.'

Clark was quite pleased with the expression on Frobisher's face as he followed the first lieutenant out of the wardroom and went to fetch his holdall.

Clark woke late next morning, momentarily confused at his surroundings. He lay in Forrest's narrow bunk and stared at the deckhead. The white paint, its matt surface irregular over the cork-chip insulation and the rivet heads, reminded him as he regarded it through half-closed eyes, of the Arctic ice.

213

His mind, drifting indolently between waking and sleeping, conjured up the vastness of the open pack ice as the ship thrust the floes easily aside and he watched from aloft, sitting astride the topgallant yard of the brigantine *Island*. He was a boy again, his life bright with promise, keen to learn and undergoing the experience that would form the man he would become.

A knock at the cabin door snatched him from reverie: 'Come in!'

'Morning, sir.' Lieutenant Frobisher, resplendent in reefer jacket, his cuffs girdled with the straight lace of a regular officer, his feet in black leather boots, ducked his blond head, clumped over the sea step and removed his hat. 'The steward's on his way up with some breakfast.'

Clark leaned on his elbow and stared at the figure looming over him. 'Do sit down, Number One.'

'Thank you, sir.'

'If you'll forgive me holding court from my bunk, I think this an opportunity to get to know each other.'

'Good idea, sir. Rather regal though...'

'What is?' Clark asked, as the steward appeared with a tray and he hauled himself up into a sitting position. Clark noticed the two cups and saucers on the tray.

'Holding court from your bed,' Frobisher explained.

'Ahh, yes.' The two officers waited until the steward had set down the tray and disappeared. Clark gestured at the door and Frobisher rose, checked the steward had gone and resumed his seat. Clark handed him a cup of tea, recalling the list of personnel Gifford had shown him at the Admiralty.

'Tell me, Number One, I know Dirk is not your real name, though it has a suitably piratical and Tudor ring.'

Frobisher grinned. 'It's an acronym. My name is Douglas Ireton Robertson Keith Frobisher. Something of a handle, especially at Dartmouth...'

'Ah yes, Dartmouth. So why, Douglas Ireton Robert Keith, are you not aboard one of his Majesty's principal capital ships?'

'Robert*son* Keith, sir,' Frobisher corrected dryly. 'Well, I've done my bit in *Warspite* as a midshipman, and I've been in destroyers since October '39, but for some reason I was asked by my captain to consider an opening in a special service vessel. I would have to serve, he said, under a reserve officer – you, apparently, sir – but it would prove a great opportunity. At the moment I am somewhat at a loss to see the faintest sign of an opportunity...' Frobisher let the sentence hang, and smiled at Clark's pyjama-ed state.

'I understand you have had some experience in combat. Hand-to-hand combat, I mean.'

'Oh that?' Frobisher's face wrinkled in distaste. 'Is that what recommended me to Their Lordships? I had hoped it was my skill in navigation.'

'That too, I believe. But what did this hand-to-hand combat consist of?' Clark asked, buttering a slice of toast.

'Oh, a bit of a scrap up a fjord in Norway. We killed a few Krauts before they did the same to us. We rather wanted to get home, sir.'

'Yes, that seems reasonable.' Clark spread the marmalade thickly, salivating in anticipation. 'And what have they told you about our present mission?'

'Nothing, sir, beyond the fact that I was expected to volunteer. I hope you're going to enlighten me, sir.'

Clark masticated furiously and swallowed a mouthful then shook his head. 'Sorry to disappoint you, Number One, but our first priority is to get the *Sheba* into commission. Now, when I've finished this and had a shave and so forth, you and I will take a walk round the ship.' He looked at his watch. 'Then at 1100 we'll clear the lower deck and hold a brief church service. Is there a dinner of any sort?'

Frobisher nodded. 'Don't ask where it came from, but there is a remarkably fat goose now roasting in the *Forest*'s galley. It will feed the lot of us. Please join us in the wardroom at 1300.'

'Thank you, I will.'

Frobisher set down his tea cup and rose to his full height. 'I'll see you on deck shortly, sir.'

'Very well, but before you go, how many of our ship's company have we got aboard?'

'Oh, all of them, sir. You were the last to join.' And picking up his hat, Frobisher passed through the door, leaving Clark staring after him, wondering where the other officers had been last night. Nor had he seen Carter, and the thought brought him roundly to his duty. Flinging his blankets aside, he dropped on to the deck.

He and Frobisher toured the little whaler, from its forecastle head with its four-inch Mark XIX gun, to its cruiser stern with its depth-charge racks. They ducked into stores, peered down hatches and remarked on the ability a dockyard had, even with a brand new ship, to leave it looking like a bombed site. It was a new metaphor to the English and their language, but one graphically apt, both in the evocation of its image and to the case in point. Although *Sheba* was newly painted, there was an air of haste and shoddiness about the work: where grey abutted black or white, the cutting-in was carelessly done and patches of grit had been caught up in the wet paint; her green corticene decking

217

was disfigured with footprints whose reproduction in adjacent alleyways was evidence of a careless migration on some dockyard matey's boots. The corners of Frobisher's mouth were pulled down in mute disapproval, while Clark could not help contrasting the obvious rush in *Sheba*'s building with the painstaking construction of the *Ernest Shackleton* in the Hamburg shipyard of their enemies.

'I hope the riveting is to a higher standard than the painting,' Frobisher said at last, provoked out of silence. 'I see they haven't bothered to give her any dazzle paint,' he added, referring to the whale catcher's lack of camouflage.

'No,' Clark said flatly. Perhaps the standard of the paint finish did not matter: they would have to repaint her anyway, once they went into the ice. He kept the thought to himself, not wanting to ease the first lieutenant's burden if only to see how the younger man coped with the challenges ahead of him. Frobisher kicked at a cardboard carton left under the depth-charge racks aft. The thing was sodden from the night's rain and merely succumbed silently to the impact of his boot.

'Well, happy Christmas, Number One,' Clark said wryly. 'Shall we take a look below?'

★　★　★

Aboard *Nottingham Forest*, Clark regarded the combined ship's companies of His Britannic Majesty's least consequential men-of-war as they sang 'Oh, Come All Ye Faithful'. The trawler's sub-lieutenant was already known to him, the other officers were, he deduced, his own. There was a stocky, grey-haired man in the uniform of the Royal Norwegian Navy and beside him a younger man in the same uniform: the engineer, Lieutenant Olsen and his fellow countryman whose name Clark could not recall. The young sub-lieutenant next to Frobisher wore the single wavy braid of the Royal Naval Volunteer Reserve. He would be Pearson, Clark's third watch-keeping officer; Clark wondered what experience Pearson had had. The youngster seemed hardly old enough to drive a car, let alone a ship.

The carol ended and Clark read the second lesson from St Luke's gospel, telling of the appearance of the angel to the shepherds, and their subsequent visit to the stable to see the Christ child in the manger. Then the congregation raised their voices and bawled 'While Shepherds Watched Their Flocks by Night'. From the merrily suppressed grins of some ordinary seamen belonging to *Nottingham Forest*, he knew they were singing, 'While shepherds washed their socks by night...'

Clark always felt uneasy about Divine

Service. Regular naval officers like Frobisher were brought up to it from preparatory school onwards until, in every warship in which they served, Divine Service broke the weeks up and they prayed to the Eternal God who alone commanded the oceans of the world and who was, implicitly, on the side of the Royal Navy. For Clark, Divine Service, more than any other established naval ritual, exposed his pragmatic, mercantile background. His deep-rooted agnosticism and his prejudice against empty forms made him approve the boy-sailors' mild blasphemy and, catching their eyes, he had some difficulty in suppressing his own smile. He shifted his glance and saw Carter among the carollers. Carter's face was pallid, his eyes deep-ringed, and then the penny dropped. Clark suddenly realised that most of his ship's company had only come aboard late last night or, more likely, first thing this morning. They were now sweating off their excesses and, judging by their slack, hungover faces, they had returned to their ship sufficiently drunk to cultivate headaches; Clark hoped there was nothing more enduring lurking in their bloodstreams.

Once the ritual of Divine Service was over and Frobisher had called the ship's companies to attention to dismiss them, Clark followed Frobisher up to the *Nottingham Forest*'s little wardroom.

220

Frobisher made the introductions while Charlie dispensed large gins. 'Lieutenant Olsen, sir, Royal Norwegian Navy and our engineer officer.'

The grey-haired man inclined his head and shook hands. 'Fridtjof Olsen, Captain. Pleased to meet you.'

'And delighted to meet you, Lieutenant. I understand there are problems with the *Sheba*'s boilers...'

Olsen shrugged. 'I do not know, Captain, but I will report to you tomorrow when I have had a good look. The water-tube boilers we have here are usually very good, but maybe a few leaks at first. Nothing to worry about, I think.'

'Good, I'm glad to hear that,' he said, relieved. 'Where are you from, Lieutenant?'

'A place near Alesund, Captain. Do you know it?'

'I'm afraid not, though I've been to Bergen and Kristiansund.'

'Ah, Bergen is good. A beautiful city. My wife is from Bergen.' Olsen's remark brought Clark up with a round turn.

'Where is your wife now?' he asked, Magda's image swimming into his imagination.

Olsen shrugged. 'I hope in our home near Alesund, but who knows?'

Clark nodded, his expression as sympathetic as it could be but his sensibilities shamed by his selfish preoccupation with

Magda.

'Do you have children?' he asked.

Olsen nodded. 'Two daughters; twelve and fourteen years of age.'

An awkward silence filled the wardroom. A wife and two daughters left behind in occupied territory was not a comfortable thought. Suddenly Clark was immensely glad Magda had cut him free. A man should not be married in such times, let alone have children.

'Lieutenant Per Storheill,' Frobisher went on, and Clark faced a pleasant-looking man in his mid-twenties.

'I'm from Bodö, captain, in the north-wards. Many years in Wilhelmsen's...'

'Of Tönsberg,' Clark finished the sentence.

'You know the ships then,' Storheill smiled with pleasure.

'Oh yes, two blue bands on a black funnel and all names beginning with *T*.'

Storheill laughed. 'Black and blue, not much to eat and plenty to do,' he quoted the old slander against his former employers.

'Good to have you aboard.' They shook hands and Clark recollected that Norwegian naval officers had all served in merchant ships as a matter of course.

'Sub-lieutenant Derek Pearson, sir. The wardroom's baby.' Frobisher grinned.

'Hello, Pearson. I'm sure you must be good at something or the Admiralty would not have sent you here.'

'He's very good with the women, captain,' Olsen said.

'Which is commendation enough,' Clark joked, raising his glass. 'May I wish you all a happy Christmas.' He waited until they had drunk to the toast and sensed that they had relaxed, the ice between them broken. 'I'm sorry we are all stuck aboard here,' he went on. 'However, we've to get the *Sheba* in commission as quickly as possible. Now, I don't anticipate much cooperation from the yard until the day after tomorrow, but by then I want you all to be aware of what you require in your various departments. Since you've only just joined, with the exception of Lieutenant Olsen and the First Lieutenant, you won't be too clear of what's expected of you, so this afternoon, after what my nose tells me is going to be rather a grand Christmas dinner, Lieutenant Frobisher and I will get down to some paperwork and we'll have the Watch and Quarters Bill organised by 1800.' Clark looked round them. 'Any questions?'

'What exactly are we going to do, sir?' Pearson asked. 'I mean, we all know that this ship,' he pointed at the carpet on the *Nottingham Forest*'s wardroom deck, 'is no ordinary anti-submarine trawler and, looking at the *Sheba's* lot, it's difficult not to come to the same conclusion.'

Clark had no idea of there being anything

223

special about the *Nottingham Forest*, though had he thought about it he would have noted the absence of any of her former peacetime fishermen and the fact that she seemed unusually pukka for an extemporised man-of-war. But this was not the time to think of the trawler.

'Well, gentlemen, I'm somewhat in the dark myself at the moment,' he fibbed, 'but I am assured that we have an important function to perform and we have to go to Scapa to start it.'

'That sounds as though we're going to be a training ship,' said Pearson with the conviction of a young man to whom the world is full of certainties and logic. 'I'll bet we end up in the Western Isles playing doggie to Western Approaches ships.'

'Well, we'll see about that, I'm sure...' Clark cocked an eye at Frobisher. 'Any chance of dinner, Number One?'

It was only when they assembled round the wardroom table and the tops were being levered off the bottles of beer that Frobisher was dispensing in a jolly but essentially false reproduction of a family Christmas, that Clark thought of the last time he had sat down properly to a meal. It had been with Jenny at the sparse little supper they had enjoyed on their last night as lovers. With a pang of remorse he realised he had forgotten all about her.

After dinner, Clark and Frobisher clambered over to the *Sheba* and made their way up into her cold wheelhouse. It smelt of new paint and sawdust and both officers stared about them with an air of frustration.

'I really expected all this to be completed,' Clark said, irritatedly gesturing round the space.

'I rather got that impression,' Frobisher said with a sigh. They leaned upon the unvarnished chart table and contemplated the list of their crew. Frobisher spread a clean sheet of paper between them and Clark fished a fountain pen from the breast pocket of his reefer jacket, handing it to Frobisher. Taking it, the first lieutenant added, 'I appreciate you can't spill the beans, sir, but tell me Pearson's got it wrong and we are not destined to be used to work up Western Approaches escorts?'

Clark looked at Frobisher. The lick of blond hair and the startling brilliance of the blue eyes made him think of his cousin Johannes and the Nazi ideal of manhood. It was a disconcertingly uncomfortable feeling and it rattled him to the extent of increasing his reticence, so that his silence provoked Frobisher further.

'Look, I appreciate that you can't tell me...'

Clark held up his hand. 'It's not that, Number One. The fact is that I can tell you little at the moment beyond saying that Pearson is wrong. On the other hand I would ask you not to press me further. You must be aware that we are not a randomly gathered bunch of officers and ratings and you will easily deduce that we are intended for something unusual. That much I can say to you because in the next hour you and I must apply that criterion to the dispositions of every man in our small ship's small ship's company.' Clark paused, allowing the importance of his deliberate tautology to sink in. 'Now, let's begin...'

Although some work was done in the yard that Christmas, no one disturbed them aboard either *Sheba* or the *Nottingham Forest*. By the evening of Boxing Day, Olsen had rigged a steam pipe and power line between the two ships. Gradually the chill was driven out of the air in *Sheba's* mess decks, flats and cabins, and below decks she glowed with electric light. At 1800 Clark ordered her company accommodated on board; two watches were given a run ashore, and the third assigned its duties. Clark had requisitioned stores directly from *Nottingham Forest* so that by that evening, when he turned in, he felt the little warship was coming to life.

Next day he began his battle with the shipyard. It was not that they opposed him but, whether it was a chargehand, a foreman, the ship manager or even the senior yard manager to whom he spoke, each and every one of them seemed like a juggler. And of all the balls each of these men were keeping airborne, that named *Sheba* was the least significant. Clark grew weary of excuses, of argument and counter-argument. But Gifford's caution prevented him from claiming the whale catcher to be a vessel of any importance, so he became a fusspot, insisting on the urgency implicit in his orders; consequently he was seen as a jumped-up second mate elevated by Admiralty order to a commander who was too big for his boots. It was as unfair as it was inaccurate, but that did not change the perception of those doggedly assigned with tasks almost beyond their resources. Clark's ship was, he was repeatedly assured, 'as good as completed...'

Until actual completion took place, Clark was permitted to occupy one of the huts behind which he had first seen Forrest's Austin saloon. Here, in a shed with *Sheba* chalked on the door, he asserted his minimal authority. Most of the time, however, he was absent on missions of cajolement and threat, leaving Pearson to handle the complex paperwork of requisitions, mail censoring and even the correction of the ship's charts, which had already arrived and grew out of date by the day, even as *Sheba's* date of going to sea seemed to recede into an ever more uncertain future.

Forrest returned from his leave. Swore ritually at the plundering of his stores by Clark, said he 'couldn't care less', and took his ship to sea. Three days later one of the corvettes slid from the slipway and entered the Tees, to be towed to the fitting-out berth. Another was brought by tugs from the fitting-out berth to join *Sheba* between the mooring buoys. Immediately the keel plates were laid on the slipway for the next hull. New Year came and went, and with it the news of the surrender of Hong Kong. It was a dispiriting time.

'The bloody Nips seem to be getting it all their own way,' said Pearson, as if the affront was personal.

'They've got rather used to that,' Clark said.

'Yah, I was in Nanking in '37,' added Storheill. 'They are bastards. Worse than the Germans.'

It seemed that all about them were the alarums of war, from which, for all Gifford's and Pound's admonitions, the wretched *Sheba* was exempt. Privately Clark agonised. What was the state of the *Orca?* More importantly, *where* was she? Still in the Baltic, which he doubted, for had not Gifford said she had already been undergoing her working-up? Was she in Norway, then? Perhaps at Alesund, in sight of Olsen's house! Would he ever get his own ship to sea?

In desperation, Clark tried a new tack, but attempts to draft *Sheba's* company into simple tasks like varnishing the chart-room table were rebuffed. 'Don't take t'bread out of our mouths, Captain,' he was told flatly by the shipyard labourers, though Frobisher, in contempt of any Trade-Union-inspired demarcation dispute, had the men clean the ship, sweeping out and scrubbing the alleyways, mess decks and cabins. Growing bolder and having located some rolls of carpet, they laid these in the wardroom, transforming the place. Then Pearson made a major discovery.

'There's a store, chaps,' he announced enthusiastically over a lunch of soup and sausage rolls. 'Inside the main store there are cages, each with a ship's name on it, you know, the corvettes and...'

'Oh, for Chrissakes get on with it, Sub,' Frobisher snapped.

'Well there's loads of kit for the ship, Number One.'

Pearson's fortuitous discovery marked the turn of the tide in their favour. Why the fact had not been drawn to their attention earlier remained a mystery. The best explanation they could come up with when they debated this over drinks that evening was that every official in the yard who knew of the accumulation of stores assumed that someone else had told the ship's officers. This seemed to assuage their curiosity and they were content with dismissive jerks of their heads, much tut-tutting and snapping of 'Typical!' Besides, they were now too busy for further reflection, while any sense of complacency was regularly interrupted by the almost nightly air-raid alarms. But Olsen's boilers were flashed-up and their warmth pervaded the ship, supplying steam to the radiators in the wheelhouse, where, to Clark's delight, varnish appeared on the chart table. On the forecastle the windlass was run, above the wheelhouse their searchlight was tested. Their Sperry gyrocompass hummed into life and the telegraphists made short, proving transmissions. Towards the end of January 1942 two men in mackintoshes arrived and Clark, Frobisher, Carter and his two Asdic operators were closeted for hours as the Asdic was set up.

On the last day of January, HMS *Sheba* slipped her moorings wearing the red ensign and, as a little flourish insisted upon by the yard, flying the white, blue-crossed flag of the Smith's Dock Company. For her trials the wheelhouse was crowded. Clark, his officers and the *Sheba's* coxswain were outnumbered by a Tees pilot, the ship manager and several representatives from the yard, the Asdic specialists, a wireless mechanic and a sinister-looking civil servant from the

Admiralty who, apart from making himself known to Clark, remained aloof from the entire proceedings.

Out in Tees Bay they worked the ship up to her full speed, making 15.3 knots over the measured mile near Redcar. Then they threw the helm hard over, first one way and then the other, timing the period *Sheba* took to reach a reciprocal course and estimating the tactical diameter of her turning circle. While these grand manoeuvres were under way, circuits were tested, alarms rung, guns traversed and elevated; down below in the engine room, pumps were run, valves thrown, extended spindles and the *Sheba's* one watertight door into her short shaft tunnel were tested.

Then the ship was stopped, a light lunch with drinks was served on the bridge and the observers watched while the boats were hoisted out. As the starboard boat was hooked on to the falls prior to her recovery, one careless seaman suffered a squashed finger. This minor disaster proved a triumph for Sub-Lieutenant Pearson, who proved an able first-aider. Next the ship was anchored, first by the port and then the starboard bowers. Cable was veered and hauled in again and the windlass brakes tested against a load. Finally a couple of dummy depth charges were fired from each mortar and the ship turned west for the Tees Fairway buoy.

From down below Olsen reported himself satisfied and the *Sheba* returned up river bravely breasting the ebb with a fine bone in her teeth.

'Well Commander,' the sinister-looking Admiralty representative said quietly as Clark rang Finished with Engines, 'I imagine you're satisfied.'

'Yes, I think so, thank you.'

'Good. I'll take your report with me then.'

Clark signed for the ship and typed out his report. While he did so the Admiralty man sat silently in his tiny cabin, smoking a pipe, an intimidating presence behind Clark's back. As Clark handed the buff envelope over, the man rose and, picking up his bowler hat, said, 'You'll commission tomorrow then?' Clark nodded. 'Good. I'll tell Gifford you're ready. You've to pick up a load of torpedoes at Rosyth and then I understand you're off to Scapa.'

'Yes, that's correct.' Clark followed the fellow out on deck.

'Good luck,' the official said and left Clark at the head of the short gangway staring after him. He never knew the fellow's name, having failed to read it properly on the identification papers he had been shown earlier that day. As he watched the figure merge into the dark shadows on the shipyard quay to which they had moored upon their return, he was seized by the most awful

232

apprehension. Suppose the man was a German agent? He had no incontrovertible proof that he was what he claimed to be! Anxiety twisted in Clark's gut and he tried to recall what he had written in his report, hurriedly returning to his desk to read the duplicate copy. It gave nothing away beyond the fact that HMS *Sheba* had completed satisfactory trials and would be commissioned at 1000 the following morning.

Leaning back in his chair, Clark lit a cigarette and composed himself. What a bloody fool he had become! He was getting nervously preoccupied, his attention divided between the details of getting the ship ready for sea and the greater purpose towards which these petty endeavours were directed. He would be glad to get away from the constraints of the shipyard, reflecting that this whole, sorry business had been initiated in a shipyard. A knock came at the door.

'Come in, Number One.'

'Your blackout needs a bit of attention, sir.'

'Does it?'

'Yes. Don't worry, I'll see to it in a moment. I take it we commission at ten tomorrow?'

'Yes, as planned. Everything went all right today, I thought.'

'Yes, pretty remarkably. Perhaps we misjudged the yard a bit.'

'Possibly.'

'What happens after commissioning, sir?'

Clark grinned. 'A nice little cargo run for you, Number One. We're off to Rosyth, to load torpedoes for Scapa.'

'Bloody hell, I hope I don't run into any of my old muckers in the greyhounds of the ocean.'

'Why not? Surely you're proud as punch of your nice little armed whaler.'

'Ha, bloody ha, sir.'

The next morning they went through the modest ceremony of commissioning. The crew were paraded on the quay, watched by a small group of managers and typists from the builder's offices, a handful of charge-hands and a few of the men who had built the ship. Clark read his commissioning order, the ensign and commissioning pendant were hoisted and Frobisher dismissed the ship's company. It began raining again, with a keen wind blowing off the North Sea. The courtesy of their presence over, the shipyard's personnel dispersed, the shivering girls running off bare-legged in the chilly breeze, the men with a resigned air. For them the esoteric act was of no great significance; there were more ships to build and their task lacked any glamour, even that attaching to a small warship: their world was bounded by the grey of their industrial landscape, not the sharp monochromes of a warship's paintwork with its bright gleam of red, white and blue fluttering over the stern in the bitter wind.

Marching off, the seamen's square collars blew up round their heads as they went up the gangway, boarding the ship officially for the first time. There were fewer than thirty of them, officers included.

Next day they were gone, the berth empty, awaiting its next, transitory visitor, the only evidence of their passing the quickening in the wombs of three careless and unknowing young women. In distant Liverpool another, not-so-young woman, was growing anxious.

As she steamed north, none of the ship's company aboard His Majesty's Armed Whaler *Sheba* gave a second thought to the River Tees, nor to those who dwelt upon its banks. Young they might be, but after over two years of war they had become accustomed to departures and inured to the pain of parting. The unthinking shaggers among them would find other willing girls and even the few disposed to fall in love could repeat the process elsewhere. In the meantime they would beat the bishop, in the time-honoured fashion.

The Admiralty, through the agency of some two dozen first lieutenants and captains scattered throughout the fleet, had done its work well in selecting the crew of HMS *Sheba*; some had viewed the request

235

seriously, most had got rid of their bad-hats. But not one of the young men who slipped easily into the routine of sea duty that raw morning was known for his sentimentality. On the contrary they were taking stock of the future and, to a man, were wondering why they had been assigned to this odd little ship with its odd and preponderant assortment of officers. All they knew with anything like certainty was what Leading Seaman Carter told them, that the Old Man was a whizz-kid on the Asdic.

As for the Old Man, Lieutenant Commander Jack Clark stood on the starboard wing of the bridge, his back to the ugly Hotchkiss gun, staring ahead. His mind was on the far north, full of his responsibilities and the intended encounter with his enemy.

SCAPA FLOW

February 1942

HMS *Sheba* proceeded independently as far as the Tyne and then received a signal to join the escort of a coastal convoy northwards to Methil. They had little to do except perform the unflattering role of 'tail-end Charlie' which surprised nobody given their unprepared and unworked-up state. Nor had they more than a token stock of depth charges and ammunition aboard, loaded shortly before leaving the Tees, but it was their first encounter with the rest of the Royal Navy and they began to feel a sense of purpose animate them. This was something familiar, something they had become masters of, unlike the endured existence 'in dockyard hands' as the naval phrase succinctly had it.

'The only time the navy surrenders is to a bloody dockyard,' Frobisher had remarked back in Middlesbrough as he saw Clark scribble the time-honoured phrase in the deck log, explaining away another day of unproductive naval service. 'How this is winning the war beats me!'

Clark merely grunted at his first lieutenant's pugnacity.

At sea, on a purposeful passage in support of a convoy, Clark began to observe his crew at work, particularly the competence of the ratings. The signallers performed with gratifying ability during this short and, as it happened, uneventful passage. The clatter of the Aldis lamp had, Clark thought, an especial significance and would linger in his aural memory as long as he lived. It was the real means by which he and his fellows communicated, in the heat of action and the relief of the aftermath. By means of its flashes they made their facetious, schoolboy jests; in its cryptic messages they received the instructions, remonstrations or compliments of their senior officer; with it they scolded the masters of merchant ships as they struggled to keep their unsuitable vessels in a naval formation, or made too much smoke, gleefully pointing out the obvious to men older and wiser than themselves. The dots and dashes of the Aldis lamps, manifested in the rapid clatter of the shutters, were like the out-reaching tip on the coachman's whip, flickering over the six-in-hand as the convoy crawled slowly towards its destination.

From the convoy anchorage off Methil

they detached to steam further into the Firth of Forth, to be briefly absorbed into a greater, grander manifestation of naval puissance. It was the first time Clark had reported to a senior officer as the commander of a commissioned warship and it was clear that no whiff of the *Sheba's* ultimate mission troubled Rosyth dockyard. The unimportance of his ship somewhat relieved him, enabling him to conceal her unpreparedness amid all the hustle and bustle of the place. After the rarefied atmosphere of the Admiralty and the intoxication of that interview with Sir Dudley Pound, the short stop at Rosyth grounded him in the immensity of the navy's task and the smallness of his own. For all Gifford's emphasis on the vital importance of the *Sheba's* mission, it seemed insignificant when set against the greater operations of so huge a force as the Royal Navy.

Then, as he lingered over a cup of tea brought by a plain Wren with straight legs and an impossible bosom, the staff officer dealing with his arrival said, 'You've heard the news from Singapore?'

Clark shook his head. 'No...'

'We've lost the *Prince of Wales* and the *Repulse*, bombed out of existence by the ruddy Japs!'

'Good God!'

'Better news from Tobruk, but the *Prince of*

Wales, for Heaven's sake...' Incredulity seemed to prevail at the loss of this brand new battleship. 'No bloody air cover, d'you see,' the staff officer went on. 'The Royal Air Force were bloody useless and the designated carrier is sitting in an American dry dock after grounding in the West Indies...'

The staff officer's tone of accusation at others' incompetence was almost venomous, taken personally as an affront. The man ground out his cigarette with the air of one who could have done better himself. Suddenly *Sheba's* mission did not seem so minor an affair. Wars were won or lost by an aggregation of triumphs or disasters, large or small: the realisation that an error in navigation in the West Indies had a decisive bearing on events in the South China Sea was a sobering thought. Clark returned to his ship in pensive mood and remained so as they loaded their consignment of torpedoes along with a quantity of shells and cartridges, depth charges, rockets and grenades. Then they made their way north alone.

Clark continued to observe the emergence of the 'characters' in his ship's company. This period, known to the navy as 'shaking-down', was as important to him in watching his crew, as it was to them in the refinement of their interrelationships on board their new ship. These, bounded in part by the constraints of discipline, were equally governed by those assertions and concessions men who were cooped up in a small space made with, for or against each other.

Clark knew, of course, of Carter's virtues and Carter was a bright enough individual to realise his strange posting was pregnant with possibilities.

'If this war goes on for long, sir,' Carter had said during a quiet moment when they had been carrying out the Asdic trials in Tees Bay, deliberately revealing the extent of his ambition and hinting at his appreciation of his and Clark's situation, 'I think we'll be needing officers with a wealth of experience at Asdic operation.'

Clark had confined himself to a knowing smile and a grunting agreement, and he knew Carter well enough to see such a curt response was all that was required. Carter was a man who understood subtleties. Afterwards Clark realised that Carter's drive was directed at encouraging his two assistant operators, Wilkins and Baker, both of whom had been recommended by their respective commanding officers. Gifford, Clark was soon to understand, must have leaned on some key men, for if these two ratings were as good as they promised to be, at least two commanding officers must be regretting the absence of able men.

You could not say that about at least four of the *Sheba's* dozen seamen. The three leading hands seemed decent enough men, ranging in age between twenty-four and thirty-one. Two, Lambert and Page, were from Western Approaches; the third, a man named Roe, had come from a cruiser. The three ordinary seamen were all men whose records had been annotated with the remarks that they possessed 'officer potential'. Educated and mature, of similar ages to the leading hands, their junior rating sat uneasily upon them. Success aboard *Sheba* demanded recognition by Clark and advancement to the status of 'CW' ratings, sailors being fast-tracked to commissions. But for the time being they occupied the lowest strata of *Sheba's* microcosmic society, the menials upon whom the six men in between, those rated able seamen, looked down. It did not help that this worthy trio possessed names like Wiggins, Oliphant and Peacock. Such apparent pretensions were grist to the mill of Harding, Black, Saunders and Collins, whose obvious selection on grounds of 'independence, initiative and aggressive spirit' had been loosely translated by their first lieutenants as 'truculence, indolence and a terrorising attitude'. No doubt these officers had been delighted to offload the free spirits in their midst with a 'good riddance'. Fortunately the remaining pair, Lincoln and Davies, were quiet, detached men who kept themselves aloof from the petty power politics of the *Sheba's* crowded little mess decks.

These dozen men, split into three watches, came under the coxswain, a man who rejoiced in the name James Cook. It amused and consoled Clark's innately superstitious soul that, quite fortuitously, his little ship's company contained the names of at least two famous explorers, Cook and Frobisher. To add his own as a third would need a respelling, Clerke for Clark, but the nearness of this third to the other two rather silly little coincidences gave a spurious meaning, by way of continuity, to his private fatalism. It was, he thought, a good omen.

As to his four 'bad-hats', he knew, with the instinct of long experience, there would come in due course a confrontation, and a confrontation with which, he suspected, Douglas Ireton Robert*son* Keith Frobisher would have some trouble. Time would tell.

Nevertheless, much would depend upon these twelve men, for upon them fell the work of tying the ship up, of letting her go, of taking away her boats, steering her, maintaining her lookouts and keeping her in working order above decks. And, when the final action for which she, and they, had been called into being as an entity came to pass, it would be they who would man the *Sheba's* guns, torpedoes and depth charges and upon whom the speed and effectiveness of the *Sheba's* attack would ultimately rely.

As for those who kept his little ship moving through the water, Clark entertained little anxiety. Lieutenant Olsen and his seven fellow Norwegians in the 'black-gang' were a bonded unit. The engine and boiler rooms were their province and Clark was swiftly made aware that any visit he made there, while not actually resented, was considered redundant. The *Sheba* might have been a British warship, but her engine and boiler rooms were Norwegian territory and a large Norwegian ensign was hung from a small galvanised block seized with wire to one of the cross bars of the engine-room skylight. Olsen dealt with whatever internecine rivalries, disputes or differences fragmented the men whom Frobisher in indiscreet moments referred to as 'the trolls'. Not that Olsen kept himself aloof, for he enjoyed the society of the wardroom, where he could speak quietly to Storheill of his private anxieties in their native tongue. The presence of Storheill was thoughtful on the part of Gifford, Clark realised, partly on account of his providing a soulmate for Olsen, but also because the young lieutenant had had some polar experience and had visited Spitsbergen on several occasions before settling aboard Wilhelm Wilhelmsen's cargo liners. Despite Frobisher's rudeness, the first lieutenant was careful to avoid any such comments in the presence of Olsen and Storheill. He considered that, as the only regular officer aboard the ship, a greater gulf existed between himself and Clark, than between Clark and the Norwegians, for all had a wider range of experience in the multiple voyagings of their merchant ships. Occasionally he would come to remark, in moments of mock pique, that they should forget their charade of being a warship and hoist the red ensign.

'Well, it would be sensible,' Pearson would put in with characteristically misplaced didacticism. 'After all, Number One, it was once the senior naval colour.'

Frobisher would curl his lip with disdain at the unseemly suggestion. 'Remember Nelson,' he would riposte.

As they steamed north, Clark, contemplating the transformation of his eclectic collection of men into a crew, concluded that they were better than he might have expected, bad-hats notwithstanding. The catering staff and the three telegraphists who completed his complement worked with quiet diligence. On the former much depended, for a badly fed ship lacked morale and, quite literally, the stomach for a fight. Day after day, irrespective of the weather, the cook would be expected to produce edible, restorative food of one sort or another. It would be a good barometer,

Clark thought, of the truculence of his bad boys, to see to what extent they moaned about the grub, and whether such complaints moved from the merely ritual to the formal. As for his communications staff, he knew Gifford's final orders would insist upon total radio silence on their part, the key to their mission being a passive role of listening and interpreting incoming radio traffic. Clark himself could not understand why anyone would want to man a radio under such circumstances. Radio rooms, or shacks as they were often referred to, seemed small, isolated and hermetic places, low on ventilation and high on claustrophobia. That wireless operators usually added to their discomfort by smoking was a mystery past his fathoming, but one from which was born an admiration. Clark had long ago learned to value particular abilities; his style of leadership relied upon harnessing them. Even his bad-hats, he reflected, had individual skills.

Now, as the darkness engulfed them on the bridge and in the wheelhouse, the subdued illumination of the radio room abaft the wheelhouse sent a sliver of light through an ill-fitting crash panel in the door. It was relatively unimportant but it irritated Clark. Leading Seaman Davies had proved useful as the ship's extemporised carpenter. Tomorrow they would have to do something about that.

'Cuppa kye, sir?'

Clark turned. A figure loomed close to him and he could smell the cocoa. 'Oh, yes please. Many thanks. Who's that?'

'Leadin' Seaman 'Arding, sir.'

'Thank you, Harding.' One of the bad-hats, Clark reflected as he sipped the scalding drink and wondered wryly what Harding had done to doctor the Old Man's nightcap. Thinking of the horror stories he had heard as an apprentice, of the seaman who, in rough weather, carried the master's tea in his own mouth until, upon entering the wheel-house, he would gob it into the empty mug and hand it to the captain; of the steward resentful of the chief officer's punishment for his drunkenness, who ejaculated into the mate's soup! Clark sipped the kye; it was hot and sweet and delicious.

Sheba lifted easily to a heavy swell and then sank into the succeeding trough. There was a gale blowing somewhere to the north of them, but here, abeam of the Moray Firth, it was a quiet enough night. Clark felt that strange relief that stole unbidden upon him at such moments of quiet reflection at sea. It was here that he felt truly himself. Jack Clark ashore was a different person, even the littoral environment of a shipyard was too obviously the concern of landsmen to please Clark's soul. Even those amphibians who dwelt amid the cranes, gantries and slipways of a shipyard failed to understand the strange symbiosis that existed between the true seaman and his ship. Such men were dropouts who regarded that rare minority whose spirits were only happy at sea as moronic throwbacks to a more primitive time. Clark knew of this, knew too that nothing came without a price and that many regarded him as 'odd'. He could not help it. He was as divided as any other seaman of his age and libido, a victim of his heterosexual lust and no fancier of his own sex. But Magda had twisted the knife in an old wound, persuading him that that peculiar, intense emotion that a few fortunate people enjoyed as love was not for him. He had assuaged his hurt in Jenny, knowing only that she had been an eager participant in their affair. It had been a mutually satisfying experience, of no great moment to either party; they had been friends at the beginning and parted greater friends at the end. He was, he concluded, a man who might enjoy temporary liaisons, but who should never marry, never bind himself with the ties of offspring. And in that unintentional smugness, the notion of self-reproach over Jenny failed to cross Clark's mind, especially upon that night at sea, as *Sheba* ran north alone. On that particular night, he recalled long afterwards, nothing could diminish his deep satisfaction at being at sea. And the pleasure

248

was peculiarly intense because he was not only in command, but he was bound north again, to the polar seas that had captivated him as a youth and which he had thought he would never see again. Happiness is only known in retrospect but that night Clark, his soul exposed, *knew* he was sublimely happy.

Given that there was a war on.

With their pendant number flying bravely, they passed the boom defences and entered Scapa Flow on a morning of mixed sunshine and showers. The breeze was from the northwest. It cut up the water of the anchorage, across which skewed the occasional fulmar, while the ubiquitous and populous herring gull screeched its familiar laughing cry, as if deriding the pomp and majesty of the Home Fleet. The flagship, HMS *King George V*, was moored to her buoy, a great grey angular shape whose outline reminded Clark of her sister ship, the *Prince of Wales*, which now lay at the bottom of the South China Sea with most of her company entombed within her.

Scattered about the flagship lay the grey monoliths of her companions in descending order of hierarchy. Beyond the heavy capital ships lay the cruisers in smaller imitation, and then the flotillas of sharp, pugnacious destroyers. The faint haze of heat rose above their funnels and the banked boiler fires below, the tiny bright coloured spots of ensigns, signal and command flags fluttered at their halliards, and among them passed the boats and tenders, busying themselves on the domestic affairs of the fleet. *Sheba* passed an outward-bound destroyer, her crew securing her upper deck as she headed for the opened boom. Across the wind-ruffled waters of the Flow the thin, persistent notes of the pipes carried; ensigns were dipped and ratings stood for a moment to attention, then HMS *Sheba*, having made her number to the signal station was ordered to a remote 'explosives anchorage' to await further instructions.

These were not long in coming, a fleet tender delivered a written order for Clark to take his ship alongside several Home Fleet destroyers and to trans-ship his cargo of torpedoes. For the remainder of that day Clark and his ship's company went from one destroyer to another, carefully swinging the twenty-one-inch weapons on to their iron decks. It was pure ship-handling and seamanship, the mooring and unmooring, the laying alongside and the working-off from each destroyer as she swung to wind and tide in the erratic conditions of the day. But there were no embarrassments and, although a gust had pinned *Sheba* alongside one ship until she slowly swung in response, Clark felt he had adequately demonstrated his skill to his crew. To have their commander's abilities confirmed was an important preliminary ritual in the delicate establishment of un-coerced discipline; so too was his message of thanks to the hands for having acquitted themselves well under the critical eyes of so many wiseacres leaning over the rails of the recipient ships.

'What about the six remaining torpedoes, sir?' Frobisher asked as he came up to the bridge in search of a cup of tea as the day-light leached out of the sky and *Sheba* swung away from the last destroyer and headed back for her anchorage. But before Clark could answer, the erratic clatter of the Aldis lamp diverted their attention.

'Signal from the flagship, sir,' the signaller reported, holding out the message pad with its pencilled upper-case scrawl. Clark read it and handed it to Pearson, who was manipu-lating parallel rules and dividers over the chart.

'We're to go alongside the depot ship,' he said to Frobisher, turning to Pearson and saying, 'Give me a course...'

Clark swung his glasses round the anchor-age and steadied them on the ungainly silhouette of an adapted merchantman. 'Ah, I've got her. Hard a port,' he ordered. 'Give her full ahead, Number One, let's get her alongside before tea time.' Frobisher straightened up from the telegraph against which he had been leaning and swung its handle. The engine-room repeater followed after a second, the jangling ringing through the wheelhouse. After a moment Clark steadied the helm and, as Pearson gave him a confirming compass course across the Flow, turned again to Frobisher.

'I expect we'll be alongside for a couple of days. We're to have some modifications done.'

'Oh, that makes lots of sense, having just come from the builder's yard,' Frobisher said sarcastically as he sipped his tea. 'And it's got something to do with the torpedoes, hasn't it?'

Clark looked at his first lieutenant. Frobisher's face was a pale oval in the twilit gloom and he could sense the sudden attention of the man at the wheel. Able Seaman Saunders would be eager for any scuttlebutt he could carry below to the mess deck.

'Once we're alongside, Number One,' Clark conceded, 'I want the officers mustered in the wardroom. Then we'll clear lower deck and I'll speak to the ship's company.'

But Clark's intended briefings were postponed. They were no sooner secured alongside the depot ship *Tyne*, than an elderly lieutenant in the uniform of the Volunteer Reserve came aboard and asked Clark to accompany him. Clark followed the elderly officer on to the old liner and was then escorted across the ship and out of her opposite side, where, at the foot of her accommodation ladder, a wooden pontoon moved uneasily in the slop alongside the depot ship. Moored to the pontoon lay a picket boat whose motion was infinitely livelier.

'Orders to spirit you off quietly to the flagship, sir,' the elderly lieutenant explained. 'I'm sure you know why.'

Clark saluted the lieutenant as he passed over the depot ship's side, and then saluted again as the elegant sprig of a midshipman in charge of the picket boat acknowledged him. A moment later Clark was somewhat apprehensively alone in the cuddy of the picket boat. The midshipman ducked his head down once to see if his passenger was all right, but otherwise they bounced across the Flow for what seemed like an age until, coming into the lee of the *King George V*, the boat steadied, her engine slowed, then stopped, kicked astern and nudged another pontoon at the foot of the battleship's after port accommodation ladder.

Clark gazed up at the towering upperworks above him. The battleship seemed huge. Her funnel and forebridge rising into the star-spangled darkness like some bizarre giant's castle in a dream, she hummed with the rumble of internal machinery. At the top of the gangway the gleam of brass and pipeclay caught his eye, but he had no time for observation. Another lieutenant, this time young and immaculate, with a telescope tucked under his arm, saluted him and led him off into a labyrinth of alleyways, companionways and flats. The lieutenant walked purposefully, so much so that his progress was unbarred, and both officers and men going about the great ship drew back from the pair of them. Clark at first thought he was to be taken aft, perhaps to the commander-in-chief's harbour quarters, but their gradual ascent told him they were going upwards towards the bridge. Clearly he was to meet a senior staff officer. In fact, and quite suddenly, he found himself on what he afterwards learned was the admiral's bridge, face-to-face with Admiral Sir John Tovey. At the intrusion the commander-in-chief of the Home Fleet turned from conversation with another officer. Clark could see a chart and some papers spread before the two men, illuminated by the lowered lamp hung over the chart table.

'L'tenant Commander Clark, Sir John,' the officer of the watch said breezily.

Clark snapped to attention and saluted. Tovey acknowledged the salute and dismissed the lieutenant. The commander-in chief introduced his chief-of-staff, then said, 'We all know why you are here, Commander Clark. We have been expecting you for some time.'

'There were some delays at the yard, sir,' Clark explained, flushing.

'No doubt. Well, I understand you are alongside the *Tyne* and your torpedo tubes will be fitted immediately. Special provisions have been made for you to draw whatever you require from the depot ship's stores – Arctic clothing and the like. Within reason, of course. I don't want you running away with the notion that you have a blank cheque.'

'No, of course not, sir.'

'Very well. As soon as all that has been accomplished, you are to proceed to sea and carry out trials. I am not proposing to complicate matters by having a special training programme drawn up for you, you know your objective and I think it best that you carry out your own programme, but if you require assistance, you are to make your request personally, by word of mouth, to the chief-of-staff here. We'll give you a submarine for a day; I hope that will be sufficient. I hear that you and your ship's company are all highly proficient.' Tovey's tone was dryly sceptical, 'I hope you are.'

'Sir.' Clark could think of nothing more appropriate to say.

'Now,' Tovey went on, 'what you ought to know about is that we have every reason to suspect matters are moving forwards. I am sure you understand.' Tovey paused.

'I think so, sir, yes.'

'Good. Well, suffice it to say that the enemy have moved the battleship *Tirpitz* into Norwegian waters. We may assume she is not alone.'

The importance of the news caused a contraction in Clark's gut. 'Quite so, sir.'

'So, it seems to us that you should not delay in working-up. I require only a formal notification by the hand of an officer that you are in all respects ready for sea duty. I shall then inform the Admiralty. You will then receive your intelligence briefing from Captain Gifford; thereafter you shall proceed and act independently.' Tovey paused and a note of irony crept into his voice. 'You are not officially under my command, Clark. However, the only obligation I am laying upon you is a signal to the effect that you have not succeeded and that your failure exposes vessels under my command, whether they be men-of-war or merchant ships. D'you understand? The Admiralty will require the same intelligence, but I am most insistent that I am informed directly.'

'Of course, sir. It is my understanding that I shall be making few transmissions, but that a failure requires a warning to be sent to both you and to the Admiralty.'

Tovey nodded. 'Good.' The commander-in-chief paused again and appeared to be making an assessment of Clark. Whatever his private thoughts the admiral concealed them and held out his hand. 'Good luck, Clark.'

'Thank you, sir.' Saluting, Clark retired and made his way back through the warren of steel passages until he emerged through the blackout on to the upper deck. He found himself too far forward and walked aft until he found his former guide on the quarter-deck. Three-quarters of an hour later the picket boat put him back aboard the *Tyne*, from where he made his way across to *Sheba*.

'The officers are waiting for you, sir,' Frobisher said as they exchanged salutes. 'We've held tea.'

'Oh, well then,' Clark said, pleased at the consideration, 'let's get on with it.'

They made their way down to the ward-room and Clark accepted the cup of tea the steward handed him. 'Well, gentlemen,' Clark began, looking round at the faces of his officers, 'I think it is time you began to understand something of what our purpose is. Most of you have already rumbled that something's up, quite what is still secret, but I can tell you that we are bound on special service and that this will take us well to the north. I shall be drawing on stores of Arctic clothing for all of us and I am asking you all to give the matter of extreme conditions some consideration. You, Fridtjof,' he said to Olsen, 'will have to keep us as warm as you can and to ensure we've steam enough to clear off any ice accumulations. Now, I cannot at the moment tell you how long this trip will last, but we must also conserve fuel. If things become protracted we'll have the opportunity to refuel, but in any operation of this nature it pays to be economical. Now, I don't need to tell you that all our equipment must be in tip-top working order. We'll be working-up in the next week or so, just as soon as the mods have been made here.' He looked round again. 'Any questions?'

'Well, quite a few actually, sir, but mainly what are these "mods"?'

'We're to have two torpedo tubes fitted, Number One...'

'Hence the torpedoes we've retained!' put in Pearson, adding the non sequitur, 'Now I understand why we've got all those bloody charts of the Barents Sea.'

'For what do we go north, sir?' Olsen asked.

The pertinence of the question struck them and Clark saw them all alerted by Olsen's query.

'I wish I could tell you,' Clark dissembled, 'but beyond saying that they're arming us with torpedoes, I am unable to enlighten you.'

The silence of polite disbelief that followed this lack of information ended in a rising buzz of speculation. Predictably Pearson initiated it; given Tovey's single revelation about the *Tirpitz*, Pearson's guess had a certain credibility: 'I bet we're to go and hide in the ice and spring out on a pocket battle-ship!'

'Don't be so fucking silly, Derek,' snapped Frobisher. 'The whole Home Fleet is waiting to do that. You don't think...'

'But we could be a sacrifice ... a what you call a decoy, yes?' Storheill broke in.

'That's more like it,' Frobisher agreed grudgingly.

'Unless we are just a weather ship for the Home Fleet,' Pearson speculated with undiminished fervour.

'What, with specially fitted torpedoes?'

'Well, that may not be such a silly notion,' Clark put in, unwilling to remain aloof in case they guessed, as he suspected they might, that he had known all along. 'With more convoys running up to Russia, the further north they can be routed, the more difficult it would be for enemy air strikes to reach them from northern Norway. Perhaps, if not weather, we might usefully report on ice conditions, even act as an ice pilot...'

'Routing a convoy through ice would not only take it out of range of aircraft, it might also make it less vulnerable to U-boats!' Pearson added relentlessly.

'Huh!' Frobisher commented monosyllabically but, for the time being, they had to be content with that.

'There is one more thing,' Clark said, capturing their attention. 'I've some forms in my cabin to enable those of you who haven't done so to make your own wills.' As a dolorous silence fell on the little assembly, Clark rose, picking up his hat and turning to Frobisher. 'Well, Number One, I suppose you'd better clear the lower deck and I'll go and repeat all this for the benefit of the petty officers and ratings.'

'Small arms, .303 ammo, white paint, K rations, Arctic kit...' Clark murmured as he ran his fountain pen down the last of what seemed to him now to have been an endless number of lists. Since he had joined the ship these had covered almost every moveable object within her fabric, he concluded, sitting back and lighting a cigarette. Then he swore, set his cigarette on the ashtray and wrote: 'paintbrushes', adding vocally, 'I'll bet we don't have enough of them in the store to paint the whole bloody ship.'

'I begin to feel like Shackleton or Worsley,' he remarked wearily over dinner, as he reminded Frobisher to indent for some more paintbrushes. 'Endless lists of stuff we might never need ... Anything else anyone wants?' he asked, looking round the table.

'Only some more packing, Captain,' said Olsen, 'and that is already on its way. They have been very good to us aboard *Tyne*.'

'Yes. I'm glad to hear that,' Clark said, regarding the mashed potatoes before him with little interest.

'Did you say Worsley, sir?' Pearson piped up.

'Yes,' said Clark, 'why?'

'Well, he taught us navigation at *King Alfred*,' responded Pearson, referring to the so-called training ship for volunteer officers at Hove in Sussex. 'She's a stone frigate, where...'

'Yes, yes, Derek, we know what the *King Alfred* is and what we have to thank it for,' Frobisher said testily, adding, 'though I heard it was just an old garage on the sea-front...'

'Well, perhaps, Number One,' Olsen cut in, 'an old garage is a modern British stone frigate.'

They chuckled and the undaunted Pearson went on, 'Old Worsley was a marvellous chap, sir. He navigated Shackleton's boat across the Southern Ocean...'

'Yes, I know,' Clark replied.

'He's a brilliant navigator...' Pearson added.

'He must be if he taught you anything,' Frobisher said with a grin at the irrepressible sub-lieutenant.

'Well we had to learn a lot quicker than you chaps at Dartmouth,' Pearson riposted sharply.

'He's got you there, Number One,' Clark said in a low voice.

'He's an impudent little toad, sir, and for his impertinence he can be duty officer tonight.'

'Oh, that's not fair, Number One,' Pearson protested.

'Little boys should be seen and not heard. Write that out five hundred times and I'll let you off.' Frobisher set his knife and fork down and looked at Clark. 'You sailed with Worsley, didn't you, sir?'

'Did you, sir?' Pearson said, leaning forward and staring past Storheill and Frobisher, his eyes wide with wonder. 'Really?'

'Yes,' Clark said, finishing his own meal. 'I was on his expedition to the Arctic in 1926, aboard the brigantine *Island*. It's a long time ago.'

'Blimey!'

'There, Derek. Now what do you say to calling the Old Man a bit slow coming alongside that last destroyer?'

'I did not say that, Number One!' the embarrassed and flushing Pearson exclaimed.

'It sounded like it to me,' Frobisher said, catching Clark's eye and winking.

'Sir, the first lieutenant is stirring it, sir. I said no such thing...'

'May you be forgiven your fibs, young man,' Frobisher said archly.

'Sir, all I said was that I was surprised that

you had, er...'

Clark burst into laughter at the young man's discomfiture and even the two Norwegians saw the amusing side of this very English scene. After he realised Clark was not angry, Pearson himself began to laugh, though he mouthed imprecations at Frobisher. As the laughter subsided, Clark said, 'Well, perhaps in the next few days you can have a turn at manoeuvring the ship, Pearson. Then you'll really have grounds to criticise me.'

Recalling the scene late that night as he lay unsleeping in his bunk, Clark thought the wardroom atmosphere very satisfactory. He could not know what Olsen and Storheill thought, of course, beyond the most superficial judgement based on observations of their day-to-day conduct, but their ready amusement at Frobisher's guying treatment of the baby of the mess augured well. As for Pearson, well, he seemed a good-hearted young man and it would not hurt him to have a little of his enthusiastic outspokenness knocked out of him by Frobisher.

The following afternoon the welders pronounced themselves satisfied. They had cut large oval apertures either side, under the flare of *Sheba's* bows, just forward of the break in the forecastle. Inboard, against these, they had lined up and secured the torpedo tubes, bolting them through the upper deck and running the pipework to a compressor squashed into the forecastle paint store. As a consequence, the hundred one-gallon tins of white paint requisitioned from the depot ship were piled on the foredeck, lashed to the racks for the spare torpedoes which had also been welded on to the foredeck. The whole lot were covered by tarpaulins to conceal them from the cameras or binoculars of reconnoitring enemy aircraft.

The torpedo tubes were placed under Frobisher's especial charge, a measure that disappointed Pearson, whose position as gunnery officer, in charge of the ship's four-inch gun, had led him to suppose that anything forward of the bridge that went bang, was his by right.

'Never mind, Derek,' Frobisher had consoled him cheerfully. 'You can look after them when I'm killed.'

While the artificers from the *Tyne* completed fitting the *Sheba's* unorthodox armament, her ship's company were busy salting away the additional stores they had embarked. This included a quantity of tinned food and additional ammunition, including twenty-millimetre shells.

Frobisher queried the supply of these with Clark, but he shrugged his shoulders and went on board the *Tyne* to enquire. He had struck up something of a friendship with the engineer commander under whose wing the armourers worked and who had had their torpedo tubes prepared.

'Sorry to bother you again, sir,' he said, locating the engineer commander in his cabin, 'but my first lieutenant's just reported a load of twenty-millimetre shells have come aboard. Unfortunately we haven't got anything to put 'em in.'

'Yes you have,' the commander replied. 'I've had special instructions to cut away your after Hotchkiss mounting and give you an Oerlikon. We've better places to put them, but you must be someone very special, Commander Clark, or you have friends in high places.'

And so they were fitted with the Swiss anti-aircraft gun and, as Pearson insisted, two spare barrels. The work delayed them further, but Clark received no prompting signals from the distant flagship. Presumably Tovey knew all about their progress, and the additional fitting of the Oerlikon.

By and large their sea trials were successful. Clark drilled his men relentlessly for three days, sending them repeatedly to action stations, but conserving his ammunition. He intended to work them up again in the Arctic, when he could reveal their purpose and practise their attack amid the ice. He was relying upon at least a short period prior to intercepting *Orca* to bring them to a high pitch of efficiency. For the time being they carried out trials of the Asdic, echo-ranging off isolated rocks until content with the kit before requesting the promised submarine. Clark let Frobisher handle the first hunt, eager to see how the younger man conducted it. Frobisher was uninspired, a by-the-book tactician, running his opponent down with a casual competence helped by the unlayered nature of the water and the ability of Carter's team. He fudged the last few yards, failing to predict the submarine's last-minute evasion, and the grenade thrown overboard to simulate the depth-charge attack was accorded a 'possible' status by the submarine commander in the debrief afterwards. At the time Carter evinced some irritation, exchanging a quick, intimate shake of the head with Clark. The small, insubordinate gesture was an indication of that symbiosis Clark and Carter had themselves achieved. Clark ignored it.

'Not bad, Number One, not bad,' he said. He handled the afternoon attack himself. The submarine commander, on his mettle following the close shave of the morning, dodged and weaved, ran deep and then attempted a bold counter-attack, but Carter, revelling in the chase, and Clark, delighted in the quick responsiveness of *Sheba*, had the measure of him. After the small detonations

266

of the grenade, the submarine surfaced in their wake and signalled indignantly: 'Ouch!'

'I think we have hunted more U-boats than he has ships,' Clark concluded in a remark to Frobisher, but which was intended as a compliment to Carter.

That evening the *Sheba* lay alongside the oiler, filling her tanks to their uttermost capacity, with ullages reduced to the minimum. In his cabin Clark wrote his report to Tovey, summoning Pearson to convey it to the flagship.

'This is to be placed into the hands of the C-in-C's chief-of-staff and nobody else, Derek, d'you understand?'

'Perfectly, sir.'

'And no lingering in the wardroom, or anywhere else on the flagship, for that matter.'

'No sir.'

'*Tyne*'s sending a motor boat for you. I'd hate to see you pulling alongside the *Kay Gee Five* in one of our horrible little punts.'

When he returned two hours later, Pearson found the wardroom a rather jolly place, filled with tobacco smoke and the fumes of gin. Clark and Frobisher were roaring with laughter over some joke made by the submarine commander and his first lieutenant. The engineer commander was also present, while Olsen and Storheill bent over a chessboard, looking up from time to time and exchanging inconsequential remarks with the others.

'Oh, I didn't know you were having a party in my absence,' a rather crestfallen Pearson observed.

'It seemed like a good excuse,' Frobisher quipped. 'Anyway, you got to go aboard the big, big battleship and shake hands with the *grand fromage*.'

'I didn't see Sir John,' Pearson said a touch petulantly.

'Any messages, Sub?' Clark asked. Olsen and Storheill looked up from their game.

'Well, the chief of staff did say he hoped we'd get our whale, sir. Bloody cheek, I thought it.'

'Did you tell him you thought it a bloody cheek?' Frobisher asked.

'No, of course I bloody didn't, Number One!' Pearson turned and left the wardroom.

'Don't be too hard on him, Number One,' Clark said.

'No, he is a good fellow,' added Storheill.

'Go and get him back for a drink, Per,' Frobisher said. 'Tell him I'm buying.'

THE LAST ESCORT

February–March 1942

'I'm sorry about all this cloak-and-dagger stuff,' Gifford said, smiling up at Clark as he settled in the small armchair in Clark's tiny cabin and accepted a glass of gin. 'Seems a bit melodramatic.'

Clark sat opposite his visitor, having turned round the uncomfortable upright chair that served him at his desk. Gifford wore a dark suit and looked every inch the senior civil servant, though a perceptive observer might have judged him a naval officer in disguise. He had arrived by air only an hour earlier.

'I can only say, sir,' Clark responded, 'that from my perspective it's fairly terrifying.'

'I can imagine,' Gifford said unimaginatively. 'Cheers.'

'Cheers.'

Gifford set his glass down and turned to his briefcase, opening it with an ominous click of its twin locks. He drew out a large, bulging Manila envelope and handed it to Clark.

'I've brought your ship's mail. We've collected it from its various addresses. I don't mind telling you it took some organising!'

Clark set the package aside as Gifford handed him a second, thinner foolscap envelope. It was addressed to him and marked, in addition to instructions as to its disposal, *Most Secret. To be opened only when above the 66th Parallel.*

Clark placed the packet on his desk and took yet a third, though smaller, envelope Gifford held out to him.

'You can open that now,' Gifford said with an amused smile. Clark withdrew a small, leather-bound book. It was musty with age and its covering boards were loose. 'I'm sorry we couldn't get a better copy, but you've the better of the two we need.'

Curiously Clark opened the book. A frontispiece showed an extraordinary engraving full of allegorical symbolism, in which the obscure imagery seemed to flood down from heaven to earth. The title page bore the even more confusing legend: *Dr Ruddick's Dissertation upon the Holy Trinity.* There was a subtitle which began: *In which Dr Joshua Ruddick extrapolates from Holy Scripture* ... Clark read no further. He looked up at Gifford.

'I presume this is the key to a code, rather

than a joke?' he said.

Gifford nodded. 'Look inside the back cover.' Clark did as he was bid and found a sheet of ricepaper which, when unfolded, showed two columns of words. On the left a list culled, he guessed, from the pages of the inestimable Dr Ruddick's thesis, on the right the Admiralty's reinterpretation. Thus 'Almighty' was rendered by 'Their Lordships', 'cypher' into 'iceberg' and 'Holy' into 'North'. Clark ran his finger down the page to find what corresponded with 'South', only to find that it had no relationship with sanctity: 'Manifold,' he read.

'We anticipate a need to send you an occasional signal. No doubt the tactical situation will demand it. The method we shall use is simple. You will receive a numerical group for each word. We chose the book not only for its obscurity, but because it contains only ninety-six pages of text – there are, incidentally, some marvellously curious engravings, several of which are missing – anyway, each numerical group will consist of five figures.

'The first two figures gives you the page number, one to ninety-six; the third and fourth the line number, one to thirty-six; the last figure the word number on that line. This will not exceed ten, so for the tenth we will transmit a zero. It's obvious if you have the book. I doubt Jerry will find it in time, even if he scours every bookshop in Berlin.'

'The Nazis have been rather efficient at burning books,' Clark said ruminatively, digesting Gifford's cypher and flicking through the little volume.

'I think I might be persuaded to chuck this one on the fire,' Gifford said with a chuckle, 'but clearly the good Dr Ruddick has a value in the Divine Plan, though not one he could have imagined.'

'Oh, I don't know, sir,' Clark said, regarding an extraordinary image of *God's Bounteous Munificence Raining down upon Mankind*, 'he seems to possess a remarkable imagination.'

'Well, that may be so, but d'you think you can manage?'

Clark looked up. 'Oh yes, certainly, sir.'

'And how's the ship?'

Clark gave a short laugh. 'We've had our tribulations, but she's shaping up well, as is her company.'

'Frobisher all right?'

'Yes, he seems a good man. Get's a bit edgy when he considers his position surrounded by we amateurs,' Clark added ironically.

Gifford laughed. 'And the Norwegians?'

'Olsen's first class, no doubt about that. Storheill knows his job, but of course I find it a little more difficult to get inside his skin. Intuition's not so reliable as with your own kith.'

272

'No, of course not. What about the ratings?'

'Oh, predictably we've a couple whose
departure must have delighted their first
lieutenants, but I'm happy enough with
them.'

'I hear your trials went well.'

'Well enough, sir, but I'm afraid I only
regard them as a preliminary to a decent
work-up in Arctic conditions...'

'Quite right, quite right.' Gifford drained
his glass and shook his head when Clark
offered him another.

'I'm trying to loosen your tongue, sir,'
Clark said with a grin, 'so that you'll tell me
the latest about our friend, which is,' Clark
looked down at the sheet of ricepaper, 'I
notice, called "conjured"...'

'A noun made perfect,' Gifford joked, 'to
dwell amongst us.' He paused. 'Well, we are
pretty certain that *Orca* went north at the
same time as *Tirpitz*. You won't know it, but
the *Tirpitz* is now in Norwegian waters...'

'I did know, sir. Admiral Tovey told me. I
presume that is why the Home Fleet is at
sea.'

Gifford nodded. 'Well then, you appreciate
the sense it makes from the German point
of view to form a formidably heavy squadron
in Norway to intercept and destroy our
Russian convoys. In addition to the *Tirpitz*
we know that the *Admiral Scheer* is already in

273

Norwegian waters, but what you may not have heard is that, to our eternal shame, the *Gneisenau, Scharnhorst* and *Prinz Eugen* with a screen of destroyers and torpedo boats got out of Brest and ran up the Channel under our noses. They're back home virtually unmolested...'

'Good God!'

'Yes, it was a piss-poor show. The PM's furious and awkward questions are being asked. They may have suffered some damage, but we are not yet certain. Their ultimate destination is, however, probably Norway, and that would add a political dimension to Operation TREE-TOP. Although this wouldn't essentially alter anything as far as you're concerned, the potential inherent in either one or, God forbid, both of these powerful battlecruisers augmenting an already powerful battle squadron in Norway – with which *Orca* would cooperate fully – only compounds *our* difficulties.'

'Yes, that's pretty clear.'

'The main thing is that, at the moment, we have a slender advantage in timing. With the Home Fleet at sea, we can maintain this advantage for a while at least. You are ready to sail and we know *Orca* has been delayed due to some technical difficulties. Naturally we don't have details but we do know this is only a short delay, to be measured in days rather than weeks. I'm fairly confident in my own mind that that is why *Tirpitz* was, at the last report, no further north than Trondheim.' Gifford's knowing expression indicated Kurt as the source of much of this information and its consequent reliability.

'I understand,' Clark said.

'Right then, we need to get you north as quickly as possible. As we speak PQ12 is on its way from Loch Ewe to Reykjavík, where she'll pick up her ocean escort. As I say, the Home Fleet is in support, so you are to sail immediately. You are notionally one of a group of British and Norwegian anti-submarine whalers assigned to beef up the anti-submarine defences of PQ12,' Gifford referred to a sheet of paper. 'In addition to *Sheba*, the *Shera*, *Shusa*, *Stefa*, *Sulla* and *Svega* are all ordered to the rendezvous with PQ12 to the north of Iceland. Several will be instructed not to join, but will be recalled and told to turn back. You will be one of them. Naturally you will disobey this order.'

'Naturally,' Clark responded ironically.

Gifford smiled. 'The difference between you and Nelson is that we *expect* you to disobey.'

'Well, history expected Nelson to disobey, sir,' replied Clark with a grin.

'That's true,' Gifford smiled. 'Anyway, you shall go first to Seidisfjord, where you will top up your fuel. You will then appear to be one of the "missing" escorts.'

'So you think it unlikely that *Orca*, with or without *Tirpitz*, will sortie against PQ12, sir?'

Gifford shrugged. 'We can't be certain. It's possible that *Tirpitz* may, but I don't think *Orca* will attack from the south. She is being saved for a *coup de main*. The Germans are not likely to go all out until they are ready. It's inconceivable that they will expose *Tirpitz* to the Home Fleet; they'll wait until they reinforce her with the *Scheer* and at least one battlecruiser from Brest. Then, with a fast and powerful battle squadron, they will be a real threat which *will* interdict our convoys. Don't forget what they did to *Glorious* here-abouts in 1940. My guess is they'll wait to inflict a real humiliation on us which will have a tremendous impact upon our relations with both Joe Stalin and the Americans. If you could see the effect this bloody Channel dash by the Jerries is having in the Admiralty, let alone Downing Street or the country in general, you'd realise that this is a pretty bloody awful time for us. Frankly it's been a real fuck-up.' Gifford expelled air, as though releasing more then the pressure in his lungs. 'No, there will be other Russian convoys.' He paused again. 'Look,' he went on after a moment, 'the important thing is that you are directed to attack *Orca*, and only *Orca*. You are not to get mixed up in

276

anything else. That's clear, I hope?'

'Perfectly.'

'Good. Well, so much for the general strategy. I can't tell you much about *Orca*'s tactical approach beyond pointing out the obvious to you. Your orders will tell you that we've been using the fjords on the ice-free west coast of Spitsbergen as a rendezvous. We've been locating a fleet oiler in either Horn Sound, Bell Sound or Green Bay, so *Orca* won't be seen on that coast. There are two German weather observing stations further north, and we've plans to deal with them when the Arctic spring comes, but the risk of our aircraft spotting *Orca* is too great for him. My guess is that he'll poke himself up, depending upon the ice conditions, in the locality of Hope Island, to the eastward of Spitsbergen's South Cape...'

'Yes, that was my conclusion.'

'It's obvious, as these things so often are, for the options are limited.' Gifford regarded the younger man. 'Now do you have any questions?'

Clark shook his head, then remembered his manners. 'Oh, only to ask if you would like something to eat, sir?'

Gifford shook his head. 'No thanks. I've an aeroplane standing by to take me back to Northolt. Besides, I must let you get away.'

'I'm at two hours notice.'

'Good. Word will be passed to the boom

defence when I report to the Admiral,' Gifford said briskly. 'Now, we've a few personal details to tie up...'

'Yes, I've the men's wills here...'

They concluded their business and stood up. Gifford turned to pick up his briefcase.

'Oh, I almost forgot. This comes with my personal compliments.' Gifford pointed to a cylindrical brown-paper parcel tied up with sisal string.

'What is it?' Clark asked.

'A surprise,' Gifford said smiling. 'But you might find it useful.' Clark's curiosity was swept aside as Gifford held out his hand, his face suddenly serious as he looked directly into Clark's eyes. 'I don't underestimate the risks, Commander Clark, nor the danger of your enterprise. I've been very frank with you, which, with your peculiar involvement in this matter, was only fair. You'd better let Frobisher know all the details, in case anything happens to you, and brief the rest – officers and men – as you see fit.' Gifford paused, then added, 'I can only wish you luck, my dear chap. It's a pathetically thin convention, but no less sincere.'

Gifford's handshake was firm and Clark felt touched by the captain's concern. 'That's very decent of you, sir.'

'We'll have dinner in London when you get back. You'll report personally to me, of course. Nothing in writing.'

'Of course.'

Gifford pulled a Burberry raincoat over his dark suit and picked up the bowler hat. They stepped out on to the windy deck. It was already almost dark. He saw Gifford down to the waiting boat, wondering what the men in the boat and those on his own deck made of the visitor. Should he tell his crew anything yet, or wait until he opened his orders? That would be after they had refuelled in Seidisfjord on the east coast of Iceland. It would be time enough.

The midshipman in the boat gave an order and turned his wheel. The bowman bore off and then he and the sternsheetsman went through their formal ritual with their boat-hooks. He saw Gifford turn his face upwards and wave. He waved back as the boat faded into the gloom, its pale wake trailing out astern of it.

'Pass word for the first lieutenant, I'll be in the wheelhouse,' he said.

They slipped through the boom three hours later. It was a raw night, with a fresh, south-westerly breeze and a lot of cloud as they headed for the passage between Hoy and Swona. By midnight they had doubled Tor Ness and had laid a course for Iceland. Somewhere to the north-west of them the eighteen laden freighters – a mixture of British, Russian and American-owned,

279

Panamanian-flagged merchantmen – headed for Reykjavík with a local escort of anti-submarine trawlers. From Iceland a cruiser, destroyers and the whalers would take over the convoy's protection. Somewhere to the north were Tovey and the Home Fleet, operating in support of convoy PQ12, anxious to bring the *Tirpitz* to battle and avenge the humiliation of – what was it Gifford had called it? – the Channel dash.

Such was the scale of these Arctic operations.

Clark went below to his cabin. Gifford had left him two letters and the cylindrical parcel. He opened the last and found himself holding a German naval ensign.

'Good heavens!' With a slight feeling of distaste he held up the woollen bunting. He stared at it a moment, then he carefully folded the Nazi colours and wrapped its own tackline round it as he had been taught as a cadet on HMS *Conway*. Next he opened his mail. There was a short letter from his father expressing disappointment that they had not met during his brief leave. Such were the vicissitudes of war, his father had written, that there would not be many such occasions. Nevertheless he wished his son well. Clark, tired at the end of a long day, imagined his father had some inkling that his present posting might be special and seemed

280

to detect some such hint in the wording of Captain Clark's letter. But it was speculation, merely the manifestation of a wish that his father, owing to his connections with Sir Desmond Cranbrooke and the Ministry of War Transport, might glean some insight into his mission. The fatuous hope arose from a desire that somehow the import of his plight would reach Magda, if only to touch her conscience.

He picked up the second letter and knew the handwriting instantly. He had seen it many times before, the small, neat and legible hand of Jenny O' Neil. He opened it with a sinking heart. He had no idea of its contents, of course, but he did not want to read of Jenny's undying devotion to him, did not want to break her heart which, in his conceit, he nevertheless rightly guessed she had lost to him. Any effusion of passion would, he thought, make him feel slightly foolish. He was already beginning to regret their affair as an embarrassment. He recognised the unworthiness of the thought, but that did not stop it rising unbidden in his consciousness. With some relief at Jenny's brevity, he unfolded the single sheet. *Dear Jack*, he read,

I miss you but I know you can't respond and I will leave it at that. I will be glad to see you when you come on leave next

281

time. The house is very lonely now, worse than it was before you came here. It would be all right but I am late and think we have made a baby. I don't want to worry you but you should know. I don't expect you to marry me or anything silly. I will have to lose my job when it becomes obvious.

Yours sincerely,
Jenny

It was the misplaced formality of the *Yours sincerely*, that struck him first. Then the tragic stupidity of the letter's true message took its visceral grip on him and he sat back in the uncomfortable upright chair.

'Oh fuck,' he murmured. 'Oh Magda, you bitch...! Look what I have done ... Poor, poor Jenny ... Oh, fuck, fuck, fuck...'

HMS *Sheba* entered Seidisfjord on a day of blustery weather in early March. The high sides of the fjord were scarred by snow and the black gashes of rock where the gradient was too precipitous for the snow to lie. On the narrow areas of coastal plain a few farmhouses were scattered. Several bore swastikas, a fact which outraged Pearson, who assumed the devices to be evidence of German sympathisers.

'Think, Derek,' Clark pointed out with an utterly uncompromising tone to his voice as they stared through their glasses at the crooked crosses. 'Their country has been pre-emptively occupied, first by we British and now we've handed the job over to the Yanks. I don't suppose the natives feel terribly bloody pleased.'

He was grimly sensitive to cause and effect, utterly heartless towards Pearson and his silly verbalising.

'That doesn't mean they have to be so obviously unfriendly.'

Clark was about to shut Pearson up with a savagery that would have been both unkind and unfair, when Storheill emerged on to the little bridge wing and prepared to take another set of compass bearings as they steamed towards the distant oiler.

'Ah, but what you do not know, Derek,' reproved Storheill, 'is that the swastika is not an emblem only for the Nazis. In our Nordic culture it is a good luck sign.'

'Huh, that's no reason to paint it on your walls,' Pearson persisted.

'It has some such significance in India too,' Clark added, mastering himself and trying to be reasonable and didactic in a commanding-officer-like way, 'and at home I've a copy of Rudyard Kipling's *Just So Stories* with a swastika decoration on the spine.' He might have added, *and a bloody great Kraut ensign in my cabin*, but he held his tongue. There was no need to unbend that far!

'Oh, why don't I keep my big mouth shut?' Pearson said.

'Is that a rhetorical question?' Frobisher asked, coming out to join them as a patch of sudden sunlight lit up the peak above them, drawing their eyes upwards in mute wonder. 'My God, what a pitiless landscape,' he said, half to himself.

'You wait until you get into the high Arctic,' Clark said. He could only look forward now. There was no point in looking back, but he resented the fact that Jenny's predicament spoiled his return to high latitudes. It was not her fault and he held only himself to blame. He had sunk to Magda's level, he thought, unless the war fucked all of them up, one way or another.

'Oiler's in sight, sir,' Storeheill reported and Clark swung his glasses ahead to where the dark shape of the tanker lay at anchor in the fjord with a destroyer alongside her. He was glad of the necessity to concentrate on the business of bringing his ship alongside the auxiliary. Not even his conscience could reprove him for giving that matter his priority. Gladly he relinquished his private misery for his duty.

'Very well, call her up and request twenty-two tons of boiler oil.'

'Ver' good, sir,' said Storeheill. 'Signalman!'

'And Pilot ... Pass word that this is the last opportunity for mail.'

They would not lie alongside the oiler for more than an hour and a half. It was just time enough for him to write a letter. Half an hour later he sat, pen in hand, wondering what he could say. Then, at last, he began a letter to Magda. For twenty minutes he scribbled the reproachful words, making several alterations until Frobisher knocked on his cabin door.

'The chief troll says we'll be finished in five minutes, sir.'

Clark was in no mood for Frobisher's joke. 'You'll get caught one day, Number One. All right, get someone to collect the mail. I've some too.'

'It's already done. There are only seven letters to go and the men seem to have caught your drift about keeping their mouths shut. Pearson's censoring the stuff. Leading Seaman Lambert is the only exception, I understand...'

'All right, Number One. I don't really want to know what Leading Seaman Lambert is up to, if you don't mind. Give me a moment or two.'

'I'll be back then.'

Hurriedly Clark shoved the letter to Magda to one side and drew another sheet of paper towards him. Thank God *he* did not have to submit his letters to Pearson's scrutiny. The resentment of married ratings roused by the compulsion of doing so to a man of Pearson's youth and inexperience was perfectly understandable. He drove the thought out of his head. He could prevaricate no longer: despite the fact that she said she expected no response from him, he *must* consider Jenny's plight.

He sighed; there was nothing to consider; he had no choice. If he was still alive after this task, he could only do the decent thing; if not he must see she and the unborn child were provided for. *Dear Jenny*, he replied to her, bending the truth for the sake of its impact on its reader,

> I received your letter just before sailing, so I only have a few minutes. I cannot say much more than to tell you not to worry. You may be wrong, but if not you must go to my father and explain to him when the time comes. Show him this letter. Be brave. He will understand.

Clark paused, feeling foolish, trapped, unable to offer her more than this cold comfort. It would be a lie to say he wanted her again. Perhaps if she were here, pushing her eager body with its plump roundness against him, he would, but she was not here, and in her distance lay more than mere mileage. He did not want to think of it; he had no time to think of it. War denied him even the indulgence of feeling sorry for himself. He was in a hurry. But he must give her some sign of their shared intimacy, particularly if a child, his child, was quickening in her womb.

Oh, Christ! he thought with a half-blasphemous savagery, why had God linked so trivial a thing as sex with so serious a matter as the making of human lives? Why could He not have ordered things differently? Why was nothing in life uncomplicated by something else? Why did he have to write this fucking letter in a hurry with Frobisher breathing down his neck? Why did he have to receive hers just when he was sailing on this mission? Why did Jenny have to conceive at all? Why by him? Why did he have to bump into her that night? Why did the fucking Germans have to bomb Liverpool? And why, oh why must he tell her a lie?

You are too sweet to be lost to me, Darling Jenny, he wrote, and pausing at the thought that his father, too, must draw some conclusions from the tone of this letter, he concluded: *With all my love, Jack*.

And then he hurriedly folded and sealed the letter before he had second thoughts, putting his name and rank on the reverse of the envelope. Picking up his hat and duffel coat, he turned off the low desk lamp and hurried out in search of the first lieutenant. Frobisher was in the wheelhouse.

'One more for the post,' he said lightly, handing over the envelope. 'Now let's get this show on the road,' he added, bending over the chart table and the black hachured outline of Seidisfjord. He had difficulty in concentrating, in seeing Storheill's pencilled line indicating their outward track.

'You all right, sir?' He looked up. Pearson was staring at him. Clark straightened up.

'I was looking for swastikas on the chart, Sub,' he said with brittle frivolity, pleased with Pearson's uncomprehending facial expression.

'Old Man's a bit battle-weary, if you ask me,' Pearson said to Frobisher later, when they met over cocoa in the wardroom just after midnight.

'Fortunately, Derek, I'm not asking you,' Frobisher said.

'I don't know why you have to be so bloody mean, Number One,' Pearson burst out.

'Because I am bloody mean, Derek. That's why I'm here.' The first lieutenant crossed one long leg over the other, lifted his mug but paused before putting it to his lips. 'Now tell me, why precisely are *you* here?'

Sub-Lieutenant Derek Pearson slammed his mug down and went to his cabin.

By this time the *Sheba* had long since cleared Seidisfjord and dropped Glettinganes over the port quarter. As they drew away from the land they felt the first manifestation of a low swell.

'Wind from the sou'west, Captain,' Storheill remarked, looking up at the dark sky. 'And the glass is dropping.'

'Yes. We're going to have a blow,' said Clark. Going below, Clark took up the envelope containing his secret orders. They had left their last contact with civilisation and, although a few miles below the 66th Parallel of latitude, he felt justified in opening them. Besides, he would not sleep without having something to think about other than Jenny and her unborn child.

An hour later he went back up to the bridge and ordered an alteration of course to due north. He had been given a series of positions as far as Spitsbergen's South Cape by which to make his passage, and at some point he had to cross the track of convoy PQ12. Thus, as the convoy swung round to an increasingly eastern heading to transit the Barents Sea, HMS *Sheba* would be to the north of it. The alteration of course brought the swell and the rising sea further round on to the port quarter. *Sheba* reacted accordingly, beginning to roll uncomfortably as she headed for Jan Mayen Island. The men of the duty watch were hunkered down at their cruising stations and he could just see the lookouts looming darkly out on either bridge wing. In the wheelhouse the chart spread out on the chart table was faintly lit, as was the compass, behind which the glim fell upon the hands of the helmsman as he passed the

289

wheel spokes back and forth. Forward, silhouetted against the glass of the windows, Storheill's wrapped-up form bulked, while the eerie, questing ping-ing-ing of the Asdic reached out into the cold waters of the Atlantic.

HMS *Sheba*, Lieutenant Commander John Clark, was at sea on special service. Then he reproached himself for being a fool! Such silly pride was asking for trouble and he was in trouble enough already. He left orders to keep a sharp eye open for the convoy and for German reconnaissance aircraft.

'Of course, Captain,' Storheill said, turning from the window.

'Let me know if and when you see anything of the convoy, and call me at any time if in any doubt whatsoever.'

'Yes, sir.'

He felt a trifle foolish telling an experienced watchkeeping officer like Storheill how to suck eggs. But then he felt bloody foolish anyway.

'Good night, Pilot,' he said.

'I hope I don't have to call you again, sir,' Storheill said.

'So do I.'

Clark took one last look about him then went below. He would brief Frobisher in the morning.

Clark was called at half past three. He had

been asleep for an hour. The screech of the voice pipe beside his pillow dragged him from a deep slumber, but he was awake instantly, his heart hammering.

'Captain, sir. Signal from Admiralty.'

'I'll be up.' He threw off the bedding, swung his legs over the leeboard of the bunk, dragged on his doeskin trousers and thrust his already stockinged feet into his leather sea boots. Pulling on a white polo-necked sweater, he made for the bridge ladder. *Sheba's* motion was a good deal livelier than when he had turned in. Storheill handed him the chit.

Clark read it. The order was for him to turn south for Loch Ewe. It took a moment for him to recall his instructions. He handed the message back to Storheill. 'Put it in the signals log, Pilot, but take no further action.'

'No alteration of course, sir?'

'No alteration of course.' Clark watched the Norwegian as he studied first the message and then his commanding officer. 'Stand on,' Clark said. 'This is to make the enemy think we have been ordered back to Scotland.'

'Do we acknowledge it, sir?'

'No. We simply stand on.'

'Ver' good, Captain.'

Clark wanted to say more, but decided this was not the moment. The man at the wheel would have overheard the exchange and by breakfast time the ship would be buzzing with the little mystery.

'Would you like a cuppa kye, sir?' Storheill asked.

'No, thank you. I'll go and get some more shut-eye.'

Back in his bunk Clark lay staring at the deckhead and waited for sleep to claim him. But the manner of his rousing had wakened him fully and it seemed he would never drop off. In his irritation he thought of Magda and the pale perfection of her long-limbed and lovely body, the smell of her hair, the hollows of her neck and the feel of her breasts under his hands. Tumescent, he turned over and drove himself into the mattress with a groan of fury. But then he was lying with Jenny, soft, biddable, running-to-fat Jenny with her pleasant, trusting face, glad to be acknowledged as desirable by dashing Jack Clark, the boss's son.

And she was, Yours sincerely, making a baby for him.

DISTANT GUNFIRE

March–April 1942

A steam ship, unlike a diesel-powered motor vessel, moves through the sea with remarkably little noise. That was why they heard the engine noise of the aeroplane while it was still some way away and above the clouds. The *Sheba* was running north with a heavy following sea as the wind increased relentlessly to gale force, with every prospect of it getting worse before long. Late that morning they had seen the convoy, a faint smudge of smoke and the jagged outline of the rearmost ships on the horizon. Clark had turned them away to the westwards. The last thing he wanted was an inquisitive destroyer rushing towards them flashing her Aldis.

'What about their radar, sir?' Pearson had asked.

'I just hope that there's enough sea clutter to obscure us at this range.'

Apparently there was; but the aeroplane was a different matter. At noon the noise of its engines grew louder and the starboard lookout caught a glimpse of it: 'Heading straight for us, sir!'

'Action stations, sir?' Pearson called from the wheelhouse as Clark strained to see what he guessed was a large, four-engined Focke Wulf 200.

'Yes! No, belay that! Keep her on course!'

Clark dashed for the ladder, bumping into Storheill as he came up to relieve Pearson. 'A bloody Condor,' he explained as he disappeared below. A moment later he was back.

'He's circling, sir!' Pearson said excitedly.

'Here,' Clark said, 'hoist this!' he shoved the Nazi ensign into Pearson's hands. 'Get on with it man!' Clark raised himself so that the men on duty could hear him. 'Look pleased to see him, you lot!' he shouted. 'Leave your guns fore and aft! Hide your caps and give him a wave if he comes low!'

'Captain!' Clark turned. Storheill stood in the doorway. 'In the German navy the captain has a white cap.' He was holding a soft white summer cap cover. 'Give me your cap, sir.'

'There the bugger is! Green thirty and coming in low!' bawled the starboard lookout, pointing.

Clark passed his cap to Storheill and turned back to the starboard bridge wing, jostling the lookout in the confined space. The big German reconnaissance aircraft was at no more than one hundred feet, the roar of her engines rapidly rising as she flew at them. In a minute that might have been his last and would have saved him from Jenny, Clark waved enthusiastically. Beside him the lookout did the same. It was Ordinary Seaman Peacock.

'Well done, Peacock,' Clark shouted, because he felt unable to remain silent as the noise reached its crescendo, resenting the racket and perceiving silence as submission. They saw faces in flying helmets staring from the cockpit of the bullet-nosed machine, then the monstrous thing had swept past and was climbing and banking.

'He'll be back!' Clark roared, turning fore and aft, and repeating the words. He was right. Pulling out to a distance of about half a mile, the Condor began to circle them. 'Oh, Christ, he's signalling, sir,' Pearson called from the port wing.

'Here, sir.' Storheill held out Clark's hat with its unseasonal white cover. Clark put it on. Then Storheill picked up the Aldis and began flashing at the Condor. Clark did not interrupt but contented himself with observing the 'received' flash from the cockpit of the Condor as she circled them and listening to the clatter of the signal lamp's shutter as Storheill operated the lamp. Then Storheill had finished and there was a rapid series of dots and dashes from the Condor in

response. A moment later the aircraft banked sharply and overflew them again.

'Wave, you bastards!' Clark roared, now
decked out in his white cap.

The Condor roared overhead, then it
climbed and banked round towards the east,
to disappear into the clouds. Clark saw it
three times; each time it grew smaller, and
each time it was still heading east.

After a moment the relaxation was palpable.

'Dear me!' said Ordinary Seaman Peacock.

'What the hell was all that about?' asked
Frobisher, rubbing the sleep from his eyes.

'A bloody great Focke Wulf Condor,
Number One!' explained Pearson.

'Oh, is that all?'

'He nearly took the mast trucks out of her,
actually, Number One,' said Clark, turning
to Storheill. 'What on earth did you send to
him, Pilot?'

'I said: "Weather Trawler on passage north
maintaining radio silence British convoy to
north-east. Heil Hitler!" '

'He didn't ask our name, then?' Clark
queried.

'Yes, that was what he wanted to know. He
replied: "Convoy seen and reported. What
ship?" '

'I sent "Good Hunting Heil Hitler" and he
seemed content.'

'Well, he'll soon find out there are no

weather trawlers out here, so we'd better be ready for him when he comes back,' Clark said. 'And thanks for remembering the hat.'

'Bit of luck, Captain. I had just washed my cap cover,' Storheill said with a grin. 'I would not have thought about it otherwise.'

'He's transmitting, sir!' The wireless-telegraphist called from the wireless office at the rear of the wheelhouse.

'I'll go and see...' Storheill disappeared, reappearing a few minutes later. 'He's reporting the convoy, sir. Then came a coded message that I couldn't understand.'

Clark nodded. 'Right. I didn't know you spoke German.'

'I speak it very badly, Captain, but I read it. Before the war I used to admire German literature.'

'Well, well.' In his conceit it had never occurred to Clark that the Admiralty had provided a second German speaker beside himself. 'Thank you anyway, that was well done.' Storheill looked embarrassed. 'But I think he will be back,' Clark added. 'Let us alter course thirty degrees to port.'

But the Condor never returned. Instead, a gale enveloped them just as, forty miles away, it overran convoy PQ12. The *Sheba* rolled and scended, her decks awash with green water, and conditions below became chaotic. Despite their best endeavours, water got into the mess decks, flushing out from obscure corners even more detritus from the Smith's Dock Company yard which they long ago thought they had scoured from the ship.

By the second day of the gale it was blowing a Force 10, with huge waves humping up astern, threatening to poop them as their curling crests were torn off and driven to leeward with the violence of birdshot. But *Sheba's* round cruiser stern rose to each wall of water and she drove forward until the great sea had passed under her and, her bow pointing at the sky, she slid down its receding back into the trough hollowing out in advance of the next comber.

And to this longitudinal oscillation she added a slow, lateral roll that drove her shoulders into the seas ahead, foaming up into the torpedo-tube apertures with a curious, unfamiliar booming sound that took them some time to locate.

Clark and Storheill managed to get an ex-meridian sight at noon. They had passed the 70th Parallel and Clark altered their course to the north-east. Daylight was now appreciably longer than when they had left Scapa Flow. Full darkness fell for only a few hours and the temperature in the wind chill had fallen well below freezing. The spray froze on the ship's upperworks and *Sheba's* roll slowed still further as her top-weight increased. Now they ran into ice. Loose, small floes began to appear, along with those small bergs known as bergy bits. At first it caused them few problems but the next day they were adjusting course and speed to avoid damaging collisions. Twice they struck growlers before Clark put the ship about and hove-to. The ice moderated the violence of the sea, but the wind-strength was now storm force and the only way to avoid damage to the ship was to dodge about, head to wind and sea.

Hove-to, the *Sheba* made hardly any headway, just enough to keep steerage way on her. At daylight all hands were called to clear the ice off the upperworks. Steam hoses were rigged, while fire axes, a handful of shovels, spikes and seamen's knives hacked at the fateful accretion as the men skidded about on the wet decks; dark, muffled and desperate figures, Clark thought, wiping the condensation from the windows as he watched them from the comparative comfort of the wheelhouse.

'What a bugger,' remarked Frobisher, the officer of the watch. Jammed in the corner of the wheelhouse he sipped at his kye.

'God knows what effect this is having on the convoy,' Clark remarked. But both men could guess. 'We'll go on to double watches, Number One, at least until this lot blows over. You and Pearson, Storheill and myself.'

'Aye, aye, sir.'

'We'll make some easting by keeping the wind on the starboard bow, but we don't want to get too far south.' Clark crossed to the aneroid barometer and stared at it for a moment. 'Well, it's risen a touch. Perhaps we've seen the worst of it...'

And so it proved. Six hours later they had turned downwind again and increased speed. As they resumed their passage, the officers reverted to their watches, though the weather remained thick and squally. In the icy drizzle that alternated with snow Clark was almost constantly on the bridge. *Sheba* was still in loose ice as he sought to drive her north-eastwards towards the South Cape of Spitsbergen along the limit of the ice pack. Jan Mayen was already many miles astern while far ahead on the starboard bow lay Bear Island.

They were not to know then, but they had been lucky. One of the other whalers, the *Shera*, while catching up with the convoy from Iceland, had accrued so much ice that she had capsized in the bad weather. Only three of her crew were rescued by their sister ship, the *Svega*. The convoy had suffered too. Apart from the disruptive influence of the ice, which caused problems in station-keeping for the columns of merchant ships, several of them straggled, while the destroyer *Oribi* had had her bows badly damaged and two men swept from her iron deck.

That was not the end of the affair, upon which the *Sheba* was a peripheral bit-player. On the following evening the shout of the wireless operator alerted Frobisher, the officer of the watch, to a plain-language distress message. It was transmitted in English, though the idiom suggested a foreign operator, for the desperate plea spoke of being 'gunned'.

Called to the bridge, Clark could only guess at the cause of the problem.

'I got a bearing, sir,' the wireless-telegraphist, a man named Hills, called out.

'Going to his assistance, sir?' Frobisher asked, half way to the chart table to lay off a course.

'No,' Clark said. He could hear Gifford's injunction not, under any circumstances, to be diverted. 'No, that is not what we are here for.'

A moment's silence followed this and then they buried their awkwardness in wild speculation. From now on intermittent radio intercepts suggested convoy PQ12 was under attack.

This was inaccurate. PQ12 had come close to disaster, but she had avoided being intercepted. Although the *Tirpitz* and her attending destroyers were indeed at sea and it was one of the latter that had gunned the straggling freighter *Ijora*, this Russian ship had not been part of PQ12. In fact she had been part of the west-bound return convoy of empty ships codenamed QP8.

A deadly game of almost-blind man's bluff was going on, an inconclusive action in which both of the convoys evaded the *Tirpitz* and she in turn escaped the Home Fleet. Later, Hills heard part of a transmission from Admiral Tovey, who, as the weather frustrated his operations, had broken radio silence.

'I *think*,' said Hills as Clark hung in the doorway of his cuddy, 'the C-in-C's having trouble with his communications. I get the impression that he's asking the Admiralty to take direct operational control of something...'

'Good God!'

Whatever the source of Hills' speculation, Clark was to recall those words years later. In fact, far to the south-west a tense drama was being played out as, between the two convoys drawing apart on their respective passages, Tovey sought to nail the *Tirpitz* with torpedo bombers from his carrier, HMS *Victorious*. But so slow were the Albacore aircraft, flying into an easterly wind, and so fast was the retreating *Tirpitz* and her single escorting destroyer, that the latters' advantage in speed was a mere 30 knots! Despite gallantly pressing their attack, the Albacores failed to score any hits and several were lost. The German capital ship vanished into the Vestfjord, heading for Narvik.

Clark's orders were now to take him and his ship out of the immediate theatre of these operations. Having made his passage, he was now to await the news that would initiate the secret British counter-stroke to Berlin's own critical operation.

That night, however, following his abrupt order not to go to the assistance of the *Ijora*, he called all his officers up to the wheelhouse at 2000 at the change of watch. As he waited for them, standing at the forward windows alongside Frobisher, they heard Pearson's voice. Frobisher sighed audibly.

'It's a bloody outrage!' Pearson was protesting as he led Storheill and Olsen into the wheelhouse.

'What is, Derek?' Clark asked wearily.

'I heard on the BBC Home Service, sir, an announcement that a large and valuable convoy – a *large and valuable convoy*, mark you, sir – was on its way to Russia! I think *that's* a bloody outrage.'

Clark looked at Frobisher, who shrugged. '*C' est la guerre*, sir,' he said obscurely.

Clark coughed and called out to the wireless-telegraphists, just then changing watch themselves, that they too should come and listen to what he was going to say. He would be repeating it shortly to the ratings below. 'I shall only detain you a few moments, gentlemen, but you may have heard that we have not diverted to the assistance of a merchant ship when she was under attack. It is time to tell you the objective of the special service upon which we are engaged. We are to seek out and destroy a large, super U-boat – a submarine cruiser, in fact – which will shortly arrive in the Arctic with a view to attacking our Russian convoys from the north.

'Accordingly we shall be making some adjustments to the ship and carrying out exercises designed to simulate various scenarios in the next few days. That is all.'

He looked round the faces. Only Frobisher still stared forward as *Sheba* steamed east through the loose pack.

'Starboard twenty,' the first lieutenant said, dodging a large growler which lay wallowing almost awash athwart their passage.

Then Pearson came forward to relieve Frobisher as Storheill, remarking on the news to Olsen in Norwegian, went below to his bunk, leaving his fellow countryman to inspect his boilers and engine.

Clark turned forward. Beyond the *Sheba's* high bow, with the four-inch gun on its platform, the Barents Sea was dark grey-blue, dotted with grey-white ice floes and bergy bits until it faded into the mist. With an almost biblical suddenness the visibility lifted, transforming the vista. The horizon, from being a milky obscurity three or four miles ahead, was now a sharp line perhaps thirty miles away. Above it a mirage lifted and distorted the fantastic shapes of distant icebergs. Closer to, the bergy bits sparkled, their odd shapes iridescent in the brilliant sunshine, the shadowed surfaces cobalt blue and emerald green in an astonishing transformation that drew an exclamation from Frobisher.

'Good grief.'

Clark smiled as Frobisher turned to Pearson, standing ready to relieve him of the watch. White glaucous gulls wheeled about and a dark cluster of little auks dotted a passing floe of old and hummocked ice. 'That's even shut you up, Derek.'

'Thank you, Number One,' Pearson said in a low voice, adding wistfully, 'What a pity we have to be at war...'

'Yes,' said Frobisher as awed as his more impressionable younger colleague, 'but then I don't suppose we'd be here otherwise.'

'No, that's true,' Pearson responded.

'How pleasant to hear you two agreeing,' Clark said pointedly. It was the first time Clark had heard the two men in accord.

Frobisher quickly changed the subject. 'The adjustments to the ship, sir. I presume you mean to paint her white?'

'Yes, that's quite right.'

'That means we could be up here some time.'

Clark shrugged. 'It's possible, certainly; but it would be foolish to bank on it. Hand over to Derek and let's have a look at the chart.' Clark left Frobisher to pass over the details of course and speed to Pearson and, going to the chart table, drew out Admiralty chart No2751. It showed the Svalbard Archipelago, better – though incorrectly – known as Spitsbergen, of which Vest Spitsbergen was but the largest and most accessible island. Drawing a sheet of folded foolscap from his breast pocket, Clark began to manipulate parallel rules, dividers and a soft-leaded pencil. He had been working for only a few moments when Frobisher joined him.

Clark stopped what he was doing and drew back so that the first lieutenant could see the chart. Just above its southern margin lay Bear Island, Bjønøya; 120 miles further north lay the South Cape of Vest Spitsbergen, actually an offshoot of the main island. Along the west coast, which trended northwards, lay the deep indentations of Horn Sound, Bell Sound and Icefjord. Running to the north-north-eastwards from the South Cape, the east coast of Vest Spitsbergen had no such inlets and off it lay two large islands named after early navigators in these remote waters, the Englishman, Edge, and the Dutchman, Barents. The strait between them was called the Storfjord; to the north of Barents Island the coast swung north-north-west, bordering the Hindlopen Strait, on the far side of which lay North East Land, an island under permafrost and from which fell the largest glacier in Europe. All round the coasts of the two large and two smaller islands, scores of lesser isles and smaller archipelagos were dotted. Clark laid his right index finger on the largest and most isolated of these, which lay to the south-east of Edge Island and on roughly the same parallel of latitude as the South Cape.

'Hopen,' he said, 'or Hope Island to you, Number One; or even Sea Horse Island, for that's what Worsley used to call it, though I understand it was named by a whaling master from Hull called Marmaduke, after his ship, the *Hopewell*. Anyway, that is where we shall make for and from where we will start our search. We are unlikely to get anywhere near the place, though if we are up here for three or four months the ice will retreat...'

'Three or four months!' Frobisher exclaimed with such astonishment that both Pearson and the man at the wheel turned and regarded them. 'I beg pardon...' he mumbled, embarrassed.

'Number One,' Clark said in a low voice, 'I have absolutely no idea how long we will be here. We may be in action tomorrow ... It may be many, many weeks ... I simply don't know. The point is that we *must* be on station before this super U-boat gets here.'

'I understand, sir.' Frobisher was contrite; the serious, professional naval officer again. For a few moments the two of them regarded Hope Island, a narrow strip of table land about one thousand feet high. Next to its name was the parenthetic abbreviation: *PA* – position approximate. Frobisher sighed. Clark might have been happy in this never-never land, but it made him uneasy and he sensed Frobisher knew it and it amused him. Frobisher looked up and stared out of the wheelhouse windows at the broken ice that strewed the sea about them as far as the eye could see. It was warm in the wheelhouse, almost too warm, and Frobisher wondered for an irrational moment if the windows were not a cinema screen and what he thought he could see beyond merely an illusion. Perhaps he felt touched by a presentiment, but Clark recalled him shuddering. Even as Frobisher drew Clark's gaze from the representational chart, with its clearly defined lines, to the bleak beauty of the reality of high latitudes, Pearson dropped *Sheba's* speed and altered course to pass clear of a huge, slowly wheeling ice floe. The deck canted slightly as the handy little ship heeled to her helm.

'Got to keep the Asdic dome in mind, sir,' Pearson said, seeing the ship's two senior officers looking up from the chart table as if reproaching him for the disturbance to their equilibrium.

'Absolutely imperative, Derek,' Clark said approvingly. 'Knock that off and we're wasting our time.'

'We're not going to do much ice-breaking then,' Frobisher remarked.

'No, but tomorrow, when we have made enough easting, we will drive north into the pack as far as we can. I'll take over from you at 0800. You can then start painting the ship. The sooner that's done the better.'

'That should be fun.'

Clark gave a short laugh. 'Perhaps. Anyway, let's make it so. Divide the ship into quarters, everything except the masts and funnel. Each watch to have one quarter with the officers doing the fourth.' Seeing Frobisher's eyes widen at his suggested impropriety, Clark added, 'It will be good for all of us.'

'Well, who'll keep watch, sir?'

'I will, but I want a pot of paint and a ladder.'

'Why?'

'Because I'll do the funnel.'

'We haven't a ladder long enough, we'll have to rig a bosun's chair...'

'No, we only want the lower part painted. The upper parts of the ship should remain grey. Something called interchange, Number

One. Think about it.' Clark gave Frobisher a knowing smile. 'All right then. Now, be a good chap and let me get on with this.' He indicated the chart. 'You go and have a word with Mr Cook.'

Clark bent to resume his interrupted task. Over the cartographic image he began to draw in a grid, based on the list of latitudes and longitudes extracted from his secret orders. The squares thus constructed were each identified by two letters and these were to be used by the Admiralty or by Clark to indicate position, should it become necessary. Such a position would be transmitted at the end of any message to which its relevance would be obvious, Clark had read. As he worked, he wondered if he would ever send the single word that meant 'success' as encoded from the estimable Dr Ruddick's dissertation upon the Holy Trinity. The word's equivalent was 'forbearance'. Clark wondered whether that was sheer coincidence, or official irony.

IN LIMBO

March–June 1942

Clark entered the wheelhouse and, having wiped his hands on a wad of cotton waste and jammed it back into the pocket of his boiler suit, picked up a heavy pair of Barr and Stroud binoculars. Clicking the medium-grade shades down, he went out on to the bridge wing and carefully scanned the horizon to the south. The sun sparkled on ice and water alike, though a bank of cloud was building in the west and would, he judged, have spread over most of the sky by the evening. There was not another thing in sight, at least nothing hostile, for just then, in one of the long leads of open water to the south he saw the faint blur of a whale spouting, followed by a glimpse of black back as it sounded.

'Bowhead or minke?' he queried to himself. Then it was gone and, with a tingle of private exhilaration, he began a systematic search of the circle of the visible horizon. To the north the ice stretched away as far as he could see, packed closer and closer, until it formed an unbroken field, unfractured by any leads. He walked back into the wheel-house, put the glasses back in the plywood box provided for their stowage and was about to resume painting, when a figure loomed in the door to the wireless office.

'Nothing at the last transmission time, sir,' reported Barrington, the senior operator. He was a serious, bespectacled young man, whose hair was neatly plastered down on either side of a centre parting.

Clark looked briefly at his watch. Barring-ton had had to break off his duties with a paintbrush to monitor the frequency allotted to them by the Admiralty. At six-hourly intervals, *Sheba's* operators listened for fif-teen minutes for any vital message from London.

If Clark had thought the code derived from Dr Ruddick's *Dissertation* smacked of Bull-dog Drummond or the pages of John Buchan, his secret instructions dispelled any notion of amateurishness. Along with the list of positions from which Clark had earlier constructed the graticule of his locational grid had come other appended documents. One tabulated all wireless trans-mission and listening times, the frequencies to be guarded and those to be used for messages, along with several coded call signs

312

which implemented the odd but secure device of utilising the theological meanderings of an eccentric, eighteenth-century cleric. It was these that translated into the routines for Barrington and his colleagues.

'We'll hear soon enough,' Clark said, sensing Barrington's reluctance to take off his headphones and resume the unfamiliar task of painting.

'Yes, I expect so, sir.'

'What were you doing before the war, Barrington?' Clark asked, certain that such practical tasks as he was now compelled to undertake were rather outside Barrington's experience.

'I was, er, teaching at a girls' school, sir.'

'Oh!' Clark raised his eyebrows. 'This'll be rather a contrast then,' he said with a smile, vaguely gesturing about the wheelhouse.

'It is, rather,' said Barrington.

'And before that?'

'Oh, Cambridge, sir...'

'Reading what?'

'Classics, sir.'

'And you graduated?'

Barrington nodded. 'A first, sir.'

'My congratulations. You know you've been recommended for a commission, don't you?'

'I do, but do you know I've turned it down, sir?' There was a hint of hesitation before the monosyllable of subservient, if traditional, respect.

'I didn't, but may I ask why?'

'I have no desire to be an officer.'

'Why? Are you afraid of the responsibility, or do you have a political motive?'

'Would it matter either way?'

'No,' Clark replied, 'not to me. But I'd be interested to know – personally, that is.'

Barrington lowered his eyes and cleared his throat. 'May I ask what you did before the war, sir? I know you're not a regular officer,' he added.

'I was the chief officer in cargo liners hauling what we called general cargo from Britain and Europe to the Far East and back.'

'Ah, I had heard you'd been in the Arctic before, sir. I thought you might have been a scientific officer engaged in research, or something similar, given the special nature of this mission of ours.'

'I've been in high latitudes before, yes, but not since I was younger than you are. Do you not consider it a suitable employment?' Clark asked, with a hint of irritation at the superior attitude of the younger man.

'Not at all. Good deal more useful than cramming the heads of young women with the works of Tacitus and Homer.'

'So, why don't you want to become an officer?'

'It's not political, sir. Not in the sense that

you mean. It's just that I really have no feeling for other people. I don't want to be set above the men. I mean, I don't want to be responsible for them or their actions. I don't mind being responsible for procedures and so on...'

Clark registered the concern of the young man. The matter was clearly preoccupying Barrington and had nothing to do with snobbery. 'So, you don't mind turning-to and doing a bit of painting then?' Clark asked with a smile.

'No, not at all. It's just that I've been a bit worried about ... well...'

'Well, forget it, Barrington. All I am truly interested in is your present role as my senior wireless operator.'

'Oh, well, that's fine, sir,' said Barrington brightening. 'You, er, you didn't mind my raising the matter, sir? Only, with the ship a bit disrupted at the moment, it seemed like a good opportunity.'

'Of course not,' Clark said, then an idea occurred to him. 'By the way, have you got any classics texts with you, on board?'

Barrington nodded. 'I've Caesar's *Gallic Wars*, the *History* of Herodotus and the *Annals* of Tacitus.'

'Good. Could you work up say four or five short lectures, either about the works, or what they contain – you know, perhaps a talk about Caesar's campaign against the Belgae, or something. I want to keep the men's minds occupied during what might turn out to be several weeks' wait up here? Could you do that?'

'Well, I, er...' Barrington considered the matter a moment, and then smiled and nodded. 'Yes. Yes I could.'

'And if there are any other glittering alumni on the lower deck, perhaps you'd let me know?'

'Would you give us a talk on the Arctic, sir?'

'Why not? Not that I'm a real expert, you understand.' Clark nodded with satisfaction. 'Well, I suppose we'd both better get back to work, or the first lieutenant will start shouting at us...'

Frobisher had discovered that it was almost impossible to break up the ship into equal areas and to run an inter-watch competition as Clark had originally suggested. Instead he announced the painting of the ship as 'job-and-finish', a task which, once embarked upon, had to be completed. It was not, he emphasised in briefing the ship's company, being undertaken from a maintenance point of view, but from a cosmetic one, designed to break up their shape, to produce a trick on the eye of any observer. 'What a German submarine commander is not expecting to see, he won't see, and for as long as he doesn't see us, he gives us the

316

advantage. Until we open fire, that is, by which time we should be on top of him, catching him with his *lederhosen* round his ankles,' Frobisher concluded.

And so they had begun that morning, wiping the accretions of salt off the ship's steelwork and slopping on a coat of mixed undercoat and gloss, which covered imperfectly, but well enough for their purposes. On the foredeck, Frobisher, as adjudicator of this inter-watch marathon, mixed the paint, quoting the witches from Macbeth and periodically emitting wild and manic laughter. Then he wandered about the deck topping up the paint kettles of the three gangs as they splattered the mixtures over every vertical surface, exhorting them to greater efforts.

The *Sheba* lay against a substantial ice floe, two mooring ropes secured to boat anchors driven into the ice so that the Red Watch could paint almost from the waterline upwards on the port side with comparative ease standing on the floe. The Blue Watch had some grounds for grumbling about the difficulties on the starboard side. Here, a smaller floe had been dragged alongside under the bow to provide a platform for the men painting forward. The rest of the side was painted from the starboard boat, lowered into the water for the purpose. Meanwhile, the White Watch grumbled about the comparative awkwardness of the deckhouse and fittings, claiming they had by far the worst of the job.

Aware of the wild fluctuations in the morale of the ship's company, Frobisher waited until the hands broke off for some sandwiches and then announced that the main brace would be spliced on completion of the job, which encouraged men to move on from their original allotted areas so that, at about one o'clock the following morning, almost the entire crew were at work on the upper deck, a crowd of zombies enjoying the midnight twilight in a mood of mild, good-natured madness. During the labours of the day someone had begun to compose what in due course was christened 'The Ode of the Shebans', in which all the varied strains of the *Sheba's* disparate cultural origins came together:

'Twas on the good ship *Sheba*,
By Christ you should have seen her,
Grey as a rug,
In a dockside snug,
With a crew of wild Hyperboreeners.

Sent north to seas polar and icy,
Oh, Jesus Christ all-bloody-mighty,
They were given a gun
To frighten the Hun,
But found only sun that shone nightly.

The skipper said, 'Chaps, we'll paint her
all white
To lurk in the ice and pretend we can't
fight,
'Til the whites of their eyes
Stand out in surprise,
As we totally turn them to shite.

There were more verses of doubtful scansion
and more dubious propriety that accompanied the rum issue and sent the tired officers
and ratings to their bunks and hammocks in
a state of mild intoxication. Clark had few
misgivings, the task was done and the
relaxation of naval discipline would do them
all good if, as he suspected, they were to
have several weeks of crushing boredom. He
stayed on the bridge all night himself, the
conclusion of the work fitting in well with
the Admiralty's transmission times so that
even the wireless operators could have a
short break. For five hours Clark was utterly
alone. From the bowels of the ship, up
through the engine-room skylight, came the
occasional clang as the duty fireman tended
the banked boilers. Olsen and his men had,
like the cook and steward, been exempt from
the labours of the day, for food and fire were
essential in these high latitudes.

As for a sudden appearance of *Orca*, Clark
considered the matter so unlikely that the

risk of exposure didn't outweigh the advantage of having the ship camouflaged. Moreover, Clark's secret orders assured him that he would 'almost certainly receive at least one warning' of the enemy's approach. This would be derived, it was implied, from a source within the *Seekriegsleitung*, the German Supreme Naval Staff. As he considered these matters, his thoughts turned once more to Kurt: Kurt in the lonely peril of his position in Berlin. Clark assumed that he was still there, able to pass on sensitive information to the British. But supposing Kurt had been transferred and sent to sea? Did that explain the dearth of information flowing out to them up here in the Arctic? And how did Kurt process information? Did he have a code as bizarre as the *Dissertation* of Dr Ruddick? Or was there a shadowy middleman, a nominally neutral Swiss or Swedish diplomat, perhaps? And what of the core of the matter, the enemy's super submarine, codenamed *Orca*? Clark wondered whether Kurt had exaggerated the threat posed by her or, if he had not, whether his pipsqueak ship would be adequate enough to counter that threat He began to agonise over the outcome, aware that the corrosive effect of his anxiety could overwhelm him.

He could only do his best, he consoled himself, but that was not enough, he argued, certainly not enough to withstand any inquiry instituted by Their Lordships! He switched his thoughts off *Orca* and Kurt, only to find them bounce back to his second obsession, Magda. Her image had, with increasing frequency, floated unsummoned into his mind's eye: Magda of the beauteous face and wide, red mouth; Madga of the luscious breasts and long, elegant legs; Magda of the smooth arms and eager hips; Magda of the delicate panting sighs and of the ultimate, consummating acceptance. And then the reality of Jenny, of her mild expression of incredulity, her slight grunt-ings, of her passionate explosions and of his withering withdrawal that came with post-coital sadness and regret.

And none of it was relevant to the small hours of that long, white night when his only duty was to keep his ship safe from surprise, when his nearest, most implacable enemy was the enclosing ice. But the pack was melting as the Arctic midsummer approach-ed. Day by day they moved slowly north-wards, pushing up towards Hope Island. Why could he not learn to enjoy the mo-ment, the pure moment of remote privilege? Was he not leader of his crew of, as they put it, 'wild Hyperboreeners'?

At 0600 he went below and called out the cook, steward and the duty wireless opera-tor.

'Never been called out by the captain

before, sir,' remarked the three-badged, regular cook.

'You've never been tied up to an ice floe either, Cookie,' he said. 'Be a good fellow and call Ordinary Seaman Oliphant when you've made some tea and tell him to report to the bridge.'

'Aye, aye, sir.'

Oliphant turned up twenty minutes later, bringing Clark a cup of tea. Clark gave him orders to call out the crew and resume normal watches from 0800.

'Very good, sir. By the way, sir, Barrington said you were looking for lecturers.'

'Yes. Got something in mind?'

'Well, only if anyone might be interested in architecture.'

Clark shrugged. 'I don't see why not.'

'I could always call it something else, sir, "how to build a house". Might come in useful after the war if Jerry demolishes much more. I was hoping to go into town planning, sir.'

'Brilliant, Oliphant, quite brilliant...'

And that is how they started their period in limbo, or – as Clark remembered it afterwards – their prelude to hell. Innocently, when they were detached enough from the reality of war to enjoy themselves. The sun did not always shine, for fog plagued them intermittently, once for ten long days at a stretch. At the end of March they endured several days hove-to, the ship's head hauled round to the south-west, head to wind, dodging the heaviest floes as a gale sent a surge of swell among the pack and the air was filled with ice spicules that blew off the surface of the pack. They gleaned from intercepted radio transmissions that a Russia-bound convoy had been scattered by the heavy weather and that several ships had been sunk. The SOS signals were piteous and there were confused indications of an action between a cruiser and destroyers, but there was nothing they could do and these distant indicators only heightened their sense of being remote.

But the gale, as well as scattering what was actually convoy PQ13, also broke up the cohesion of the pack ice, which, with the slow but inexorable warming of the Arctic air, was drifting slowly south as March gave way to April. Clark began a series of training exercises in this looser – but heavier – pack, focusing on the judicious use of the Asdic and acclimatising Carter, Wilkins and Baker to the background responses of ice and, on three memorable occasions, of whales. As the ice drifted south in the aftermath of the gale, fog wafted about them again, often that low form of 'sea smoke' that made the sea appear to be about to boil, where the ship's deck was engulfed in wraiths of water vapour, above which the mastheads were in clear air.

In such conditions they found the cold, damp air far worse than the dry cold experienced previously, even though it was several degrees warmer, if the thermometer was to be believed. They were almost entirely unaware that, far to the south, convoy PQ14 had been broken up by the ice and most of it had returned to Iceland, joining the homeward-bound QP10.

During May, as Russia-bound convoys PQ15 and 16, with their returning counterparts QP11 and 12, fought their way east and west through the Barents Sea miles to the south of HMS *Sheba*, the whaler was honing her skills in the gradually dispersing ice to the south-west of Hope Island. Frobisher carried out dummy firings of the torpedo tubes and Pearson was permitted a few practice rounds from his precious four-inch gun. Whatever the private preoccupations of their commander, most of the hands agreed they had got a good number. Opportunists like Harding thought they were on a fool's errand and Their Lordships had 'fucked-up'. Not that he was complaining, he explained to his messmates, he was all for a 'soft billet' and a 'cushy war', because, mark his words, there were 'plenty of bastards at home having a cushier time getting their legs over other blokes' wives while seeing if they'd like some nylons'.

The only thing worse than 'having one's bint poked by a black-marketeer', Harding assured his appalled audience, 'was having her screwed by an RAF officer'. 'Those bastards,' Harding stated with unequivocating certitude, 'were no more heroic than anyone else in the fighting services, and, bugger me, they get home every fucking night! And where d'you think home is, mates? In some poor sod's bed, that's where!' Such assertions were usually concluded by a general instruction to 'bugger the Brylcreme boys', a pleasing alliteration that seemed to satisfy Harding's sensibilities, even if it did unnerve one or two of the older, married men.

'It ain't the Brylcreme I worry about,' Able Seaman Collins admitted quietly one evening, 'but those bastards peddling nylons and chocolates – well, they take some beating for cheek, an' no bleeding mistake.'

These unpleasantly disturbing considerations were displaced only in part by the better-intentioned lectures of Oliphant and Barrington. Frobisher spiced things up by giving lessons in unarmed combat, in which he and Able Seaman Saunders demonstrated a disturbing ability, while Clark's talks on the Arctic were received with a respectful interest.

'Fucking ship's like a bleeding uni-fucking-versity,' remarked Harding with that dismissive tautology so beloved by certain denizens of the seamen's mess. 'It's just fucking propaganda to divert your fucking minds from what's really fucking happening back home while we're stuck aboard this fucking heap of crap.'

Sometimes such a diatribe was countered with a rendering of the 'Ode of the Shebans', to which additional verses were added as time passed. Pearson was immortalised, along with a mention of a polar bear too obscene for publication. On the other hand, Able Seaman Saunders, with his ability to disarm the lanky first lieutenant armed with a bayonet, was said to have out-hugged a male bear, only to get his comeuppance when required to perform, in its place, the dead animal's marital duty.

Indeed, they might have supposed that the war in the Arctic had died away. For almost the whole of June they heard nothing, not knowing that the Home Fleet had been called upon to provide much of its strength to Operation HARPOON, a major effort to resupply Malta in the distant Mediterranean. But June was not entirely uneventful, for early in the month Pearson, on watch one morning, spotted huge footprints on a large ice floe and, about half an hour later, spotted a large male polar bear heaving itself out of the water on to an ice floe. Thereafter they saw several of the magnificent white mammals – including a mother with two cubs –

but none came near the ship and their closest neighbours were several species of seals, guillemots, auks, kittiwakes, fulmars and the voracious glaucous gulls.

Their latitude had been increasing as they slowly made their way north and east, stemming the polar current as it drove the breaking ice down from the Arctic Ocean. Just as the last vestiges of the warm Gulf Stream, known as the Norwegian Atlantic Stream, washed the west coast of Vest Spitsbergen, so the counter-current of cold water drained out of the Arctic basin, eventually sinking beneath the remnant Gulf Stream somewhere to the north of Bear Island. On midsummer day they came within sight of Hope Island. The flat table land was dark under its mantle of snow, a narrow strip of rock rising out of the sea and surrounded by ice. Clark and Storheill took sights and laid off bearings in an attempt to ascertain its exact position. 'So that we might achieve something concrete while we are up here,' Clark remarked as he and the Norwegian officer bent over the chart.

It was at that moment that they heard the engine noise. Both men looked at each other for a split second, then made for the bridge wing. At the same moment the lookout shouted, 'Aircraft, green one five zero!'

Clark raised the glasses and stared out over the starboard quarter. 'Low down, sir!' the lookout said, pointing urgently. 'Just above that greenish-blue berg...'

'I see it, sir!' Storheill exclaimed.

'Got it!' responded Clark.

'Condor!' said Storheill.

For several tense minutes they watched as it flew east, all thinking the same thing: was it searching for them?

'What is your opinion, Pilot?' Clark asked as it droned away, out of sight.

'He's going along the edge of the heavy pack. He's not looking for us.'

'No, I agree.'

'But why exactly?'

'Because he wants to know, or somebody in Norway–' Clark was about to say *or Berlin*, but he bit the words off in time – 'wants to know for operational reasons.'

'Ja, that's right, Captain. Maybe our time is coming.'

'Maybe it is, Pilot, maybe it is.'

'It is good, for Fridtjof is worrying about fuel.'

'Yes, I know.'

Clark went back to the chart table, his heart thumping. He worked out an estimate of the aircraft's distance from them and the probable ice limit of the heavy pack ice. It was possible that the Condor was reconnoitring for *Orca*. The submarine would operate on the surface as much as possible and, just like themselves, the fringes of the

328

pack would provide her with the best cover. But, unlike themselves, she would not need to conceal herself from anyone other than the convoy – or so she would assume – which would have cruiser cover and therefore a measure of air reconnaissance from the cruisers' Walrus amphibian aeroplanes. But she would not wish to tuck herself so far away that she could not strike at the convoy. Perhaps her commander would have as many anxieties as himself, Clark thought consolingly with a smile. Taking up a soft lead pencil from the rack, he drew a line approximating the limit of the heavy pack. Storheill stood beside him and he explained his reasoning.

'I think you are correct, Captain,' Storheill said.

'So, somewhere along here we may well find our quarry.'

'Yes, but when?'

'That is a question I cannot answer. I only wish I could.'

'Was it von Clausewitz who said, In war the simple becomes quickly complicated?' Storheill asked.

'I've no idea, Pilot,' Clark said, putting the pencil back in the rack, 'but it certainly sounds as if he ought to have done.'

ALARM!

June 1942

Immediately after the sighting of the Focke Wulf Condor, Clark had warned Barrington to be especially alert as they monitored the Northern Zone frequencies. He was certain the Admiralty would soon transmit some information, if only as a wake-up call, for there must have been some anxiety in London, or at least Clark hoped so, even if it was only on Gifford's part. If Olsen was growing concerned about the run-down of fuel, so should Gifford, for all their long-range tanks. Sooner or later, if things dragged on much longer, they would have to steam to Bell Sound and refuel from a fleet oiler. But that ran the twin risk of their being off-station at the critical moment or attracting the attention of German reconnaissance aircraft like that damned Condor!

He had also closed the ship up to defence stations, placing the ship's company on a higher state of alert than hitherto. The change in tension was palpable and he found himself worrying about minor details, like the discharge of the ship's garbage.

'It must go in the water, Number One,' he insisted. 'I don't want it chucked on to passing floes where it could conceivably attract notice.'

Clark began to appreciate the virtues of those old sea officers of Nelson's day who had remained on blockade duty outside the great French naval arsenals for months, even years, at a time, irrespective of the weather and with no thought of their personal lives whatsoever.

Two days later, still having heard nothing from the Admiralty, they suffered a minor breakdown. It was nothing much, Olsen informed the bridge, and would take about an hour to fix. Clark, having seen the *Sheba* drift safely against a large, flat adjacent floe, returned to his cabin and a book. Half an hour later Frobisher appeared in his cabin doorway.

'Excuse me, sir. I've just come down from the bridge. They've had word from the engine room that Olsen's going to be another half an hour. Apparently it's taken longer than expected.'

'Blast it!'

'Look, the ship's safe enough nudged up to this big floe. D'you mind if I let the men have a kickabout on the ice? I'll run some moorings out.'

Clark stood, stretched and peered out through his cabin port. 'If they think they can play football on that, good luck to them,' he said, yawning dismissively.

'You don't mind then?'

'No, do 'em good.'

When Frobisher had gone, Clark stared for a while longer at the expanse of ice visible from his port. It was a big floe and the area immediately alongside was flat enough. About a hundred feet away it hummocked up. Rafts of old ice had obviously impacted during previous years and the whole lot had frozen into one amalgamated mass. A watery sunshine played across the ice, brighter patches alternating with the grey cloud shadows. It was not the Arctic at its best, Clark concluded and returned to his book. Shortly afterwards he dozed off to sleep.

He woke suddenly, his heart thumping with premonition. For a moment he looked down at the book, as though it was the source of his alarm, then at his watch, for the hour for the Admiralty's transmission was approaching. Then he heard the shouts and laughter of the men and the thump of a football on the ship's side somewhere below him.

'Here, Charlie, pass it to me...'

'Hey, Spud...!'

'Oh, you tosser, Charlie...!'

And then a cheer as the ball hit the side of the ship again. Someone had scored a goal against the shell plating.

Shaking his head and thinking himself a fool, or even a tosser like Charlie, Clark rose to his feet and, rubbing his eyes, went and pressed his forehead against the damp cold of the armoured port glass. His cabin was too hot, that was why he had dozed off. The other goal was directly abeam, on the edge of the rafted ice, made up of two piles of duffel coats. Harding was keeper there and immediately below him he could see the back of Barrington's head as he guarded the goal against the ship's side. The rest of the men were dodging about in midfield, skidding on the ice, slipping and sliding, happy as the boys they had all once been, mucking about in a park. Somewhere, heaven knows where, they had acquired a real football and, as this spun into view, it immediately provoked a fiercely contested tackle in which two men collided, one of whom was left tumbling on the ice. Clark could see him roll over and nurse a knee. He was swearing.

'Lincoln, you bollocky bastard, I'll get you for that!'

'Get back in defence, you little bugger,' Harding was roaring as the tussle round the ball moved towards him. 'You've no fucking business playing forward!'

Clark chuckled, then, looking down at

Barrington again, thought of the next monitoring period. He frowned, thinking Barrington should have been on watch and then wondered who was manning the wireless office. Perhaps he should go on the bridge. He rubbed his eyes. He ought to clean his teeth first, after falling asleep. Having once sailed with a master who suffered from the most appalling halitosis, he hated the thought of exhaling foul breath over anyone. He took one final paternal look at the lads as they contested Harding's goalmouth.

And then Clark saw the bear. 'Shit!' he exclaimed, cannoning out through his door and making for the wheelhouse companionway.

Frobisher had the watch and he turned from the rail where he had been leaning, watching the football game. 'What on earth...?'

'Stand clear!' snarled Clark as, eyes blazing intently, he cocked the rifle he had snatched from the small arms rack at the rear of the wheelhouse, steadied it against the Hotchkiss mounting and took aim.

Frobisher spun round, staring over the heads of the footballers. Then, just as the Lee Enfield bellowed in his ear, he saw the bear. It must have been watching and stalking the men for some time, for it was almost on top of Harding. At the moment Clark fired, it reared up, though whether in agony at the impact of the bullet or in preparation for striking Harding, they would never know.

What happened precisely in the next few seconds was afterwards the subject of wild speculation. From the bridge wing Frobisher and Clark saw the huge bear rear up and turn away, saw it land heavily on all fours and run off, hidden a moment later behind the hummocked ice on the far side of the floe. Clark reloaded and stood ready, his heart thundering in his breast, his breathing laboured. He was roused to a pitch of concentration after the exertion of his extraordinary dash up the companionway and his seizure of the rifle. Only two minutes earlier he had been slumped in his chair, dozing stupidly over his book.

While Clark watched for any further sign of the bear, Frobisher's attention was drawn to the men. Up until the point of the rifle fire, the footballers had been utterly oblivious of the presence of the polar bear. They had all been concentrating on the half-serious, half-amusing scrap for possession of the leather ball, a dozen men in grunting concentration. The goalkeeping Harding had been dancing from one foot to the other, sliding occasionally as he strove to keep his balance, his woolly-mittened hands held out in anticipation of catching the ball as the opposing team booted it for the net. The heavy crack of the gun brought the game to an abrupt stop: the men straightened up and looked wildly about them, seeking the source of the explosion. The ball, escaping their kicking feet, rolled away inconsequentially as some saw Clark and Frobisher on the bridge wing, the gun smoking between them. Others saw the bear, some claiming they had heard it roar as it reared up, others that they saw the red of the wound, that the impact of the bullet had thrown the gigantic animal backwards. Others thought that preposterous, the bear had been too big, larger than they had ever imagined a polar bear could be.

Perhaps Barrington, as the unoccupied goalie, with his back to the ship's hull and already facing the other end of the extemporised field, had the best view. He was intent on what was happening, though not as much as the threatened Harding. Barrington thought he had shouted a warning even as the gun went off above his head, but he was quite certain that the bear had reared in order to strike down at Harding.

As for Harding himself, he scarcely knew what had happened. His first impression was confused. Aware of the tearing wind of the passing bullet, he bellowed with instinctive outrage, fearing the ball had flown past him. Then the smack of the rifle's discharge made him look up to see the two officers and, for

an outraged second, all the force of his class-
conscious hatred persuaded him that the
Old Man had gone mad and was trying to
shoot him. This seemed right, for the game
in front of him had stopped, and everyone
seemed to be staring at him. Had he been set
up? Were they all staring at him expecting
him to die? He was aware of his wavering
popularity, though he would not have attributed this to his bullying ways below decks,
only to the bad luck that had dogged him
since boyhood when his mother had died
and he had outgrown the last pair of shoes
she had saved for from the pay packet of his
drunken father. Now the bastards had
ganged up on him to have him shot! And the
fuckers were smiling now...

'You lucky sod, Harding!' someone shouted.

'Look behind you!'

After that split second of gross mispercep-
tion came another of uncertainty: he had
misjudged, as he had misjudged before. Just
when he felt his deep-rooted anger justified,
something happened to rob him of triumph.
They were not trying to kill him, it was a
joke. 'Look behind you!' was an echo of his
one childhood treat in a music hall on the
Caledonian Road. But some reflex deeper
than his self-centred and impulsive instinct
for suspicion, compelled him to spin round.
He saw the rump of the bear as it moved off

at a run and began to chase it.

'Stand fast, Harding!' Frobisher screeched from the bridge wing, but Harding had reached the first summit of the hummocked ice and saw the great animal slide, almost without a splash, into the dark water on the far side of the floe. A moment later he was flanked by the panting footballers, some muttering oaths and blasphemies, others silent as they watched the retreating bear. Then it was gone behind another nearby chunk of ice and they did not see it again. The tension broke. There was an explosion of relief, of more oaths, of backslapping on Harding's shoulders, of smiles and acclamation of Harding as 'a lucky sod'.

'The bastard nearly got you...'

'Yeah, it was right on top of you...'

'Who the fuck shot it?'

'The Jimmy, I reckon. That bastard'd shoot his mother!'

'Surprised he didn't run out an' give it a flying toe hold...' They chuckled companionably, recalling Frobisher's enviable brilliance at unarmed combat.

'It was right behind you, Harding, and much fucking bigger than you are!'

'Made a better goalie – you let two in, you bugger!'

Walking behind Harding as the crowd wandered slowly back towards the ship, Leading Seaman Roe got up on tiptoe, stretched his hands above his head, pulled a face and made what he thought was a polar bear noise. Round him the others laughed again. From the other end of the field Barrington came towards them, his face white behind the black circles of his spectacles.

'Seen a ghost, Barry-boy?' someone asked.

'Don't be silly,' Barrington replied with that stiff formality that separated him from almost every other rating on the ship. 'Are you all right, Stephen?'

Harding looked at the leading wireless operator. No one ever called him Stephen and he wondered if this toffee-nosed cunt was taking the mickey. Then he found he was shaking uncontrollably and the laughter and chaffing of his messmates was rather a long way off.

'Christ, he's passing out!'

'Well, I'll be buggered...'

'You might have been, after that bear had finished with Harding,' one wit persisted as Harding slumped on to the ice. They were organising Harding's recovery on to the fore-deck, when the first lieutenant's voice came down from the bridge wing.

'There are some duffel coats and a football out there, chaps. Somebody ought to go and get them.'

One or two of the men not actively engaged looked up, then turned and stared back over their football pitch. The surface of the ice floe was wet with little pools of melt-water, marred by skid marks and the furrow-ings of their game, yet it was inhospitable and they shuddered at the prospect of returning across the few yards that separated them and the two piles of coats that were no longer goal markers, but cairns in the Arctic wilderness. They might have been a hundred miles away.

'Go on, Roe. You and Wiggins go and re-cover that gear. I'll keep you covered,' Fro-bisher added with a grin, holding up the rifle.

Clark had handed him the gun a few minutes earlier as the men had gathered round Harding. 'Here,' he had said, 'you take this!'

Somewhat surprised and thinking Clark was suffering from some nervous reaction, Frobisher took the heavy weapon and watch-ed Clark disappear into the wheelhouse. 'Well, well,' Frobisher muttered to himself, returning his attention to the footballers.

Then Clark was beside him again, a pair of Barr and Stroud binoculars clamped to his eyes. 'There he goes,' Frobisher heard him mutter, but on looking up he could see noth-ing moving on the ice, only the inexorable closure of the lead lying to leeward of them as the windage of *Sheba's* hull pushed the ice floe against which they lay to the north-east.

Clark watched the polar bear until its swimming head was just one more indistinguishable white speck among all the others. He was seized by an overwhelming sadness that it had to be him who fired a shot in anger, and that it had been at nothing more hostile than a polar bear. True, the polar bear would have killed one of his crew, but it was they who were the alien invaders. Clark sighed and lowered the glasses.

'I don't know if I winged him, poor thing, but he's not dead yet.'

'He was a bloody monstrous animal,' Frobisher said. 'He must have been ten or twelve feet tall; twice the height of Harding, and he's no dwarf.'

'Yes, he was an adult male, I think. They're usually wily and reluctant to take risks. Perhaps he was old and hungry, not having had much luck with seals lately.'

Frobisher watched Roe and Wiggins pick up the duffel coats and hurry back to the ship, throwing glances over their shoulders. He smiled. Beside him Clark sighed again.

'You all right, sir?'

Clark nodded. 'Yes, I'm all right, but I'd rather be shooting at Jerry than a magnificent specimen like that.'

'Didn't you shoot them when you were here before?'

Clark shook his head. 'No. Other members of the expedition did. They killed a female and kept the cub, but I could never bring myself to do it, perhaps because I was never threatened by one like that before. Mind you, they are bloody dangerous. One swipe of a paw will take your face off...'

'Might have improved Harding,' Frobisher joked.

'That's not funny ... I expect,' Clark went on, thinking of the polar bear's acute olfactory nerves, 'that that big feller could smell the men and found them irresistible.'

'That's not funny either, sir,' Frobisher riposted.

'*Touché*, Number One...'

'Sir?'

Both officers turned. Humphries, the junior wireless operator, was standing in the wheelhouse doorway holding out a signal chit. It lifted in the light breeze.

'Signal from the Admiralty, I think sir. Repeated by Reykjavík. It's in code, sir.'

Clark took the signal chit and saw the groups of numerals. Just then the telephone from the engine room rang. Holding the signal, Clark lifted the handset. A moment later he put it back on the hook. Seeing Frobisher's inquisitive expression, he said, 'It never rains but it pours. That was Olsen. He wants another half an hour. I'll go and decipher this.' Clark waved the signal and made for the companionway. Frobisher exchanged glances with Humphries.

'Looks like a change in the weather,' Frobisher said enigmatically.

In his cabin Clark took Dr Ruddick's *Dissertation* from among his books and, drawing a sheet of foolscap writing paper towards him, took up a pencil and began work. He instantly recognised the Admiralty's coded identification and *Sheba's* call sign for June, a group of five letters preceding the first numeric cluster. This was a date and time group and it was followed by the text of the message. He opened the *Dissertation*. The terse words of the brief text grew across the page. When he had finished he sat back and stared at his completed transcription. Blowing his cheeks out and then exhaling the air he read it through again:

ADMIRALTY TO *SHEBA* 26/1900 GMT BATTLESHIP POCKET BATTLESHIP CRUISER CRUISER NORTH NORWAY GALE WARNING ENDS

And that was it! No reference to *Orca* whatsoever. What was he to make of it? He settled down and read it again. The excitement of the incident with the polar bear had knocked his judgement. Gifford was not a fool and Clark was certain that it had been Captain

Gifford who had drafted the signal, that was the whole point of a book-based cipher.

Firstly, of course, this was an alarm call, the preliminary contact transmitted to alert them to further traffic. Clark was forbidden to acknowledge receipt of it, but so be it. Next it told him that he was not forgotten, an important factor as he was, as Gifford had doubtless calculated for himself, growing concerned for his oil reserves. Then, though there was no direct reference to *Orca*, there was a precise assessment of a German concentration of heavy ships in northern Norway. A battleship, clearly the *Tirpitz*, a pocket battleship, the *Admiral von Scheer*, and two cruisers, the *Hipper* and one other, perhaps the *Prinz Eugen*, he supposed – incorrectly as it happened. Supported by U-boats and aircraft, such a battle squadron could fall upon the next Russia-bound convoy and destroy it, with or without the help of the nebulous *Orca*. But then there were those last two words: *Gale Warning*. Did they refer to the battle squadron, the passage of the next Allied convoy, or to *Orca*?

He had no idea and consulted the appendices to his orders. The only possible reference to anything associated with such a phoney meteorological report was a short list of definitions. These were for the adjectives *imminent*, *soon* and *later*, words customarily prefixing gale warnings and signifying the probable time of its onslaught. They referred to timescales: *imminent* meant within the next six hours; *soon* signified six to twelve hours and *later* indicated a time beyond that. Clark was puzzled. Was the message *just* a warning? A signal that something was up, but that Gifford could not yet be specific?

Clark dismissed the idea that the words had any reference to a convoy. Gifford had sought to distance him from any direct association with any convoy. Clark reminded himself that his only task was the location and destruction of *Orca*. But that very thought alerted him to Gifford's probable thinking. There had been no wireless traffic up to that moment, so presumably there had been nothing to say specific to Clark's task. Yes, that was better, more logical; he felt intuitively comfortable with the notion, so Gifford had omitted a direct reference to *Orca*, because, at the moment of despatch, there was none. On the other hand there was a concentration of heavy ships and that alone was evidence that something was at the very least on the cards. And Clark thought as, the polar bear forgotten, the logic kicked in and his assumptions crystallised into 'facts', it argued that the enemy were waiting for *Orca* to reach her station and then for a convoy to come through the constricted alleyway of the Barents Sea.

Clark ran his finger down his list of 'translated' words. *Orca* was signified by the obscure word 'trimorphism'.

'God bless Dr Ruddick,' Clark murmured, putting his papers away and locking them securely in his safe. Then he sat stock still, hardly crediting the fact that he had forgotten the Condor.

Of course! The appearance of the aeroplane had been the stimulus for his 'intuition'! How could he be such a fool? The incident with the polar bear was hardly enough to warrant such a failure in his thought processes.

'Never mind,' he muttered to himself. 'It is the independent emphasis that I need.'

Satisfied and with a score of considerations now crowding into his mind, Clark again ascended the steep companion ladder to the wheelhouse. Back on the bridge he summoned Frobisher, and the two men leaned, heads together, over the chart table.

'We've had an alarm call from the Admiralty, Number One. Nothing much at the moment except that the Germans are concentrating heavy ships in north Norway. I think we can assume that means a sortie is being prepared.'

'That bloody Condor seems to suggest that to be the case, yes...'

'Exactly,' Clark said wryly.

'And our baby?'

Clark shook his head. 'It's my,' he was about to say *guess*, but that would weaken his case and belie his inner conviction. 'It's my assessment that even now our baby is on passage north, crossing the Barents Sea.' He looked up and raised his voice. 'Humphries!'

'Sir?' The young man's face peered at them from the wireless office. Tethered by his headphones, he lifted one to hear Clark.

'I want you to monitor the convoy frequencies carefully,' he said. 'We've heard nothing for some time but I anticipate another convoy coming through very soon. I want to know the minute you are aware of anything, all right?'

'Yessir.'

'Captain?' Olsen hauled himself wearily up the ladder and confronted Clark. He looked exhausted and his boiler suit was covered in oily grime.

'Oh, Fridtjof,' Clark said, then faltered, seeing the expression in Olsen's eyes. 'Are your engines still playing up?'

Olsen shook his head and managed a wan smile. 'No, Captain, we are all ready for your orders.'

'Oh, that's good. What was the trouble?'

'A blocked oil duct; a lot of shit, swarf and God knows what else. Bloody shipyard...'

'Bloody *British* shipyard you mean, eh?' Clark suggested with a sympathetic smile.

'Maybe,' Olsen conceded with a shrug.

347

'Anyway we can move when you want. Did I hear a story about an *isbjørn*?' he asked, one grey eyebrow raised.

'Yup,' Frobisher put in, 'and the captain shot it.'

'Have you got the skin?' Olsen asked, visibly brightening.

'No, sorry. Unfortunately the thing ran off. I don't even know if I hit it.'

'Oh, you hit it all right, sir. It nearly ate Leading Seaman Harding,' Frobisher explained to Olsen.

Olsen nodded. 'Pity about the skin,' he said, turning to return to the engine room. 'I'll ring stand by when I get below again,' he called over his shoulder.

'Gosh, I thought he was going to say we were stuck here for the bloody duration,' Frobisher said as Olsen disappeared.

'So did I,' Clark said. 'He looked at the end of his tether.'

'I agree, he didn't look good.'

'He certainly didn't look well ... You don't think he's ill?' Clark asked Frobisher and they exchanged glances.

'I'll have a word with Storheill.'

'Try and keep it subtle, Number One.'

Frobisher smiled. 'I'll do my best, sir.'

'Right, before we get under way, clear lower deck and muster the men on the foredeck.'

A moment later the telegraph jingled, the

engine-room pointer stopped on 'Stand by'. Clark answered it as Frobisher mustered the ship's company on the tannoy. A few minutes later they all stood shivering on the foredeck and Clark addressed them.

'Well, lads, we've just received a signal. I think we can assume things will be warming up from now on.'

'That's good news, sir,' someone called out.

'Quiet there,' Frobisher snapped.

'We'll go to action stations every time we change watches as a precaution,' Clark resumed. 'I want you to do it in your sleep and without a lot of noise. Noise can carry in these latitudes, and if we're hunting a U-boat on the surface I want us closed up very quickly. We'll use the tannoy, not the alarms, is that understood? If you see anyone lingering in their hammock, turn them out! That's all. Carry on, Number One.'

Later, on the bridge, Clark found himself yawning. 'What's the time?' he asked Pearson, who had taken over the watch two hours earlier.

'Ten, I mean 2200, sir,' Pearson said, shaking his head. 'I just can't get used to this constant daylight.'

'No, one just doesn't feel like sleeping, even when one ought to.' The sun rode above the horizon to the north, approaching the polar meridian. 'I suppose it doesn't help to be keeping the ship on GMT ... I say, sir, I'm jolly miffed that I missed seeing the bear. Unfortunately I had my head down for an hour.'

'So did I, Derek. I just happened to wake up and look out of my port. No idea why I did, but,' he shrugged, 'it was lucky for Harding.'

'So I heard.'

'Well, let's work the ship off this floe,' Clark said, reaching for the telegraph handle. 'And Derek, instruct the lookouts to keep ears and eyes open, for submarines in the ice and Condors flying over the stuff.'

'Aye, aye, sir,' said Pearson cheerfully.

How easily young men went to war, Clark thought as he tugged the telegraph handle back and forth, setting it on 'slow astern'.

THE ASSYRIANS

July 1942

Clark headed *Sheba* south-east, aiming to reach a position within the loose pack both east and slightly north of *Orca*'s assumed patrol line. This he would have to judge to a nicety, but he guessed his adversary would lay this patrol line just within the ice limit, hiding on the edge of the pack ice to conceal his submarine from Allied radar. He also guessed *Orca*'s conning tower would be painted white.

The ice field was opening up rapidly, the conditions improving day by day, and it was important that the little whaler did not work her way too far south, for she was already returning to the latitude of Hope Island, which she had crossed days earlier. The *Sheba* shoved her way through the pack, shouldering aside the grey and white ice, occasionally having to back off astern and work her way round the more obdurate

351

floes. Amid the relatively flat and hummocked rafts, bergy bits and the low, eroded growlers were an increasing number of large and distinctive bergs. These had been sculpted by erosion, melting and refreezing over a succession of summers and winters. They loomed fantastically out of the mist, assuming weird transformations as they slowly revolved or *Sheba* steamed past, so that it was possible to conceive out of their silhouette first a crouching lion and, a few minutes later, a castle. But in bright sunshine they were sublime, assuming the most dazzling colours, amazing and delighting even the most impervious soul among *Sheba's* hardbitten sailors.

During their weeks of pushing north, all three of the watch-keeping officers had become remarkably proficient at handling the ship in ice, developing a patience that was constantly mindful of their Asdic, disturbing only the voracious gulls that had discovered *Sheba* as a source of sustenance. Their constant presence troubled Clark, who saw his ship as he might have done a trawler, with a white cloud of birds hanging about her stern. There was little he could do about it, other than issue a standing order that permission must be granted by the bridge before gash was dumped and instructing his officers to ensure that no enemy was in sight at the time.

'I thought we were always supposed to make sure of that?' asked a puzzled Pearson as he steadied the *Sheba's* course into a long lead of open water, giving the helmsman a course to steer down the dark polynya.

'Just obey the last order,' Frobisher growled. The first lieutenant was scenting the air for an enemy. Although off watch, he was on the bridge, sitting in the chair provided for the commanding officer, cleaning the Lee. Enfield so spectacularly employed by Clark the previous day. To his disgust he had found it returned to the rack uncleaned; Frobisher reprobated such a lack of discipline, attributing it to Clark's reservist, or merchant-service, sloppiness. He had, withal, an indecent affection for small arms, especially as he was in momentary anticipation of encountering their mysterious enemy. At the very least, Lieutenant D.I.R.K. Frobisher wanted a mention in despatches from the engagement he felt, in his water, to be inevitable.

Daydreaming of glory, Frobisher was nevertheless startled when the voice of one of the lookouts shouted out: 'Aircraft, green zero six zero! Condor, sir!'

Frobisher's feet hit the deck with a thump and he ran out on to the starboard bridge wing, still carrying the rifle, to where the muffled lookout was pointing to the south.

'Stop the ship!' he ordered, dashing back

353

into the wheelhouse to call Clark, but Clark was already at the telegraph and staring ahead at the uninterrupted lead into which the ship had broken at this least auspicious of all moments.

'Hard a-starboard!' he ordered and *Sheba* heeled as she turned under full helm while Clark rang the telegraph. The clang of its orders could be heard coming up from the engine room by way of the skylight. A moment later the duty artificer answered and the way began to run off the ship, but the *Sheba* was heading for the ice.

All on the bridge realised the necessity of their not exposing themselves, for the longer the *Sheba* steamed down the open lead the longer and more conspicuous the white wake she trailed behind her. Such a wake would be highly visible from the air.

They could hear the roar of the Condor's four 1000hp BMW engines, but there was little time to take much notice of the crescendo, for they were almost knocked off their feet as the *Sheba* ploughed into the ice flanking the polynya.

'Shit!'

The next moment the Condor flew right across their bow, perhaps four miles away and about one hundred feet above the ice. Clark, Frobisher and Pearson, with the man-at-the wheel behind them, followed its progress. As the noise of the aeroplane's engines diminished they all sensed something was wrong. An instant later they turned at Carter's shout: 'The bloody Asdic's knackered!'

'*What?*'

'We've damaged the Asdic in the ice, sir,' Frobisher said.

Clark closed his eyes and, mastering his irritation, replied as coolly as possible, 'The question was purely rhetorical, Number One. Keep your eyes on that Condor.' Raising his voice, he called out to Carter, 'Thank you, Carter.' Then he picked up the glasses and stared after the dwindling dot. For a moment or two no one spoke, their attention devoted to watching the big aeroplane.

'She's banking!' Frobisher called out and they strove to see whether he was right, and which way the aircraft would turn. If to port, towards the north, she would almost certainly pass over their heads, if to starboard and the south, they would be clear of danger.

'She's swinging north,' Frobisher commented, his voice becoming harsh.

'Oh, Christ...' Pearson breathed beside Clark.

They watched the big plane as it turned, then it seemed that the swing was arrested. 'He's climbing,' said Clark, uncertain as to what the enemy intended.

'And steadying,' added Frobisher. 'He's

heading about north-west.'

Recalling both Gifford's remark about German weather observers and the chart to his mind's eye, Clark divined the German pilot's flight plan. 'I'll bet he's going to over-fly Vest Spitsbergen from north to south and spy out the land ... See if we've a tanker lying in the sounds, or even drop supplies to any weather station they may well have.'

'Doesn't really matter, sir, if it gets us off the hook,' Pearson said, with renewed cheerfulness.

'Could you try and think of something intelligent to say, Derek?' Frobisher said with amiable contempt, lowering his glasses.

Clark rang half astern and with a reluctant trembling, *Sheba* drew herself off the submerged ice shelf. Ten minutes later she was again steaming at eleven knots down the polynya and Clark had handed over to Pearson. Then he went to see Carter.

'It's no good, sir, the transmissions have ceased. I can have a look, but I don't think ramming the ice helped.'

Clark expelled his breath. 'Don't make your point with too heavy a hand, Carter,' Clark said. 'Tell me, are you able to hear anything ... I mean, can we use it passively, as a hydrophone to listen for an enemy.'

'I won't know until I hear one, sir,' Carter grumbled, 'or I *don't* hear, if you know what I mean.'

'All right, all right,' Clark responded sharply. 'I'll have to think about it,' and he left Carter muttering discontentedly. It was the nearest naval propriety came to allowing Carter to call Clark a stupid fool.

Clark had scarcely stepped foot back in the wheelhouse when Barrington announced that wireless traffic indicated the early passage of a convoy. 'It's a long way off,' he said, 'but there's no doubt about it.'

There was much that they would not know about in the coming hours, but, while they were not certain of its sequential number, what they knew aboard HMS *Sheba*, was that a convoy was at sea bound for north Russia.

It was called PQ17.

Three hours later Wireless Operator Humphries shouted out: 'Signal from Admiralty, sir!'

Storheill, the officer of the watch, strode across the wheelhouse and grabbed the voice pipe, whipped off the whistle and blew down it. At the other end he heard Clark's voice.

'Signal from Admiralty, sir,' he repeated.

'I'm on my way.' The noise of Clark replacing the whistle at his end rung for a moment in Storheill's ears. He had hardly replaced the flexible tubing before Clark was on the bridge. He was in his stockinged feet, Storheill noted, stripped to his shirt and minus collar or tie, an oddly youthful, dishevelled figure in his braces.

'Humphries is just taking it now, sir.'

Clark nodded and went into the wireless office. Humphries was just completing the commanding officer's copy and, sensing Clark's presence, turned and held out the small sheet of paper.

Clark took it, saw the *Sheba's* call sign for July and took it below. Out came the faithful Dr Ruddick. Clark felt a slight jar as *Sheba* nudged a floe and he heard the engine-room telegraph clang as Storheill adjusted speed and manoeuvred the ship. After a few moments he regarded his handiwork:

ADMIRALTY TO *SHEBA* 02/1300 GMT
IMMINENT TRIMORPHISM
ASSESSMENT E5

It was clear enough this time!

Clark ran up to the bridge and bent over the grid drawn on the chart of the Svalbard Archipelago, running his finger along to grid square E5. The grid was constructed from the 75th Parallel northwards and eastwards from the 19th Meridian. Each box was ten miles square and E5 was centred some ninety-odd miles to the north-north-east of Bear Island or about fifty miles south-west of Cape Thor, the southern extremity of Hope Island. Relative to *Sheba's* present position,

Orca lay 140 miles to the west-south-west. But that, Clark reflected, was when she had been reported – and *that*, he presumed with a degree of certainty, cannot have been by air reconnaissance, but must have been by radio-location, or perhaps by some method Kurt used. He had, of course, no idea of the Ultra decrypts available from Enigma-generated signals, but he guessed that *Orca* was heading north-east, just as *Sheba* had done weeks before, in search of a hiding place along the ice edge.

He straightened up from the chart table. There were only so many options, he thought, and matters were falling into place with a precision that was chilling. He stared ahead, through the wheelhouse windows. At the binnacle and telemotor the helmsman concentrated on steering the course, on either bridge wing the lookouts were alert, and up and down between them paced the officer of the watch.

Somewhere to the far south-west a convoy had set out from Iceland, and in the fjords of northern Norway, the heavy ships of the Kriegsmarine were raising steam. In distant Berlin Kurt would be consumed by anxiety while, Clark imagined, he played the part of a serious and devoted naval staff officer. In London Gifford and Pound would be watching the plot of the convoy's passage; the Home Fleet would have left the Orkneys to provide cover to the convoy. Even if Admiral Tovey intercepted the German surface warships, the field would be left clear for the Luftwaffe's Heinkel torpedo bombers and God knows what else besides; and all the time the U-boats would be tracking the convoy, ready to call in their brother wolves and make their attack in a pack. And then there was *Orca*, whose sudden appearance in the midst of the convoy with her torpedoes and heavy-calibre guns, would utterly overwhelm the convoy's defences. It would be a repeat of Otto Kretschmer's daring initiative of night-time surface attack inside a convoy's defensive screen, only on a bolder, more brilliant scale. Moreover, Clark was convinced it would succeed. With all his experience as convoy escort, the plan was brilliant in its simplicity. If Germany had a hundred of such long-range, heavy super submarines, they would win the war in a month, but Germany had only one. Nevertheless, the success of that single boat might arrest the flow of supplies to the Red Army at a significant moment. Upon such a critical interdiction, the fate of the world might turn.

The thought made Clark's blood run cold.

From 1600 that afternoon Clark doubled the watches. Owing to the slight friction between Frobisher and Pearson, he took the younger man under his own wing and left Storheill on watch with the first lieutenant. To give Storheill a break, he therefore brought Pearson's watch forward four hours, delaying Frobisher's so that he and the Norwegian came on duty at 2000. Pearson and Clark therefore took over at 1600.

At the same time *Sheba* turned back to the west and, at slow speed, with lookouts on either bridge wing and in her crow's nest, began to methodically comb the ice as she headed for grid square E5. Far to the south the masthead lookout could see open water.

'Keep an eye on the funnel, Derek,' Clark warned his young watch-mate. 'I've spoken to Olsen about not making smoke and he's too experienced a campaigner to take the matter lightly, but a slight sulphurous haze can be seen for miles if there's no wind.'

Pearson went out on to the bridge wing and looked aft. 'There's the shimmer of hot gases, sir, but I think there's enough breeze, with the ship's movement, to be all right.'

'Excellent,' Clark said. He had got over the enormity of his task now that he was engaged in keeping a lookout. He left Pearson to con the ship, preferring the more important role. In the Asdic compartment Baker was closed up, listening intently. As he scanned the horizon ahead, Clark did a few elementary sums. Say the Admiralty signal was its maximum of six hours out of date, with an assumed speed of fifteen knots *Orca* would be six times fifteen miles closer than the 140 miles he had at first estimated. But, until 1600, *Sheba* had been steaming southeast, and that would reduce the speed of closing range a little, altering their relative bearing a touch, but not much. Clark guessed *Orca* would now be heading east, as *Sheba* steamed west; nevertheless, as a worst case, the German submarine could be no more than fifty miles away!

And at the moment, Clark estimated, staring out through the crisp, clear air, the visibility would be about thirty miles. He levelled his glasses. On the horizon refraction cast distant bergs into slightly elevated shapes so that, within a few moments, he saw ten, twenty *Orca*s!

'Put her on slow ahead, Sub,' he ordered, keeping his glasses level. There was no point in rushing on to the spearhead of the enemy, he thought poetically.

The watch passed slowly. The ship wove through the ice field, shuddering from time to time as a slowly rotating floe nudged them. Forward the duty gun's crew hunkered down round the gun mounting, keeping warm in their scarves, mitts, balaclava helmets and their ugly fawn duffel coats. He could see them chaffing each other, the occasional piece of short-lived horseplay and visits to the deck to relieve themselves over the side. The gun layer sat reading a book, which he laid down from time to time, to routinely traverse and elevate the gun. Elsewhere, out of sight of Clark, other men stood to their posts, similarly bored and diverting themselves, similarly cold and similarly dreaming of home, a girl, a wife, or just a pint of beer in their favourite local.

The duty watch officers ate on the bridge and smoked their postprandial cigarettes in silence. The air in the wheelhouse was one of relaxed concentration, a taut and heightened awareness which passed the time speedily. It was when men relaxed from this vigilance that boredom set in and, Clark knew only too well, they would be able to maintain it at this peak of efficiency for no more than a couple of watches.

Still, fifty miles was no distance at all...

Nevertheless, they had seen nothing unusual when Frobisher and Storheill took over at 2000. Having passed over the relevant details of their course, speed and his estimate of the enemy's distance, Clark said, 'We could well see her in your watch.'

'Let's hope so,' Frobisher replied curtly. 'We don't want too much of this. Too much strain.'

'I was just thinking the same thing.' Clark paused, then added, 'I'll go and put my feet up. You know what to do.'

'Yes.'

363

But Clark did not go below immediately. Instead he went out on to the port bridge wing and lit a cigarette. The distant horizon to the south seemed clear of ice. Open water, he thought, rubbing his forehead and squinting to relieve his eyes as he leaned back against the steel side of the wheel-house. Close by the new port lookout had just assumed his duties, which, with the close proximity of the commanding officer, he was performing with impressive assiduity.

Clark smiled, the restorative properties of nicotine allowing him to unwind. In a moment he would go below, peel off the outer layer of clothing, kick off his boots and relax. A gin would be wonderful, but just for the time being he embargoed alcohol. He took a last drag on the cigarette, then pitched it overboard with a practised flick. Staring at the horizon abeam he exhaled slowly, the smoke a faint blue cloud as the wind caught it...

But there was a grubby yellow smudge dancing before his eyes...

'Number One!' he called, then held out his hand. 'Lookout, give me your glasses!'

Clark was staring out on the port beam, frantically adjusting the lookout's binoculars as Frobisher filled the port wheelhouse doorway.

'Sir?'

'Clap your eyes on the port beam! Can I

see a diesel exhaust?' There was a tense moment of silence as the deprived lookout strove to see what his commander was staring at through his commandeered glasses. He thought he could see something himself now...

'By Christ...' breathed Frobisher.

'Action stations, full ahead ... Asdic! Can you hear anything?'

'Not a thing, sir. Oh, shit, yessir – er, red one hundred, moving left fast.'

'Too damn right it is!'

Frobisher swung the telegraph and slammed it down hard on the stops. After a slight pause, the engine room responded, then Frobisher repeated the order, the double ring of imperative command. The helm was already over and Clark could hear the tannoy calling the men out. Those on deck were already aware of the change of course, of the surge of the ship as she no longer gently nudged aside the obstructing ice, but crashed into it, her bow lifting as she forced her way through. Clark was vaguely aware of men in a flurry of activity forward, clustered about the open torpedo tubes, and of Frobisher leaning over the starboard bridge wing shouting orders at them.

Clark handed the glasses back to the port lookout and picked up his own from the box in the wheelhouse.

'Midships,' he ordered. 'Steadeee. He

peered into the gyrocompass repeater. 'Steer one five zero.'

'Steady on one five zero ... Steering one five zero, sir.'

'Very well.' Clark levelled the glasses and picked out the submarine easily now: the feather of smoke from her diesel exhaust betrayed her. She was long, very long, with a huge, extended conning tower, stepped down at its after end and bearing a bristling armament far exceeding the usual U-boat's light weapons. He could see too that this lower, after part of the conning tower was large enough to house an aircraft, while forward she bore a gun house. He could see the flat steel flank of the thing, though it was, he had to admit, well camouflaged with diagonal slashes of blue and grey breaking up the shape so that, unless one anticipated a submarine of such size and configuration, the eye would be entirely deceived. As it was, he could not determine how many guns that turret contained, but it was a sure-fire bet that it bore a minimum of two, and they would be heavy-calibre weapons, eight-inch at the very least, entirely outclassing their own four-inch toy.

He watched the foreshortening of the submarine as she too dodged ice floes, but she was in much looser pack than the pursuing *Sheba*.

Above the tall section of the conning tower

Clark could see an irregular array of aerials and vertical pipework. Below them, he assumed, stood her deck watch. God grant they did not look too closely out over their port quarter. Frobisher straightened up from the azimuth ring.

'Bearing's still opening, sir. She's going at quite a lick.'

'Sixteen or seventeen knots at a guess. The water's more open where he is. Ring the engine room ... Shit!'

The jar as they stemmed a floe threw them all off their feet as *Sheba's* bow rose and then bore down on the rotten ice. Ahead of them a jagged split shot away from their bow and then, screw thrashing, they broke through.

'Ring the engine room and see if we can have more revs. I'm going to get astern before trying to catch up, hide our racket in her wake and use it to pursue.'

'Aye, aye, sir.'

Frobisher ought not to be on the bridge as they went into action, Clark realised. His station was forward with the torpedo tubes. The first lieutenant put the phone down.

'Olsen says he'll give you what he can, but the valve's fully open. I suppose he'll reduce the safety...'

'Yes, yes, that's fine, Number One. Now I want you forward.'

'I'm on my way,' Frobisher responded and ducked out through the starboard door.

Clark could hear him quoting something:

' "The Assyrian came down like the wolf on the fold ..." ' A moment later Frobisher's lanky form strode forward to join the torpedo party under the break of the forecastle. The tubes were already loaded with an armed torpedo and on the platform above them, Sub-Lieutenant Pearson was staring ahead as the four-inch gun was laid on the target.

Ten long minutes later the *Sheba* broke out into more open water and Clark swung her into *Orca*'s wake. The German submarine had created a long lead fringed with small pieces of broken ice, into which the whaler turned. Free of the floes the *Sheba's* speed increased, her lean hull almost leaping out of the water as she pressed after the long, low shape ahead of her. It was now only a matter of time before someone on that conning tower looked astern but, before she could hit her pursuer with her heavy-calibre weapons, the enemy would have to swing round, thereby exposing her side and presenting Clark with a perfect target.

Leaning over the bridge wing Clark called out to Pearson and Frobisher, 'Stand by!'

FIRE AND ICE

July 1942

At that moment Clark remembered the *Orca* would have stern torpedo tubes, just like a conventional U-boat, and as quickly dismissed the thought. If the enemy commander did use stern torpedo tubes, the chances of them passing clean through the broken ice were slim, while he himself could probably comb their tracks. The imperative was for Clark to close the distance and hope that he could hit *Orca* before she swung and used her heavy guns on *Sheba*. If he could force her out of the ice into the clear water to the south, then his own torpedo tubes might be brought to bear faster than his enemy's.

He had no idea what speed *Sheba* was now doing, but judging by the opening bearing of a medium-sized and oddly shaped berg that must have taken several years to migrate down from the far north, and by the broken the ice floes streaking past her, she must be

369

topping sixteen or seventeen knots, far faster than she had managed on trials. He ducked out of the wheelhouse and stared up at the funnel cowling. Olsen was doing his job to perfection, the boilers were producing hardly any smoke, only the unavoidable, sulphurously yellow exhaust fumes that rose in a pall above and behind the racing *Sheba*. Sooner or later the enemy must see them...

'She's turning, sir!'

Clark swung round, almost bumping into Ordinary Seaman Oliphant, who, as starboard lookout, was watching the *Orca* through his binoculars. For a moment Clark could not see the white-painted conning tower amid the floes, but then, as Oliphant called out unnecessarily loudly in his excitement, 'She's going to starboard, sir!' Clark saw the elongation of the huge submarine.

His heart was hammering as he scanned the ice to starboard. He had to get *Sheba* out of the ice as quickly as possible. As the *Orca* turned under what looked like full helm, she slowed down, so that with every passing second the range was closing. Then Clark spotted his opportunity, a narrow lead four points on the starboard bow.

'Starboard easy!' he ordered.

The measured response came from the man on the wheel. Clark headed the racing whaler for the slender polynya, steadied her and called out 'Brace yourselves!'

370

'Shall I phone the engine room?' Oliphant asked.

'Too late!' Clark snapped as *Sheba* shuddered and the ice squealed on the steel hull as the little ship forced her passage. The *Sheba* faltered, her bow rose and she shook as the racing screw thrashed. She was buffeted as she slowly rotated the floes and then they gave way and she blundered through, the displaced ice grinding and rumbling in protest as the floes were thrust outwards, one or two riding up and over their neighbours, the rotten, half-melted edges giving way under the impact.

'Lookouts, man your guns!' Clark called as Oliphant dropped the glasses on their strap and moved behind the bridge-wing Hotch-kiss.

'I think I can hit her, sir!' Pearson's voice came from the four-inch gun platform forward and Clark spared a quick glance over the bridge dodger. He held up his hand.

'Hold your fire, Sub, just a little longer.' He hoped his voice sounded cool. His heart pounded in his chest with such violence that he thought it could not stand its own action, while the adrenaline poured into his bloodstream. Clark had to force *Sheba* out of the loose pack, into clearer water. He raised his glasses and studied the enemy. The *Orca* had almost completed her turn, but her guns remained trained fore and aft! Clark could

371

scarcely believe their luck, for it was clear the Germans had not yet seen them. A quick look astern showed why, for they were almost in transit with the fantastically castellated berg they had rushed past a moment or two before, and now ran down the line of bearing between it and the enemy. Against the berg they would be difficult to see unless that treacherous pall of rising exhaust gasses...

'They've seen us, sir!'

Even without glasses Clark could see what Oliphant had spotted. The heavy gun turret was foreshortening as *Orca* completed her turn. She was clear of the ice field, though a few loose floes lay around her. The *Sheba* had yet to break out of the mass of ice into the relatively clear water to the south.

'Open fire!' Clark bellowed. As the four-inch barked, Clark went back into the wheelhouse and bent over the azimuth ring. The gun smoke whipped back over the wheelhouse windows and then the target came in sight again.

'Steer one four three!' he snapped.

'Steer one four three, sir!'

They headed directly for the *Orca* and, as Clark saw the orange flashes of her heavy-calibre guns, he straightened up, leant over the dodger and shouted at Frobisher: 'All yours, Number One!'

Pearson's gun barked again but the noise

of the discharge was somehow lost in the enormous splash and detonation of the enemy shell close to the starboard quarter. At least Clark thought it had detonated, for the whole ship shook as though in the furious grasp of a gigantic hand and the cold splash of water cascaded down on the after-deck. Clark had no idea what had happened to its twin, though afterwards someone said they had been straddled on the port quarter.

Clark never heard Frobisher's call that the torpedoes were running, though he caught a glimpse of the sunlight upon one of them as it left the starboard tube. Immediately, he called for full port helm to confuse *Orca*'s gunnery and to tuck themselves inside her turning circle to avoid a counter-attacking torpedo, for the big German submarine was swinging again, her image foreshortening.

A weird zinging sound filled the air and he saw the streak of tracers: the *Orca*'s light-calibre armament was now strafing them. Clark steadied on their course again and Pearson's gun fired another shell.

'We've got a hit, sir!' Oliphant shouted and a thin cheer seemed to come up from the foredeck, but Clark did not share their triumphalism. Hit or not, the German guns would destroy the little *Sheba* in a matter of seconds, for the range was under two miles. He could press on and risk utter destruction before getting in close enough for the kill, or he could withdraw. He had to destroy *Orca*, not wound her.

He grabbed the engine-room telephone and, as soon as he heard Olsen's voice, ordered: 'Make smoke!' Then, turning to the helmsman he said, 'Hard a-port!'

As the ship heeled under the influence of her spade rudder, the *Orca*'s second salvo plunged into the sea alongside her. Had Clark not put the helm over, his ship would have been destroyed. As *Sheba* swung round, the barrel of the four-inch traversed fast, then struck the stop with a thud. Behind the wheelhouse the Oerlikon burst briefly into life and fell silent as the thick black cloud of smoke settled astern of them.

Back in the wheelhouse, clinging to the gyro-repeater, Clark knew immediately that he had done the wrong thing. He had thrown away the advantage of surprise and, now his presence was known to his adversary, he might never get another opportunity. He felt a sudden clammy sweat pour out of him, physical evidence of the enormity of his tactical error. A sudden terror, not of the enemy but of ignominy, overwhelmed him and at that moment the man at the wheel called out, 'Helm's still hard a-port, sir!'

The reminder was fortuitous. Under Clark's nose the gyrocompass card ticked round as the lubber's line moved to the west. For a moment he stared at it and then he

374

had his moment of inspiration. If only...

'Hard a-starboard!'

'Hard a-starboard, sir!'

He glanced down on to the foredeck. If only...

From the starboard bridge wing he roared at Pearson as *Sheba* heeled violently to port, canting to the outside of the turn: 'Train twenty to starboard! I'm breaking out again!'

Pearson's hail of 'Aye, aye, sir' was followed by Frobisher's.

'Starboard tube reloaded!' Half an apple was better than no apple, Clark thought as his misgivings faded.

'Midships! Steady!'

Clark had executed a Williamson turn and brought his ship back on as close a reciprocal course as he could. *Orca*, if she had continued on her course, would have shifted her bearing further right, hence his order to Pearson to train on the starboard bow. The *Sheba* now headed back towards her own smoke, trailing a veil behind her. He prayed that Pearson might quickly find the exact range and bearing as they emerged south of the smokescreen. Astern of them two columns of water showed the fall of the *Orca*'s third salvo: it was guesswork. The shells threw great shards of ice upwards where, tumbling in the air, it briefly caught the sunshine in a thousand splintering flashes before the smokescreen obscured it.

Then they were engulfed in the oily black, stinking cloud, choking on the foul stuff before they burst again into the sunshine, the ship juddering from a glancing collision with a loose floe.

For a moment Clark thought he had lost his mind, for the sea was empty, then Oliphant spotted the white conning tower, no higher than a small berg, but betrayed by the array of periscopes protruding from it: *Orca* was diving.

'Starboard!' Clark swore as *Sheba* again answered her helm and the four-inch gun barked. But it was too late to loose a torpedo, for by the time the *Sheba* was heading for where they thought the enemy might be, all that could be seen was a swirl of water.

'Asdic!' Clark called out, cursing the fact that they were reduced to passive mode.

'Possibly moving to the right, sir.' Carter's voice lacked conviction.

Clark swore again. Was he now being stalked? Or was *Orca* retreating under the ice? Apart from that solitary old berg, it was mostly flattish pack and *Orca*'s commander could dive deep. It all depended upon why he had submerged: to escape, or to resume the hunt?

He could only be escaping if they had in fact hit him. Had one of Pearson's puny shells hit him? He asked Oliphant what he had seen.

'A flash at the base of the conning tower, sir.'

It had not been enough to inhibit the submarine's heavy gunfire. 'Starboard easy,' Clark said, phoning the engine room and cancelling the order for smoke. Then he concentrated on taking *Sheba* back into the relative protection of the ice.

Sticking his head into the Asdic compartment Clark caught Carter's eye. 'Well?'

'Well what, sir?'

Clark ignored the insolence. Carter had not forgiven him for wrecking his precious Asdic.

'Well, what do you think he's doing?' Clark responded, a warning edge in his voice.

Carter looked at the gyro-repeater. 'He's going north, sir, back into the ice. I'll lose him there in a few minutes: there's too much noise from the ice field and there are some whales about, I think.'

'Whales?'

'Yes. I'm afraid I can't tell you what species though, sir.' The sarcasm was mutinous and Clark stared at Carter who quickly quailed under the scrutiny. 'I beg pardon, sir,' he apologised, flushing.

'Very well,' Clark said, withdrawing.

Twenty minutes later, as *Sheba* was once again surrounded by increasingly dense pack ice, he reduced speed and stood the ship's company down to defence stations. On the bridge he was joined by the officers. Their mood was almost as brittle as Clark's own. Frobisher's eyes were defiant with indignation. It was not difficult to judge that he considered Clark had mismanaged the encounter. Pearson, hardly able to keep his mouth shut, clearly sought recognition for his gun crew's achievement while Storheill, black from the smokescreen, came up from the afterdeck reluctantly, assuming that his depth charges would yet be required.

Clark took the bull by the horns; he had little choice. 'I'm sorry we didn't give your torpedoes a better chance, Number One,' he said in a conciliatory tone, then, before Frobisher could respond, asked him, 'Do *you* think we scored a hit?'

'I didn't see, sir...'

'We did, sir!' Pearson broke in.

'Derek's correct, sir,' Storheill said and, as Clark turned to regard him, added, 'I happened to be looking forrard, sir.'

'Are you certain?'

Storheill shrugged, 'As certain as I can be, sir. But I think we have driven him underwater...'

'And he too is heading into the ice,' Clark added reflectively.

'I think we *must* have hit him,' Frobisher said. 'Not badly, but badly enough to have done some damage. It is otherwise inconceivable that he did not hit *us* at that range. It's my guess that we may have hit his gun-laying apparatus...'

'I suppose that's possible,' Clark agreed half-heartedly.

'But we've no Asdic and not a clue where he has gone,' Frobisher said, his tone accusatory.

'Not that the Asdic would be much good in the ice, though,' put in Pearson.

'If we have hit him and his task is to strike the next Russian convoy, he will want to repair his damages,' Storheill said. 'I don't think he would have seen us return from our smoke, so he will think he has driven us off and made us frightened.'

'Well, he can't repair damage underwater and there are no dark hours to take advantage of on the surface,' Frobisher said somewhat dismissively.

'So he's got to surface in the ice,' Clark said as Olsen came into the wheelhouse. 'He could do that a few miles from us and we'd never know.'

'But we found him before and he will think we have radar, so he may not risk it,' said Pearson.

'Are you all right, Fridtjof?' Clark asked Olsen.

'A bit bruised from all your ice-breaking, Captain, but otherwise yes. Can you tell a poor engineer what is happening?'

Clark smiled and explained. As he concluded, Frobisher added, 'And the bugger escaped us, Frid.'

'I think he's going to come back into clear water, or nearly clear water along the edge of the ice limit,' Clark said. 'I think he'll go west to get nearer the convoy and then surface to effect repairs.'

'It's still risky, sir. Suppose there's clear water to the north,' said Storheill. 'This lot's sweeping down from Erik Erikson's Strait and there could well be large expanses of open water to the north.'

'That's true,' Clark mused, casting his mind back to his time in these latitudes years earlier.

'Yes, but he'd have to *know* there was clear water to the north. He couldn't gamble on it.' Frobisher was dismissive.

'Perhaps he's just come from it,' said Pearson, receiving a withering glance from the first lieutenant as a consequence of this contradictory opinion. 'And it might no longer be there,' Pearson added with a kind of dogged courage.

'Perhaps,' said Storheill, clicking his fingers with inspiration, 'he's been *told* there is clear water there!' His glowing eyes caught Clark's. 'The Condor, sir...'

'It flew off to the north-west, towards the Storfjord!' Clark said, catching on. 'By God, Pilot, you have a point! It's worth a gamble, for I confess, I don't know what else we can do.'

Frobisher grunted but Clark ignored the impropriety. He moved across to stare a moment at the chart. Storheill moved beside him and a moment later *Sheba* steadied on a course of north-west at a speed of eight knots.

'I suppose you are going to go bumping about in the ice again, Captain?' Olsen asked with a wan smile.

'I suppose I am, Fridtjof.'

Long afterwards, when he had time to reflect upon the affair, Clark wondered if he would have followed the hunch had it been his own. That it originated with Storheill seemed at the time to give it a validity that was entirely imaginary; Clark had come to admire the Norwegian officer and to rely upon him and his navigational skill. Storheill had proved himself a seaman par excellence, a man utterly without pretension who was simply very, very good at his job. So when Storheill deduced his solution to the problem of the *Orca*'s disappearance, Clark saw no good reason to doubt the assertion. Furthermore, the logic of Storheill's argument chimed in with some instinctive feeling of his own. The two of them possessed a pool of knowledge about the Arctic, and Clark was only too aware that Storheill's experience was not only more recent and extensive than his own, but Storheill had acquired it as a mature sea officer. Besides, Storheill's was the only working hypothesis they had to go on.

Thus, while Frobisher went off shaking his head, Clark adopted an almost defiant conviction that they must head north. In his recollection of this confidence, Clark was assisted by another fact. It was their fourth piece of luck, if one took the sudden encounter, the failure of the Germans to see them as they approached and Pearson's hit as the first three. As they blundered northwest through increasingly thick pack ice, Carter emerged into the wheelhouse asking for the captain. Pearson, who had the watch, summoned Clark, who had been dozing in his cabin.

'Well, what is it?' asked Clark, rubbing the sleep from his eyes. He was not pleased to see Carter, whose manner had irritated him earlier.

'I think we've got the Asdic working again, sir.'

'What?' Clark stared at the rating, shaking his head.

'I think we've got the Asdic...'

'Yes, yes, I understand what you are saying, but how...?'

'Well sir, the collision destroyed some of the circuitry. Baker managed to get to grips with the problem and after a bit of repair work and the replacement of a couple of valves...'

'Well done, Carter! Well done!'

Carter smiled shyly and dropped his eyes. 'Didn't want to let you down, sir.'

Clark regarded the younger man for a moment and wondered if he and Baker would have exerted themselves had Carter not overstepped the mark. Nevertheless it was gratifying that Carter dispensed credit where it was due. Carter might be apologetic, but he was not abjectly so; he eschewed taking the credit himself and refused to be obsequious.

'I'd better look after it a bit better then,' Clark joked.

'Well, it would help, sir.' They smiled at each other.

'Right, well, I think we'll leave it passive for the time being. I'd rather not advertise our presence...'

'I'd like a few practice pings, sir, perhaps astern or close to a berg.'

Clark nodded. 'Very well.'

He felt very tired now, and wanted to go below and turn in, but he felt compelled to hang about on the bridge. When he did go below, it was to sit and doze in his chair, unsatisfactorily trying to rest, but all the time with one ear cocked for the summons to the bridge. And so, in a state of heightened vigilance, they drove north.

Before long the pack ice assumed the character it had in the vicinity of Hope Island, stretching away to the horizon, broken only by the seams of narrow polynyas. The horizontal planes of sea ice were thrown up at shallow angles as successive years of rafting and overriding created a landscape of haphazard regularity, for the pilings were whimsical, while the fractured sheets of ice often possessed an almost geometric regularity. This young ice was in contrast to the worn hummocks and rounded shapes of older ice. Some of the impacted sheets were turned almost on end in small irregular ice hills by the inexorable pressures. Such formations were called, in Russian, toroses. As they pressed deeper into this wilderness the ice blink grew more intense and, as the hours passed, the weather deteriorated and the sky clouded over with a light veil of altocumulus cloud. This decreased the distance to the horizon but proportionately increased the white glare. They now had to crease up their faces and squint, the issued sunglasses proving ineffective, and they developed headaches in the process. Then it began to sleet, a thin, chilling precipitation that was part rain, part melting snow, slushy enough to make the decks lethal underfoot.

In the wheelhouse warmth prevailed, supported by a seemingly endless supply of cocoa, but around the guns the men huddled in a damp and freezing misery in which even the hottest kye soon lost its warming properties. Once again the *Sheba* was forcing her way through the thinnest ice her officers could find. It took twelve hours to make forty miles and Frobisher was increasingly dubious as to the wisdom of Clark's course of action. To him the increasing disorder of the ice meant only that conditions were worsening, a logic that seemed incontrovertible in the face of the evidence of ever-slowing progress. Twice he called Clark to the bridge, protesting that they were at a standstill, and twice he roused Clark's own dogged perversity. Taking the con, Clark withdrew, turned the ship and made a detour a mile to the east, then pushed *Sheba* north again. He seemed able, Frobisher thought as Clark handed the con back over to him, to 'read' the ice, a knack Frobisher himself despaired of developing.

On the second occasion Frobisher had the grace to apologise for troubling Clark. Clark shrugged it off. 'It's no trouble,' he said.

'But how are you so damned certain that it's going to clear further north?' Frobisher persisted.

'I don't know for certain,' Clark explained, 'but this impacting of the ice may well be evidence that the current is pushing down from the north-east and this ice is, so to speak, trying to overtake the mass of floes in front of it. That's why one can usually find a way through at this time of the year...'

'I see,' said Frobisher, not at all sure that he could.

But Clark, or perhaps one should record that it was really Storheill, proved correct. At 1100 the next morning, with the visibility down to about 300 yards, they suddenly found themselves in almost completely open water, a dark, swirling sea containing small fragments of rotten ice and decaying growlers, over which the glaucous gulls shrieked, for the bloody remains of a seal sailed past on one small bergy bit, evidence of a polar bear disturbed by the approach of the ship. Slowly, the ice field disappeared into the murk astern of them.

Informed of this dramatic breakthrough, Clark clambered wearily back up to the bridge. In the incessant daylight that robbed 'day' and 'night' of all meaning, he had just dropped off into a deep slumber occasioned by the sudden end to their buffeting through the ice. Now he stood bleary-eyed at the wheelhouse windows as a curtain of wet snow fell in white swathes out of a grey-white sky. Close by a solitary floe of pancake ice drifted past, dotted with the huddled shapes of little auks. It seemed to him that, anthropomorphically, they exuded a quality of sympathetic discontent.

'Stop engines,' he commanded, too weary to bother to adjust the telegraph himself. Pearson did as he was bid and the *Sheba* lost way and glided to a stop amid the white whirling of the snow.

'Asdic!' he called. 'Hear anything?'

'Not a thing, sir.'

'Hmmm.' Clark stirred and looked over his shoulder. 'That'll do the wheel for a while,' he said drowsily, jamming himself between the radiator and the gyro-repeater. 'Go and make us all some cocoa.'

'Aye, aye, sir.'

They drifted on. Under his elbows the gyro-repeater ticked as *Sheba*, finally stopping dead in the water, fell broadside to the wind. He wondered where exactly they were, then decided he could not care less. The wheelhouse was warm and the low visibility cocooned them from the outside world, where, even in these remote waters, the horrors of war awaited them. His mind began to wander; he was on the verge of sleep, or hallucination. He could not remember when he had last slept properly, and the endless daylight made the passage of time unreckonable. When the sun shone it did not matter, for one seemed invigorated by it, able to go without sleep at no physical cost, inspirited by the vastness of the Arctic vista, dwarfed yet exhilarated by its remoteness. In contrast, this damp cold, with its circumscribed and indefinable horizon, drove one into the soporific warmth of the wheelhouse where it lulled one to sleep. Clark felt like Odysseus under the spell of Calypso, safe in her spacious cave. Somewhere behind him he was vaguely aware of Pearson handing over to Storheill. The matter need not trouble him; nor did he want to be troublesome to them. They could get on with it. Just let it continue snowing, as long as hot water streamed through the radiator on the forward bulkhead...

'Sir?' The voice was uncertain and a long way off. Clark roused himself with an effort. 'Kye, sir – and Asdic are asking if you'd mind stepping in there, sir.'

'Oh, oh thanks.' Clark took the hot mug of cocoa and went through into the Asdic office. Carter was on duty and he motioned Clark to listen. Clark picked up the second headset and put it on. He had none of Carter's ability to discriminate the many strange noises that seemed to fill the sea and make of it a vast acoustic soup, but he tried to identify some of them. There was a background rumble, like the blood one hears in the ears when lying awake on a quiet night; that, he presumed, was the working of the pack ice. Then there was an odd squealing that he could make nothing of, unless it was something grinding against something else, perhaps another distinctive ice noise.

He could see Carter's mouth working and he took off the headset. 'Pardon?'

'Can you hear it, sir?'

'I can hear a rumble which I presume is the distant pack, and a squealing that sounds like more ice...'

'That's some sort of whale or porpoise – no, the hammering, a mid-tone, regular hammering. It's a diesel engine.'

'A diesel?' Clark clapped the headset over his ears again. Was he imagining it? They could not both be imagining it, but he could certainly hear it now, now that it was pointed out to him.

'Any idea of direction?' he asked Carter.

Carter nodded. 'Due west.'

'Very well.' Clark dodged back to the wheelhouse, summoned the helmsman and rang half ahead. 'Steer two seven zero.'

If that was a diesel engine aboard *Orca*, was she lying stopped on the surface repairing damage, charging batteries, or both? Or was she under way? And how far away was she? A mile? Ten miles? Twenty? Sounds carried vast distances in water, but how much was that modified by ice? But was there any ice, or much ice, on the rhumb line between *Sheba* and *Orca*?

'How the hell do I know?' he blurted out loud in answer to his own thoughts.

'How do you know what, sir?' Storheill asked.

'Oh, er, nothing Pilot, nothing. I'm, er, thinking aloud.'

'Aye, aye, sir.'

Nothing woke a man up quicker, Clark thought savagely, than making a fool of himself. He went through to consult Carter again. Carter lifted one earphone of his headset.

'Are we getting nearer, d'you think?' Clark asked.

Carter shook his head. 'Noise level pretty much constant; still quite a long way off. Bearing's about the same though. I reckon we've got the direction right, sir.'

Clark nodded. 'I hope so. Very well. Thanks.'

'My pleasure,' Carter mouthed after Clark's retreating back, snapping the lifted earphone back over his ear and turning again to his dials.

It stopped snowing just before the end of Storheill's watch. Clark, again ensconced between radiator and gyro-repeater, had resumed his trance-like state, but he stirred when he saw the relief watch emerge on the foredeck and climb up to the four-inch gun platform. The men coming off duty stomped circulation into their frozen limbs, flogging their arms about their bodies, grinning at their wretched shipmates who would have to freeze for the next four hours. Clark suddenly realised that he could see the gun platform more clearly and that not only had the snow stopped, but the visibility was improving rapidly by the minute. The shock of the change woke him.

'Call the hands to action stations on the tannoy,' he ordered and heard Frobisher's voice summon the men. The handful of men by the four-inch gun looked round expectantly. Clark was already on the starboard bridge wing, his glasses level as he carefully quartered the horizon.

'Sir!' The voice came from the other side of the wheelhouse. Clark skidded on slush, caught his balance, bumped into Frobisher as he dodged the gyro-repeater and emerged on the port bridge wing. He focused his binoculars out on the port quarter in the direction the lookout was pointing. The enemy submarine lay stopped amid the ice.

'We've waltzed past the bastard,' Frobisher said facetiously behind him.

'Shouldn't you be on the foredeck?' Clark snapped. Frobisher recollected himself and was gone.

'Hard a-port, half ahead.' Clark looked round for Pearson, caught sight of him climbing up to the gun and waved in the direction of the enemy submarine. *Sheba* trembled slightly as she turned and increased speed. A watery sun broke out, throwing faint shadows. Clark wondered whether Storheill had yet left the bridge, but then the Norwegian officer was beside him, his sextant cradled in his right arm, a pencil held like a long cigarette in his mouth.

Clark turned to the wheelhouse and steadied the helm. 'Can you see the enemy?' he asked the man at the wheel.

'Aye, sir.'

'Steady on her!'

'Can I...?' Pearson was shouting as his crew rapidly traversed the four-inch gun.

'Shoot!' Clark shouted.

The roar of the gun's discharge was followed by the rattle of the discarded charge and the frantic activity of reloading.

'When you bear, Number One!' Clark bellowed, but his voice was lost in the crash as the first of *Orca*'s shells hit them. It passed right through the forward paint locker and Clark actually saw it as, emerging through the starboard bow, it went spinning away into the sea.

Then all was confusion. An instant afterwards, *Orca*'s second shell hit the *Sheba's* boat deck, passed through the wooden boat in the port davits and burst against the engine-room skylight, tearing a great hole in the fiddley and the lower part of the funnel. This swayed for a moment, held up by the two forward guys. Forward, Frobisher fired both torpedoes, then a third shell struck them and the whole ship forward of the bridge seemed to disappear in the flash of the explosion. The detonation of the shell countermined the warheads of the remaining torpedoes, so that a series of almost instantaneous blasts tore through the vessel. Clark recalled rough-edged but otherwise indistinguishable chunks of steel flying through the air, and myriad noises, none of which amounted to an explosion. All he sensed aurally was something akin to a deep sigh, which came with a tremendous tightening about his chest. Only the brilliance of the flashing lights attested to an actual explosion, and even this was so bright that his eyes instinctively closed. He felt his body lifted and he was flung backwards on to the deck. A second later the lookout fell on top of him. The wretched man's fall had been delayed by his first hitting the Hotchkiss mounting before being spun round upon Clark. He was already dead.

As he opened his eyes, gasping for breath, Clark could see the funnel as it tottered before it fell overboard behind the wheelhouse. Again, there seemed to be no noise and Clark's deafness seemed to confer upon the world about him the qualities of a dream. None of it was real; he would wake in a moment and find himself the victim of a brief nightmare, induced by the excessive heat of the wheelhouse radiator and his anxiety.

But the weight on his chest oppressed him, and was impeding his breathing. Suddenly he was stirred by an even more primitive instinct. Heaving the lookout's deadweight off him, he rose to his feet and staggered to what remained of the rail. The fore part of the ship had ceased to exist and was ablaze; by some quirk of the blast, the front of the wheelhouse had been forced backwards; where the wheelhouse door had been there was now a roughly diamond-shaped aperture. Ducking down, Clark went inside without difficulty. Storheill was alive and, amid the dust and distortion, he was already gathering up the confidential books and stuffing them into the weighted bag provided for the purpose of jettisoning them. Clark picked up the chart as Storheill tossed the bag overboard. He was saying something, but Clark could not hear him. Carter was there and so was the wireless operator, but the man at the wheel was dead, something having come in through the wheelhouse windows and killed him, for he was unrecognisable.

'Abandon ship!' Clark shouted, but he could only just hear himself. He went to the main alarms and rang them. It was all he could think of to do. He knew there were other things to attend to, but he experienced difficulty ordering his mind. Then he felt the deck under him move, and realised the

Sheba was settling in the water. Somehow he reached his cabin and grabbed the blankets off his bunk. He was already wearing his duffel coat and a heavy, white submariner's sweater. He could think of nothing else and stood stupidly for a second or two until the ship gave another lurch. Something made him turn to his desk and he recalled Dr Ruddick. Carefully he took the ancient leather binding and ripped out the sheets; then he tore them in half and scattered them round the cabin. Lastly he drew open the drawer of his desk and removed his secret orders. These he stuffed inside his duffel coat with the chart.

Taking a last look round he went out into the flat. The after door to the boat deck through which he had, weeks earlier, conducted Gifford, hung half-open upon broken hinges. He stepped through it on to what was left of the boat deck. Below lay a chasm that had once been the engine room. Steam and smoke rose out of this and far below he could see the licking of flames which grew in extent and intensity even as he watched. He later recalled being disappointed that he could not see the Norwegian flag, then he remembered that he needed his lifejacket. He had forgotten all about it and turned back to his cabin. Grabbing the thing he put it on and, while doing so, it struck him as odd that no one else was about.

Where had Storeheill and Carter got to? And the wireless operator? Barrington, he thought it had been. He wondered how best to proceed and decided that he must return to the bridge and recover command of the ship.

He was never quite certain how he got from the bridge to the narrow strip of boat deck that remained alongside the starboard bridge housing, but he recalled that it was from here that he looked down into the water and saw that it was much closer than it should have been. He did not want to leave the ship and jump into the sea. He turned: great gouts of steam were now rising out of the engine room as the inrush of seawater extinguished the boiler fires. Beyond, he thought he could see what might have been the Oerlikon platform, above which flew the white ensign. That was something, he supposed.

'Sir! Here, sir!'

'Captain, over here!'

Men were shouting at him and he was ridiculously happy to hear other human voices. They seemed a long way off, however, and he began to sob. Then, with a tremendous effort, he mastered himself and began to think clearly again. With the sound of the men's voices came other noises: the steady screaming hiss of steam escaping from the boilers, rising from the engine room, the erratic roaring of the fire forward and the popping of small-arms ammunition exploding.

'Captain, sir!'

Now he could see them, three of them in a Carley float, about twenty yards out from the ship's side, two of them wielding paddles. He began to climb up on the rail.

'Hold on, sir, don't jump!' It was Storheill. No, he must not get wet. It was better to keep dry. Much better.

The Carley float bumped alongside. It was only four feet below him. Clark heard Storheill say something about 'paddling like fuck' and then he went over the rail and fell on top of them. After a moment's grunting confusion the two paddlers resumed their work with a frantic urgency and then stopped. Clark looked round as they watched *Sheba* sink.

She was unrecognisable, an angled and jagged grey shape, her whole forepart underwater, her stern slightly elevated, so that her depth-charge racks stood out against the grey pall. Further forward the Oerlikon platform was silhouetted, the ensign a drooping rag, half-shrouded in the clouds of steam as the wreckage of the wheelhouse slipped below the dark surface of the sea. A sudden boom convulsed the sinking hull and sent a shockwave through the frail Carley float as seawater found the whaler's boilers. Then, in a crescendo of roaring and hissing, the depth-charge rails swung vertical, the spade rudder, screw and curve of the cruiser stern stood up stark for a moment, hung, and disappeared as *Sheba* plunged into the deep. A cloud of slowly dissipating steam hung over the swirling disturbance in the water.

Then they were alone on the dark surface of the Barents Sea.

THE ENCOUNTER

July 1942

For several minutes no one spoke, then Storheill said, 'That was very bad. So quick...'

'The poor bastards didn't have a chance.' The voice belonged to Able Seaman Harding and Clark nodded.

'Where were you stationed, Harding?' he asked.

'Depth charges, sir.'

'Oh, yes. Of course.'

'He got this thing over the side, sir,' Storheill patted the hard cork of the raft.

Clark nodded and caught the last man's eye. 'You all right, Carter?'

Carter nodded. 'Think so, sir.'

'Where's Barrington?'

'He jumped into the sea, sir. I think he banged himself. I didn't see him come up.'

'Oh...'

For a further moment they digested this news, then Clark stared about them. An ice floe loomed about fifty yards away. It was a large bergy bit, perhaps twenty-five feet high. He indicated that they should paddle towards it.

'We may be able to find a way of climbing on to that berg. We'll be able to see if anyone else is in the water from up there,' he explained.

'I've not heard anyone shouting, sir,' Storheill said flatly, though he plied his paddle obediently.

'An' no whistles, neither, sir,' Harding added.

'There's someone there!' Clark said, pointing. The others stopped paddling and turned to stare. Beneath the pale orange curve of the lifejacket there was an expanse of neck, but the head was underwater and the motionless corpse was already attracting the notice of the glaucous gulls. Clark looked up at them, aware that he could hear better and better as the moments passed. 'We'll still have a look round from that berg,' he insisted.

Clark began to feel the bite of the cold

now. In his privileged position he had been too long cosseted by the warmth of *Sheba's* wheelhouse and, as his hearing marked a return of his senses to normal, he began to be assailed by terror. They were as good as dead, for no one would come and seek them out. Sir Dudley Pound and Captain Gifford had given them a one-way ticket: 'Go and sink the *Orca*, or don't bother to come back'!

As their fearful predicament insinuated itself into Clark's consciousness by degrees, he suddenly wanted to see Magda again ... And Jenny and the child of his that she was carrying...

Or did he?

Was there not a savage satisfaction in dying up here in the remote and lonely cold of the pure Arctic? Damn Magda! And damn Jenny and her ill-begotten bastard! What was the purpose of it all anyway? Life was a futile gesture, a fart against thunder; what was the point of opposing death, since death was inevitable? To demonstrate courage? Ha! And who was there here to record it? Courage was a silly chimera about which great lies were told. Why, somewhere up here he had had his boyhood scandalised when, aboard the brigantine *Island*, he had heard the old hands talk of Captain Scott's courage in the most contemptuous tones. It was all lies, they asserted, to maintain the image of the Empire.

For what remained of their pathetic lives they would have to seek moments of incremental advantage, like Scott. But unlike Scott they were not seeking kudos or prestige; they were on active service. There was no comparison and Clark shrugged off the oppressively distracting thought. His first consideration must be his duty to his men. He coughed and cleared his ears. Only a hissing remained to impair his hearing; a residual tinnitus, he thought, smiling wanly at Storheill.

They must take stock from the low eminence of the iceberg, and to this end they paddled closer. They found nowhere to land on the near side and worked round it in search of somewhere suitable. As they came clear of the berg and doubled its northern corner, they saw a sight of horror.

The noise Clark thought was tinnitus resolved itself into an updraught of flame that spewed from the conning tower of the German submarine. She lay on the water a mile and a half away, her bow a wreck and lying low in the water, her stern already lifting as, like her opponent, she settled. If Pearson's gun had winged her, one of Frobisher's torpedoes had struck her forward. God knew what carnage it had caused within the great steel tube, but the interior must be an inferno to vent with such horrendous vigour through the conning tower. The big guns were trained towards them, but the turret seemed unmoving and impotent, the gun barrels at different angles of elevation, abandoned or served by a crew already burnt to calcined and disintegrating skeletons. A handful of men gathered on the casing, where Clark could see two large rubber boats had been inflated and slipped into the water.

Storheill, Carter and Harding stopped paddling and stared at the enemy. 'We wrecked her, sir,' said Carter, a sudden brief brightness in his voice.

'Or the other way round,' Harding added sullenly. 'An' they sure fucking outnumber us.'

'But she is sinking,' said Storheill. 'And that is what matters.'

'Yes,' said Clark, looking at each of them in turn, 'that *is* what matters.'

'I'm fucking glad to hear it, sir,' said Harding. 'And now what are you proposing we does, sir. Go over an' take 'em all fucking prisoner?'

There was a silence in the raft and the three of them looked at Clark. The next incremental decision had to be taken.

'I suggest that we go and make common cause with them. It is our best chance of survival. We're not going to get very far in this thing and they might be picked up by aircraft. The choice is pretty simple: we can die here by retreating behind the berg, or we can paddle over and give ourselves up as prisoners of war. You have a few minutes to make up your minds.'

'Well, it's one way of getting back to Norway,' Storheill said.

'I'm not too keen on the idea of dying, sir,' Carter said.

They all looked at Harding. The big sailor stared back. His face was begrimed with soot and oil and he was beginning to shudder with the cold. 'What's the fucking Norsky beer like then, Lieutenant Storheill?'

'Pretty good,' Storheill responded with a lopsided grimace.

'That's settled then, sir.'

'Right we had better start paddling again,' Clark said. 'And keep quiet when we meet up with them. I speak German quite well.'

They began paddling again. Clark suddenly recalled he had stuffed his orders into his duffel coat. With a beating heart he pulled them out and began to tear them up into tiny pieces which he dropped into the bitterly cold water. He was engaged in this when he heard shouts. Looking up he saw the giant U-boat's stern rising up and the venting roar from her conning tower change its note as gasses now poured from the open hatch. A moment later the noise was snuffed out and, with a strange hiss, the tapering after part of the big submarine dived with accelerating speed into the abyss.

There was a silence and immobility as the three bobbing craft lay still with their remnant crews staring at the empty sea. One man rose uncertainly and flung up his arm.

'Heil Hitler!' he shouted and a few arms snapped out in salute. Then the farther inflatable swung round and someone saw, beyond their fellow survivors, the British Carley float. A shout went up and suddenly the occupants of the nearer inflatable turned and saw Clark and his men. The U-boat's rubber boats began heading towards them. In all they bore twelve or fourteen men. In the nearer, one man wore a white-covered cap.

'Hey, you British bastards!' the voice came in heavily accented English.

'Take care!' Clark hailed back in German.

The German inflatable drew closer to the Carley float, her consort still a few yards astern. Clark could see at least three machine guns pointing towards them. 'Keep paddling,' he said to his own men in a low voice. 'I'm going to raise my hands. Whatever happens, just remember we were a weather ship, up here gathering weather information.'

'Do you surrender?' The voice came again in English.

'You outnumber us and you are armed.'

'You speak German. Tell your men to stop

paddling and you must all raise your hands!'

'Do as he says,' Clark said. Storheill, Carter and Harding stowed their paddles and put up their hands. The Carley float spun slowly until the German inflatable bounced alongside and their grab lines were seized.

Clark stared at his captor in stunned disbelief. 'Good day, Fregattenkapitän Petersen,' he said in German, recognising his cousin Johannes. 'It is fate.'

'My God! Jack?' Clark saw the frown of incomprehension clear and Johannes almost smiled. Then he recollected their circumstances. 'You have sunk my boat and killed a lot of my men...'

'You are going to shoot us then, are you, Hannes? Just like a good Nazi...'

'That was a foolish thing to say!' snapped Petersen.

'But necessary,' Clark said, slipping into English, 'to stop too many questions by your men.' He resumed German, adding, 'You have sunk my ship and, with the exception of the handful in this abominable raft, killed all mine. They were good seamen like yours.' He paused and let the effect of the words tell on the enemy, who were regarding the exchange between their commander and this English officer with incredulity. How had he known their commander's name? Was that why his ship had lain in ambush?

Clark quickly nailed any suspicion, lest the notion that he had had any special intelligence about the super U-boat should grow, by looking at them and saying, 'This is an incredible coincidence: first we are up here gathering weather data and we find you here too and finally your captain is a distant relative of mine. I suggest, if we are to stand any chance of survival after having done our duty, we pool our resources. We are unarmed and, if it makes you feel better, surrender to you.'

Petersen looked at Clark, his face full of suspicion. 'You were in command of a weather ship?'

'Why not? I was a merchant-marine officer before the war and I have been to the Arctic before.' Clark shrugged. 'It is more incredible that you are here, not me, and in a U-boat the like of which I could not imagine! My God, what calibre were those guns? No, don't tell me, you can't, but what are we to do now, eh? You have airbases in Norway...'

'They will not help us.'

'Why?'

'They do not know we are in trouble. Our only chance is to make for Spitsbergen. We may get to a weather station or find a British oiler in Hornsund.'

'So, we make a truce between us, eh?'

'Yes. We will take you aboard here. There is

room, and your float–' Petersen looked with contempt at the net floor where their feet were immersed in seawater – 'is not good for you. You will have frostbite in your feet soon. Come.' He beckoned them and they clambered into the German craft. Clark noticed the smell of the German sailors, the foreign smell engendered by a lack of washing in their confinement and a different diet. They would be thinking the same about their un-invited guests.

'Be good boys,' Petersen said in English as Storheill, Carter and Harding took the places assigned to them among the German sailors. Some – no most – seemed mere boys, Clark thought.

'This is not a British officer,' Petersen said, pointing at Storheill's insignia.

'I am Norwegian,' Storheill said in passable German, 'in British service.'

'Ah, you are a *patriot*,' sneered Petersen.

'He is entitled...'

'Don't tell me what he is entitled to,' snapped Petersen at Clark. 'Just make certain he does not do anything stupid.'

'I have a chart, Kapitän Petersen,' Clark said, drawing the folded paper from his breast. 'I suggest we agree on our position and strategy.' Clark unfolded the sheet and spread it on his knees, Petersen motioned for the sailor next to Clark to move over and then squatted down next to his cousin.

'This is our weather grid,' Clark said, 'along the ice edge. I think we are here.' He pointed to the last plotted position of the *Sheba*.

'Hmm, I think we may be a little further west. But it does not make much difference.' Petersen then pointed to a spot some forty miles to the west-north-west. 'I think we should land here. Most appropriately, alongside the Hambergbreen, the Hamburg glacier. We may then make a march over the isthmus to Hornsund. It is less than twenty miles to Gashamna.'

He pointed to a section of wooden thwart, one of three that traversed the rubber craft as a stiffener. 'We have a compass let into that and some provisions. We are better provided for than you in that raft.'

'I am not intending to argue with you, Johannes.'

'Good. And I am not only your captor, but I am senior in rank, I think, so you will oblige me by not directing me, notwithstanding your earlier experience in high latitudes. And don't call me Johannes.'

Clark smiled. It was the first lifting of his spirits since the moment he knew he should not have turned *Sheba* away from the enemy.

'You are sure you were a weather ship?' Johannes asked in English, his voice low as he bent briefly, as if to study some detail of the chart.

'Of course I'm sure.' Clark feigned indignation convincingly: he did not like being questioned in this manner, especially by his Nazi-fied cousin.

'But a weather ship with torpedoes?'

It is a characteristic of the Arctic, at least in the vicinity of the Svalbard Archipelago, that its climate is less extreme than that of the Antarctic. Notwithstanding this fact, the men huddled in the inflatable boats adrift upon the waters of the Barents Sea felt the cold strike them. Many were partially wet, the British in particular, all of whom had suffered from wet feet from the defective design of the Carley raft. This chill misery was to dog them in the days that followed, to influence all their thoughts and actions, ruling their morale and dominating their ability to respond to the vicissitudes of their situation.

Clark was almost immediately impressed by two things, the first of which was the determination of the German sailors. Their youthful energy and the discipline of their conduct ensured that the two inflatables were paddled and shoved to the north-west with an assiduous care and remorseless persistence that seemed to guarantee their conjoined survival. The second was the effect that this had upon his own two seamen, Carter and Harding. Both had, for entirely different reasons, displayed tendencies that Frobisher, in Harding's case, had described as 'pure Bolshie'. While this would not be a description applicable to Carter, the young man's self-esteem encouraged him not to suffer fools gladly, even when the perceived fool was his own commanding officer. This manifestation had not overly troubled Clark. A commanding officer had too many considerations to let the single-minded contempt of an individual rating rattle him, provided that rating did not exceed the boundaries of a reasonable propriety. Besides, Clark had, as has been related, trodden upon Carter's insolence. Now Carter was no longer in the familiar environment which had, with its advanced technology, called him to manhood. He was a frightened survivor in enemy hands. Harding was made of tougher stuff, set from boyhood against the world and in no wise fazed by the overwhelming number of the *Herrenvolk*. On the contrary, Harding's perverse perception of life diminished the barrier between himself and his commander. He wanted only to outshine these youthful ambassadors of the new world order, to demonstrate a tribal superiority quite as fascist as his captors', and to emphasise that superiority by his own individual tenacity.

Carter followed his lead, noting too that neither Clark nor Storheill shrunk from the task of paddling, for the invigoration gained thereby was essential to their existence, particularly as snow and freezing showers of sleet again fell from the dismal grey sky. After eight hours the two craft met increasing floes of ice, into which they drove their frail boats, seeking out the leads that led north-westwards. From time to time these turned into narrow dead ends and, cursing and splashing, wet and chilled, they got out on to the ice, dragging the rubber boats behind them. In this way they made seven portages of varying length, struggling over the rafted and hummocked ice, slipping and falling in their care not to puncture the vulcanised rubber fabric. Eventually, discovering a new lead, they would shove their boats back into the water, scramble in, and resume the monotonous routine of paddling. There were sufficient paddles for about one third of each party to occupy themselves and, by making their stints short, Petersen kept them all tolerably warm.

To assuage their thirsts, they found adequate supplies of fresh water lying in pools upon the ice, but for food they soon became desperate, for neither party had had time to provision their boats. All that the British had was a small quantity of water and a stock of biscuit which had been put into the *Sheba's* Carley rafts before leaving Scapa Flow.

From time to time they saw seals and walruses, but such was the clumsiness of their approach that, though a few rounds of machine-gun fire were sent in the direction of the frightened mammals, the animals soon dived beyond reach. No better success was enjoyed against the numerous birds that they saw, for the German rapid-fire weapons did not lend themselves to sharpshooting. The need for food became critical once they reached the thicker ice, for their expenditure of energy in the portages put extra demands upon their bodies.

On the early evening of the second day the weather cleared up and the sun shone from a blue sky, broken only by a few wisps of cloud. Looking up, Clark saw the sharp peaks of Vest Spitsbergen breaking the horizon ahead. He pointed them out to Petersen, who nodded and uttered a few words of encouragement to his men.

'They are a long way off, Captain,' Clark cautioned in German, adding, 'and we have to cross them to reach Gashamna.'

Petersen merely nodded. Clark caught Storheill's eye and the Norwegian shrugged. He turned to Harding, who happened to be one of the paddlers. 'Land's in sight, Harding. A good way off yet, but it's good news of a sort.'

'What land's that then, sir? Not Norway?'

'No, Spitsbergen...'

'Bloody hell. No beer on Spitsbergen then, sir.'

'Not that I know of, though, if there is, it'll be lager.'

'I'm not drinking that Kraut piss,' Harding said, digging his paddle in with a savage lunge. Clark looked at Carter. He was dozing and Clark left him in peace.

An hour later the wide polynya up which they had been confidently proceeding grew suddenly narrow, turned a corner and ended in a massive rafting of ice. The sight which met them seemed like a warning from nature. On either side of the lead, eroded floes, rising up to a yard above the water, their edges melting and dripping in the sunshine, lay upon the sea in a relatively flat surface. The hummocks and irregularities that rose and fell upon this bleak and impermanent terrain had been formed from successive changes of season as the ice migrated west and south, spinning with an infinitely slow patience around the Boreal pole. Partially melting in summer and refreezing in winter, it had split and broken up, collided with and either mounted its neighbours or itself been overridden. In the summer the warmer sea had melted it and in the winter the wind had scoured its surface as it gradually moved towards the east coasts of the Svalbard Archipelago.

From time to time much larger pieces of ice formed individual bergs. These, subject to similar attrition from collision, melting and refreezing, often assumed fantastic shapes. Occasionally, as now, a berg and a mass of overridden and rafted ice became pressed by the tremendous forces at work within the pack into a compact mass. This natural castle, hidden from their low viewpoint by the metre-high floes, confronted them with a startling suddenness.

Clark heard the oaths, but also the expressions of wonder made by the young German seamen. One spoke in awed tones of the Wagnerian quality of the obstacle, another likened it to paintings by Caspar David Friedrich. Then Petersen caught his eye and Clark noticed the uncertainty in his cousin's expression. In their childhood games this was the point at which Kurt would have instructed them. The abstraction brought Clark to his senses. He looked from Johannes to the mass of ice and then back at his cousin.

'I think a camp, for twelve hours,' he said. 'We can send out hunting parties and reconnoitre the ice from up there,' and Clark pointed to the summit of the ramparted ice, about thirty feet above them.

Petersen nodded curtly and began giving orders, shouting across to the second inflatable that just then followed them round the corner into the cul-de-sac. Clark passed the decision on to his own men.

Half an hour later they had managed to

find a floe upon whose surface both boats could be drawn up, and the men flopped down to get their breath. Petersen and one of his three petty officers – besides Johannes the most senior men to escape the conflagration aboard the *Orca* – drew aside. Clark and Storheill walked towards them. Petersen was instructing the petty officer to select a hunting party and he looked up at the approach of Clark and Storheill. Next to him the petty officer, armed like his commander, brought his gun muzzle up to cover the enemy officers. Clark noticed that Petersen's eye was suddenly caught by something beyond them.

'Hey,' he shouted to two men and Clark turned to see a pair of the German sailors wandering off towards an angled sheet of ice some three feet thick that formed a natural buttress. 'Where d'you think you're going?'

'We are going for a shit, Captain!' they called back, hastening forward with some urgency so that the men lying about on the ice laughed, and one or two also got up, similarly moved.

Clark turned back to Petersen. 'About the hunting party, Captain,' he said, preserving a strictly formal distance between them, 'Lieutenant Storheill here is a good shot. Like most Norwegians, he is a hunter...'

'You are asking me to trust a Norwegian patriot with a gun, Lieutenant Comman-

415

der?' Petersen responded sarcastically.

'I would go myself,' Clark riposted, 'but the horse and hounds are absent ... I will stand surety for Storheill. It strikes me you cannot have a lot of ammunition.'

'We have enough,' said Petersen, unslinging his own machine gun, cradling it and patting its chamber with his gloved hand. 'And enough hunters not to trouble your lieutenant.'

Clark spread his hands and shrugged his shoulders, turning away and pulling Storheill with him. The Norwegian officer was about to say something when there was a piercing shriek. The men lying down jumped to their feet and everyone stared about them for a moment until, round the corner of the up-thrust ice, beyond which a latrine had been formed by common consent, rushed one of the shitters, his hands holding up his breeches. The laughter that greeted this ludicrous spectacle was short-lived, for the screaming grew louder, and was then abruptly silenced. Beside Clark, Storheill spun round.

'Isbjørn!' he snapped, and grabbing the machine gun from the hands of the petty officer, he ran towards the terrified, half-breeched seaman. Then, in full view of them all, he turned and fired a short burst behind the buttress of ice, after which he held the gun out at arm's length and waited until one of the German seamen ran up and relieved him of it. They were all running forward then, all eager to see what had happened behind the ice.

As Clark and Petersen came up and shoved their way through the little cordon of puking seamen, they were confronted with a hideous sight. A gigantic male polar bear lay dead, sprawled out against a slope of ice, its paws together as if in slumber, but its head thrown back at an unnatural angle. Beyond the head, the bloody contents of its skull lay thrown out upon the ice mound. But Storheill's intervention had come too late: at their feet lay the remains of – Clark learned later – Oberfunkmeister Otto Wahlen. His body lay face down in the snow and ice, surrounded by the paw marks of his assailant and the footmarks of his last struggle. Wahlen's legs and buttocks were bare, his ankles encased in his leather trousers and boots. Beyond the corpse a small pile of faeces and a puddle of urine steamed. His arms were flung out and his face, turned towards them was a bloody pulp. But most horrific was his waist, which was almost torn in half by the stroke of the bear's paw and the insertion of its hungry jaws.

As the noise of retching subsided and silence fell on the horrified company, Petersen said sharply: 'Bury him!' and turned away.

The men turned and began to drift away while a petty officer called out the names of a burial party. Clark felt Harding loom alongside.

'Plenty of meat on that bear, sir,' he murmured.

The thought occurred to the Germans soon afterwards and all ideas of hunting were dismissed. There was nothing out on the ice from which to make a fire, but the butchered carcass soon yielded some raw steaks. At first few men would touch the red meat, but those that did soon grinned up at the others through bloody stubble and praised the taste of the meat. A number of hungry seamen gathered about the bear, above which a growing flock of glaucous gulls was already noisily assembling. It was then that Clark recalled the danger.

'That meat is poisonous,' he called in German, rising to his feet from the ice block upon which he had been resting, head in hands. Casting about to locate Carter and Harding, he repeated the warning in English. Harding was already on his way to get his share and Carter was hesitating in his wake.

'It's poisonous, Harding,' Clark repeated.

'If it's good enough for eskimos, it's good enough for me, sir!' Harding called back over his shoulder.

Clark swung round and confronted Storheill. 'You know it's poisonous to humans, don't you?'

Storheill shook his head. 'I don't know, sir. I've never had to think about eating it before. Now, if we could shoot a whale, even a beluga, I'd not hesitate...'

'You get some damned bug from it,' Clark said, turning away and striding off towards Petersen, to whom he made the same protest.

Petersen shrugged. 'The men are hungry, so they have to eat. What is it you say, beggars cannot be choosers, eh? Come, eat.'

Clark shook his head. 'No, this is folly. You will regret it...'

'All right!' Petersen said sharply, 'perhaps a few men will get an attack of diarrhoea, but that is better than starvation.'

'Send out your men to find seals or walrus,' Clark remonstrated.

'Why, we already have four or five hundred kilos,' Petersen said, moving off in the direction of the bear's carcass. 'If you won't, I am going to eat.'

Clark went back to his own men. Harding was already befouled by blood and Carter was taking tentative bites at a thick slice of red meat, his hands all sticky with gore. Only Storheill held back, biting his lower lip.

'I'm going to look for a seal,' Clark said decisively. 'If we can find a few on the ice, we may catch one before they get back into

419

the sea.'

'No, don't forget, sir,' said Storheill, putting out a hand to restrain Clark. 'The smell of the dead bear may well attract more. It will be very dangerous out on the ice alone – or even with two of us,' he added hurriedly.

Storheill proved right. Within an hour, three bears were prowling within sight. An occasional shot warned them off, but Petersen was driven to ordering them all to move on. Having hacked off a quantity of meat from the bear's carcass, they continued their portage. Even before the last man had left the site, the other polar bears were closing in on their dead fellow.

'They will dig up the German too,' Storheill muttered as they trudged off, wincing from the pain in their feet.

The portage turned out to be their worst, lasting twenty hours and resulting in damage to one of the boats. Surveying the tear in the vulcanised rubber fabric, Petersen ordered the thing broken up, some sheets cut from it for tents, the thwarts split for a framework and the compass removed. The rest was set on fire and some of the remaining bear meat was roasted, filling the still air with a delicious aroma and reminding them all of home.

Clark and Storheill were greatly tempted by the delicious smell and the joyous enthusiasm of the sailors, an enthusiasm which was shared equally by Carter and

Harding.

'It's absolutely smashing, sir,' Carter said, his eyes bright. 'It's saved our lives...'

Clark opened his mouth to speak. He could not recall the details of the warning he had been given all those years earlier, perhaps he had never been given them and had remembered only an old whaler's cautionary tale, but there was enough of a conviction in the yarn to make him apprehensive and, after Carter had shrugged his shoulders at his commander's obduracy, Storheill nodded.

'I think you are right, sir,' he said, frowning. 'I remember something about bear meat being bad, and something about it killing men. There were some Swedes they found up here, a balloon expedition to the pole that ended in disaster. They ate bear...'

'You mean the Andrée Expedition,' Clark said, recalling the story.

'They found them on Kvitøya ... You have the chart?' And the two navigators sublimated their hunger by poring over the chart. But they failed to locate the White Island.

'It is too far to the east,' concluded Storheill at last, pointing off the chart's margin to the east of North-East Land. They could remember little else, beyond the conviction that the meat of the polar bear was dangerous.

'But what *are* we going to eat?' the ravenous Storheill asked after a long silence.

THE BEACH

July 1942

It was two days before Clark and Storheill ate anything, two days during which their stupidity at not having joined what, in the war-shortened memories of these young men, had already come to be called 'the feast of Wahlen's bear' was often brought to their attention. Invigorated by the meat, the young U-boat sailors burst into snatches of patriotic song as they laboured, dragging the remaining boat over the ice field towards the distant spires of Spitsbergen's sharp peaks.

At the end of the second day they came upon another lead and tumbled once more into the boat. But the polynya led them south-west and their progress was hastened by a perceptible current. Clark was dozing when the machine-gun burst split his oblivion and he regained full consciousness to the unruly cheering of the German sailors, for they had rounded a large floe upon which a score of fat harp seals had been basking in the brilliant sunshine. The resulting carnage guaranteed the entire company not only plenty of meat, but a means by which to cook it, for Clark succeeded in making a primitive blubber stove using the biscuit box salvaged from the Carley float. Many of the German seamen, assuming a bravado forced upon them earlier, disdained the cooking of their meat and ate it raw, but Clark insisted Carter and Harding joined Storheill and himself in eating only cooked meat. This they cut into slender strips, finding they cooked relatively quickly and could be savoured. Seeing their obvious enjoyment, Petersen and several of his petty officers and ratings joined them. As they finished the first seal it began to snow and Petersen ordered his men to erect the remnants of the first boat, incorporating irregularities in the ice to provide a shelter for the men. The wind, a katabatic gale from the heights to the west of them, blew for several hours before it gradually abated and they roused themselves to press on.

Six hours later they found themselves a lead to the west but within an hour they reached its end and again began a long portage. Once again the inflatable boat was hauled out. The constant scuffing was reducing the airtight qualities of the rubberised fabric and increasing use had to be made of the small foot-pump which the Germans had brought with them from the *Orca*. It was clear that, with only one craft available to carry them all, they were now engaged in a race for survival. It would all depend upon whether the boat failed or they reached dry land. In addition to the burden of the inflatable, they had to drag the bodies of the dead seals that constituted their larder. The bloody trail attracted a following of polar bears, but these were kept at bay by an occasional short burst from the machine gun of Bootsmaansmaat Straub, Petersen's second-in-command.

It was during this tedious trek that the diarrhoea attacks began. At first the sufferers withdrew to the side of the trail, sent on their way with ribald puns about their 'bear behinds' so that Petersen, not wanting to lose another man, ordered the column to halt until the defecators rejoined. But as the hours passed, an increasing number of men left the column and anxious shouts of 'How long do we have to wait, Captain?' began to ruffle the morale of the *Orca*'s crew.

'We wait as long as necessary,' snapped Petersen, his expression grim.

'Then we'll never get anywhere,' a voice responded.

'Then we'll die together, for the Fatherland!' Petersen shouted, and even Clark's flesh crawled at the cry. Yes, they would, he thought as they trudged on at last, admiring them despite himself. He was himself in a poor condition now and walking was an agony, for, in common with Storheill, Carter and Harding, his feet were in a bad state. Although he had managed to dry their socks over the blubber stove during the storm and – having bound them up in his torn-off shirt tails – they were easier, they still pained him. At least, he consoled himself as they halted again and half a dozen men fell out of the line to crouch shivering and pallid while they shot yellow faecal liquid on to the ice, at least he had not yet succumbed to this help-lessness!

It was when Carter fell out that the trouble started, for Carter was alone and, without a German companion to join him in his humiliation, the U-boat's crew were not sympathetic or in favour of stopping. Up to that moment they had suffered the enemy in their midst with a good-natured tolerance. The British were prisoners and while there was nothing to eat they might as well help to paddle or pull. At the feast of Wahlen's bear only half of them had eaten anything and they had been ratings, men like themselves. If the British snob Clark and his treacherous Norwegian familiar wished to starve them-selves, then that was their own affair and meant there was more for themselves. The consumption of the bear and then the seals had thrust back the fears of starvation that each man entertained. They were going to make it to land, and then things would work out. They were young men, too young to die among this wilderness of ice.

Only when Petersen had called on them to die for the Fatherland had the first of them realised this was a battlefield which might claim them as much as any other. It was an inglorious prospect and one made even more so by the sudden indignity of diarrhoea.

But when the Englishman Carter sat shitting by the wayside with the rest of them staring at him, fear lent an urgency to their pleas to press on. Reaching Spitsbergen was their objective and they could see the summits of the mountains in the distance. Carter could catch up.

'No, we wait!' Petersen called out and they stood shuffling or sat resentfully on the sagging sides of the boat. When Carter did himself up and rejoined the group, he was cheered. They picked up the inflatable and began to shuffle forward again.

'Are you all right, Carter?' Clark asked.

The Asdic operator shook his head. 'You were right, sir, that bear was poisonous. I feel awful...' Carter's face was white, his skin pearled with sweat and he was shaking. They had not gone 300 yards before Carter fell out again. A groan went up and for a moment a savage murmuring ran among the German seamen. Then another man dropped out, followed by another and another until almost half of their number squatted, squitting hot yellow jets on to the ice.

Petersen walked back towards Clark. He too wore an unhealthy pallor. 'Is this the bear meat?' he asked, as if Clark was personally responsible.

Clark nodded. 'I think so. It's a bacterium in the uncooked meat. I can't remember what it's called...'

'God damn that!' Petersen broke in. 'It's what it's doing to us that troubles me.' Petersen paused a moment and then asked, 'How far do you think we are from land?'

Clark sighed. 'It cannot be more than ten miles,' he replied.

'That may be ten miles too far,' Petersen said. 'If we gain the land...' He shrugged and moved away again. 'Hold your arseholes tight!' he ordered with a savage and impressive authority. 'We'll stop every hour. Now, let's get moving!'

'That's very German, don't you think, sir?' Storheill remarked ironically. 'Very *organised.*'

Despite the gravity of their situation, Clark smiled, and even Carter, who overheard the exchange, managed a wan grin. They moved off again and, by an almost superhuman effort manifested by sundry grunts and pale faces, they staggered along with their burden, their shaking legs banging against the rubber tubes of the sides of the boat. Then an agonised voice cried out, 'Surely the hour's up, Captain?'

A chorus of assent joined in. Suddenly, as if on a signal, the inflatable was dropped and the men bearing it turned aside and tore at their breeches. At the head of the line, Petersen himself succumbed and bent to discharge his bowels in a foul stream. Clark turned away from the stink. A wedge of rafted ice fifty yards to their right offered a low eminence from which he might determine the lie of the land. As much to avoid the stink of his companions and gaolers as to spy ahead, he clambered up on to it. What he saw made his heart leap with joy.

Half a mile beyond an ice ridge which, from the level of the trail, marked the western horizon, lay a wide, dark lead. It was dotted with the remains of bergs, and beyond the water bergy bits lay grounded upon the shallow bottom which rose on to a rocky, heavily pebbled beach. Odd splashes of green showed where the low Arctic scrub of lichen and scurvy grass clung to the level rock faces. Rising behind this wide and broken littoral strip, upon which a herd of seals lay sunning themselves, was a range of low foothills, grey-green against the sky until they disappeared in a thin veil of cloud. Far away, beyond the cloud, rose the peaks of

Spitsbergen.

'Land, thank God! And an easier country to traverse,' Clark muttered and, turning about, took the good news back to the miserable party.

They camped exhausted on the beach that night, making a prodigious bonfire out of the quantities of pine and fir logs that littered the foreshore, borne thither over countless summers from the Siberian rivers down which they had long ago been swept. So ground by the ice were these tree trunks that they might have been machined as telegraph poles. As the survivors ate roasted seal steaks and withdrew for their by now regular defecations, the mood swung from desperation to relief. Even the endless squatting of the shittery was turned, in sailor fashion, into a joke once more. They would get over it; they were young and tough and they had made dry land!

As the fire crackled and burst into life with a jolly orange glow in the shadow of the hill, Petersen called Clark over. He was clearly unwell and had a better appreciation of their plight than his men. The two cousins began to walk up the beach and over a low ridge where the large stones of the shingle beach gave way to rock and a thin boggy layer of moss and lichen which constituted the 'soil' of this remote island. Thus drawing Clark off a little, Petersen lay himself down on a mossy bank, cradling his machine gun, his knees drawn up a little, his face damp with sweat. Behind him a narrow valley, seamed by a dry gully, led upwards into the low hill that rose behind the beach.

'This is bad, Jack. I don't know where we are and, while we are safe for a bit, we have miles yet to go to Horn Sound.'

'Twenty or thirty at the most,' Clark said encouragingly.

'Over those goddamned mountains behind us,' Petersen said through clenched teeth as a spasm took him. 'Oh, Christ!' he scrambled up and withdrew into a fissure between two slabs of rock. As Petersen groaned and Clark heard the wet fart and the sudden eruption of the discharge, he found himself staring at a tiny orange flower, an Arctic poppy. It was the last to bloom in a small, delicate clump, for its companions had already turned into seed pods. For some reason Clark put out his hand and picked them, slipping them into the folded sheet of the chart in his breast pocket.

Petersen returned. Clark saw for the first time the hollow eyes and the first occlusion of death, that misting over of the cornea that signalled a spiritual surrender which would turn physical in its conclusion. 'We must camp here, make the best of our situation.' Petersen was gasping. 'Some of us must go on and find help at Horn Sound. You must go, I trust you. I should go, but if I do who will look after my men?'

'You are not fit, Hannes. I will leave Storheill, he is in good shape. You can trust him, you know...'

'I am not an *idiot*, Jack...' Petersen said venomously, using the noun with all the implications it had in German.

'I will give him an order. He will obey me. We are still your prisoners.' Clark indicated the machine gun.

Johannes smiled and shook his head. 'You are not a fool, Jack. You could take this gun and shoot me before I could lift a finger. I am done for and so are most of my men. They cannot march over those mountains...'

'Then let Storheill and I go...'

But his cousin did not seem to have heard him, for Petersen went on, following his own train of thought. 'No ... I do not know what to think. You British are a puzzle. You did not eat the bear meat and look, you are fit and ready to march over the mountains...'

Clark thought of the pain in his feet and said, 'Let Storheill and I go. We can get help...'

'Just shoot us, Jack!'

'Don't be silly!'

'Shoot us! It takes courage to throw off your civilised values, but you should not find it too hard. If I was a Pathan or an Indian

you British would shoot me without thinking. It might take you a little more courage
to shoot us, Jack, your German cousins, but
you, you have German blood in you! Come!'
Johannes held out the machine gun with
both hands. 'Take it! Shoot me, Cousin!'

'Get a hold of yourself, Hannes!'

'Why did you have torpedoes on your little
weather ship, Jack?' Petersen asked, his pale
face sodden with perspiration even while he
shuddered helplessly.

'What has that got to do with us now?'
Clark felt himself flushing from guilt as the
piteous sight of his cousin touched him.

'Why did you have torpedoes, eh? You
came after me, didn't you? You came because you British knew of our mission to
attack your convoys to Archangel! You think
we are stupid? I am correct, aren't I, eh? Why
else should you, my cousin, meet me and my
U-cruiser in the Barents Sea? And how do
you know where to find me? Why, because of
that God-forgotten swine of a brother of
mine!'

'That is rubbish!' Clark said. 'Mere silly
conjecture, and it is entirely a coincidence
that we have met like this...' That much was
true, Clark thought, for he had had no idea
of the identity of the *Orca*'s commander. As
he looked at his suffering cousin he
wondered if Gifford had known. Perhaps...

'You are smiling,' Johannes went on. 'It

doesn't matter for you, you have accomplished your mission and I have failed.'

'I have accomplished nothing...' Clark began, but he knew Johannes detected his lie.

'It *was* Kurt, wasn't it? He's been supplying information to you British for months, God damn him!'

'How the hell would I know that?' Clark said, turning aside. 'Even if it were true – which I very much doubt – I've been in the North Atlantic, where I made a name for myself hunting U-boats. The Admiralty thought I was quite good at it and all the time I owed it to young Carter...'

'It *was* Kurt, wasn't it?'

'Look Johannes,' Clark said, rounding on his cousin, his eyes blazing, 'how the bloody hell would I, a mere lieutenant commander, know? D'you think Their Lordships summoned me and told me all about it...?'

'Yes, that is precisely what I think.'

'Hannes...' Clark met his cousin's eyes. The occlusion had gone and they blazed at Clark with such ferocity that he could not submit to their glare and, as he looked away, Johannes sighed. He knew the extent of Kurt's treachery.

'Shoot me.' Again Petersen held out his gun. 'All you have to do is point and fire it.'

'Don't be a fool...'

'Jeesus!'

Shaken by another spasm, Petersen dropped the gun to fumble at his belt. There was a sudden bang; the shot ricocheted away off a rock. Clark jumped back with shock, unfamiliar with the deficiency in the German machine gun that, once cocked, could chamber and discharge itself if the butt was struck sharply upon hard ground. He leaned forward and caught the gun as it clattered on to the frozen rock and slid towards him, intending to hand it back to Petersen, but Petersen himself was again thrusting his leather breeches down over his thighs. As he exposed himself, Clark saw his stained under-linen and caught a whiff of the stink. Petersen closed his eyes and turned away.

'Shoot me, Jack,' he pleaded as he evacuated himself. Clark averted his eyes.

'What's going on?'

Clark spun round. Twenty yards away Bootsmannsmaat Straub, Petersen's right-hand man, stood upon a rock with his machine gun at the ready.

'Your captain is ill, Herr Straub.'

'Where is he?'

'He is here, shitting.' Clark pointed behind him.

'I cannot see him.'

'He is in a small hollow behind me,' Clark explained, suddenly realising Petersen was invisible to Straub.

'You are lying! You have shot him, you bastard!'

'No!' Clark swung on Petersen to find his cousin staring up at him. 'Say something, Johannes!'

'Shoot me, Jack! Shoot me with my arse hanging out!' Petersen gasped.

Clark turned round again. Straub was closer and was craning his neck, trying to peer past him.

'There!' Clark called. 'You heard that ... He is ill...'

'You turned your head away. You speak German – you have killed him...'

'For God's sake ... Stand up, Johannes!' Clark called, his eyes fixed on Straub in wild disbelief that the petty officer could think him capable of ventriloquism at such a moment! Clark's nerves were strung taut as a bowstring. Instinctively he sensed the impending crisis inherent in the imbalance of Johannes' mind, the conviction of the German petty officer and the tension in his misunderstanding of the situation.

Clark flung himself backwards. He would have twisted his ankle had he not fallen against Johannes who was leaning forward, one hand on the rock supporting his body, the other across his rebellious and uncontrollable belly.

As Clark rolled over, away from the faecal stench that filled his nose, he was still

435

holding Petersen's discarded machine gun. He was face to face with Petersen's ordure and the stench brought him retching to his knees, just as Petersen stood up. Straub fired a short burst before realising his error and, as Johannes collapsed backwards with a cry and slumped sideways, Clark stood and shot Straub, the machine gun leaping in his hands with a life of its own.

Clark ran forward as Straub was flung backwards with a cry, dropping his own gun with a clatter. Fifty yards away a dozen men stood on the beach, watching what was going on in uncomprehending astonishment, for it had happened so quickly. Then several of them began running forward. At Clark's feet Straub twitched then lay still. The pool of warm blood steamed as it ran out over the yellow-green of the lichen-covered rock. The stink of blood and shit rose from Straub's body.

Clark looked up. On the left of the line coming towards him one of the men was armed. He bore the third of the machine guns rescued from the *Orca*.

'Stop!' Clark shouted in German and when they had obeyed, he lowered the muzzle of his gun and added, 'There has been a terrible accident. You have my word on it. Bootsmannsmaat Straub thought I had killed Captain Petersen. In fact his gun went off by mistake when he was shitting...'

'That is a lie! You are lying!' someone shouted and the men began to move forward again.

Clark saw the flaming stutter of the gun on the left of the line. The rocks behind him exploded as the spray of bullets traversed. He dropped like a stone, ducking backwards again, hidden from his assailant. Behind him Johannes lay quite still. The butt of a Luger gleamed on his hip and Clark quickly withdrew it and shoved it into his own pocket, then he fell back into the narrow gully Petersen had been using as a latrine, his boots slithering in Petersen's shit.

The gully was an old watercourse down which meltwater from higher up had worn a deep furrow in the hillside. Bending low, Clark retreated up it, gaining a little height until, behind the low vegetation of a patch of ground willow, he paused and looked back.

Below him was the beach. A few men, too weak to take any part in the proceedings, lay near the camp, staring anxiously to their left. He could see Storheill standing close to one of the reclining figures, whom he recognised as Carter. Harding was also on his feet close by and they were all staring at the backs of the Germans as they cautiously advanced on the rocky hump upon which the dead Straub was spreadeagled. It was clear they expected Clark to be hiding directly behind Straub, in the declivity into which the narrow watercourse dropped and where, between two confining rocks, Freggatenkapitän Johannes Petersen also lay dead.

Clark saw the slow advance, more an approach by nervous and suspicious strangers than an attack, led by one man, the machine-gunner. It was Straub's fellow petty officer, the last one left after Straub's death. Clark wished he could remember the man's name, he might thereby save him, but then there were Storheill, Carter and Harding to be thought of. If only he could remove the threat of that last machine gun...

He could not have many shots left; crouching, he aimed carefully and fired. The shattering chatter of the short burst sent a crowd of auks skywards from the beach, where they had just settled after the last discharge. He could not have many shots left and now he had missed! Ducking back, he shifted his ground again. A burst of bullets fired upwards from the beach sprayed wildly over the scrub and rock, sending the whine of ricochets over his head. He climbed higher, still partially hidden from the beach, hoping to work round before dropping down again to get back to Storheill and the others. He was torn by a fury to end this ridiculous situation and get those remaining to safety, but then he heard a voice call, the echo of it eerie as it reverberated up the narrow valley.

'Captain Clark,' it called. 'Come back and

surrender. We have your men here as hostages.'

'Do you hear us, Captain Clark?' queried a second voice.

Clark sat back and stared up at the sky. It was clouding over again but he did not notice, he was desperate to know what to do and was filled with a sinking feeling of despair. This was where he must die, he thought, here in the Arctic that had captivated him as a young man...

But he could not abandon Storheill and the others. He was not finished yet! Perhaps, if he disappeared into the hinterland for a few hours, he could stalk them so that when the opportunity offered he might gain control of that last gun. There was not one of the Germans fit enough to follow him. Yes, that was the thing to do, he would simply go to ground, until they had dropped their guard; then he would return to sort the matter out and get Storheill, Carter and Harding out of the mess.

Then he heard the next shout. 'Sir!' It was Storheill, hailing in English. 'They are going to shoot us. Carter and Harding are both bad and still shitting. I will die for Norway! Remember my reputation!'

'No!'

Clark was moving now, back the way he had come, at a fast lope, unheeding of his painful feet. He knew now that he must die, like his cousin. Their fates were inextricably intermingled – Johannes, Magda, Kurt and himself – a metaphor for this useless, fruitless war, and into this familial maelstrom they had sucked the luckless Jenny and her unborn bastard. Was that what all this was about, this new life in Jenny's uterus, utterly ignorant of all that had gone into the genetic accident of its birth?

Clark dumped these abstractions. He no longer cared. He was cannon fodder, like both his cousins. If he had escaped the indignity of diarrhoea it was because he was being saved for a different ignominy. As he hobbled forward, he heard the staccato chatter of the gun and Storheill's defiant cry: 'God save Norway!'

Clark was furious: why did men have to justify their miserably futile existences by such grandiosities?

Oblivious to the pain in his feet he leaped out of the gully and began a slithering, scrambling descent down over the ice-splintered rock talus. Only a few feet below him spread the beach and he saw Storheill falling in obscene jerks as the petty officer fired relentlessly into him. Clark scrabbled down towards them firing the machine gun from his hip; the petty officer had hardly completed the destruction of Storheill when he fell himself after a ridiculous little dido in which his legs collapsed and he flopped down upon a pelvis shattered by good German bullets.

Clark slid to a standstill. The petty officer's machine gun dropped in front of him. Clark stood over him and swung his own weapon round, emptying the magazine into the German sailors as they approached. When he had run out of ammunition, Clark bent to pick up the petty officer's gun. When that too was emptied, he threw it aside. Then he knelt beside Storheill. The Norwegian was quite dead and Clark extended his own fingers and drew Storheill's lids down over his staring eyes. Carter lay next to him. He had been dead for some moments, Clark thought. He looked up, seeking Harding. The man lay a few yards off; he had been cut down across the midriff, but he was still breathing. Clark drew the Luger, cocked it and knelt beside the big, Bolshie seaman. He placed the muzzle at Harding's temple. The man must have felt something, for his eyes fluttered open for a moment.

'I'm sorry about this, Harding, but it's all I can do for you,' Clark said as he pulled the trigger.

Then he rose and walked back along the beach. One by one he shot the wounded as they stared up at him, several caught by death in the act of defecation. One man had escaped the machine-gun fire and fell to his knees in a gesture of supplication.

'I'm sorry,' Clark said in German, and shot the sailor. He was about nineteen years old. Then Clark looked up at the sky. It was beginning to snow and he called out in a loud voice: 'May God have mercy on me!'

When the echo of his cry had died away he was weeping. Sniffing as he went, he rescued the compass, the improvised blubber stove and a sheet of vulcanised rubber. Recovering what ammunition he could find on Petersen for the pistol, he made a bundle of it all.

Then, consulting the compass, he began walking towards the north-west.

He found the ruins of an old whaler's hut on the southern shore of Horn Sound near what the chart called Gashamna. Here he waited for four weeks, shooting seals with the Luger and subsisting on seal steaks and salads of scurvy grass until one morning a British fleet oiler glided into the sound through the sea smoke and anchored a mile offshore. It took Clark all morning to attract the attention of the tanker, burning old oil-sodden rags to make smoke, anxious that his cigarette lighter was almost out of fuel and he might never succeed.

But at last he saw the welcome and acknowledging flash of an Aldis lamp and, an hour later, the fleet auxiliary's motor lifeboat chugged ashore and grounded on the shingle. Clark walked down to the boat, dropping the Luger into a rockpool as he went. It fell through a thin sheet of ice. At the boat a rather nervous young third mate asked, 'Are you British, Norwegian, Russian or German?'

'I'm British,' he said. 'My name is Clark.'

They helped him aboard and he sat alongside the young officer, his face seamed by tears.

'Were you in PQ17?' the embarrassed young man asked, raising his voice above the noise of the engine as the motor lifeboat ran out towards the rusty grey tanker. Clark met the young man's eyes and then he looked away. 'You must have had a terrible time. What a mess!'

'I don't know much about it,' Clark said, his voice indistinct.

'Bloody Admiralty cocked it all up, they say,' the young man affirmed. 'Lots of ships lost.'

Clark shut his mouth. He was aware that he could not think straight. He would find out all about it in due course. All he wanted to do now was to sleep, and that is what, after a hot bath, they let him do aboard the oiler. He did not care that they had put an armed guard upon the door.

EPILOGUE

'How did you cover your tracks?' I asked as Clark finished his story sometime in the early afternoon of the next day.

He smiled. 'I have tried to do that ever since,' he said with a weary, enigmatic air, 'and I should have succeeded, but for your book and the fallibilities of age. For most of life one tries to forget and one is very largely able to do so. But old age brings unwanted things back unsummoned; the memory plays tricks, the past seems so close you can hear it breathing. Every night I hear the pistol shots I fired as I executed all those men. Judge, jury and hangman...

'Your generation has counselling, though what good it does, I have no idea. My generation simply remembers...' He fell silent for a moment, and I was left thinking over what he had said until he rallied. 'Oh, you asked how I kept the secret, didn't you? Well, the master of the tanker was a very decent fellow. "I'll have to report that I've picked you up," he said, and I said, "Can't you wait until we get to Scapa, or wherever you're

444

going?" and he said he couldn't really, so I said that I wasn't in PQ17. That's when he told me what had happened and that the convoy had been scattered and then the merchant ships sunk piecemeal. I found it difficult to believe after all I had gone through, but the Admiralty weren't to know we had succeeded in our mission, and it was clear then, as it is clear to me now, that Pound had acted on the assumption that we had failed.

'Anyway, I told the oiler's master that I had been involved in a secret weather mission connected with covering PQ17 and that our ship had been lost in the ice. I said that I was the only survivor and had been first lieutenant. I said I had a codeword to transmit if we had problems and was anxious to send it as it should have been transmitted before we lost the ship, but the circumstances didn't allow it. He was sympathetic, as a seaman is when another has lost his ship. Even though I think he nursed a suspicion that I was a spy, it was harmless enough. Perhaps if he'd been a regular naval officer, he might not have been so relaxed, I don't know.' Clark shrugged. After a little, he went on. 'Anyway, I sent the Admiralty the single word *Forbearance*. It was far too late, of course, but someone picked it up and, in due course, it must have been passed to Gifford, for an armed guard was waiting for the tanker when she returned to Loch Ewe and I was taken in conditions of considerable secrecy to London.

'I met Gifford once more and told him what had happened. He looked tired, over-worked and disappointed. He told me not to make a formal Report of Proceedings and that he would pass on the information to Sir Dudley Pound. I asked if I could report to the First Sea Lord and he said, rather curtly I thought, "Certainly not!" Then he said that I was in line for promotion to commander and that I would be sent for a refresher course in anti-submarine warfare. He re-minded me that the source of the intelli-gence that had started my wild goose chase into the Arctic remained valuable to the Allied cause and that I was to observe secrecy for the rest of my life.

'I remember telling him, a little curtly myself by now, that he had no need to con-cern himself. I understood the importance of an official secret.

'A month later I was in command of a corvette, and six months later I received a brass hat and moved into a new frigate, where I found myself senior officer of an ocean escort group. I saw the war out in the Atlantic; a grey war fought by grey men in grey ships; a desperate business.

'D'you know I didn't really care about things after PQ17 ... But you know all about the aftermath of *that* affair ... It's in your book.'

He sat back in his chair and dabbed at the corner of his mouth with a handkerchief. The story seemed to be over and I was scribbling what I thought was to be the last of my notes. It grew silent and I thought he had dozed off when suddenly he said, 'I forgot to tell you the cause of the diarrhoea.' I looked up. 'It was trichinosis, caused by a parasite called *trichina spiralis*. It is found in polar bears and pigs, and some seals too, I learned later. Thank God we cooked those we ate...'

'And what brought you here?' I asked.

'What?'

I repeated my question, adding, 'What happened to you and Magda, and Jenny...?'

'Oh, I told you all that, did I?' He sighed, then went on: 'I sold up the big house on the Wirral after my father died in 1951...' He sat for a moment and stared out of the window. Charlotte was pruning roses in the overgrown garden. He gave a short, dry and bitter laugh. 'Dead roses,' he said, 'for a dead man talking.'

'Did you marry Jenny?' The question was an impertinence, blurted out before I could stop myself, but I wanted to know the end of the story – *his* end, not that of the official secret.

He did not seem to mind and merely shook

his head. 'No. She married an American seaman. I married Magda.' He paused a moment after that admission and I was left to imagine how their reconciliation had come about. It would have been an impropriety to pry further. 'We adopted the little girl; the American didn't...' He failed to finish the sentence and I could see no point in pursuing the detail; it was not important.

'Magda had found this house when she had been having a fling with a Yank herself. He was an airforce colonel, East Anglia was stiff with them then. He abandoned her, of course, when he went back to his young wife and child in Connecticut. We were happy for a few years, then Magda decided to emigrate to Israel. She died of cancer about twelve years later. When my daughter lost her husband she came and joined me. She loves the house...'

He fell silent and I sensed the story had ground to its end. I remember looking down at my notes. For some reason, Storheill had fascinated me, perhaps because Clark seemed fond of him.

'I have told you a great deal,' Clark said, as though deciding himself that the matter had now reached its conclusion.

'What did Storheill mean about his reputation?' I asked.

Clark frowned. 'Oh, yes, I told you that too, did I? His last words were something about God saving Norway and that I should remember his reputation.'

'I wondered what he meant by it?'

Clark rubbed his forehead. 'Out on the ice he had said to me, "Do you know what the old Norsemen said of a man's life?" I admitted I didn't and he said, "All men, their kinsmen and their cattle die; but a noble name, praise and reputation are immortal." It was a curious fancy, don't you think?'

I nodded and jotted Storheill's words down. And I remember thinking how difficult it must have been for a man to bury such a reputation as Clark had acquired in life. But then I had not shot a dozen helpless, unarmed men.

I stared at him for a moment and, catching my eye, he said, 'Perhaps you can save Storheill's name for him, eh? I should like you to do that.'

'Of course.'

Then there was just one other question.

'What about Kurt?' I probed, anxious not to leave a strand untucked in the last splice he was making of his life.

But Clark shrugged. 'We never found out. Did the Gestapo get to him before the Russians? Was he implicated in the Stauffenburg Plot alongside Admiral Canaris?' Clark shrugged again. 'Who knows? I am inclined to think he was executed in the aftermath of the Rastenburg explosion. We shall never know. Perhaps he escaped then died in the awful mess Hitler left the Germans in...

'In the end we were unimportant. We were all killed long, long ago. I have been dead ever since I left that beach, but–' and here he smiled with a quiet haunted certainty that I cannot get out of my mind's eye – 'dead men never know when to stop talking.'

As I left him, I sought out his daughter to let her know I was going. She was still in the garden, where a chill had set in under the shadow of the high holly hedge.

'Thank you for coming,' she said simply, removing her leather gardener's gloves. 'It is good of you to take the trouble.'

'It was no trouble,' I said. 'I'll be in touch.'

'He told you everything, I suppose,' she said.

'Yes,' I said, looking straight at her so there could be no misunderstanding. 'Everything.'

She coloured slightly and lifted a strand of hair from her face. 'Did he tell you about the poppies?'

'That he picked them, yes.'

'Come, I'll show you...'

We walked to a small area where a few stones were piled. A small plant of a pale green, with tiny brown seed pods trembled in the chilly breeze.

'Arctic poppy,' she said, *'Papaver dahlia-num.'*

I tried to equate the tiny plants with the ring of shots echoing about that remote Arctic beach and found that it was beyond the power of my imagination. And then it occurred to me that the act of picking the delicate and frail things had been the last act of an innocent man.

Charlotte walked me to my car, where we shook hands. She was still a handsome woman and her smile was open and attractive. I tried to see her mother in her face but she seemed to bear her father's features. I wanted to ask her about Magda as a stepmother, whether she had children of her own and how long she had been widowed, but I felt I knew more of her life than I had a right to.

She stood watching me as I got into the car and backed out of the drive. I had the curious sensation that she did not want to lose sight of me, that I bore off something precious to her. Ever since she told me of her father's death I have wondered how she copes in that remote old house.